Women in the Background

There was absolutely no doubt about it. The girls were regarding Derek with a special interest. He was stirred by the way they so boldly looked him in the eyes with little lewd conspiratorial smiles. They could see past the double chin, the receding hairline, the less than spotless skivvy, the shoulders with their cutaneous confetti. Driven by a kind of uterine fury, they were clearly at the party for one thing and one thing only: they were trawling for it, *screaming* for it. It was Celebrity: the monosodium glutamate of sex.

Barry Humphries was born and educated in Melbourne. Since the late fifties he has divided his time between England and his homeland, performing in a series of one-man theatrical events, and, more recently, television appearances which have won him the Golden Rose at Montreux. He is the subject of two individual biographical studies and the author of several books, including his autobiography *More Please* (winner of the J. R. Ackerley Prize for Autobiography), which Auberon Waugh described as '[An] extraordinary cocktail of a book . . . a literary masterpiece.'

Women in the Background is his first novel.

By the same author

The Traveller's Tool by Les Patterson
My Gorgeous Life by Dame Edna Everage
The Life and Death of Sandy Stone
Neglected Poems and Other Creatures
More, Please (autobiography)

Women in the Background

a novel by

BARRY

HUMPHRIES

'Who is this chap?
He drinks, he's dirty,
and I know there are
women in the background!'

FIELD MARSHAL SIR BERNARD MONTGOMERY
ON AUGUSTUS JOHN, 1944

Mandarin

Published in the United Kingdom in 1997 by
Mandarin Paperbacks

1 3 5 7 9 10 8 6 4 2

First published in the United Kingdom in 1996 by
William Heinemann

Mandarin Paperbacks
Random House UK Ltd
20 Vauxhall Bridge Road, London SW1V 2SA

Random House Australia (Pty) Limited
20 Alfred Street, Milsons Point, Sydney
New South Wales 2061, Australia

Random House New Zealand Limited
18 Poland Road, Glenfield
Auckland 10, New Zealand

Random House South Africa (Pty) Limited
Endulini, 5a Jubilee Road, Parktown 2193, South Africa

Random House UK Limited Reg. No. 954009

A CIP catalogue record for this book
is available from the British Library

Papers used by Random House UK Limited are natural, recyclable products made from wood grown in sustainable forests. The manufacturing processes conform to the environmental regulations of the country of origin

Printed and bound in the United Kingdom by
Cox & Wyman Ltd, Reading, Berkshire

ISBN 0 7493 2218 7

For Lizzie

Disclaimer

It is the custom sometimes of ghosts and demons to assume the form and likeness of real persons to achieve an evil purpose.

Similarly, the characters in this work of fiction may, from time to time, resemble living beings known to the Reader.

Do not be deceived.

The personages which you perceive you know, or think you recognise, are mere illusions; the embodiment of your own fancies and obsessions. They have no existence beyond these pages. They are chimeras: as real and mischievous as ghosts.

When people have been more than usually disappointing,
we turn with an added tenderness to things.

HOWARD OVERING STURGIS

1

Inge

MRS PETTY WONDERED what Vanessa would be like in bed. Imaginative, she decided. Vanessa was her make-up artist and Pru Petty watched her in the mirror, moving around the dressing-room in her loose, blue smock. Although she was certainly over forty, and already quite grey, Vanessa was probably what Americans meant by 'foxy'. She had high cheekbones, a Tenerife tan, and her throat bore only the faintest lateral striations and as yet no trace of scaling or wattling. A mole, just above the right corner of her forelip, imparted a look of coquettish asymmetry. There was a husband somewhere in the background, but something told Mrs Petty that, under favourable circumstances, this attachment was unlikely to prove an impediment.

Was she imagining it, or did Vanessa meet her gaze a little too directly with those grey, humorous eyes? Did her hands – smoothing in the Max Factor before a show – sometimes linger upon her face longer than was necessary? Mrs Petty felt an almost irresistible impulse to reach out and touch the younger woman; to knead a buttock, for example, or slide her hand in under her breast and feel the nipple graze her palm. Would Vanessa bring a sexual harassment charge or merely lock the door and step out of her clothes? Mrs Petty would never know.

She was interrupted in the midst of these agreeable, if never to be proven speculations, by the sound of laughter. The warm-up man had begun his routine. On a television monitor in her dressing-room she could see the studio audience; five hundred of them on the steep bleachers, tittering indulgently. Alistair Toogood was doing his stuff. In the sixties it was said that Alistair could have been – nearly was – the seventh Python, but something had gone wrong.

Alistair worked hard; his routine generally concerned his sexual inadequacies, and a brutal catalogue of his wife's dissatisfactions. He had extrapolated a routine from his own failure. In a few minutes he would really start the warm-up: coach the audience in applause, whip them up into frenzied ovations. All rather unnecessary in Mrs Petty's case, because tickets to these final tapings in the *Petty Quarrels* series were as scarce as hens' teeth. The audience were clamouring for Mrs Petty and a warm-up man, however adroit, was an irksome obstacle to their pleasure. She was the hottest show on TV.

Mrs Petty examined her maquillage, skilfully applied by Vanessa, in the mirror. She always liked to do her lips herself. With pencil poised, she pouted into the glass. Her skin was certainly her best feature, she decided, and her teeth were of an uncanny perfection, well worth the money. However, under the exquisite make-up, an incipient jowl could still be discerned, and beneath her melancholy and expressive eyes, the letter Y was embossed, more deeply with each passing year, in the soft upholstery of her cheeks. In the candid light, she observed the delicate corrugations of crow's-feet. They divaricated from the corners of her eyes like deltas. What had Auntie Ruby always called them? 'The dried-up beds of old smiles.'

As Mrs Petty deftly applied her lip-liner, she surveyed her long fleshy nose, the septum discreetly tussocked. There it was again, a long undulating brown hair with a kink in it that sometimes emerged from her left nostril like a daddy-long-legs waving.

'There it is again!' exclaimed Mrs Petty. 'I thought I'd got it last week with the nail scissors, but it must have been lying low.'

Vanessa inserted her cold forfex, and extirpated the nasal antenna.

Hugh, the floor manager, appeared at the dressing-room door. 'We're ready in the studio if you are, Mrs Petty,' he said, looking appreciatively at the spectacular diva in mauve taffeta.

Mrs Petty took a deep breath and winked at Vanessa. 'My public awaits,' she said.

By 7.30 it was over. 'Mrs Petty, you were wonderful,' said Vanessa. 'Listen to them.' They stood in the dressing-room and listened to the Nuremberg Rally on the tannoy. The perspiring star resumed her seat at the dressing-table. 'And that's only a tiny studio audience,' said the younger woman, coming quite close behind her and slipping her cool fingers over Mrs Petty's ears to remove the bobby pins.

Vanessa then carefully peeled off the marvellous mousey wig. Sweat, trapped under the gauze membrane, trickled down like tears. 'Another great show in the can,' she said. 'Well done, Derek.'

Derek Pettyfer depressed the doorbell. For the second time. Was the party so noisy that they couldn't hear it?, he fretted, stamping and hunching his shoulders as much from impatience as the unseasonal cold.

The porch in which he waited, with ebbing equanimity, belonged to a tall redbrick semi-detached in the vicinity of Fitzjohn's Avenue, Hampstead. The neighbouring houses were subdivided to accommodate the confessionals of psychotherapists whose female patients Derek had glimpsed, not seldom, as they fled bawling into rosettes of Kleenex from those sombre and cypress-flanked portals.

Not far himself from tears of rage and frustration, Derek put his finger on the doorbell for a third time and held it there. He was, at best, a man who, on raising his right arm at the kerbside of a busy street, felt genuine pain – even a faint paranoia – when taxis failed to scream instantly to a halt.

He was glaring at the big green door; at the Neighbourhood Watch sticker and at a circular ideogram which adjured against smoking, when it was flung open and a dishevelled Fergie look-alike in jeans and a bloodstained apron stood before him.

'Sorry about that, I'm Emma, I'm only the caterer,' she yelled. 'It's a miracle I heard the bell, I'm in the middle of a fricassee of hare for sixty bods.'

Derek hurled his coat and scarf on to a pyramid of mantles in the narrow hallway and gave himself a roguish glance in the mirror. He had come straight from the studio and he hoped the gathering wasn't too dressy.

'Sorry about that,' Emma was saying, looking down at her ensanguinated apron. 'It's just the blood for the gravy.'

After a precautionary 'huh' into his cupped palm, Derek insinuated himself into the party. The noise in the front room was deafening – the ugly sound of many voices trying to dominate each other – and in spite of the admonition on the front door, a lot of people seemed to be smoking. As he squeezed between the guests, Derek pretended not to notice the discreet little stir his arrival had inspired. He even tried not to feel elated by it and adopted his modest, hang-dog posture, although it was impossible not to overhear his own name whispered on either side and the more raucous giggles of recognition. Once these exclamations had irritated him, but over the years he had grown more sanguine: after all, he was a comedian; as much a figure of fun off-stage as on. It was the price of fame.

The tall room was run-down tasteful, befitting artistic subscribers to the *Independent.* A sixties Morris wallpaper of writhing acanthus leaves in sage green and plum seethed across the walls, its lower expanses scuffed and abraded by malicious dwarves, or children. There were two high bookshelves from Habitat, accommodating a heterogenous library, amongst which he noticed the romances of A.S. Byatt, John Fowles and Margaret Atwood. Around the room comfortable, loose-covered chairs and sofas were disposed, on which a herd of people were perched, seated and sprawled, shouting upwards at others who, standing with their drinks, were obliged to bend almost double to hear their interlocutors. Suspended over the fireplace was a large, abstract canvas by Auerbach, so loaded with pigment that if it were to fall off its hook, Derek conjectured, some hapless reveller would be flayed alive by the impasto. Elsewhere the walls were hung with drawings and watercolours in that debased expressionist style favoured in north London. There was an overframed Chagall lithograph which looked like a sickly agglomeration of boiled sweets. Folding doors separated this room from another chamber equally large, where tables were arranged for supper.

In a far corner Derek could see his hostess Inge pinned to the wall by Woody Weinglass, the famous agent. Poor Inge. The presence of an agent at any social gathering – even with a Garrick tie – was enough to convince Derek that he had found his way on to the 'B' list, but it was too late to turn back. He was pressed, not altogether disagreeably, like Parsifal among the flower maidens. There certainly seemed to be a lot of pretty girls, and all shouting at each other.

'I was gobsmacked . . .'

'Barbados basically . . .'

'FANTASTIC!'

'It was a nightmare basically . . .'

'*Gobsmackingly* good . . .'

'Phoebe's seeing a lot of this rather splendid young Ugandan student . . .'

Overhearing this last fragment of dialogue, Derek wondered what 'rather splendid' meant in that context. Black, undoubtedly, possibly of diminished intelligence, and almost certainly unemployed.

'Could I have a cup of tea?' Derek bellowed at a tall, bald youth with long spindly wrists covered with black hair, who was proffering *méthode champenoise.* One of Emma's gay little helpers, he surmised.

Inge liked to be 'At Home' every now and then when her husband was on tour, just to prove she had a few friends of her own. From afar, in an ice-blue low-cut number, she waved at him. She was not really waving but drowning, he apprehended. Drowning in Woody's conversation, which was always calculated to impress you with how *European* he was; how much the cosmopolitan Londoner. A boy from the Bronx with an account at Harvie & Hudson's, Dougie Haywood's, Tricker's, and Turnbull and Asser's. Henley, Crufts, the Chelsea Flower Show, Wimbledon, Ascot, Glyndebourne: Woody was always there, furiously networking and bestowing upon all and sundry his favourite epithet of approbation – 'smashing'. It was really a wonder he had any time for his poor clients since, by some mysterious process of osmosis, he too had become a star. Long ago Woody made the useful discovery that most people can be persuaded to accept you at your own estimation of yourself.

All those compressed human bodies had squeezed Derek with an inexorable, almost vortical force across the room, so that he now stood a few inches from his hostess, who seized his hand as he ducked to avoid the terminal ember of Woody's dangerous cigar. With her short, ash-blonde hair and Nordic looks, Inge resembled more than ever his adolescent idol, Kim Novak. Simultaneously, he reflected how few people in the room would have the faintest idea what he meant had he made that comparison out loud. Derek observed a split second of deep mourning for Kim Novak and slightly longer for his own vanished youth.

Tonight, Inge's *décolleté* was especially inviting; a simple crossover of Fortuny pleated silk within which her large breasts loitered impatiently; but there was something different about her teeth.

'Don't tell me you've let Pinky and Perky into your mouth again, Inge,' he said. 'What's happened to that sexy little gap up there?' He tapped his upper anterior incisors.

Pinky and Perky were, in reality, a married couple. Two fashionable New Zealand dentists called Hugh Bremner and Trevor Watson who were practically Dentists by Appointment to the Covent Garden Opera, the Royal Ballet and the upper echelons of show-business. A wag had once said that they performed before the crowned teeth of Europe.

'They closed it, darling. They did the same thing to Meryl Streep's little gap ten years ago, so how could I complain? The trouble is,' Inge lamented, 'I can't talk without spitting. At dinner parties people put their hands over the soup and the other day some wit told me he'd asked for the news and not the weather.' Derek had noticed that when Inge smiled or laughed, as she often did, a dewy cat's cradle of saliva veiled the aperture. 'Talking of teeth, where's your lovely lady?'

'Pam's worried about her mother, but sends lots of love'. Inge looked at him shrewdly. Derek's girlfriend had never, to her knowledge, exhibited the least inclination to filial devotion, and she had never sent lots of love, love, or even kind regards to anybody. Derek in turn wondered why he always felt compelled to invent gracious little exculpations for Pam. He hadn't kissed his hostess yet, but as he attempted to remedy the omission, someone pushed him from behind, driving his nose against Inge's face.

'Cold nose warm heart,' aphorised Inge, submerging her forelip in a glass of wine. 'Have you met Derek's lovely lady, Woody?'

Why did 'lovely lady' always sound so patronising?, Derek wondered. 'Come to dinner and bring your lovely lady!' It really means your latest screw whose name I can't be bothered remembering.

'Stunning – smashing.' Woody might have been extolling any old lovely lady. With his round bald head, polished nut-brown by the suns of St Moritz and Palm Beach, Woody Weinglass must have been well over sixty and his receding jowl was mantled with a whitish, almost pubic stubble in the mode of Mr Arafat. Woody was always in exemplary female company, in spite of an unprepossessing, indeed potato-like physiognomy and large nostrils in which the hairs rattled like twigs. But Inge seemed to like him, or tolerate him. She had a penchant for ugly men. Lionel, her husband, was certainly no oil painting.

'How long have you been off the sauce?' Woody enquired as the emaciated waiter thrust a cup of Earl Grey at Derek over somebody's shoulder.

'About ten years.'

'Bully for you, old boy,' exulted the agent, giving Derek a slap on the arm that sent most of his tea into the saucer. He didn't really mind. He generally preferred not to drink anything at parties and he couldn't stand Earl Grey. Derek put the Earl Grey well up there with Stalin and Hitler in the pantheon of monsters. Anyone who could persuade large numbers of respectable people to drink tea flavoured with bath salts had to be truly evil. But they always offered it to him automatically, and it riled him to be thought of as an Earl Grey Man. It went with chesterfield collars, art deco and tasselled loafers. If they gave you Earl Grey they probably also assumed you were an only child and that you couldn't drive.

'My God! you mean you quit at forty!' Woody was saying. 'What willpower – smashing! Don't you use these either?' The American flourished his double corona and blew a trumpet of smoke into Derek's left eye.

'Actually,' said Derek looking straight at Inge and trying not to sound pompous, 'I thought that having made one big decision to go on living, it was logical to make the next.'

'So what *do* you do, dear?' said Inge whimsically, cocking her head and making a lump in her cheek with her tongue.

Derek hoped the question was rhetorical. He was feeling distinctly off-colour, as Woody embarked on a long anecdote about Shaun Griffiths, his most famous client, who had collapsed in the middle of his acclaimed Macbeth a few months before. Woody had dozens of stories about the thirsty actors he represented. Indeed, it seemed that very few of his clients were not institutionalised.

'. . . I tell you, the man makes me laugh; even in intensive care he makes me laugh. Griff's talent is *awesome*.' Awesome was another of Woody's words. The agent pulled out a silk handkerchief from his top pocket, applied it to his big brown glistening eyes and dusted the witch's brooms from his nose.

'Why did they do the liver transplant so late? We all thought he was a goner in September.'

'No fresh organs, Inge dear,' said Woody, briefly fellating his Monte Cristo. 'Luckily a couple of kids coming home from a Christmas party had an argument with a Porsche on the M1 outside Luton and within five hours old Griff had his new software. I tell you Derek . . .' – the agent had discovered lint, or worse, on Derek's shoulders and was thoughtfully flicking it off – '. . . if you ever need an organ transplant in a hurry, try to sync up with Santa.'

'How did he look?' said Inge.

'Was Griff in *good form*?' asked Derek disingenuously. He knew that to a man of Woody Weinglass's sensitivity, even the terminally ill were 'in good form'. Christ on the Cross would have been in good form in Woody's estimation, and if he'd met Dylan Thomas a few minutes before he collapsed for the last time in the bar of the White Horse, Greenwich Village, Woody would have proclaimed the poet as having been in *smashing* form.

'Funnily enough, Derek, Griff was in smashing form: even cracked a bottle of bubbly.'

'But, champagne . . . I mean alcohol . . . did the doctors . . .?'

'Since when did old Griff let a few doctors spoil his fun? C'mon, Derek, you reformed alkies are a bit of a pain in the ass sometimes. Wouldn't you celebrate if you'd just got a couple of free-range eighteen-year-old organs under your belt?'

Inge looked thoughtful. 'But he died three days later, didn't he?' she said.

Woody assumed a long-suffering expression, as though the fact of whether his famous client was alive or dead was a matter of irrelevance. 'He died like he lived, Inge dear heart – with a glass of Dom Perignon in his hand.' He glanced down at his own glass of *méthode champenoise* with an unguarded grimace and pronounced with finality, 'He lived hard and he played hard.' How Griff would have lapped that up, Derek reflected. It was the drunk's most coveted epitaph.

Derek felt like being sick. Why did he go to these parties? Hadn't someone at an AA meeting once told him, 'If you escape from the lion's den – don't go back for your hat'?

A Very Nice Man accosted him, his face wreathed in smiles. 'If I said the name Ian Polkinghorn,' he ventured, 'would that mean anything to you?'

Derek ransacked his failing memory. 'I'm afraid . . .'

'Not to worry, not to worry,' said the Very Nice Man. But Derek had felt the chill wind of hostility. He had dropped a catch, and lost a fan for ever.

Two rather attractive women, however, had obviously just recognised him. Not too young and silly, either: dressed up to the nines and probably desperate – divorcees perhaps – undoubtedly nymphos, or part-time lesbians, or even art historians doing a bit of phone sex of an evening to put their kids through college.

But there was absolutely no doubt about it. The girls were regarding him with a special interest. He was stirred by the way they so boldly looked him in the eyes with little lewd conspiratorial smiles. They could see past the double chin, the receding hairline, the less than spotless skivvy, the shoulders with their cutaneous confetti. Driven by a kind of uterine fury, they were clearly at the party for one thing and one thing only: they were trawling for it, *screaming* for it. It was Celebrity: the monosodium glutamate of sex.

'Could I ask you . . . could we . . .?' One of them, the less pretty but more desirable because of a neurotic, rabbit-like tremor to the upper lip and a slight cast in her eye, common in sexually famished women, thrust a paper napkin towards him. 'It's not for us, it's for our husbands, they're BIG FANS.' Derek saw two smirking thugs over the girls' shoulders, accountants probably. 'Chris and Jeff are too shy to ask.' The women dissolved in giggles.

They never had pens, these cows, he thought, the paper napkin was a turn-up for the books. He fished for a biro. 'Be my guest,' Woody intervened, turning round so Derek could rest the improvised autograph book on his Harrods' best cashmere shoulders, and he scribbled:

'For Geoff and Chris
hugs and kisses from
Mrs Petty'

The two harpies snatched at the inscribed tissue. 'You've got it wrong,' said the mad one. 'It's Jeff with a J.' But she was swept away in the rush for supper.

In the room beyond, Derek could see the array of candle-lit tables. There was no *placement* and he found himself next to a woman with an enormous bum in flowing garments of taupe and aubergine layered like an inverted artichoke. Her face was defiantly innocent of cosmetic improvements. A Hampstead author, he wondered? A publisher of books for handicapped children? A colonic irrigator? He was about to engage her in conversation when, with a perfunctory 'sorry about that', Emma thrust between them a plate on which some iridescent constituent of a dead hare had been submerged in a chocolate-coloured syrup.

'Mashed swedes coming up,' Emma said brightly,

and soon all present were gazing warily at the unidentifiable repast. Derek remembered the raddled apron at the front door and the caterer's ominous phrase came back to him '. . . *only the blood for the gravy*'. But his neighbour was already tucking in, her wispy grey hair which had escaped from a red elastic band flicking across the viscous sauce. The colonic irrigator looked up for a moment from her trough. 'I suppose,' she said, 'you don't much like being recognised so I'm not going to recognise you, but you *do* give us all such a lot of pleasure.'

Derek lowered his chin modestly and covered the filthy meal with a napkin. Why did people like Emma feel they had to cook for people? Couldn't they just answer telephones in empty art galleries like all those other Emmas, Camillas and Arabellas?

'It's a lovely job making people laugh,' said Derek for the thousandth time, hoping it still sounded warm and genuine. 'I feel rather privileged, actually.'

'We ran a nice piece on you in our mag last year. I'm Pippa Billinghurst by the way.'

Derek grasped her proffered hand, to which a quantity of hare's blood greasily adhered. 'Of course,' he said, 'how silly of me; you wrote it?'

'Ah no, alas. It's sweet of you but I only do the headlines. But that's quite a special skill though I say so myself.' Derek was mesmerised by the stalactite of mashed swede suspended from Pippa's right dewlap. He was cheering up.

'Would I, er . . . know, I mean recognise, any of your er, headlines?'

'ABSEILING MAKES THE HARTZ GO FONDUE.'

'I'm sorry?'

'It was a travel piece about food and recreation in the Hartz Mountains, one of my better efforts I think, although I'm pretty proud of THE REMAINS OF THE DEJA. That was a piece about the old quarter of Deja in Majorca that they haven't fucked up yet. I suppose purists would say I was cheating a bit with the "the".'

Derek was impressed by a journalistic growth industry of which he had been, hitherto, unaware.

'. . . and A STRITCH IN THYME was all about Elaine Stritch cooking with herbs.'

'This taken?' A slight young man in a grey suit seated himself beside Derek. 'Jesus!' he said, 'I can't believe it, are you Derek Pettyfer?'

'I'm afraid so.'

'It's incredible, I was reading all your cuttings this afternoon, I just can't believe this. I'm a journo, I'm actually writing your obituary!'

'I hope there isn't a deadline,' said Derek, rather proud of himself.

'This is just mind-blowing, very much so. I mean, I'm your number one fan. I feel I know you from all those cuttings, though so far I haven't got past your twenty-fifth birthday. I just want it to go on and on.'

'So do I.' Looking at that cheeky little fox terrier face, Derek was curiously shaken, and alarmed. 'Sounds like you're going to give me a big spread when I finally go to my reward, but I've got news for you, Mr . . .?'

'Gro-co, Kenneth Gro-co. Well, it's actually *Grocock*

but Dad changed the pronunciation some time in the twentieth century.

'Isn't it still the twentieth century, or am I going mad? Listen . . .'

'Kenneth.'

'Listen, Kenneth, I have no intention of dying for a very long time so I can assure you that when I finally do drop off the twig I will be so totally obscure that your paper won't be faintly interested in running my life story.'

The journalist's face lit up as he grasped Derek by the shoulders. 'That's where you're wrong, Mr Pettyfer, that's where you're wrong. The *Evening News* loves publishing the obituaries of forgotten people!'

'Well, good luck, Ken,' said Derek, rising.

'Kenneth, it's Kenneth.'

Now they were standing facing each other he realised that his obituarist, who grinned up at him batting his sandy lashes, was only about five-foot-four.

He had to get out of here. It was definitely the 'B' list. Who were these people? They didn't seem to be musical – or specially artistic or psychiatric or even vapidly fashionable. How did Inge know them? Were they just people she'd bumped into at Sainsbury's? He'd ring her in the morning.

But Inge, trapped at a far table, shook her fist at him. 'Can't you hold on until Alan Bennett arrives?'

Derek shook his head and mimed a phone call. 'Beauty sleep!' he yelled.

As he edged towards the door, Derek was conscious of an importunate plucking at his left sleeve. It was Pippa.

'It's me again, how bor-ring! No, seriously, did you see last month's *Harpers* – the profile on Sir Lancelot Green the famous bone surgeon? That, I think, was my masterpiece.'

'Astonish me,' said Derek.

Pippa dipped her head, looked up coyly, and said in the voice of Blossom Dearie: 'THE SIR LANCE OF THE LIMBS.'

'I'm sorry . . .?'

'*Silence of the Lambs*, get it? Tina Brown wants me on the *Tatler*.' She seemed to be rising on point, her garments fluttering, her plain, whiskery face upturned for the caress of praise. If she had been a performing seal he would have flicked a sardine down her throat.

Somehow he excavated his coat from the pile in the hall without attracting more than the attention of Emma, who, with the help of the arachidic butler, was loading a Peugeot estate with the gory accoutrements of her trade.

'Sorry about that, sorry about that,' they said as they traipsed back inside with plastic trays of lime and pistachio mousse in a chocolate casing. 'I'm a major fan, Mr Pettyfer,' said the thin butler, coming a bit too close, 'but I suppose everyone says that.'

Derek smiled self-deprecatingly and delved for his keys.

'Could you just say something funny as Mrs Petty so I can tell my flatmate?'

Through the open door, the London night, borne to him over the dark and tousled heath, smelled cool and clean and slightly chemical.

As he drove home Derek thought to himself: it's an odd sort of Ken who insists on Kenneth.

Pam

INGE PINKHILL PUSHED an invisible trolley. Her early training as an SAS stewardess still informed her every gesture. When she was not in an attitude of stooped solicitude, her strong brown arms were, perhaps unconsciously, indicating exits. She was still a hostess, but now a far more illustrious one than the opulent blonde hefting a duty-free wagon at 30,000 feet. She was now the wife of the cellist, Lionel Pinkhill, who had one day, flying between the Finzi concerto in Zurich and the Elgar in New York, looked up from his *Newsweek* and seen Inge across the aisle, one knee on an arm-rest, reaching up awkwardly to fetch a pillow from an overhead locker.

It was a concupiscent mental polaroid: that glimpse of upper thigh, a bruise the size of a thumbprint discernible through the translucent pantihose, and it had been the turning point in his life. At that instant, as she stretched upwards within a few inches of his first-class seat so that he could have reached out and slid his palm up her inner thigh until his index finger, renowned for its *pizzicato*, came to rest along the humid groove, he had mentally divorced Joan, given her and the children the house in Barnes, the Volvo, the old English sheepdog and the Klimt drawing, survived the prurient molestations of the media, and installed this gorgeous creature in a heavily mortgaged love-nest in north London.

When she turned back towards him to switch off the call button, he had seized her hand and pressed it to his crotch. Her quick glance across the aisle to see if they were observed told him all he needed to know.

Derek was thinking about Inge as he drove home. Why did she throw these ghastly parties for people she hardly knew? He supposed old Lionel encouraged it, probably on the advice of a neighbourhood analyst: something to do with giving her 'her own space'. It also probably took the focus off some of his own recreations. On tour he was supposed to be a bit of a 'pants man', in a quiet way. Gerontophiles couldn't be as thin on the ground as most people supposed. But Derek had got off pretty lightly that night; still only ten o'clock.

Yet he was grateful to Inge. Hadn't she introduced him to Pam at a party, and a slightly better one too than the one from which had just escaped? He thought ruefully that at another time, in another place, he might have preferred it if Pam had introduced him to Inge.

She had said: 'I've got someone special over there I want you to meet.'

Derek had glanced across the room and seen a rather bad-tempered girl with a lot of hair and wearing a slightly butch blazer.

'She's a sculptor, did Martin Amis last year and I *think* she might be flattered if you sat for her.' Inge had winked broadly.

'Why doesn't Lionel sit for her? Surely a senior cellist . . .?'

'Enough of senior!' Inge had said, 'Lionel can't sit still even when he's fiddling. He's as ugly as sin, and besides dear, Lionel isn't lonely.'

'What is that supposed to mean?' Derek had replied, knowing what it meant. He *was* lonely and he liked young girls who sculpted or painted. Some of them were very pretty indeed and it was amazing how much value you could get for the price of a picture. Or so he had heard. This one appeared to be a tougher customer than most, but she looked poor. Needy. Yet she had looked interesting as well and there was a challenge in her large green eyes that aroused him. It was strange to think she was now living with him.

Derek's BMW pulled up at the red lights at Regent's Park and he regarded himself in the rear-vision mirror without disapproval. Thus, sympathetically lit, and with the skivvy pulled well up over the chins, he looked far from fifty. More like a slightly dissipated forty. 'A long time to go yet, Kenneth old lad,' he said aloud. He always talked to himself in the car. People in parallel vehicles sometimes looked across at him quizzically, but for all they knew he might have been singing along with the radio, assuming the radio was relaying a performance of *Wozzeck*. Derek's soliloquies were usually more expressionistic than the average transmission.

He took both hands off the wheel and tackled a recalcitrant spot on his chin until a loud blast from the car behind told him that the lights had changed.

Derek put his foot down. He was feeling rather guilty about Pam sitting there at home. She didn't seem to mind him going to the odd party without her and she trusted him. In retrospect, he certainly could have taken her to that one. He might have enjoyed himself with his own 'lovely lady'. Two precious hours out of his life and not even an interesting phone number scribbled on those empty January pages where women never thought of looking. He pictured Pam back there in the mansion flat at Victoria, waiting for him. Lately she had taken to meditation and he would sometimes enter the room to find her cross-legged on the floor: irritatingly unreachable.

The large mahogany door of Derek Pettyfer's flat went 'thunk' behind him. It was a sound he loved. He stood still in the hall for a moment, savouring its reverberation, then opened the door once more and let it swing closed with the same satisfying sound: 'thunk'. Derek flicked the light switch and heard the throb of the dimmer as his pictures – artfully spotlit – sprang into view. He walked across the hall and touched each in turn: his Piranesis. In pride of place over a small Biedermeier table was his first Piranesi, bought when he was a schoolboy from an antique shop in Adelaide. It was a prison scene in the first state from the famous *Carceri* series. A nightmare fantasy of dark cages and vertiginous staircases. It had cost six pounds. These days he paid as much as two thousand pounds for a good print; sometimes he paid what a dealer called 'tomorrow's price'. There were more engravings in other rooms, fastidiously mounted and framed; they hung three tiers deep in the drawing-room, in the study and in his bedroom, and in a wide-drawered Victorian print cabinet were countless proofs and duplicates in large portfolios. He possessed all but four of Piranesi's one hundred and thirty-five *Veduti di Roma*, in first state and mint condition.

From a remote part of the flat he thought he heard the phone. The instrument had been turned down, so it might have been ringing for some time. It sounded as telephones do when they are about to stop ringing. He ran into the next room and snatched up the receiver. It was Inge.

'You old shit. You might at least have waited until Alan Bennett arrived.'

'How is he?'

'He didn't come, but you might have waited all the same. You could see I was having an awful time.'

'Inge darling, it was your party. Didn't Abraham Lincoln once say, "Most folks have as good a time as they make up their minds to have"?'

'God, you can be boring.'

'You want a salon, but all you've managed so far is a saloon,' he said, appropriating, with little risk of discovery, a Wildean quip.

'I found Pam for you, didn't I? Don't forget you met her at one of my parties.' Inge was extremely proud of her matchmaking skills and this had been her masterstroke – pairing off the perennial bachelor Derek with her old friend from Yoga class. She and Pam had bonded several years before over pelvic floor exercises. 'Where is she by the way?' she continued.

'Probably asleep,' said Derek wearily.

'What's all this about her mother? I thought she loathed her mother.'

'I've never met the woman.' Derek lowered his voice: 'They seem to have a love–hate relationship. Typical Birmingham working-class family stuff. I saved her and she is eternally grateful, that's all.'

'Don't pretend to be a bastard, Derek dear. I know you're smitten – why else would you go home so early? I can read you like a book.'

That old threat of his mother's, rehashed by a *parvenue* Swedish air hostess, really irritated him. Sometimes Inge spoke to him with the intimacy of an old lover and that was even more annoying, considering that nothing like that had ever passed between them. Unfortunately, they were just good friends, though there had been a few scurrilous rumours. It was appalling what ugly people said behind the backs of attractive unavailable women.

'Well, I want to speak to her in the morning

because she left a message on the machine and she sounded a bit odd, frankly.'

'Well, she is a bit odd, frankly,' said Derek. But Inge, silly girl, had rung off.

Derek threw himself on a sofa and let his irritation subside. Why ever bother to go out, he wondered, when here was the most comfortable, the most *gemütlich* flat in London.

The light in the hallway cast a dim lambency on the objects around him; it glinted on the serried Piranesis and on the tall vitrine which protected his other treasure, his collection of Roman glass. Derek could never go to bed without giving at least one of these most precious and most ancient objects a voluptuous caress. Lighting a lamp, he ran his hand along the high bookshelf where he kept the key. In a moment the vitrine was open and he held in his palms a miracle of late second-century glass.

Just as some people, people he never understood, liked to come home to the sticky embraces of children or the bestial yelping and the wet obsequious noses of dogs, he preferred those more reticent sentinels who dwelt all day in the silence of the large apartment; those fragile and iridescent cups and beakers, flasks, amphoras and scent bottles, with their exquisite patinas of frosty viridian, mauve and *Fabrile* gold. He licked his finger and gently rubbed the foot of a greenish coloured flask which had been found in a grave at Koblenz. For a second he smelt again the cold, earthy odour of antiquity on his fingertip. This was the object – the gem of his collection – which the British Museum and later the museum in Cologne had borrowed for their 'Glass of the Caesars' exhibition. The flask had a rounded rim and a piriform body with a short-stemmed foot-ring and a pontil mark. There was a single spiral trail round its neck at the narrowest point and eight double 'snake-thread' trails on the body, tooled flat with horizontal corrugations. The flask was intact, except for one small chip in its rim, a few strain-cracks in the body, pin-prick bubbles, a flaky iridescence and a trace of incipient crizzling on the foot. It was miraculous to think that this delicate object, except for the patina of age, had survived unbroken for 1,700 years.

Once he had visited a German museum with an artist friend and they had marvelled at some drawings which had somehow survived the holocaust. 'Why, of all things, have those been preserved?' Derek asked. His friend had replied, 'Because somebody loved them enough'.

He locked the vitrine and replaced the key, well out of reach of his cleaning lady Amerika. Amerika had been coming to him for five years now, ever since he had bought the flat. But for the past three months she had been rather taciturn, even huffy; ever since Pam had moved in. 'I like it better when you by yourself,' she had said at last, looking at the Hoover. 'She not your type, Mr Petty'. 'Thank you, Amerika,' was all he'd said.

With mixed emotions Derek remembered that he was no longer the sole inhabitant of that beautiful mansion flat in Victoria. Curled up in his enormous bed was the waif, Pam. He could see the CD player winking at him in the dark. She'd left it on again. Probably Piazzolla; she played little else as she padded around the flat wearing a towel and with her hair up, secured by a toothbrush. There was something wrong with Piazzolla; too vagrant. It teetered annoyingly on the brink of real music.

Derek thought back to that other party at Inge's, when she had introduced him to Pam.

'This is Pamela Black.'

She had been a tough customer at first. He had done all the usual things: seemed offhand, talked art, feigned surprise when she told him what she did. Said, without having seen it: 'Not that fantastic head of Martin in the Royal Academy last season!' Left early. Sent roses (mixed, not red) and a note suggesting lunch sometime. She had taken a week to call back, which was much longer than usual.

Lunch at the Caprice hadn't gone all that well. She was taciturn, a bit truculent really. Very pretty, but one of those waifs from the provinces whose lives had been somehow blighted by women's lib. Then she had insisted on paying for her half of the meal. She was appallingly dressed in fawn tweed and he had soon realised why she didn't smile much. Two of her top teeth overlapped. But Derek had made enquiries. She was unmarried, and she was talented.

'Why are you so nice to me?' she had said a few weeks later at the end of the first lunch she had allowed him to pay for. Looking across the table at those large green eyes, his heart had given a little jump. He had felt such a sudden tenderness that he could only reach across the table and tentatively put his hand over her cold and unresponsive hand.

'Be my guest,' was all he said.

The phrase sounded vulgar and unconvincing, but he couldn't help it. Whenever Derek wanted to succeed with a woman he felt he had to impersonate someone else; someone more urbane and likeable.

The time came when he asked if he might see her studio. She worked in her flat in Chiswick, but he could come round any time if he wished. Again, that odd diffidence. It had been worrying, but challenging.

The flat turned out to be in Acton – almost Chiswick. Derek decided to follow the infallible rules of seduction as codified by the most successful philanderer he knew, his Australian friend, Ross Gibb.

'Always look around at her stuff and ignore her,' the rake had counselled. 'Peer at the books' (Greer, Doris Lessing, Erica Jong), 'admire the pictures, although they're sure to be shit' (Giacometti prints, photos of her own work and Elizabeth Frink's). 'And mate, once they see you gawping at the crap in their bedsit as if you were in Aladdin's fuckin' cave, they'll start creaming their jeans!'

Shamefacedly, Derek followed instructions. Pam said: 'Didn't your mother tell you it's rude to stare at other people's things?' But Derek could see she was stirred, if not exactly flattered. She was too intelligent for that. There wasn't much furniture in Pam's flat and the walls were grey. A discouraging colour, if it was a colour. But he was touched to see, in the midst of all that asceticism – or perhaps genteel poverty – a Waitrose cake and a bottle of wine on the table; presumably in his honour. She had forgotten that he didn't drink, but he would not ask for tea in case it was Earl Grey.

She led him into the studio, another grey room filled with tall stools on which, presumably, her clay sculptures stood, swaddled in wet rags. Pam unpeeled one and stood back as Derek recognised the features of the author and TV personality Melvyn Bragg. It was breathtakingly good. Yet he found it strange to imagine Melvyn sitting for hours in this cold, dim studio.

'It's a commission,' Pam said. 'He's sure to be made a Lord when we get in at the next election.' Derek assumed 'we' referred to the Labour party and its righteous supporters. It seemed somehow consistent; even the taste for ennoblement. 'Do you want to see Clive?'

Staring at Melvyn's muddy bust, Derek realised with a sinking heart that he too would have to attend innumerable sittings, and shell out unspecified sums, if he was really serious about getting this girl into bed. 'No thanks, not yet,' he said as Pam began to unwrap what looked like a heavily-swathed boulder.

Was this the moment, he wondered, to put into effect Ross Gibb's allegedly foolproof 'photo in the briefcase' manoeuvre. A ploy that melted the coldest heart and parted the most inflexible legs.

Ross had explained it this way: 'Listen mate, if you've only known some hornbag five minutes, but you want to propel her into the cot, tell her your wife has found her picture in your briefcase.'

'But what if you're not married?' said Derek.

'Don't come the raw prawn, pal. They'll know you're married. Everyone's fuckin' married! Most of them feel safer with a married man, for Christ's sake. Anyway, they always blush like buggery when you tell them about your briefcase. Fancy that, they think. He hardly knows me and he's got my snap in his Samsonite. It's like they're in the middle of a red-hot affair with you and they haven't even taken off their panties.'

'Wouldn't they run a mile?' said Derek.

'Pig's arse they would!' replied his tutor. 'They've known you ten minutes and already they're the Other Woman. On top of that, your little wife *knows all*, so why not be hung for a sheep as a lamb!'

'And that works?'

'Oldest one in the book, pal, a lay-down *misère*. You've already got the motel key in your pocket, and you're in like Flynn.'

Yet did he really want Pam?, Derek wondered. It was the perfect moment to turn back. But it was surprising how quickly and with what a deep sigh and a whispered name she responded when he took her in his arms. Their lips met with a faint clash of teeth and he thought he felt the flick of her tongue. He noticed then, as he noticed thereafter, that her eyes were closed. Were always closed.

At that moment Derek had felt submerged in a wave of pure happiness. It was odd, though, that whenever he resolved to break off a relationship he then made an irreversible commitment.

In the weeks that followed, he began to feel like

Henry Higgins growing accustomed to Eliza Doolittle's face. It was not just Pam's talent that attracted him, but her diffidence and offhandedness. She diffused a tantalising aura. When they met she rarely spared him more than the ghost of a smile and when she finally slept with him after the third sitting, she was compliant yet curiously detached and silent. But before the bust was completed she had moved into Ashley Mansions and she had two new dresses and an appointment with Pinky and Perky.

Derek switched out the lamp in the sitting-room and went into the bedroom. Pam was curled up and sleeping like a child. That was it; she was like a child. A pretty, grateful kid. When he climbed into bed beside her he noticed she was still wearing those striped flannel men's pyjamas that he particularly disliked, and airline shades! Her own tiny flat, he remembered, had no blinds or curtains. Before he fell asleep he wondered if she had really been waiting up for him to return from the party. Miraculously, she probably hadn't. He felt a surge of love for her.

I don't deserve to be alone, Derek thought.

Denise

ROSS GIBB WORKED from home. A large thirties Tudor bungalow in Weybridge. The name of the house, 'Denross', in *repoussé* copper, glinted on the gatepost. Ross drove a Jaguar and had a snooker table in his modestly baronial hallway. His wife Denise, also from New South Wales, had, since her arrival in England twenty years before, made a slightly more strenuous attempt than her husband at phonemic assimilation. In spite of this she still let slip a few Sydney giveaways: said 'Oo-er' if she nearly dropped something, 'haitch' for aitch, 'r-i-gh-t!' for yes, and occasionally, when she wasn't thinking, enjoyed a 'fillum'.

Derek sprawled in the comfortable kitchen while Denise, in her tight Versace jeans, got him a cuppa. Here, mercifully, was the only place on earth he never had to stipulate 'no Earl Grey'. Here, also, with these nice, warm, bawdy Aussies, he felt relaxed and at home. After all those years in tight-arsed, toffee-nosed Albion, he could be an Australian again.

Ross Gibb was not merely Derek's unsolicited adviser on amatory matters; he was his business manager and friend. They had first met in a dentist's waiting-room in 1974. That was long before Trevor Watson and Hugh Bremner had moved their practice to Cadogan Mews and struck gold, platinum or merely plaque in the mouths of divas and prima ballerinas. In the old days, Pinky and Perky's surgery was in Earls Court – Kangaroo Valley – and their patients were mostly expatriate or itinerant Australians.

One morning in the waiting-room, as Derek prepared himself for an emergency root filling on the National Health, he had noticed the tall, bearded figure of Ross Gibb in jeans, a leather jacket and an 'I love Australia' T-shirt, slouched in a corner reading *Punch.* They got talking and Ross had asked him if he had 'wheels'. He explained he was in the motor business and could get him a dead-set deal.

Derek guessed Ross was from Sydney. They were always more pushy. You would be unlikely to find an Adelaide man hustling in a dentist's waiting-room. But Derek had felt a surge of amused patriotism, and they had met later in the pub – the only one in London that sold draught Fosters. Once he got the message that Derek wasn't in the market for a set of 'wheels', he had relaxed and regaled him until closing time with sardonic tales of the used car trade.

Ross Gibb flogged second-hand VW kombie vans to naïve antipodean tourists. Conveniently these vehicles usually broke down in France, Italy or, with any luck, Greece, and there was small print in the warranty which exonerated Koala Motors, West Kensington from all responsibility.

In the months that followed, their friendship developed, and over a few and many drinks, Ross told outrageous stories of irate and anorak'd couples trying to get their money back. 'For every van we sold, we always chucked in a complimentary length of rope,' said Ross, 'though sometimes you couldn't help feeling sorry for the bastards.'

Derek had liked Ross's girlfriend Denise, too. In those days she was like a beautiful yobbo, still dressed in the flattering mode of the sixties: back-combed Julie Christie hair, black mini and a big laugh. Not so much a dolly-bird, as a dolly-kookaburra. Now, years later and after two children, she was still attractive in a tough, wiry way, though her long hair was clipped short *au garçon* and coloured gold by Daniel Galvin in George Street.

Ross had changed a bit over the years, too, since the days he had shuffled bombs in Earls Court. His hair was short and crinkly now, almost white, and the beard had been abridged to a still-blonde moustache that extended below the corners of the mouth in a style pioneered by Dennis Lillee and perpetuated by Merv Hughes. But Ross remained trim and fit, with a Coeurcheval tan and a Missoni sweater.

That morning, in the Weybridge kitchen, with its gleaming Poggenpohl appointments, Ross took a long pull on his coffee and said, 'Who's this Pam you're shacked up with, mate?'

'She'd have to be an improvement on Belinda,' contributed Denise. 'Rossie and me always said she behaved like she had a poker up her arse.'

'I thought you liked her,' Derek lied.

'Listen Dek,' said his friend. 'To be perfectly honest with you, what can you say when your mate is married to the wrong sheila? You wouldn't have thanked us if we'd told you to shoot through.' Derek's manager grabbed his wife, and flinging her on his lap with much kicking and giggling, whispered some inaudible ribaldry. Derek observed them glumly from across the kitchen table.

Not bad after ten years of marriage, he reflected, and he still has plenty on the side. He was almost jealous of his manager: the big if ugly house, the nice cars, the still frisky wife. Even the children, Andrew and Simon, who probably thought of themselves as English and had no memories of heat and dust and surf and Vegemite to yearn for. Whenever Derek started to envy Gibbo's domestic bliss, he consoled himself with the triumphant observation that they had no taste whatever. There wasn't a single thing on the walls he would ever want to take home, and that included the Nolan.

'I suppose you thought you were marrying a bit of class, you poor old bastard!'

'Listen you two, lay off. I haven't lived with Belinda for over ten years, so why are you giving me a hard time now?' said Derek, feeling for a cigarette packet, as ex-smokers sometimes do.

'You'd have to be a sucker for punishment. Is this Pam a pom as well?' enquired Denise, plonking a

Fortnum's fruitcake on the table. 'Not ashamed of your roots, are you, Dekka?'

'We never had no roots we was all that ashamed of, did we mate?' said Ross, putting a conciliatory arm around Derek and looking up at his wife with an expression of mock outrage.

Derek always enjoyed his friends' infantile sexual banter. Sometimes Ross would make some lewd reference to a girl he had slept with, forgetting the incident had occurred since his marriage, but Denise never seemed to mind.

'Jesus, Dekka, see what a randy old cunt-struck bastard I married!' They always called Derek 'Dekka': it was strictly an Australian hypocorism. Ross was always 'Rossie' or 'Gibbo'. As a laconic abbreviation, Derek had once reflected, Gibbo actually took longer to say than Gibb. It was, so to speak, a diminutive of magnitude.

Derek noticed that on the fridge door someone had blu-tack'd a page ripped from a skiing periodical. The headline read:

A REMEMBRANCE OF THINGS PISTE.

'Who do we have to fuck for a second cuppa?' said Ross.

'I'd like one too,' said Derek.

'R-i-gh-t,' said Denise, 'not a problem.'

'Mrs Petty likes it much better at the BBC.'

No longer to his own surprise, Derek always spoke of his famous TV creation in the third person. Ross Gibb had long ago adjusted to, then ceased to notice this eccentricity. He even went along with it. He said; 'Mrs Petty would have had a real shitty on me if I let her do another series with Grosvenor Television.'

Derek and his manager had retired for a business chat to the study, if a room innocent of books may be so called. They sat in an expensive, uncomfortable, green leather buttoned chesterfield, under a big, framed photograph of Derek shaking hands with Princess Diana, with Gibbo grinning in the background in a ruffled dress-shirt and attached wing collar.

'That new Controller of Programmes is a fuckin' dickhead,' Ross vituperated, 'a mini-cab driver in the back seat of a company Rover'.

'I never thought he liked me much,' said Derek.

'To be perfectly honest with you he's a piss-ant, mate,' proclaimed Ross. 'He doesn't know what he likes. He wouldn't know a tram was up him until the bell rang. Anyway, the BBC is giving you top dollar.'

'What about the tax?'

'Leave that to Gibbo, pal. Haven't I set up a sexy little structure for you in the Caymans?'

'I'd like to see this structure sometime,' said his client. 'You make it sound like a cross between the Eiffel Tower and the Sydney Opera House.'

Ross laughed and stroked his Dennis Lillee. 'Give us the low-down on this new hornbag of yours?'

'Pam?'

'Did you slip her the old eight inches?' Ross made a priapic gesture with his Missoni-clad forearm. This was another of his foolproof aphrodisiacs, but the eight inches referred to the length, not of some conjectural virile member, but of a standard business-class British Airways ticket. The small print thereon – according to Gibbo – unconditionally obliged the recipient to participate in any form of sexual intercourse, lawful or unlawful, which the donor of the ticket might propose at journey's end. Although all women knew this, they preferred to go along with the fantasy that they were a last minute replacement for a sick secretary, accepting a spare ticket for a hot Broadway show, or merely yielding to a Romantic Impulse. In Ross Gibb's experience, however, it was inevitable that their legs would be pointing at a transatlantic hotel ceiling within an hour of touchdown. The old eight inches had worked again.

'She required no such inducement,' said Derek primly. 'Pam loves me for myself and I don't have to bribe her with frequent flyer points to get her into my bed.'

'Don't you believe it, mate. To be perfectly honest, I've checked her out. She's a quiet one, but the quiet ones are often as cunning as shit-house rats.'

'Charming,' said Derek, the actor.

'Listen, mate, we've known each other for yonks now and to be perfectly honest with you, it gives me the shits to think what your career would be like if it wasn't for me.'

Derek raised his hand and tried to say something.

'Shut up for once, will you, mate. I'm not giving myself the big rap, I'm thinking of you, because you're the goose that lays the golden fuckin' eggs, and if it wasn't for them eggs the old head of the war office in there,' – Ross flicked his thumb in the direction of the kitchen – 'wouldn't have the Cartier watch, the Harrods charge card or the BMW! Are you with me?'

Derek inaudibly concurred.

'Your career was rat-shit until you let me take over the reins and run you like a fuckin' business. Now you're a hot property; you've got a beautiful flat, objects fuckin' d'art and a sexy structure in the Caymans, and I don't want you pissing it away on some little beatnik with the arse out of her flares.'

The beatnik rather dated Gibbo, Derek thought, as did the flares; but it was all true. He hated to think where he would be without his friend's shrewd, if brutal, guidance.

Ross leant forward and grabbed Derek by the wrists. 'Look, mate, you've still got that Belinda living it up like Lady Muck somewhere out there in the English outback. You thought she'd give you a bit of class, and all you ever got was aggravation, right? Now you're on your own, with a big new series coming up that'll pull you in a squillion. I don't care who you root, but don't let them shack up with you, or they'll take you to the cleaners.'

'You ought to know, Gibbo, that Pam is nothing like this rapacious monster you've invented. You've got her completely wrong. She's so independent she'd drive you mad. She earns a perfectly respectable living as a sculptor, she insists on going Dutch in restaurants, and when Pinky and Perky did some work on her teeth last week she picked up the tab behind my back.'

'I've said my bit, mate. It's your life anyway – up to a point – but don't come whinging to me when she's shafted you.' Ross stood up. 'Don't forget there's plenty more fish in the sea.'

'I never seem to meet them,' said Derek ruefully. 'All the beautiful women seem to be attached to somebody else.'

'Don't you believe it, mate!' Ross put his face close to Derek's and growled lecherously. 'Take a tip from me, and if you want it, go for it. However beautiful a woman is, there's always some stupid bastard who's sick of fucking her.'

Derek attempted to absorb this gem of old Australian wisdom, then returned to his defence of Pam. 'But you'd *like* her, Ross, you really would! I'll arrange a dinner,' exclaimed Derek. 'As a matter of fact, she's got a great body, but not much clothes sense. Perhaps Denise . . .'

'Listen mate, if you let my wife loose with your bird in South Molton Street, I'll have to get you a booking in Vegas to pay the Amex bill! Are you with me?'

Derek was with him.

'Is my husband giving you a hard time?' Denise had come into the room and stood beside Ross, pushing her fingers through his white crinkly hair. It was like Persian lamb, Derek thought.

'Rossie's being a bit of a bore, as usual.'

'Someone's got to ride shotgun while I lock this new deal away.' Derek noticed, not without affection, that Ross had incorporated his two favourite phrases in this last pronouncement. He was always locking things away and riding shotgun, though rarely simultaneously.

'If that new bird of yours wants to look at a few clothes next week,' said Denise, 'I'll give her a bell, but not Tuesday. I've got my aromatherapy Tuesday morning.'

'What did I tell you, Dekka,' exclaimed Ross, 'Den's taking your ceiling inspector shopping! You're a dead man.'

The three of them were laughing as Derek climbed into his car.

'Shit,' said Denise, 'I nearly forgot. My aromatherapist is called Veronica Evans, she'd be pushing fifty, bit of an old hippie, and she reckons she knew you in Adelaide in the sixties. Ring a bell?'

Derek remembered instantly. 'Cast your mind back, Denise,' he said through the car window as he started the engine. 'Just before she does whatever aromatherapists do, does she say: "May I?" '

'Don't think so darl, why?'

'Nothing,' said Derek, 'but it used to be her nickname. I'll tell you the story sometime. See you on the phone.' He backed the car down the long drive.

'Thanks for the cuppa,' he yelled back at Denise and Gibbo.

'Not a problem.'

'R-i-gh-t.'

As Derek drove home, he thought about May I. She was the first English girl he had ever slept with. Her father had been in the British Army and, if he remembered correctly, was Secretary of the Adelaide branch of the English Speaking Union. But May I had lived alone in a small neat flat and worked at the university library. She was famous for her good manners in a society where even passably good manners are conspicuous. He had known her name was Veronica but everyone called her May I. She wasn't obviously sexy, far from it. In fact, she looked rather like Vera Lynn, or how one imagined Enid Blyton in her nubile phase. But she was bit of a dark horse; indeed, the equine comparison could have been unkindly extended. She was a big girl, full-chested and twin-setted, and with long teeth which she seemed able effortlessly to retract when the occasion demanded.

But she was really famous, in undergraduate circles at least, for her Olde Worlde manners in the most intimate of human connections. She would invariably, after the preliminary embraces, slide abruptly out of sight into a genuflective position. Then she would look up with wide, appealing blue eyes and the winsome smile of a polite child requesting confectionery, and utter her famous entreaty: 'May I?'

Another of her accommodating phrases was 'Be my guest,' an invitation no less heartfelt or hospitable for being muffled by a pillow.

After Derek had left for England, he heard on the grapevine that May I had become a hippie and had set off, patchouli'd and discalceate, for Goa and Katmandu. She had written him a few psychedelic letters in green ink on musky aerogrammes. One of these had related her adventures in Delhi, where she lost her money and her passport and threw herself on the mercy of the Australian Embassy. Luckily, Our Man in India, Stuart Murphy, a failed journalist and leftist lickspittle, had known May I in her genteel incarnation. She was given a bath and a comfy bed in the servants' wing of the Australian compound.

At about three in the morning, May I was surprised by an importunate visit from His Excellency who had furtively extracted himself from his wife's bed, and far beyond the call of duty, scurried to the pallet of the indigent hippie. He had been sweating profusely and trembling with fear, lest Joyce Murphy discover the lengths to which Australian functionaries are sometimes prepared to go in order to alleviate the distress of youthful taxpayers, far from home.

May I's nocturnal visitor was now the Australian High Commissioner in London, Derek remembered with satisfaction. If he ever needed a visa in a hurry, or an extended work permit, he knew the magic words.

Belinda

KENNETH GROCOCK JABBED at a few characters on his keyboard, and after a moment's electronic stridulation, the green text flashed up on the screen of his superseded Amstrad. Leaning forward, his elbows on the desk and his small chin in his hands, he reread the morning's work.

> DEREK PETTYFER
>
> The entertainment world today mourns one of its brightest stars. The death of Derek Walkerville Pettyfer, which occurred on ? after a long/short ? illness/accident ? marks the end of an era in British comedy. Famous in the United Kingdom and Australia and increasingly popular across the Atlantic for his brilliant comic invention Mrs Petty, he was also a character actor of distinction. His appearance last autumn in the new one-man show, *Memoirs of an Old Bugger,* based on the letters of Patrick

White, won him the coveted *Evening Standard* Award for the Best Play of 1994 and universal critical acclaim for his performance as the eponymous curmudgeon of Australian literature.

Derek Pettyfer was born in Adelaide, South Australia on 11 February 1945 and attended St Peter's College and the University of South Australia, although he was always reluctant to advertise his antipodean roots. Failing to complete a degree, he was nonetheless active in student revues and undergraduate theatricals. His first success was in a student production of Shelley's *The Cenci.*

Like so many Australians of his generation, Pettyfer went to London in the late sixties, soon after he left university. After a stint in repertory theatre, he officiated at the death throes of the self-styled Satire Movement before embarking on a series of one-man shows which coaxed high comedy from such unlikely literary subjects as the diaries of Søren Kierkegaard, the *Trivia* of Logan Pearsall Smith and the scabrous journals of Frank Harris. However, his television appearances in the drab guise of Mrs Petty, the puritanical but hilarious housewife, will prove to be his lasting claim to fame. With this character he extended out of all recognition the theatrical possibilities of the pantomime dame.

Unlike his peers, he granted few interviews and although quite gregarious, little is really known about his personal life. There was a period in the late 1970s when his habits of intemperance gave serious concern to . . .

Kenneth lent back gingerly in the swivel chair and put his hands behind his head and his feet on the desk as he had seen journalists do in films of the 1930s. If he had had a Lucky Strike he would have lit it.

Not much to show for all that research, he thought, but having met the man himself only last night at Inge Pinkhill's party he was spurred on to further efforts. He was certainly determined not to be caught on the hop as he had been over John Osborne and Peter Cook, though Pettyfer had looked extraordinarily well, if a bit tired and irritable. Perhaps he should quietly interview a few friends of his subject and get the real low-down: even a little dirt. His editor liked that kind of obituary because it generally provoked indignant letters – even protests from the wives and children of the defamed stiff. In short, a catty obit sold papers.

Perhaps he could pump Inge; take her to lunch on the pretext of thanking her for the party, but he didn't know her that well. In fact, not at all really. He had only been there because he had persuaded Pippa Billinghurst to ask if she could bring a friend.

Funnily enough, Kenneth had already started writing an obit on Lionel Pinkhill, Inge's husband, and enjoyed revealing that the Bradford-born cellist had changed his name from Rosenberg in 1945. She was very attractive, Inge, and it seemed unlikely that she was totally faithful to that old, sinister-looking and frequently absent husband of hers. Pinkhill played like an angel but he was an ugly bugger. In Kenneth's hearing some drunken hack had once referred to Mrs Pinkhill as 'Inge the finger', a sniggering allusion to digital dexterity at some climactic moment, Kenneth presumed.

Another useful source might be Derek's estranged wife, Belinda Pettyfer, whose existence seemed to have been well hushed up; she didn't even rate a mention in Derek's *Who's Who* entry. Perhaps he thought it might cramp his style with the bimbos. Belinda lived in Devon, near Bideford, Kenneth remembered. A painter. Did painstaking portraits of people's country houses. And wasn't there a child?

Kenneth Grocock was beginning to think in terms of a book, a full-length, unauthorised critical study. Warts and all! He knew there were a few pretty respected people around town who had stated, out loud, that Pettyfer was getting a bit too clever for his own good. That his was a facile talent in sore need of revaluation. Kenneth reckoned that through a couple of his friend Polly's contacts, he might get a nice fat advance; that was if the material were juicy enough. Not a hatchet job, of course, but a balanced assessment of a nearly great career, with a few startling, and preferably sexual, revelations.

Soon after, on a hot morning in August, Kenneth took the train to north Devon. The journey from Paddington was much longer than he imagined, with a change at Exeter, and even when he got into

Barnstaple at noon, it was a long taxi ride to Belinda Pettyfer's isolated residence.

'As soon as you see the pub, you're there,' she had said brightly on the telephone. But the steep lane which ran off sharply to the right, directly past the Ostrich, was far too daunting for Kenneth's elderly driver. He paid him off and walked. Kenneth knew from experience that most destinations 'you can't miss' were always extremely missable unless you happened to live there. The house was on the left and not the right, and the 'pretty garden' a sour and neglected wilderness. The dwelling itself was a child's drawing: two eyes and a big blue nose, at which Kenneth now stood and rang the doorbell.

A woman's distant voice cried, 'Coming, coming,' as Kenneth's journalistic eye observed the wreckage of a bicycle, a ruined pram filled with nasturtiums, and what looked like six months' supply of rotting pink and yellow junk mail trampled to *papier mâché* on the step. At length the door opened and Belinda Pettyfer stood before him with a radiant smile.

'Come in, Mr Grocock, come in,' she said as he stood transfixed by the scale, the colour and, he now perceived, the aroma of the personage before him. 'I'm afraid I had to start without you.' She looked down with an expression of vague surprise, first at the cigarette in her left hand, then at the glass of amber liquid in her right. Kenneth noticed that a great deal of cigarette ash had embedded itself in the folds and smocking of her voluminous maroon caftan. It was clearly a favourite garment which had proved most practical in the enshrouding and exuviation of Belinda Pettyfer's difficult body.

She led the way into a small and frowsty sitting-room, wherein every surface seemed to be heaped with books, magazines, dirty plates, old clothes, empty cigarette packets and overflowing ashtrays. With a sweep of her naked foot, Belinda cleared a pile of rubbish off a small chair and bade Kenneth sit down. The grime-mottled calf and ankle, which he had briefly glimpsed, were monumental; rather like the hefty terracotta limbs of Picasso's neo-classical bathing beauties. He noticed, too, that she had mauve feet.

'I knew it was only a matter of time before one of you chaps came down here to interrogate me about Derek,' she said. 'And I think I should tell you, Mr Grocock, that I haven't seen my husband for six and a half years. His loss, not mine.'

She took a long drag on her cigarette and thrust a glass into Kenneth's hand. He noticed a sticky crimson puddle in the bottom and a flake of ash.

'We'll have a quick one here and a nice tête-à-tête down at the Ostrich. I'm sure you fancy a ploughman's after that ghastly trip.' With something like grace, Belinda plucked up a half empty Johnnie Walker bottle from the cluttered hearth and splashed some into his glass.

'Cheers,' she said, draining her own and attempting to stifle a terrible cough. At this she failed, and as Kenneth gazed anxiously at the beverage he was expected to consume, she leaned her large frame against the doorjamb and abandoned herself to a long bronchial paroxysm. When she had sufficiently recovered and mopped her streaming eyes with a dubious Kleenex, Kenneth was standing, ready for a stroll back to the pub, having deftly emptied his glass on to a dead potted hyacinth.

He was relieved they were lunching out, having glimpsed Belinda's kitchen through another door.

'That's a nice picture,' said Kenneth, who knew nothing about pictures. He was peering at a large and gloomy print of Roman ruins, the glass of which was broken and repaired, it seemed, with Band-aids and Sellotape.

'Oh, isn't it fun!' said Belinda, lighting another cigarette and glaring at the picture through her fringe of implausibly yellow hair. 'It's a Piranesi; all I have left. Derek took the rest of my collection, though he wouldn't know a good picture from a hole in the ground.'

She poured herself another aperitif. 'I put him on to Piranesi soon after we met, but he pinched the lot when we parted and he's welcome to them. I hate possessions, I'm afraid, Mr Grocock. It's an old saying but a true one that possessions end up possessing you.'

The Obituarist could not but agree with this apophthegm as he glanced around at the stupendous chaos.

'Of course, Mr Grocock, I earn a little pin money from my own topographic watercolours which I may show you later, but it's not much fun being a deserted mother and if I'd had a few Piranesis to sell, wee Timothy might have had an easier childhood.'

It was the first mention she had made of Derek Pettyfer's son, and Kenneth pricked up his ears. 'You mean he didn't support his own child?' exclaimed the journalist with effortless sanctimony.

'None of this is for publication, Mr Grocock, you understand. I have been silent all these years, and until my book is published, I shall remain silent.'

A book! She was writing a book. If only he could see it and paraphrase a few choice extracts. Money would probably do the trick, but he must win this old bat's confidence first. A few more drinks might help open the floodgates.

'Let's adjourn to the Ostrich,' she said as if in answer to his thoughts, 'and we can talk there. But remember, off the record, Mr Grocock, *off the record!* What you intend to write will only appear when Derek is dead, but what I'm writing I want him to read.'

The public bar of the Ostrich was almost deserted, and it was clearly Belinda Pettyfer's home from home.

'How be young Timmy then, Mrs P, doing his sums right?' said the black barman with a strong West Country burr. He wore a University of Idaho T-shirt.

'If Mr Grocock is a gentleman and gives me a good lunch, he may be meeting our Timothy later today,' said Mrs Pettyfer in cryptic reply, as she settled herself on to a bar stool upholstered in red vinyl and proceeded to rupture the cellophane on a new packet of Benson and Hedges. 'A large red Johnnie I think today, Graham,' she added, as though her choice of beverage was a matter of caprice; tomorrow it could easily be ouzo and Pepsi Cola, or water! But Graham had already put a glass of mahogany fluid on the bar. Hastily, Kenneth called for a Chardonnay and slapped ten pounds on the counter as a guarantee of good faith.

After the first urgent gulp, Belinda Pettyfer turned her large and startling countenance towards him. It was the first time he had looked at her full on, in a good light.

You could tell that she had been pretty; beautiful perhaps, but she appeared to have performed her *maquillage* in the dark, or on some violently moving piece of heavy machinery. Her entire face had been distempered a deep, St Tropez orange which stopped abruptly at the neckline, and her rouge and lipstick, of an unfashionable cyclamen, had been applied with a careless regard to facial congruity. Beneath her xanthic fringe, false black lashes, carelessly fastened to turquoise lids, sheltered her pale-blue bloodshot eyes.

Only when she smiled, as she did now upon her visitor from the Press, did she reveal her *pièce de résistance*: a set of magnificent teeth; a portcullis of the purest Royal Doulton. Grocock, who had been a showbiz hack, was reminded of images of Carol Channing and Brigitte Bardot.

Belinda Pettyfer fluttered her substantial nylon lashes. 'You've seen me before, haven't you, Mr Grocock?' She took a famished suck on her cigarette, which she held in the crook of two nicotine-varnished fingers. 'How clever of you to recognise me from Francis's picture. I suppose it's my claim to fame – apart from being ditched by Derek. A ploughman's for my host, Graham, and I'll try the shepherd's pie, if it's nice today.'

Probably no nicer than it was yesterday, thought Kenneth uncharitably. 'I'm not sure what picture you mean, Mrs Pettyfer,' he confessed, sipping his warm wine.

'Of course you do, you crafty little man, and it's Belinda if you don't mind awfully, and not too much shepherd's pie please, Graham! Just a taste. Must remember my regime.' She turned back to Kenneth, and in a fruity whisper, accompanied by gusts of cigarette smoke borne on a zephyr of whisky, she resumed: 'No one down here has heard of the Screaming Woman Triptych, surprise surprise, but I hope it stays in Britain, Grocock, don't fancy hanging on a wall in Malibu.'

The penny dropped.

'Screaming Woman'! Kenneth recalled the controversy, still raging, about Francis Bacon's late masterpiece and the national appeal to stymie the Getty and buy it for the Tate. 'It's you, Mrs . . . Belinda! Didn't David Sylvester call you Bacon's Mona Lisa?' Kenneth Grocock, who had little visual memory, nonetheless remembered that painting as one would remember a road accident; a triplicate portrait of the woman beside him in this rustic pub, though it more accurately resembled three generous dollops of placenta on a billiard table.

'I introduced Derek to all the right people in London, you know, Mr Grocock. Francis, of course, and Liz Smart and dear Colin MacInnes. I got him into the Colony Room, too, but nobody liked him; couldn't hold his drink you see – never cultivated a *second stomach.* If you're going on to Appledore ask Dan Farson what he thinks of Derek and he'll keep you there till closing time. But I first met him through Jeff and Penny Craig or Jeff Bernard or Bimba MacNiece or someone at the French Pub and he'd just come over from Australia and looked at us as though we were all barmy which we were Mr Grocock which we were but he was very good-looking in his duffle-coat and he didn't talk strine cobber me old kangaroo dundee mate not likely and we had this scene together as they called it then and next thing I was married again though Francis said I'd watch that one dearie and Dan couldn't stand a *bar* of him.'

Belinda paused for refreshment and continued: 'By then he was well and truly into the demon drink and Muriel barred him darling barred him and he was always off drinking with those Australians with that Gibb that Ross that Ross Gibb ghastly creature with no style darling rough as bags common as dirt but I had their number Mr Grocock and I tried to get him to the old Alcoholics Hieronymus God didn't I try to get him to cut down darling cut down and he did in the end after he walked out on Timmy and me and what a bore he is now what a CRASHING BORE doesn't touch it now they tell me and boring with it boring with it and Ian God rest his soul said he'd bar him again for being sober darling and a bloody bore!'

Mrs Pettyfer laughed so much at this that she

started to cough and, with Kenneth's assistance, had to heave herself off her stool and stand in the middle of the bar with her yellow hair and her big bare violet feet. She coughed until the tears streamed down. When she was sufficiently recovered, she took Kenneth's arm rather violently and demanded they go home then and there. Her shepherd's pie remained untouched on the counter except for a Benson and Hedges butt projecting from the crust like a crooked, lipstick-stained periscope.

Kenneth was paying, and trying to explain to Graham his need for a receipt. 'You see,' he was saying to the bewildered barman, to whom a request for a receipt in a north Devon pub was as common as a request for Fernet Branca. 'You see, I need one for my editor, for my expenses.'

Belinda Pettyfer, meanwhile, swaying at his side, had allowed her reminiscences to assume a more darkly misanthropic complexion. 'Has he told you about his precious Roman glass collection, has he, Mr Grocock? I suppose he's told you about his Roman glass collection, has he?' She spat out the words.

'I don't actually know him that well basically.'

'Let him tell you about his Roman glass except it's *my* glass darling, all of it and thank God I kept some hidden away that I could sell to feed my son and feed his wife and I bet he said he invented Mrs Petty did he tell you that darling did he say he invented Mrs Petty but he would wouldn't he say that when it was *me* who wrote all those scripts and gave him ideas and gave him the contacts and it's all in my book all in the book in the bank under lock and key because he'd come down here and steal it if he could darling wouldn't want the truth about Mrs Petty leaking out would he my darling and who is he living with now Mr Prick Mr Cock who's the scrubber he's bedding up there in his flat with my glass and my pictures he'll put her through hell darling just like he put me through hell and he can't be alone oh no he can't stand it he has to have someone some scrubber have anything woman or animal *boys* more than likely oh yes he's a dark horse that Derek . . .'

Kenneth, alarmed, even for a journalist, at the sinister direction of Mrs Pettyfer's monologue, glanced anxiously at Graham the barman, who was just leaning on the counter and laughing tolerantly at what Kenneth realised must be a regular cabaret turn, as the enormous bulk of Belinda Pettyfer, a drink in one talon, wambled into an inglenook and slowly collapsed.

'Don't go, Mr Dick! Don't let that black bastard send you away,' she cried from the floor. 'This pub is a dump it's a big crock of shit. Do you know what he likes? Shall I tell you, your Derek your teetotal Derek! Print this if you want to, put this in your paper . . .'

Her voice was rising to an eldritch scream. Kenneth, scared to death, decided to make a bolt for it, but the barman grabbed his arm. He was still laughing. 'Don't worry about Mrs P, sir. It happens every few days. She passes out cold and young Timmy collects her around teatime.'

Kenneth shuddered. 'Poor little devil,' he said,

looking down at the foundered hulk of Belinda Pettyfer. 'Poor little bugger.'

'He's not exactly a kid, mister, not our young Timmy.'

But Kenneth Grocock's brain was reeling. For a mad moment he entertained the notion that Graham the barman might *actually* have studied at the University of Idaho as his T-shirt proclaimed; that he was even a brilliant African-American dropout doing esoteric field work. A lawyer perhaps.

'. . . not exactly a kid, not Timmy. He's Mrs P's boy by her first husband. He's the local bank manager.'

Mercifully, there was a bus stop directly outside the Ostrich and a cluster of people: three schoolchildren, a district nurse, a Down's syndrome teenager, a pregnant Indian girl and an old man on a Zimmer frame. They peered up the road to where a green bus distantly loomed. Kenneth joined them as though he were rejoining the human race. He realised with a pang that he had left his pocket Philips dictaphone running on Belinda's mantelpiece three hours before.

Suddenly she appeared, horribly resurrected in the doorway of the Ostrich. A heaving monolith of bordeaux red crowned with unruly yellow. She was Bardot by Botero; Mother Courage run amok.

'MR CUNT!' she bawled. The little queue of commuters froze. They regarded the apparition of Belinda Pettyfer, swaying perilously in the entrance to the pub, with silent stupefaction. She had a cry like a coronach. 'You know what he used to like in bed, my darling? Know what he used to like?'

As public transport drew noisily nearer she raised her voice to a stentorian level. 'A hot scotch and MY TONGUE UP HIS ARSE!'

They were all glad of the bus.

Yvette

AT NINE ONE morning, some weeks later, Derek had a final fitting for a full-length, bias-cut, midnight blue, satin ball dress. For the next episode of *Petty Sessions,* they were recording a scene in which Mrs Petty was presented to Royalty. The script was very very funny.

Derek climbed carefully out of bed and went into the kitchen to make himself a cup of tea. It was still only seven o'clock and Pam would be dead to the world for a couple of hours yet. He had the flat to himself.

As usual, he stood for a few rapturous moments before his shelves of Roman glass, to which had been recently added an important bluish green cinerary urn from the first century AD, with a folded rim, a broad strap handle attached to the shoulder, and slight iridescent patches of silver-grey weathering. The beautiful object, found near Flamersheim, had been sold to him by a respected dealer in North

Audley Street. He always gave Derek first refusal before offering a special item to the Corning Museum of Glass, New York, or the Romisch-Germanisches Museum of Cologne. It had cost roughly the price of a new Audi Quatro and, once again, Derek had been forced to go cap in hand to his manager. Ross had sighed and groaned, but finally, with another of his 'You've got the dough, mate, so you might as well spend it, you're a long time dead' speeches, Ross had arranged payment from one of Derek's off-shore accounts which he managed so shrewdly. How that worked was beyond Derek's comprehension, but it was all above board and went like clockwork, so long as fifteen million people still laughed at Mrs Petty every Saturday night, prime time.

Derek always said a tacit good morning to his green, fifth-century unguent bottle, because it was the first piece he had ever bought. When he first arrived in London with a little money left to him by his father – an Adelaide estate agent – he had seen this exquisite object in a shop near the British Museum, and the pilot light of acquisitiveness was kindled. Even then, this small bottle had cost him most of what he owned; nearly all the money that was meant to tide him over in London until he found work. It was fortunate that job at the Lyric Hammersmith had turned up when it did. Derek was lucky like that, although the tiny actors' bar on the dress circle level, accessible by a spiral staircase in the proscenium arch, had been a bit of a trap.

Belinda had never shared his enthusiasm. 'What's

that funny old broken bottle?' she had said. 'You must come down to Cornwall and meet Bernard Leach. English Pottery, *that's* what you should collect if want to collect anything. How do you know it's not a fake?'

But Derek knew it was 'right' and the idea of pottery – turds really, however nicely shaped and glazed and burnished – left him cold.

But when they had split up during Derek's horrific drinking days, Belinda had changed her mind about the six pieces of glass he had managed to assemble, though in a boozy row there had been one terrible casualty: an inscribed globular flask with a tapering neck found at Populónia in Tuscany was smashed to smithereens. Belinda had decided she loved these things after all, and when Derek stumbled home one night they were gone.

Two years ago, at Christie's, he had bought four of them back at an enormous price, including his precious unguent bottle. He had paid dearly for them; he had paid twice.

Now Derek reclined in a comfortable chintz window-seat, sipping his warm and sapid beverage, and gazed out at his 'view'. Mostly, it was a view of another large block of mansion flats, but he had an impressive glimpse of Westminster Cathedral's Siennese campanile, beautifully lit by the morning sunshine.

Who lived in all these mansion apartments?, he wondered. Who else lived in his building, for that matter? Who lived next door? The enormous appeal of a soap like *Neighbours*, he supposed, was that it was a melodrama set in a remote, all-white society, where people still knew who lived next door. Well, it was an Australian show, all about a place he came from. A place he had forsaken for England.

He had turned his back on Utopia; all that neighbourliness and back-slapping and too-easy intimacy, but for what? Literate newspapers – except a fellow Australian was now doing something about that. Marvellous art exhibitions – except he always missed them. Great theatre – but it was usually disappointing, and going to the theatre anyway felt too much like 'shop'. Civilised pubs – except he didn't drink any more, and it was amazing how sordid the best pubs looked through the bottom of a glass of ginger ale. And awful weather.

Derek noticed an ominous rag of indigo cloud resembling Scandinavia, creeping across the sky behind the Cathedral. It even looked as if it might rain. Derek's nostalgia returned.

Yes, he decided, cynicism apart, Australians *were* somehow more trustworthy than those pallid, closed-off poms. There were exceptions, of course. Take his accountant, Roger Wainwright, of Nimmo, Nimmo, Blackburn and Tricker. There was a classic product of the English public school system, somewhat eccentric, but solid as a rock and a tax whiz-kid, according to all reports.

Derek had been in England for nearly twelve years before he received the tip about Roger, and in a mood of scepticism met him in his Dickensian chambers near St Paul's. He was an overgrown schoolboy, a bit stage-struck, but he had an impressive list of clients and when it came to tax he was immaculate; he knew all the wrinkles.

Of course Derek had checked him out with Ross Gibb, and after a few enquiries, Ross had given Roger two thumbs up. 'To be perfectly honest, mate, you couldn't do better,' Gibbo had said. 'I'll lock up a deal with him, but I'll ride shotgun just in case.'

Before taking a shower, Derek did a quick tour of his Piranesis. The light on one wall was too strong. He drew several curtains and adjusted a blind; he didn't want any of his four magnificent *Grotteschi* getting accidentally 'sunned'. Soon he must consider having special ultra-violet filter glass installed in the windows of the apartment. Gibbo would tear his hair out when the bill for that arrived.

But how had his passion for this artist begun?

He remembered, of course. When he was nineteen there was a French girl at the university called, absurdly, Yvette. Her parents had come to Australia after the War, though the French community in Adelaide was minuscule. Frenchmen who elect to live outside their native France are usually suspect – failures or fugitives – and Parisians who emigrate to Adelaide would have to be on the run from something. But Yvette was deliciously, and of course self-consciously, French. She had studied at the Leslie Caron–Gigi École de Gallic Charme. In sultrier moments she could impersonate Juliette Greco. She favoured cobalt stockings, short skirts, snug angora tops and black *grosgrain* chokers. One evening, after their first date, when Derek drove her back to her parents' home in a drab suburb, he had no sooner switched off the engine than she had methodically unhitched her bra and permitted him a systematic manipulation of her breasts, spasmodically lit by passing cars.

For the three months which followed, and after innumerable attendances at the films of Ingmar Bergman, Derek was in love. A more experienced student, a youth Derek privately detested, had once told him that girls were more inclined to 'go all the way' if you told them that you loved them. Derek, in this case, had no need to dissemble: he adored this exotic and much coveted creature, and he told her so at every opportunity. But though his physical desire was satisfied, uncomfortably and not seldom in the back seat of his mother's Vauxhall, Yvette made no reciprocal confession of love, or even affection.

An unfrequented and sparsely lit street would be selected; the car would be parked in its most penumbral precinct, and then the two would clamber into the back seat and commence their desperate struggle with zips, clips, clasps, elastic, buttons and finally with each other. Gradually, a sense of hopelessness, even despair took possession of Derek. The words he longed for never came, and their erotic rituals ceased to have any real meaning for him. Thus began their slow estrangement.

But as it happened, Yvette had given him, on his birthday, a parting gift. She knew he admired the writings of Aldous Huxley and she had found, at Beck's Bookshop, an essay on Piranesi's *Prisons*, illustrated with plates, published in a limited edition. It was the finest book Derek had ever possessed. It bore Huxley's signature on the colophon, but he looked on the flyleaf and preliminary pages in vain for a personal inscription from the girl he thought he loved. Just a fine book, gift wrapped, left at his parents' house without a word. He never saw Yvette again. He wrote thanking her, of course, but his tone was guarded, cool and self-protective.

The impersonal gift, so perfectly chosen, hurt him more than had anything previously in his life; but it set him on the trail of its subject, the eighteenth-century Venetian artist, Piranesi. Derek no longer possessed the book, of course. It was lost somewhere, in one of his countless moves, upheavals, excursions and alarms.

Like all Australians, even apostate Australians, Derek liked to shower; and beneath a forceful stream of hot water. Not for him those tepid aspergations favoured in British bathrooms. A special motor had been installed in the roof of his bathroom which, though noisy, guaranteed an intense inundation. As Derek stood in the glass cubicle enjoying this most un-English amenity, a stinging sensation reminded him of his rash. It was a minor but disagreeable inflammation in a vulnerable place which had troubled him once before that morning. Perhaps he had also been conscious of it on the previous evening, when he and Pam had made love, and he had dismissed it as some slight abrasion, acquired in the Lists of Venus. On examining himself more closely in a strong light, he noticed what looked like minute pustules on a field of angry red flesh. Could this be herpes, he wondered, *or worse?* It was an affliction from which Derek had hitherto been spared, though of course one read of little else in those Women's Magazines in Pinky and Perky's waiting-room. He recalled a grisly headline in *Cosmopolitan*: MANY HERPES RETURNS!

Now, he knew the author of that embarrassing conflation, but who was the author of his present discomfort? Pam? At that moment the subject of these anguished conjectures appeared in the bathroom, a blurred figure in Derek's red Sulka dressing gown. Derek saw her through the trellis of steaming water.

'Is that you, Pam?' he cried superfluously.

'Can I have the shower in a minute, Derek? I've got to get to my studio by nine.'

'It's yours!' he yelled, stepping out of the cubicle and flinging a towel around his waist. Pam's naked form flashed past him and the glass door slammed. Derek darted to the bathroom cabinet, grasped a bottle of Listerine and furtively applied it with a cotton bud.

'Would you get me a cab on your company account?' Pam cried above the thunderous deluge. 'I can't have Simon Rattle standing on the studio doorstep waiting for me, he's only giving me three sittings as it is.' But Derek was clutching the marble-topped vanitory unit, recovering from a spasm of excruciating pain. If he was going to broach this sensitive matter with Pam, the moment had passed.

Obediently, he ran back to the sitting room, picked up the phone and dialled the black cab hotline. Mercifully, the agony was slowly fading.

Minutes later, it seemed, Pam stood in the doorway fully dressed. Fully dressed in the sense that no item of her attire seemed to be absent, yet paradoxically, she wore nothing Derek felt he would miss if she never wore it again. Pam was indeed a strange sight in a baby-pink loose-knit polo-necked sweater over a full, floor-length, mustard-coloured rayon skirt decorated with green and orange cubist roses, beneath which peeped the sturdy toes of her Doc Martens. Over her shoulders she wore a very old man's jacket in fawn Donegal, and over her head, which projected from this pyramid of dissonant apparel, Pam had pulled a black knitted balaclava concealing most of her face. She looked like a terrorist emerging from a lampshade.

But perhaps this motley was perfect, Derek thought, for someone who would be mucking around with wet clay in half an hour, and considering what her wardrobe was like when he had met her, he decided that Rome wasn't built in a day. Denise could take her shopping again; Inge was probably being polite when she had said 'she scrubs up well, your Pam!'

'Surely it's not cold out now, is it?', were the only words that Derek could muster to express his dismay at the balaclava. But Pam's mood was stern.

'I better go down now or the taxi will come and go.'

'I'm off in a minute too,' said Derek unconvincingly. He was still slumped in a chair wearing nothing but a large bath towel.

'Are you all right?'

'Perfectly,' lied Derek. 'And don't panic, Tom the caretaker always rings up when the cab's here. You should get rid of that awful little flat, Pam. It's too far away.'

'I need a studio,' Derek,' she said in a hard voice he hadn't heard before. 'You're not the only artist around here. How would you like it if I moved all my stuff into your awful little drawing-room?'

'I didn't mean it was awful exactly, I'm sorry, Pam, I just think you deserve something better. More, well, salubrious.'

'I haven't got time to look that word up now Derek. Bye.'

The front door went 'thunk' more loudly than usual as the phone started ringing.

'She's on her way down, Tommy,' said Derek. Then he had a brainwave. 'Tommy,' he added, 'do any places ever come up in this building? I mean, small flats with one decent sized room? *On the floor directly under me!* How long has that been on the market? What's the guy's name again? Thanks Tommy, won't hurt me to ring the doorbell, a man can't be blamed for asking. See you.'

As Derek dressed he realised that he actually knew his subjacent neighbour, Mr MacDermott. They'd met in the lift a few times, and when the bathroom was being redone very noisily to Australian specifications, he had made a few placatory trips downstairs with the odd bottle. Mr MacDermott's name had lodged in his mind because someone, Amerika perhaps, had said he was a dermatologist, and Derek was always amused to find a clue to a man's calling embedded in his surname. He would be a popular boy on Pam's birthday if he could give her the key to the MacDermott apartment.

The door was opened almost immediately after he touched the bell, and closed again with a rather ugly 'bang'. This was not the only respect in which the MacDermott flat differed from his own. To begin with, it preserved its original gloomy decoration; a high, treacle-coloured wainscot, worn, undulating parquet and funereal lights of cracked alabaster, suspended by chains. All easily smashed up and stripped out, thought Derek with Cromwellian relish, mentally rolling up his sleeves.

Mr MacDermott greeted him with such geniality that Derek wondered if Tommy hadn't already tipped him off that the rich actor upstairs was an interested buyer. By now MacDermott might have calculated the celebrity surcharge, thought Derek glumly. But he *was* a very nice little man, all the same. A spry seventy-five, white-haired, and almost certainly retired from Harley Street. Derek guessed he had a cottage in Hampshire and half a mile of good trout fishing on the Test waiting for him as soon as he had flogged the flat.

'Mr MacDermott,' Derek began, as his neighbour offered him an armchair.

'*Alan*, if you don't mind,' the old boy interrupted,

'please call me Alan. After all, I think we all know *you*, Mrs Petty. You give a lot of people a lot of pleasure.' And Alan MacDermott chuckled away at the very thought of it. 'Well noo . . .' Did Derek detect a hint of Caledonia? '. . . I don't mind saying that wee Tommy downstairs indicated a while back that you might be interested in extending your holdings here at Ashley Mansions'. Derek realised he had been right twice, but as he looked across at this particularly charming old widower who was on the verge of asking a telephone number with an international dialling code up front for his sadly dilapidated abode, Derek had another idea.

It was unbelievably fortuitous; providential! Here he sat, in total privacy, with a distinguished specialist in diseases of the skin: he, who had only just discovered, on the most sensitive region of his anatomy, a disturbing irregularity. Derek coughed.

'Before we speak about this Mr . . . Alan, I have a more pressing problem which, if I may, I would like to discuss with you in confidence.' Alan MacDermott frowned slightly but it was a frown, Derek recognised, of professional concern.

Derek stood and walked to the window, noting how inferior was the view to that from his own quarters. 'I know that when you have an architect to dinner, it's not the done thing to ask his help in redesigning your kitchen . . .'

'I'm sorry, I don't quite see what you're driving at,' said the dermatologist.

'Well,' continued Derek huskily, his back still turned. 'I do know you're retired, and perhaps I should have dropped you a note, but the problem has just flared up and frankly I'm worried sick, and I just hoped, I mean wondered, if you could take a quick look at this.' Derek swung round, holding his cock in a trembling hand, two feet from Alan MacDermott's face.

To his amazement, the old man uttered a hoarse cry of horror, leaped out of his chair and ran for the door. 'What the hell do you think you're up to, man? What the devil do you take me for, you dirty bugger? Put it away man, put it away and get the hell out of here, sir! Get out of this flat, and God help you, sir. God help you!'

Derek was immobilised. What had gone wrong? Some terrible breach of etiquette perhaps. He should have written this chap a letter first, or discussed fees . . . 'About the flat, I mean, er, can we talk later? I, I'm being fitted for a frock in fifteen minutes.'

'That does not surprise me, Mr Pettyfer. Not in the least,' said Mr MacDermott stonily, pushing the door harder against the shoulder of his departing guest. 'And this flat is not for sale, you understand, sir? It is not on the market.'

Derek had completely forgotten about his fitting until then. Had the BBC sent a car?, he wondered. At the porters' lodge, Tommy told him the car had already been waiting twenty minutes.

'How did you get on with MacDermott guv? I know he's keen to sell.'

'No he's not, I think he's a bit of a nutter actually,'

said Derek waving at his cab driver. 'Was he ever meant to be a good doctor?'

'What do you mean, doctor?'

'Doctor. He's a dermatologist, a skin specialist.'

'Sure, Doctor McDermott's a skin specialist all right, but he's in flat 10C. Alan MacDermott's an accountant from Price Waterhouse, or he was. He's a real gentleman, don't you think, Mr Pettyfer? I'm sure if you make him a reasonable proposition, he'll give it some serious thought.'

I'm sure he will, thought Derek, crawling into his cab. *For a long time to come.*

6

Vanessa

PINKY AND PERKY conducted their thriving dental practice from a large mews house in the vicinage of Harrods. It had been completed gutted and converted by one of their Sydney friends – a fashionable architect – who had redesigned the front of the building in his own vernacular with the reluctant approval of the Cadogan estate.

The façade was a blank brick wall painted a deep salmon pink and pierced by one extremely narrow door, the architect's trademark, which unconsciously betrayed his penchant for a tight entry. Nonetheless, through that slender portal passed a procession of London's most famous theatricals.

Trevor Watson was tall and thin and grey, and his colleague Hugh Bremner, short and fat and pink. Their first words, on peering into the mouths of new clients, were invariably, 'My God, who did this work?' When Derek first went to see them for a lost filling, he had to confess that the incompetent he had last let into his mouth was Mr Raymond Nash of Wigmore Street; it was another of those euonyms Derek enjoyed; a name which echoed its owner's vocation.

Pinky and Perky were generous to their poorer patients and young male ballet dancers sometimes had their teeth capped for next to nothing, but the partners' richer clients, many from the Arab Emirates, frequently stepped into the chair with a minor toothache and emerged with a full set of gold and platinum-backed porcelain crowns and a bill for thirty thousand pounds.

Derek had been sitting in Pinky's chair once when Perky ran in from the adjacent surgery and placed a wafer-thin gold wristwatch, with two ivory faces framed with diamonds, in his lap.

'What's that?' Derek had tried to ask.

'Patek Philippe, custom made,' declared Mr Watson exultantly. 'I got it off the old camel driver's wrist next door.'

'Won't he miss it?'

'She'll be out for another hour easy. Just thought you'd like to see it.'

'You'd be amazed,' said Mr Bremner, 'the tricks *some* dentists get up to when the patient's gone sleepy-byes. Remember when you had Baryshnikov in the chair, Hugh?'

'My lips are sealed!' giggled Derek's dentist, and resumed his orthodontal probe.

They were outrageous, but everyone liked them. At first nights at Covent Garden you couldn't miss them, standing in the best seats looking back over the stalls to see who was there. And when the curtain rose there was barely a smile they hadn't had a hand in.

Since their humble origins in Earls Court, whither they had travelled from their native Auckland, they had acquired, besides the mews surgery and their home in Glebe Place, a comfortable holiday villa near Marbella. The London house had been exquisitely decorated by one of Covent Garden's star designers in exchange for a great deal of free and complicated dental work, for Pinky and Perky rather wisely believed in the efficacy of barter. Their residence was filled with what they liked to call 'nice' things: an enormous amount of Biedermeier furniture and rather too many obelisks. The pictures were conservative, generally of livestock: eighteenth-century watercolours of sheep and cows with attenuated torsos, and all with picture lights. In deference to a more modern taste was their assembly of art deco vases and Clarice Cliff tea-shop trumpery. At the brunches thrown by Pinky and Perky for their more starry patients, Derek Pettyfer, as a fellow glass collector, always feigned admiration for their large holdings of Lalique; kitschy and come-coloured.

This morning, the waiting-room, tastefully furnished with chrome and black leather Eileen Grey reproductions and framed Victorian chromolithographs of New Zealand volcanoes in eruption, held only one occupant. It was Kenneth Grocock's first visit, for he had decided to suborn as many of Derek Pettyfer's acquaintances as he could muster to spill the beans on his subject. The comedian's chatterbox dentists were high on the list. To secure this early appointment he had casually mentioned on the phone that he was Assistant Arts Editor on the *London Evening News.* It was a white lie they would be unlikely to check. He sat nervously reading a travel feature in *Vogue* about a new restaurant attached to a Greek art gallery. The puzzling headline read:

HOUMOUS WHERE THE ART IS.

Raewyn, a dental nurse from Christchurch, accosted him. 'Come this way, thanks, Mr Cocoa.'

'It's Gro-co. Spelt G-r-o-c-o-c-k.'

'Sorry about that, Mr Gro-cock.'

'The cock is silent, it has been for about fifty years. It's Gro-co.'

Raewyn looked perplexed. 'Sorry about that. Anyway, the dentists just need a wee x-ray of your teeth first. It's a wee formality.' She conducted him to the x-ray booth and invested him with a long leaden apron. This offered protection, not so much to the patient as the dentist, since it shielded him from litigation by irate patients when they gave birth to children with gills.

Once Kenneth's chin and forehead had been aligned with a machine resembling a sophisticated Iron Maiden, or scold's bridle, the nurse said: 'Keep still, thanks, it'll only take a wee minute.' Then she ran like the clappers to some remote refuge and pressed a button.

It was over.

'That didn't hurt much, did it?' said Raewyn. 'Now all you have to do is fill in this form, Mr Grocock, and Mr Bremner will see you in a wee while. Oh, and we always like to know who recommended you, thanks.' Raewyn pronounced it 'thinks'.

'Well, actually no one, basically. But I suppose, now you mention it, Derek Pettyfer pointed me in your direction.'

Raewyn melted. 'Oh, Mr Pettyfer, isn't he a scream? Are you watching his new wee series? Didn't you love it when Mrs Petty went in to have her legs waxed and discovered . . .'

The nurse's summary of Derek's most recent television triumph was interrupted by Hugh Bremner himself, his chubby form wrapped in a chartreuse surgical overall with matching skull-cap, and his white Bally loafers encased in sterile paper booties.

'Come in Mr Grocock, come in,' said the dentist, beckoning with a latex covered finger.

'It's Gro-co actually.'

When Kenneth was in the chair and the dentist had donned his surgical mask and an expensive looking visor incorporating miniature binoculars, Kenneth explained that there wasn't anything in particular wrong with his teeth. 'Basically just a check-up, actually.'

From an invisible source, rather loud ballet music percolated into the surgery as Pinky's rubbery fingers inserted a steel instrument into the obituarist's mouth.

'My God, I don't know who did this work, Mr Grocock, but you're sitting on a time bomb in here. Your mouth is an accident waiting to happen.'

This was not how Kenneth Grocock had envisaged the consultation at all. He had only made the appointment in the hope of pumping these dentists for a little valuable gossip about one of their celebrity patients, Derek. He had come to extract information and now it looked as though he might become the victim of extraction himself.

Kenneth struggled to say something, but the chair, of the most modern American design, had been tilted backwards, and a funnel-like rubber membrane had been clamped to his lips.

'Please raise your finger if you feel anything, but I doubt you will,' said Pinky's voice. 'We like to give our patients a little cocktail just to keep them happy while we do the first assessment.'

Kenneth felt his sleeve being deftly rolled up and a mosquito sting on his right triceps. As though playing a porcelain xylophone, the dentist strummed a sprightly *danse macabre* on his teeth with a metal rod.

'I'm rather concerned about one, four, six, upper left seven occlusal, upper right canine and watch lower left bicuspid, Raewyn.' But Mr Bremner's voice seemed a long way off, and soon Kenneth heard nothing.

As he slumbered, Dr Hugh Bremner took an impression of his condemned teeth, whilst his nurse, Raewyn Mackle, after a brief search through the patient's pockets, took a precautionary impression of his Barclaycard.

On the evening of his mortification at the hands of the spurious dermatologist, Derek was called for some night shooting for the next episode of *Petty Sessions.* The film location was the stage door of the London Palladium, on the occasion of a Royal Gala. Mrs Petty, the star of this fictitious event, was meant to be accidentally locked out of the theatre, and the script required Derek, in full make-up and wearing a blue satin ballgown, to run at high speed around the theatre, frantically trying all exits. Here, some trick Keystone Cops speeded-up photography would be employed, and Mrs Petty's desperate efforts to get past the Royal security guards were to be risibly explored.

Derek sat in his caravan in Great Marlborough Street feeling miserable. This 'standing by' for half the night seemed particularly pointless, since most of the dangerous or acrobatic stunts were usually performed by his cockney double, Stanley, a true son of Stepney with muscles of steel, even under a frock. It was only eight o'clock and he was already in full make-up when Harold, the director, informed him with many apologies that someone had made a cock-up. In order for the scene to be set up convincingly, and the extras and Royal lookalikes assembled, shooting would have to be postponed until two in the morning when the area, just south of Oxford Street, was relatively deserted. The police were co-operating.

Derek received this news politely, but when Harold had gone, poor Vanessa, his make-up lady, took the brunt of it.

Whose fault was this balls-up anyway? He could have been at home or in a decent restaurant, and where was his manager? Ross never turned up at these stints, although for twenty per cent you'd think he might. He was always quite frank about it: 'Too boring, mate. You don't want me hanging around like a fart in a phone box.'

Derek was about to give Vanessa an earful when he remembered being in a film with Terry-Thomas in the actor's declining years. The recollection of a star unleashing his bilious tantrums on defenceless underlings and wardrobe ladies was a chastening one.

But he was unhappy all the same. It had been a ghastly day. His intimate ulcer remained unexplained, undiagnosed and untreated. Moreover, Pam had not come home before he had left for location.

Now he had been called six hours early. Grumpily he sat there in his make-up, periodically punching out his own telephone number on the mobile. Pam's flat had, incomprehensibly, never been on the phone, and when he suggested getting her a mobile, she had dismissed the offer as 'élitist'.

On each occasion, Derek only got his answering machine. To his surprise, the voice on the tape was Pam's: flat, brief and matter-of-fact.

What had happened to his own witty message introduced with some stirring chords of Richard Strauss? Instead: 'Neither Pamela Black or Derek Pettyfer can come to the phone right now. Leave a message after the beep.' Not even 'please', Derek fretted. And was it entirely fair that Pam had put her own name first, or, for that matter, reprogrammed the machine without asking him?

'Penny for them,' said Vanessa, 'it's not the end of the world. What's the matter with you tonight?'

'Nothing,' said Derek. Then, 'Why the hell did they call me so bloody early? I'll have to shave again at midnight. Can't I go home?'

'No, apparently. The director wants another word with you about Maggie.'

'What's the matter with her?' he snapped. 'She's getting six grand for a spit and a cough, isn't she?'

'She doesn't like her material, she says it's not funny enough.'

'It's only a celebrity cameo, for Christ's sake! All she has to say is "Where's Mrs Petty? The Queen's party is backstage" – and a few other things.'

'That's just it, love,' said Vanessa, giving Derek's pepper-and-salt wig a mollifying stroke. 'She wants to funny it up, that's natural isn't it? You can't pay an arm and a leg for someone like Maggie to do a cameo and then give her nothing to do.'

'It's the writers' fault,' said Derek. 'You're right of course, Vanessa. Should we call her agent?'

'Her agent is here already, love, giving everyone an earful.'

At that moment, the door of Derek's caravan flew open and Woody Weinglass stood before him, as hastily dressed as a General Practitioner hauled out of bed on an emergency call. He wore a tracksuit of white *velour* to which was affixed a top-of-the-range, eighteen-carat, red-enamelled, Cartier AIDS Awareness ribbon. A Monte Cristo smouldered between his fingers.

'Hi Derek. What's the scoop?'

Woody combined the most blood-curdling *agentese* with his post-Bertie Wooster Anglicisms. It was an unappetising hybrid.

'Maggie's chuffed to be in this concert, don't get me wrong . . .'

Did English people still say 'chuffed'?, Derek wondered.

'Look old boy, can't you call Ian Davidson or someone to give her a few smashing lines?' Woody struck a copy of the script with the flat of his hand, sending his cigar ash into Derek's face powder. 'This stuff you've given her is about as funny as a pork chop in an orphanage.'

An odd silence followed this Delphic utterance, but Woody was clearly getting worked up. The black twigs in his nostrils rattled ominously. Sitting there in half drag, Derek felt at a distinct psychological disadvantage.

'I'm here to tell you, old squire, that if your lads don't pull their fingers out, you've lost Maggie.'

Harold, the director, had entered the caravan. 'We've got two top writers travelling as we speak.'

'Smashing,' said Woody, 'rewrite it and she's yours. Schmooze her, you guys! But I'm here to tell you that with the script in its present form, you've got a snowball's chance in a synagogue of bringing her round.'

Derek assumed that somewhere between his last interview with Maggie and this visit to Derek's caravan, an intricate electrical circuit in the agent's brain had temporarily malfunctioned.

When Woody had disappeared in a cloud of cigar

smoke, Vanessa had a brainwave. 'I know what you need, young fellow m' lad. You need food. Your blood sugar's too low.' She opened the caravan door and summoned a runner. 'We've got some new caterers, not much variety but rather grand.'

'Any good?' Derek suddenly realised that he was quite hungry.

'Well the crew didn't like it much, I have to say. Hare stew I think, hard as rocks and covered with gunge, but it was tasty.'

Derek had a terrible memory of grumous gravy. 'What did they look like?'

'The crew?'

'No – the new caterers. Is one of them a redhead?'

'There is a thin bald man with an earring.' Derek saw the strigose wrists. 'And there's a jolly girl who looks like Fergie, only upper class.'

'Perhaps it *is* Fergie.'

By then a plate of steaming brown lumps had been set before him on the dressing table. A card, like a flag, had been attached to its summit on a toothpick. The card read:

COLHERNE CORPORATE CATERING

and beneath, near an umber thumbprint, the scribbled words: 'We're thrilled to be part of your team. Love, Emma and Jake.'

Vanessa and Derek both looked at the congealing coprolith.

'I think I might just have a nibble of swede,' said Derek.

*

The writers succeeded in injecting enough humour into a minor role to placate Woody Weinglass's client, but it was a long night, and at half-past three in the morning Derek was still capering around the block in high-heeled shoes and a sweat-soaked ballgown. Finally however, it was over, and the director put his arm around Mrs Petty's damp shoulders and assured her they had some 'marvellous stuff' in the can.

One hour later, numb with fatigue, Derek let himself into the flat. There was an unpleasant, livid stain in the sky behind Westminster Cathedral. It was the dawn. Derek went into the bathroom, locked the door and re-examined his little problem. Perhaps it was spontaneously healing. It was hard to tell. He risked another agonizing application of Listerine and experienced that feeling of spiritual desolation which only seems to come with bereavement or chronic diarrhoea. It's going away, he thought, but so did syphilis.

It was a miracle, Derek reflected, that he had reached the age of fifty without ever getting any of those nasty little bugs which afflicted people far less promiscuous than he. Twelve years ago, at the nadir of his drinking, there had been a period of satyriasis which he preferred not to think about. It had been an interlude of dubious clubs, squalid encounters and *liaisons dangereuses*, of which only a few hideous snapshots remained in his memory. They made his flesh crawl, those grainy stills of 'private hotels' in Shepherd Market and Bayswater, and of beds stained with the rennet of drunken whores.

Derek undressed in the bathroom, and without switching on the bedroom light, crept into his side of the bed. For some time he lay there in the dark listening to the distant rumble of early morning traffic at Victoria. Finally he reached out to touch Pam, but there was nothing there, just a cold pillow. It was an hour before he slept.

Meanwhile in another bed, in Islington, Polly Garland woke up again. She had been up most of the night. It was impossible to sleep through all that groaning in the next room. She climbed out of bed, and in her faded Laura Ashley nightie went into the kitchenette and brewed a soothing cup of camomile. With that, and two homeopathic arnica tablets in the palm of her hand, she nudged open the door of her poor wounded flatmate's room. Sitting on the edge of the bed, she said softly, 'Just try to sit up and sip a little of this. There's some nice honey in it and you better swallow these as well.' Her gentle solicitude was met by even louder lamentations, and she switched on the bedside light.

'Turn it off, for Christ's sake. Turn it off,' cried a sepulchral voice. It broke her heart to see Kenneth's pale face on the pillow and those poor bloodied lips, and beyond them, the sparse crenulations of his few remaining teeth.

Kenneth Grocock, as in a bad dream, remembered the voice of Mr Bremner before he had stumbled out into Knightsbridge and somehow caught a cab.

'You wouldn't have thanked me if I'd left those in a minute longer!'

Kenneth groaned.

7

Polly

'I MET HIM in a toilet, how could I ever forget it!'

Pam laughed, even though she had been crying. 'How come?'

'Well,' said Inge, 'Lionel was being interviewed on one of those talk shows at the BBC and I went to the loo.' Inge sat back in the big squashy sofa in her bedroom and laughed at the recollection of it all. She wore a *peignoir* of peach silk from La Perla, and nothing much underneath. Pam didn't think she had ever seen a more beautiful woman.

On a large coffee-table piled with books about Poussin, Parrots, Hungarian Castles, Mozart and the Unknown Tasmania, several bottles stood on a silver tray.

'Would you like some orange juice, champagne, or champagne and orange juice?' Pam thought she was flying first-class, and Inge, for a moment, had forgotten she was not.

'Nothing thanks, but what happened?'

'Oh yes. Well, when I'd done what I went in there to do, I saw this weird woman in fuschia Thai silk touching up her lipstick over the basin. I took a closer look when I washed my hands and realised it was that comedian the children are all mad about – Mrs Petty!'

'Why in the Ladies?' said pragmatic Pam.

'Well, he could hardly have a pee in the Gents, could he, dolled up like that?' Both women laughed, though Pam then started to cry again; silently. 'He was recording his show in the next studio and we met during his comfort stop.'

'That was all?' sniffed Pam.

'Absolutely. Just good friends – always. Isn't it marvellous?' Inge lent forward and helped herself to a glass of champagne. One opulent breast fell out. Nordically, Inge didn't care. The nipple was like a mulberry in a little pool of *café au lait*.

'All the same,' she said, 'I do feel rather responsible, Pam. I introduced you both.' A black toy poodle, clipped in a lion cut, scampered into the room and looked up imploringly at its mistress. Inge dipped her finger in some champagne and the dog licked it off. She said: 'If you come here and ask to stay the night every time you two have a row, I suppose I've only got myself to blame.'

'It wasn't a row exactly, but Derek's such a male chauvinist pig.' It was an oddly old-fashioned phrase, Inge thought, like a Bee Gee's song. 'He thinks he can dress me up like a Barbie doll, he's insulting about my old studio, and frankly, I think he takes me for granted.'

Inge thought how very good-looking Pam was without make-up; those large green eyes, such fine white skin and all that black, unruly hair. 'Perhaps he wouldn't take you for granted if he thought there was a little competition.'

With the frayed cuff of Lionel Pinkhill's Mandarin Hotel bathrobe in which she was enveloped, Pam brushed off a tear. 'What do you mean?' she said.

'A little jealousy,' suggested Inge cautiously, 'sometimes works wonders.'

Pam smiled one of her rare smiles, revealing Watson and Bremner's recent handiwork. 'Well,' she said, 'there's Bob. He might do the trick.'

'Who's Bob?'

'The man I live with. He shares the rent on my flat in Chiswick.'

'I never knew there was a Bob, Pam. What does Derek think about him?' Inge was, to her own surprise, deeply shocked.

'Derek doesn't know about Bob because he's never asked. He's totally self-centred and he's got tunnel vision. If he wants something, like me, it never occurs to him that there might be an obstacle in the way.'

Inge realised she didn't know this girl at all. Not at all. What had she let Derek in for? 'What does this Bob, I mean *your* Bob, do?'

'He's a sculptor too, and has a studio in a warehouse in Gunnersbury Park. We've pretty well known each other since I was seventeen. We both went to art school in Birmingham.' She pronounced it "berbi-gum" in an exaggerated nasal accent, to demonstrate her emancipation. 'Bob was never there when Derek came around, and Derek didn't seem faintly curious. He doesn't want to know about my past. He thinks things like women, pictures, Roman glass, and money are just waiting around for him to acquire.'

'Did you mind being acquired?'

'Hell no. I've been bored by Bob since day one. We're poles apart artistically, but you get to need people after a while. We encouraged each other. In work I mean. He helped pay the rent too. Rich people like you wouldn't understand that.'

Pam glared rather arbitrarily at several objects in the bedroom, on the walls of which two girls called Susanna and Caroline had once stippled and stencilled their worst. Sulkily she observed an equivocal Epstein watercolour of two wrestling female nudes, a Tiffany lamp, an eighteenth-century Burmese Buddha and Inge's toenails. Pam had never known a woman with such beautifully enamelled toenails. Saskia, the poodle, lay ecstatically still on her back while Inge stroked her tummy with a long naked foot. 'I suppose you've got a slave who comes round and paints them,' she said aloud.

'You're being very hostile, Pam, and I'm only trying to help you.'

'Anyway, Derek just assumed that when he snapped his fingers, I'd walk out of my flat – out of my life – and come and live with him.'

'And you did.'

'Well, didn't *you*? Didn't Lionel pick you up on a plane? Didn't you get him to ditch his wife?'

'*He* made that decision, not me,' said Inge coldly.

She didn't like to be reminded of her days as a stewardess by this little snob from the wrong side of the tracks.

'I'm sorry I spoke like that, Inge, but the fact is, Lionel did divorce his wife and marry you.'

'So what?'

Something dawned on Inge.

'Wait a minute,' she said, turning the other woman's face towards her with her fingers. 'You mean, you're pissed off with Derek because he's still married to that cow in Cornwall or somewhere and you don't think you stand a chance!'

'I don't want marriage. I'm never getting married. I hardly know him anyway. He's only the third man I've ever done it with, he's too old, and my career is the most important thing in my life,' said Pam.

'I bet you'd marry him all the same – like a shot. Do you love Derek?'

Pam was silent. 'I wouldn't tell him if I did,' she said after a while. 'Men lose interest when they think they've got you hooked. Derek would, anyway.'

'I'm not so sure, Pam, he's not all that secure. But on a rather mundane level, he could help you with your career.'

Pam looked crestfallen. 'What career? I don't sell much; hardly anything. I write off to famous people and if they are vain enough, they sit for me. When I tell them they can buy one of my sculptures for a thousand pounds, they run a mile. I'm doing a head of Simon Rattle right now.'

'Good for you! Who's arranged that?' exclaimed Inge disingenuously.

'Derek.'

Inge gave a small "no comment" smile, and rose from the sofa. She took the other woman's arm. 'Have a nice long bath, dear, and then go back to him. I've dug out some clothes I never wear; Jaeger, St Laurent, Bruce Oldfield, a few bits and bobs. Try them on, we're pretty much the same size in most places, they're yours if you like them.' And then she added, surveying her friend, 'You know, you scrub up rather well when you make the effort.' It was Inge's kindest revenge for the airline pick-up story.

Two very Scandinavian-looking children of about five and eight erupted into the room with Junewyn, their New Zealand nanny.

'Just taking them to school, Mrs Pinkhill, back in a wee while.'

'Miranda and Joshua, this is Miss Black.'

'Ms,' corrected Pam, primly.

'You have a lovely day at school, darlings, and when you come home, Daddy might be back from San Francisco. She embraced them and the children left jubilantly, banging down the stairs.

'He's got guest towels and coffee spoons and a real percolator and too many CDs and Bang & Olufsen and cable television and linen sheets and monogrammed slippers and hand-made shirts with his initials on the pocket and stationery with his address in raised writing and dimmers on the lights and he can tie his own bow-tie . . . it's *sickening*!' said Pam, bursting into tears again.

'It's how the other half lives, Pam. You ought to try it sometime. You might even get to like it.'

'I doubt it,' said the *Guardian* reader. 'He's even got a son.'

'He's got a stepson he hardly knows by that fruit-cake in Cornwall, and he'll be grown up by now.'

Pam was standing at the window. She had tweaked back the Colefax and Fowlers and was gazing at the street below. 'Your children are beautiful, Inge. Are you having any more?'

'I don't know,' said the other, leading Pam across the bedroom into her own fragrant bathroom, and vigorously turning on the taps. 'Lionel's getting pretty long in the tooth by now, I don't think he can manage any more,' she said, laughing.

Pam slid out of the cellist's bathrobe and tested the water with a rather ugly, blunt toe. Inge noticed the long appendix scar, and Derek's blue fingerprints on her triceps. Pam bundled up her hair, abstracted a toothbrush and speared the copious chignon. Inge saw she didn't shave; there was a slick of black hair in each exposed armpit, and as Pam stepped over the edge of the tub, she glimpsed the poignant wick of a Tampax. It explained a lot.

'Have a good soak, you'll feel better, and for God's sake, please use up some of my Penhaligon's.'

As Pam lowered herself into the water she looked at the pretty flasks and bottles and phials beside the bath: the ottos and attars and essences. It was another world.

Closing the bathroom door, Inge said, as an afterthought, 'I think I *would* fancy one more child. A nice quiet little girl who likes having her hair brushed.'

'And do you love Lionel, Inge?'

But Pam's hostess had shut the door so her reply reached the younger woman muffled, and through steam. 'Of course not! He's a filthy lech and a bastard, and I hate him.'

Pam wished she could have seen her friend's face then, to know if all that was true. In a way, she hoped it was.

Derek prowled around his flat feeling miserable. Luckily Amerika had arrived so he was not physically alone. Like every Spanish woman he had ever met, of any class, Amerika was married to a vain, idle shit. He was generally to be found watching TV at home, feigning illness of every kind, from whiplash to prostate cancer, while his wife toiled at all hours and seasons through flu, varicose veins and hysterectomy.

For the past few months Amerika had wasted no words on Derek. Her hostility to his new 'arrangements', as his mother used to call his girlfriends, was patent. Derek pretended it was the extra work she objected to; the feminine mess. Pam left towels on the floor, dishes unwashed in the sink – she had never found the dishwasher – CDs out of their covers were scattered on the floor, and there were footprints of grey clay from Pam's Doc Martins all over the brown broadloom Wilton. No matter what he tried to tell himself, however, he knew that Amerika's disgruntled mood was due to one thing only: she couldn't stand Pam. Gone was her old banter, her false chiding: 'Mr Derek, you killing me! What you wearing that shirt again today for, when I iron you a beautiful silk one!'

Now she came, did her job with many a deep sigh, picked up her money and left. Was he imagining it, or was his side of the bed made up better than Pam's?

He looked at Pam's bedside table. Camille Paglia, Michele Roberts . . . what did she read for pleasure?, he wondered. Barbara Taylor Bradford, probably. He could not watch her with books. She licked her finger and read them like magazines. He winced to hear the pages snap by, and she even marked her place by turning down the corners. At mealtimes she held her fork strangely and when she finished eating in a restaurant she would shove the empty plate away from her as though she had just choked down gruel at an orphanage.

The more Derek catalogued her faults and solecisms, the more his sadness and self-hatred seemed to grow. Amerika's verdict came back to him: 'She not your type, Mr Derek.' His anger spilled over on to everyone who had caused him recent inconvenience. Woody Weinglass for instance. Couldn't that joke of an agent have let them all know sooner that Maggie had some worries about the script?

Derek dialled a number.

'MTO, this is Tracey.'

'Woody Weinglass please.' Why did she have to tell him her name?, Derek wondered. And how mean, how horrible it was, that flat London voice fed on Silk Cut and sausage rolls.

'Would you tell me what it's regarding?' said Tracey.

'No.'

'I beg your pardon?'

'If it was anything you could help me with, Tracey, I'd tell you, but as it isn't, I won't.'

Shit, thought Derek, I've blown it. Now she'll tell me he's in a meeting.

'Mr Weinglass is in a meeting. What company are you from?'

'A company in the Cayman Islands actually, and I'm ringing him about his birthday.'

'His what?'

That always did the trick, thought Derek. They always assumed if you knew about their birthday, you were family.

'Just a moment Mr . . .?'

'Pettyfer.'

'His assistant's phone is now free.'

I'll bet his assistant's a real raver, thought Derek; Woody's secretaries were rarely selected for their computer literacy.

'Mr Weinglass's office, Garryl speaking.'

It was a low and attractive American voice. Derek had expected something English and Sloany, an Arabella or at the very least a Camilla. 'Garryl?' he said.

'I'm new, I used to be with William Morris in LA, but I felt like a challenge.'

'You'll certainly get one now,' said Derek. He wondered if, as she spoke, she wasn't squelching up and down on Woody's lap. It was an embarrassing name: her father was probably Gary and her mother, Cheryl. 'What is your last name, Garryl?'

'It's Garryl Curtis.' The name was a bit smudged over the phone, but he didn't get her to repeat it. He was quickly forgetting the purpose of the phone call as he tried to guess what Garryl looked like.

'I suppose Mr Weinglass is at lunch?'

'Woody is not at his desk at this time, Mr Pettyfer, but I'll be touching base with him momentarily.'

Derek said he would call back.

'Wonderful,' she said.

'But,' he added, 'tell Mr Weinglass I'm keen to talk to him.

'Wonderful,' she said, 'you bet.'

Derek tried to imagine what epithet she would select to describe something – like a sunset – that really was wonderful. 'Neat,' he decided.

Derek put down the phone having now completely forgotten why he had made the call. He had also, for the first time, noticed a blue envelope bearing his name behind the telephone. It was a note from Pam on his best Smythson's writing paper, which he had obviously been meant to see last night.

He sat on the bed and read the brief missive; the writing was black and savage, like barbed wire.

Derek,

I think I need my own space. Don't try and find me. We may have been a bit too hasty with this relationship. Take Care.

Regards,

Pam

With a loud growl of anguish, he read it again. For a long time he sat on the bed and yielded to feelings of emptiness; of desolation.

He remembered a far-off afternoon in childhood when he had come home from school and found the house empty, his mother gone.

In fact, she was visiting a sick neighbour and had been detained longer than expected. On her return two hours later his mother had laughed apologetically and hugged the frightened child, but he had never forgotten the feeling.

Could this be why he had chosen an actor's life – company, full houses?

Derek was angry now. Why should he be tossed aside like this? He remembered a warm American voice; a tacit hint of invitation. Then, guided by instinct, he made another phone call.

Fifteen minutes later, just as Derek drove off towards the West End, a taxi drew up at Ashley Mansions and Pam, still fragrant from Inge's bath, alighted and ran up the steps.

Kenneth, sipping a nutritious liquid through a straw, glared at the screen of his word processor. Beside him on the desk was an invoice from Watson and Bremner and a long list of the appointments which had been arranged for him. They seemed to stretch into the following year and involved, as far as the journalist could perceive, titanium implants, bone grafts, periodontal therapy, intricate bridge-work, and finally, fifteen gold platinum and porcelain crowns. The estimate given was roughly equal to the cost of a small Cezanne watercolour. However, there was a note attached, in a florid red holograph (blood?) suggesting that Kenneth might care to make an appointment to 'discuss' the bill. It seemed a strange invitation, but typical, he surmised, of the New Dentistry.

Accordingly, that afternoon, and in defiant mood, he journeyed to Cadogan Mews and stood before the stark pink façade of Watson and Bremner's clinic. The nurse, Raewyn, had said on the phone: 'You're lucky, Mr Bremner can squeeze you in at four.' It was an apposite phrase, Kenneth thought, looking up at the dark narrow entrance; though he felt less than lucky.

He had no sooner entered the waiting-room than Mr Bremner's surgery door opened and a Luciano Pavarotti lookalike emerged ashen-faced and holding his jaw as though, if he removed his hand, it might fall to the floor and shatter like an expensive cup and saucer. Pinky gazed after him rapturously. Again, the latex finger beckoned, and Kenneth was once more in the electric chair of Procrustes. Mr Bremner smiled down at him benevolently.

'You might have noticed just then the class of client we have here, Mr Grocock, and at the end of your treatment my colleague will show you our VIP visitors book. It's a *Who's Who* of opera, ballet and theatre, fully illustrated.'

'Illustrated?'

'Yes, we get a polaroid of everyone who sits in that chair.' He indicated the *chaise-longue* Kenneth occupied. 'Naturally, they're asleep when wee Raewyn snaps them; we wouldn't want to intrude on their privacy. This is a pretty special practice.'

'It certainly is,' said Kenneth with some feeling. 'Which rather brings me to the matter of your bill.'

'If it seems on the high side, let me remind you, without wanting to sound melodramatic, that we did save your life.'

'My life!'

'Look at these x-rays.' The dentist touched a button and on a TV screen appeared the enlarged rictus of a skeleton. 'That's you, Mr Grocock.'

With a flourish of his expressive rubber fingers he indicated specific areas on this grinning *memento mori*. 'Here, here, here, here and here were, in dental terms, the equivalent of five hydrogen bombs on the verge of exploding. Active oral volcanoes!'

Kenneth thought he now understood the suggestive purpose of that picture of a New Zealand volcano in the waiting-room. It was a cautionary metaphor for an acute, apical, periodontal abscess.

'No, Mr Grocock, the Arts Editor of a major newspaper needs a good image.'

'Arts Editor?' Kenneth had completely forgotten about that harmless deception.

'An Arts Editor can't spend the rest of his professional life without teeth.'

'Whose bloody fault is that!' Kenneth nearly said. But he felt vulnerable in the chair. Pinky might easily throw a switch, and Raewyn, one of her curare darts.

'Ours is a word of mouth business.' As he spoke he was actually holding an instrument with a little round mirror on the end of it, like dentists used to do in halitosis ads. 'Mr Watson and my good self specialise in helping media people, high profile show business personalities, singers and dancers, and we are constantly striving to upgrade our client list.'

'So why me?' said Kenneth with pathos.

'Come now, Mr Crocock, don't be modest. You're a senior journalist with a theatre background . . .'

Kenneth interrupted: 'I'm not exactly senior, Mr Bremner, though I suppose I've had a few lucky breaks.' He had made an attempt at honesty and decided against it.

'Exactly! You must have friends in the entertainment industry: films, opera and so forth. If you can deliver us some of your best, shall we say "contacts" – a star or two – we'd be happy to finish off your mouth for nothing!'

There was a long silence, during which the labyrinthine progress of the dentist's lunch, and the peristaltic rills, tricklings and eructations which accompanied it, could be plainly heard.

'Basically, you want me to pimp for you,' said the journalist bluntly. And bravely.

'Come, come, that's not a very nice way to put it, Mr Grocock. But a man like you must know Hugh Grant, for instance, and Sting, and Emma Thompson, and Kenneth Branagh . . . To be frank, Mr Grocock, when we first saw you in our waiting-room the other day on our closed circuit surveillance system, we thought you *were* Kenneth Branagh! Has anyone ever . . .?'

'Hundreds of times, I'm afraid,' said the lesser

Kenneth, 'but since my last appointment with you, the resemblance is far less striking.' He snarled at Mr Bremner, exposing his discontinuous occlusion.

The dentist exchanged a look with his nurse and the chair gave a sickening lurch backwards. Kenneth found himself at an invidious angle.

'All right, all right! Basically I'll do it, that's to say I'll do my best. I've got the odd contact at Covent Garden . . .' He was improvising wildly, clutching at straws, but the dentist was smiling, or had been before he pulled down his mask and adjusted his inimical visor. Kenneth felt his sleeve retract and the prick of steel.

As Raewyn's stupefacient sent its tendrils through his veins, he heard Pinky say: 'Excellent, Mr Grocock, excellent. But I'm slightly worried about that upper sixth bicuspid.'

Polly Garland was in her leotard doing *t'ai chi* when Kenneth got home to the flat in Islington. He was no sooner in the door than he flung himself on to the couch and screamed. She broke off in the middle of her oriental discipline and ran to his side; now he was beating his fists against the wall.

'What am I going to do, Poll? It's bizarre.' He failed to successfully pronounce the last word and merely produced a tragic trickle of incarnadine saliva. 'My mouth is a disaster, and I'm being held to ransom by a couple of queer Kiwis!'

Polly bridled. 'Now don't be sexist, Kenneth, what do they want?'

'They want to be paid, basically, though they'll probably lose the cost of my mouth in the bills of a few unsuspecting towel-heads. But that's not the point.'

Polly cradled the obituarist's head in her arms and put her cheek against his damp, sandy crown. 'What do they want?'

'Basically, if I can deliver them a rock-star or a prima-ballerina, or Elizabeth Hurley, I'll get the lot for nix.'

'Is that professional?'

'It's barter, Poll, everyone is doing it. The trouble is, I said yes.'

'What!'

'I said I had contacts at Covent Garden. I told them my best friend was Antoinette Diggins.'

'Is she?'

'Of course not. I could never understand why people rave about ballerinas anyway. No tits, skinny as scarecrows, scraped-back hair, pointy chins and they walk like ducks.' To Kenneth's dismay, Polly burst into tears.

'You're so cruel and beastly.'

'What's wrong, Poll?'

'I was a dancer once, don't forget. I can't help the way I walk. And I like scraping back my hair, and I enjoy being thin and having a pointy chin and some men don't like boobs.' She wept again.

Kenneth sat back and looked at her. 'You know, Poll, you're a dead ringer for Antoinette Diggins. Did you know that?' Polly blew her nose and managed a wan smile.

'Dame Antoinette Diggins is forty-five but she is still beautiful.'

'Well Poll, you're only thirty-five but you look a lot older.

Polly thumped him. 'You bastard, Kenneth! Am I beastly to you? Take a look in the mirror before you start being hateful to me.'

But the journalist was no longer listening. He had jumped up excitedly and was pacing the room. 'I've got an idea,' he said. 'It's innovative, it's mould-breaking and it could even be in-your-face. Basically, *you* pretend to be La Diggins!' He ignored the exclamations of protest and incredulity from his flatmate.

'We book an appointment on the phone under her name, right? Pinky and Perky will go berserk.' On the last word there was another effusion of pink drool, which Polly caught with a Kleenex. 'Let me finish! You're always complaining about your teeth, right? This way you'll get the lot done for nothing by Trevor Watson, while I get mine fixed up for free by Hugh Bremner. They'll never check it out, and if and when they do, we'll be home and dry with new toothy-pegs.'

'I'm not sure, it feels wrong,' said Polly, remembering a recent toothache.

'These two dentists are stage-struck loonies. They'll never twig you're not Dame Diggins in a hundred years. You know all about ballet jargon and they won't expect you to look beautiful without your make-up. They know the stars look pretty ghastly off-stage.'

Polly gave a shriek of rage and ran at Kenneth

with hammering fists, but Kenneth Grocock grabbed her bony wrists and looked at her hard.

'It's uncanny. You're the spitting image,' he said. 'Shall I stuff a few pairs of socks down my Y-fronts so we can do a *pas de deux*?'

'You are a silver-tongued bastard,' said Dame Antoinette's understudy. 'You've twisted my arm.'

8

Garryl

DEREK REALISED IT was silly to have considered driving to the Ivy. Jeremy might get it parked for me, he hoped, otherwise I'll be in more strife than Speed Gordon. He smiled, in spite of himself, to see other motorists glancing at him in the heavy traffic. He watched the double-takes: he was a man in a car chatting away to himself. And then there were the grins of recognition, when the smart ones realised it was Mrs Petty in mufti. Not all that many of them however. His disguise had guaranteed him more privacy than most.

'More strife than Speed Gordon.' It was a phrase from his Adelaide childhood; or his father's. It was folklore. Well, he was in strife all right this morning. There was the note from Pam; she needed her 'own space', did she? Derek wondered if she would get a better offer than his from anyone else. And 'take care'. Uggh! Derek gripped the steering-wheel, clenched his teeth and uttered an enraged roar. A woman in a Volvo next to him at the lights in Piccadilly smiled and waved. 'Take care.' What an uncaring valediction that always was. Cold people said it because it *sounded* warm. And then the final insult – 'regards'. Not even a hypocritical 'love', or the more recent, paradoxically less intimate, 'lots of love'. How could a woman make love to you one minute and desert you the next, and then send her 'regards'? The reason was obvious: women were Martians, aliens.

And here he was, the morning after his first real row with Pam, taking another Martian to lunch. It hadn't even been a row, he reflected; Pam had taken irrational offence at something well-intentioned he had said, and nursed her grievance, as women did. Whenever Peggy Pettyfer, his mother, seemed upset, Derek had always said 'You OK, Mum?' 'Fine,' she had invariably replied, 'it's nothing, darling, nothing at all.' Now he knew that this was not stoicism or feminine courage in the face of emotional distress. It was not even a noble effort to spare the feelings of a child. It was a kind of usury; it was banking a resentment and enjoying the interest.

My thinking is stinking, decided Derek as he walked into the restaurant, shrugging off his venomous mood like a Burberry at the door. Jeremy greeted him.

'A very late lunch I'm afraid, Jeremy.'

'You're not late, just early for dinner. Good to see you whenever.'

'Is my friend . . .?'

Jeremy indicated a corner banquette. 'I've given the lady a drink.'

Derek walked among the tables, saying a word to Alan Bates and another to Peter Hall, but he had already seen her at the corner table in a cool pistachio linen suit by Donna Karan, bare legs and strappy, high-heeled sandals.

'I'm Derek. I'm sorry to be late but, like a fool, I actually drove here from Victoria.'

'Where on earth did you park?'

'There's a funny little hotel around the corner near Seven Dials. I know the doorman.'

'Ah, influence!' She raised her champagne glass to her lips and looked at him over the rim, a large amber ring, with an insect in it, winking on her finger. She was thirty-eightish, blonde, full-lipped, and glamorous in the old-fashioned American sense. Perhaps even a touch overripe. The *maître d'* hovered.

'Another drink I think for Miss Curtis, please Lawrence.'

'Kurdish.'

'I'm sorry, we met on a bad line. Kurdish?'

Garryl Kurdish nodded.

'I've worked out,' Derek said, his heart beating palpably, 'where the "Garryl" comes from.'

She laughed, and passed her tongue across her top teeth. With a serious look she said: 'Isn't it a kind of dorky name? But I guess I'm stuck with it.'

'I like it,' said Derek. He loved it. 'Mind you, Garryl, with a name like that I doubt I could trust you with a secret.'

'Excuse me?' She asked the question anxiously. He remembered, of course, that Americans are all literal-minded. Why should he be so sentimental as to suppose she might be an exception?

'Can't trust you with a secret – you know – *garrulous!*' It sounded so corny when you spelled it out like that. Was she sending him up him with that immoderate laughter?

'Love it, love it! You're too bizarre,' she said, laughing again so that a few people looked across at them and smiled. He guessed they thought Mrs Petty must be a giggle a minute.

'Well, kind sir,' said Garryl, after they had both ordered the same thing; arugola salad with bresaola and the fish cakes. 'How did I get my name?'

'Your father was Gary and your mother was Cheryl.'

She tasted her wine but declined to clink glasses. It was unlucky, she said, since he was only drinking San Pellegrino. 'Wrong!'

'Well?'

'My father was Gary and his boyfriend was Daryl.'

Derek went blank and then assumed his broad-minded expression. 'How Californian.'

'But aren't you . . . a bit . . .?' Again the tip of her tongue performed its swift transit.

'Excuse me?' Derek had slipped into her dialect; he was a chameleon sometimes.

Garryl sucked in her cheeks, narrowed her eyes and gave Derek an amused and knowing look. 'Gay? Aren't you just a little bit gay?' When she said the word she made those little quote, unquote scratching movements with her fingers. Of all human gestures, including nose-picking and arse-scratching, it was the one he most loathed. It went with astrology and green ink and circles over i's instead of dots.

'Is that why you came, a nice safe lunch with one of the boys?' he said pompously, hoping she was joking.

'But that Mrs Petty shtick, it's so . . . *epicene!*'

Derek, annoyed, was nonetheless pleased to see she was learning how to increase her word power.'

'You couldn't be Mrs Petty without being a bit of "both".' Again she made the appalling signs. Derek sat back and took a deep breath to forestall cerebral haemorrhage. Americans were so simplistic, so banausic! If she'd seen Ralph Fiennes's Hamlet, did she assume he was Danish? Was Tom Hanks really a cretin? She worked for the second biggest agency in the world and she didn't know what *acting* was! She was probably a fag hag on a recruiting drive.

How screwed up Americans were. The Pilgrim Fathers had a lot to answer for. Here was the most inhibited, puritanical society on the planet, yet it could not make a movie without at least one 'cock-sucker' and a couple of 'motherfuckers' in it. Even their profanity was infantile. Individually, Americans could be so witty, so cultivated. But when it was all stirred up into the national intellectual product, what a sickly, vulgar, unappetising soup it was.

But Garryl had not read his thoughts, or his body language, or, it seemed, heard his groan of exasperation. 'I just think you're a genius to know what some of us are like, and not be . . . *you know!*' she winked. Derek could forgive a lot when he heard the G-word.

'Is it fun working for Woody?' he said, keen to get as far off the subject of culture as possible.

'Smashing,' she said, winking again.

'What's he really like?' Lawrence asked Garryl if she'd like another *coupe de champagne.*

'Wonderful,' she said. Derek realised wonderful was just hyperbole for 'yes', like 'absolutely' had been in seventies London. 'He's neat. Have you been to his home?'

'His house? No, why?'

'I won't spoil it, but it's worth a visit.'

'He hasn't been to my house.'

'Has he missed anything?'

'I thought you might care to be the judge of that after lunch.' Derek's heart was thumping: he had never impersonated a Lothario so boldly, so soon, while eating.

'That is a proposition, isn't it? But I don't screw on the first date.'

'You don't?' said Derek huskily. His mouth was very dry.

'No, I'm afraid if we went to your place, I could only go down on you.'

All around them, the crowded restaurant carried on as normal; people, some of whom he knew, yelling at each other over food. The usual luncheon ritual. And here they were, quietly, politely talking dirty. Derek hoped they would not be leaving right then and there. He would have to assume instant disc trouble, and leave the restaurant in a hunched position to conceal an embarrassing erethism. He would have to walk to the car like Groucho Marx.

Then he remembered his problem. Perhaps it was better now. He couldn't feel anything, nothing pathological, but what if it were visible to the naked eye? Or the naked woman. Oddly enough, since his cathartic interview with the spurious dermatologist, Derek's little problem seemed to have cleared up of its own accord. Perhaps it had been psychosomatic.

'Aren't you supposed to be playing Mr Weinglass's assistant this afternoon, Garryl?'

'Oh no. I've got a dentist's appointment, haven't I? A long one.' And as she devoured the last forkful of fish cake, Derek felt Garryl's foot moving up his leg under the table and coming to rest on his crotch, where the long toes dabbled. Over the coffee Garryl said: 'When you called me the second time and asked me to a late lunch, were you surprised I said yes?'

'Yes, I was even more surprised you turned up.'

'Woody's in Rome. I had over an hour to think about it while I was shopping around Soho.'

'Soho?'

'I always shop in Soho. Don't forget the MTO office is in Poland Street.'

'What did you buy?'

'Goodies. You'll see them if you're lucky.'

'At my place?' Derek hoped Amerika had come and gone. This could be awkward.

Garryl's foot resumed its kneading under the table. 'Not your place, not now. I feel like something anonymous and a tad seedy.'

'Sounds like my place,' said Derek. It wasn't funny,

but the blood supply to his joke-making apparatus seemed to have been diverted elsewhere. He was also thinking how oddly off-putting the word "tad" was. That old pedant, his unconscious, was probably throwing up pusillanimous little objections to the inevitable.

'What's that small hotel called around the corner, where you left the car? Is it the Kemble?'

Derek looked nervously over his shoulder but no one seemed interested in their arrangements. 'Garryl,' he said. 'We can't just book into the Kemble together. Everyone knows me. Well, if they don't, they always do when I want to be invisible.'

'Gotcha!' said Garryl. 'I know. I'll check in and call you here with the room number. Hasn't the Kemble got a car lot in the basement? And an elevator?' She winked. She seemed experienced in intrigue, thought Derek. But why were they being so bloody circumspect?, he wondered. He wasn't married, not really; but was she?

'Just think,' said Garryl, standing up coolly and deftly slipping one foot back into its sandal, 'you can have a nice sticky English pudding, another cup of coffee and in about twenty minutes – me!' She was off through the restaurant with her rippling blonde hair and her creased green linen. A few men turned slightly to watch her and exchanged appreciative smiles. Derek swallowed hard and called for the *carte des desserts.*

Earlier that morning, before Pam left Inge's, she had

phoned for a cab on Derek's account. She had once noted the account number on his desk, and quoted it now to the controller. He had promised a taxi in fifteen minutes. It was as easy as that. What the hell! She was going back to Derek, wasn't she? A miserable cab fare from Hampstead to Victoria was a pretty small price to pay. It would be nothing to him, and he never looked at bills anyway. They all went to Gibbo.

In the back seat she stretched out her wrist and admired the Cartier watch he had given her. Perhaps it was, as he had insisted, prettier than the larger one she had admired. It was more . . . tasteful. But as a general rule, she said no to fancy presents. She didn't like this business of Derek dressing her up, or of changing her into some other kind of person that would not prove a social embarrassment. Beside her on the seat was the Marks & Spencer's carry bag containing Inge's cast-offs. It was nice of Inge; perhaps she really was a good friend. But it made her feel like little Orphan Annie all the same.

Pam asked the driver to reroute via Harrods, and when he protested that it was somewhat out of the way, she insisted. After all, wasn't it on the account? He waited while she visited the Knightsbridge store. She went to the florists department and bought a dozen long-stemmed red roses. The woman in front of her had purchased some exotic orchids and had snapped on to the counter a piece of green and gold plastic.

'I'd like these on my husband's account,' she had said in a rude foreign voice.

Another sold-out female, thought Pam. Another rich man's chattel, deluding herself with the bogus independence of a credit card.

Pam let herself into the flat. She dumped the roses by the sink, went into the big room and rummaged amongst the CDs for her favourite disc. Soon the sound of a tango by Piazzolla reverberated through the apartment. She moved around the room trying out several chairs like Goldilocks, but they were all either too low and squashy or too antique, expensive and uncomfortable.

On the walls, the Piranesis proliferated grimly. In the locked cabinet, the flasks and bottles and bowls and amphoras softly glinted. Pam shuddered. It was a bit like an empty museum, she thought, without so much as a weedy attendant sneaking a smoke behind a column. She picked up a posh colour supplement and licking her finger, idly leafed through the pages before casting it aside.

In the bedroom she found the torn blue envelope beside the bed, and her note, crumpled on the floor. She smiled. Perhaps she had been too hard on poor old Derek. Inge had said 'he's not that secure'. Perhaps, up to a point, she was right. It would be a lesson to him anyway, not to take her for granted. She thought over her friend's advice. Perhaps Bob might come in handy; she might phone him. It would be a nice surprise for Derek to come home and find her entertaining a tall, scruffy sculptor with a grey ponytail who rolled his own cigarettes. It wasn't difficult to imagine how he would react to Bob's work.

'Derek, I'd like you to meet Bob Dooley, he makes large conceptual installations using hair, perspex, plastic cutlery and lasers. Oh, and I meant to tell you: we've been living together for seven years.' Thinking about this, Pam laughed and gave a little skip around the room to the music. She couldn't do it to him, of course. She was too much of a softy, but Derek never talked much about Belinda either, except to say he couldn't stand her. Well if he couldn't stand her, why didn't he divorce her? They'd lived apart for long enough. He probably still nursed a secret passion. Men were like that, not to be trusted, and there were always two sides to a story.

Pam went back into the kitchen and started bashing the stems of the roses. They would be waiting for him in a vase on the big table in the sitting-room when, and if, he came home from wherever it was he might be sulking. As she brought the steak mallet thumping down on the stalks of the beautiful, scentless flowers, she wished Derek was there now so she could make love to him. She fought off the irritation of tears.

A long way off, the telephone seemed to be ringing.

'Do you want your car then, Derek?' The doorman's cry stung him on the back of his neck like a dart. Derek ducked.

'No thanks, I've just got to go down and get something off the back seat.'

The doorman of the Kemble Hotel gave him a

friendly salute before he turned back to minister to a swarm of importunate Japs. There was nobody on the second level but for some reason Derek went through the absurd pretence of unlocking his car and looking inside. In the eyes of God, if to no other, it gave a sort of credence to the lie. Perhaps he *did* need something off the back seat. But in his erotic reverie of the past hour and a half he had forgotten about the letter.

As he had left Ashley Mansions, Tom had given him his post: one long envelope from his solicitors. They were pleased to inform him that his application for a Decree Absolute, filed several months before, had been uncontested. In short, he was now divorced from Belinda.

It was ironic. If Pam had waited one more day, might things have been different? Or might he have forgotten to tell her? The advantage of the married state, a cynic had once told him, was that it was a prophylactic against remarriage. Fortunately, Pam wasn't the marrying type. But she had, nonetheless, often taunted him over the absurdity of that legal connection with his ex-wife. Well, now he was technically free, yet skulking in a hotel car-park before an assignation like an old, guilt-ridden husband!

Derek entered the narrow car-park lift. At the entrance level the elevator stopped dead. To ascend to the room Garryl had breathlessly nominated on the telephone, he would have to run the gauntlet of Reception. Fortunately, the small lobby was thronged with tourists. Were some of them Russian? If anyone recognised him it would make interesting gossip in Tokyo and St Petersburg.

At last he took refuge in a larger lift, which limped upwards. Yes, the hotel had certainly seen better days; it was seriously in need of what the management would call 'refurbishment'. The lift's interior was scored with initials, one large swastika, and the letter F scratched with a coin and crudely erased. On another wall was a sign exhorting guests to SAMPLE OUR GOURMET CUISINE IN THE MRS SIDDONS BRASSERIE. This was illustrated with a coloured photograph of two people in smart-casual attire staring at each other across a table in what looked like a deserted cafeteria. Between them stood an inanely grinning waiter – Derek recognised Terry, the doorman – holding a platter on which lay an enormous lobster surrounded by a garish yellow and green salad. The red insect seemed to be waving a monitory mandible. Below this, there was another image of the same couple. They were in night attire and photographed from a very low angle, posed rather stiffly in a bedroom and watching television. Its caption read: CABLE AND VIDEO FACILITIES AVAILABLE IN ALL SUITES.

When the lift juddered to a halt on the fifth floor and the doors opened, Derek saw there were arrows and numbers on the wall ahead. Yet even though he knew he was looking for room number 52 he could not decide whether to turn left or right. He set out down the long, narrow corridor, shoving his way through a series of redundant fire doors. It was extraordinary how buildings in urgent need of incineration seemed to be the most assiduously protected. Cheap and sagging chipboard panels had been suspended beneath a once high ceiling, to accommodate electrical ducting and the rusty nozzles of the fire extinguishing system. There was a smell of stale smoke. It was all sufficiently seedy, he hoped, to meet with Garryl's exacting requirements.

As the last greasy fire door swung shut behind him with an ominous *whoomph*, Derek's palms were sweating and his heart had started thumping again. He felt curiously light-headed as he tapped on fifty-two. A chain within rattled and the door opened and closed. She wore a short, limp, porridge-coloured bathrobe, no doubt provided by the management with the respectful reminder that an identical garment, in luxurious Turkish towelling, could be purchased at reception for £40 as a lasting souvenir of your stay at the Kemble.

'Hi Guy,' said Garryl, pushing him against the door.

As Derek adjusted to the darkness of the room and the unfamiliar salutation, she pulled the jacket off his shoulders and covered his mouth with hers. Enjoyable though this was, there seemed to be something odd about the lighting in Suite 52. It flickered. As they moved, locked together, towards the bed, Derek could see that the only illumination in the room came from the television screen, on which he observed what seemed to be three very busy people with orange skin, filmed from the floor. Garryl laughed as she leant across to turn up the volume with one free hand. It was one of those videos of the 'yeah, yeah, oh yeah!' school.

'Is that with the hotel's compliments?' asked Derek, helping Garryl help him to take off his shoes and socks.

'No way,' said Garryl, 'just one of the little goodies I picked up on my shopping expedition in Soho.'

Derek fell back on to the bed and allowed Woody Weinglass's personal assistant to remove his trousers, then his underpants, which she tugged off in spite of an inelastic obstacle. He felt her cool nipples graze his thighs, her hair brush his belly and her warm engulfing mouth.

Then, to his surprise, Garryl seemed to change her mind; for she suddenly abandoned him, and with a snap of her fingers and an exclamation of someone who has overlooked the obvious, she began rummaging in a shopping bag beside the bed. From this she produced something which, by the light of the television, resembled to Derek a pony's bridle in black leather with innumerable attachments in jingling chrome.

'These goodies I bought today are giving me some wild ideas. Just lie there and amuse yourself a tad, while I slip into something more interesting.' And with that, Garryl seized what he presumed to be the bag of Taiwanese merchandise, and vanished into the bathroom.

Derek lay half-naked on the polyester sheets, watching the tableaux on the TV screen; its loud, guttural accompaniment interspersed with implausible squeals. The pillow beneath his head smelt as though it had done long service in an emphysema clinic. He decided that he had better remove his shirt and tie before tackling Garryl's equivocal apparatus, which appeared to have come without multilingual instructions.

The video continued to unfold its rudimentary tale and seemed to date from the Woodstock era. It appeared to be of venerable age. There were sartorial clues. Two female hitchhikers in flared jeans were now being picked up on a Los Angeles highway by a lorry driver with shoulder-length hair and a beaded Indian headband. There was an ugly break in the film, which then jerkily resumed in a motel bedroom.

Unlike his highbrow friends, Derek never affected to find such entertainments boring. On the contrary, to him they were so riveting that sometimes, when lodging in German or Scandinavian hotels, he was obliged to spend whole nights without sleep, mesmerised by the tireless cavalcade of lubricity.

But what was Garryl doing?, Derek wondered. He hoped these toys were her idea of fun, but her earnestness disturbed him. There was an ominous lack of humour about it all. And why did she address him by the generic 'Guy'? Was it just a creepy Californianism, or did she prefer her lovers to be mere ciphers?

Garryl's voice came from the bathroom. 'How you doin' out there, Guy, having fun?'

Still watching the television screen, Derek's attention wandered to the periphery of the main action. He relished the prosaic domestic details; the amateur touches. The girls' grimy soles, the red bedside phone, the power point on the chipped skirting-board, the glimpse of late sixties traffic through the half-closed, duck-egg blue venetian blinds, the mustard shagpile and the two paperbacks on the bedside table. He recognised the mauve cover of *Zen and the Art of Motorcycle Maintenance* and the spine of Hermann Hesse's *Steppenwolf.* One of those girls whose faces were temporarily invisible must have been an intellectual. Derek wondered what might be the favourite bedside reading of troilists in the nineties. *Wild Swans? The Fist of God?*

From behind the bathroom door Garryl said: 'Fuck!'

'What's going on in there?' Derek called at last, not without impatience.

'Sorry, Guy, but this goddam belt is a real drag, it was built for Roseanne Arnold. It's a bring down but I'm trying to make another hole in it with my nail file.'

'Belt?' cried Derek weakly, over the resumed troating of the video performers.

'What I've got in mind won't work with a loose buckle.'

All the excitement and anticipation which Derek had felt in the Ivy – all the romance, for Christ's sake – seemed to be ebbing away. Behind the door of a gimcrack hotel bathroom, a recently desirable girl was almost certainly disguising herself as Messalina on roller-skates. He experienced that rare phenomenon: *pre coitus tristis.*

A muffled telephone sounded. Derek knew from his filming days that a scene was sometimes interrupted by a rogue phone call from an instrument which the second assistant had forgotten to silence. Now the telephone on the screen had started up and the valiant porno stars had decided to carry on regardless.

Then Derek realised that the pulsing signal came from nearer at hand. It was his own mobile calling to him from the jumble of clothes on the floor. It took him some time to extract the instrument from the inside pocket of his tangled jacket.

'Derek?'

Derek cleared his throat. 'Speaking.'

'What's that?'

'What's what?'

'That noise? All that grunting?'

'I can't hear you. Got to turn off the TV.'

'Who's that, Guy?' Garryl's voiced called. 'Who are you talking to? I'm coming ready or not.'

With difficulty, Derek silenced the orgiasts. 'Who is this?'

'It's Pam. I don't care where you are or what you're doing, but your sister Jill has just rung from Adelaide.'

The bathroom door burst open and Derek's worst fears were confirmed. Standing in the wedge of yellow light was the girl who had once been Garryl Kurdish. Noticeably chubbier in her lattice of leather, she resembled an hermaphroditic hell's angel or, if the comparison may convey anything, *La Belle Dame sans Merci* in rubber.

To her credit she seemed, to some extent, aware of the absurdity of her accoutrements.

'*Voilà, monsieur!*' she laughed, raising her arms like a showgirl. 'Now, you and me have got a little unfinished business.'

'Your mother died two hours ago,' said the voice on the phone.

Bronwyn

IT WAS EARLY evening when Derek let himself quietly into the flat. He knew Pam was there somewhere; he could hear the soft throb of the Piazzolla. For a moment he stood in the hallway amongst his Piranesis wondering when grief would assail him. Instead he felt only gratitude. To be home at last, safe, with someone to come home to. A person who might be wilful, volatile, even unreasonable, but a sane person.

Derek thought of his narrow escape in Suite 52. Poor Garryl. It was amazing how complicated, not to say loopy, a lot of attractive women could become. It was staggering also to think that on the strength of one lunch invitation Garryl could have blown at least three hundred pounds in a Soho sex-shop, plus the room charge. Derek thought he might just have survived the experience if it had not been for that wagging pink truncheon, absurdly harnessed to her loins.

As gently as possible, he had told her his news, and regretted that it looked as if they would have to take a 'rain check'. Derek was afraid he might even have employed that awful phrase. As though mollifying a wanted erotomaniac, he had repeated that he was very sorry, but mercifully stopped short of adding 'after all the trouble you've gone to'.

'It happens,' said Garryl. The poor girl just sat on the edge of the bed, in full kit, sobbing, as he dressed and let himself out.

'It sure sucks about your mom,' she had whispered, and then, as he closed the door, 'Take the best care.'

When he entered the drawing-room, Pam was sitting in his favourite chintzy window seat looking out towards the cathedral, which had caught a vertical stripe of late sunlight. In the tall vitrine, a first-century Roman cup picked up the auric glint. Pam did not turn at the sound of his footstep, but said in a quiet, steady voice: 'Did you phone Jill from wherever you were?'

'Yes, but we couldn't hear each other. I'll use a real phone.'

'Would you like a cup of tea?'

'I thought you'd gone for good. The note and all that. It seemed so . . . final.'

'Your sister didn't know who the fuck I was. She called me Belinda.'

Derek stepped towards her. 'Jesus Pam, you know

I haven't been very close to my family. Not for years. They live in another world down there.'

'You've never mentioned them, actually. Though you've given me a gutful on your dear wife.'

'We're divorced. I got the news this morning from the solicitors. Your letter, then his.'

'No wonder you were celebrating in some flop-house.'

'Pam, I'm going to have to fly to Australia in the next twenty-four hours. I should go to the funeral.'

'That's up to you,' said Pam. She rose in the darkening room, and still without looking at him, went through to the kitchen. He heard the kettle being filled and the clink of cups.

Derek lit one of his lamps with a blue Chinese base and a yellow silk shade and collapsed into an armchair, his head in his hands. Through his fingers, he saw a dishevelled supplement on the Isphahan rug, opened at a feature about Al Pacino and his projected remake of Kurt Weill's *Threepenny Opera.* Beside a large photograph of Pacino by Snowdon, the caption read:

AL'S WEILL THAT ENDS WEILL.

He flung the magazine across the room; then he saw the crimson roses in their tall vase by the window, catching an oblique ray and subtracting the last richness of the day. He had made up his mind about something.

'Can you hear me, Pam?' he called.

'Just,' she said from the kitchen.

'If we went down to Caxton Hall tomorrow morning . . .'

'I can't hear you.'

'I said, IF WE WENT DOWN TO CAXTON HALL TOMORROW MORNING . . .'

Pam entered the room and put a hot mug of tea on the surface of a signed Gallé marquetry table. Derek whipped it off but went on talking.

'. . . and managed to get an emergency licence, would you marry me?'

'Yes,' said Pam.

But they still did not touch.

'I'll kiss you when you've had a hot bath and cleaned your teeth,' she said at last, 'and hadn't you better ring your poor sister?' Obediently, Derek took his tea into the study and dialled Jill's number. As he listened to the sound of the phone chiming in a grieving house in a far Adelaide suburb, Derek took a long healing swig of tea. It was Earl Grey.

Denise Gibb was crying.

'You are a prize bastard, Dekka,' said Ross, putting his arm around his wife's shoulder. 'Don't you think you could've given us all a smidge of notice before you decided to tie the knot?'

Derek and Pam Pettyfer sat in the back of Gibbo's Jaguar on their way from Caxton Hall to Weybridge. Derek's suitcase was in the boot.

'What else is new?' said Pam. 'He only told me last night.'

'I'll tell you what,' said Ross, withdrawing his arm from his wife's shoulder as he swung the car from West Hill towards the A308 for Kingston Vale. 'You were both bloody lucky there were a few Petty-boppers down at the old registry office or you two would have been living in sin for the next few weeks. To be perfectly honest with you, I didn't think we'd make it until I managed to swing you the VIP express service.'

'We're separating anyway tonight, when Derek goes to Adelaide. It's a trial divorce,' said Pam.

'We're really sorry about your mum, mate,' said his friend. 'I guess it's been coming a long time.'

'No,' Derek replied, thinking how comparatively talkative Pam was since that austere ceremony in the registry office half an hour before. 'My sister told me on the phone last night it was very sudden. She was pruning the camellia or something.'

'Shit, mate, death's a bastard whichever way you look at it. Anyway, Den and me are real sorry, aren't we Den?' Denise stretched her arm back over the comfortable leather seat and squeezed Derek's hand. It was a decent-sized rock on her finger, he noticed.

'If my mother had been dying for the last two years they would never have told me. "Mustn't worry Derek," they'd say.'

'I heard something like that,' chipped in Denise. 'A friend of mine got back to Sydney after a few years overseas, and bowled up at her parents' house to find it was full of dagos! She tracked down her cousin in the end, who told her that the oldies had been killed in a car crash yonks ago and the house and contents sold off.'

'What's this racist dago crap, Den?' said her husband. 'Some of our best friends are greaseballs.'

'What happened?' asked Pam.

'Get fucked, Gibbo. Well, my friend went apeshit. Why didn't anyone in the family tell me?' she said. 'And you know what they said?'

'What?' came three voices.

'*We didn't want to worry you.*'

'That sounds like Australia,' said Derek. 'Envy and hostility masquerading as compassion.'

'Come on, mate,' said the driver. 'Would you be being a pain in the arse by any chance?'

'It's true, Pam,' said Derek. 'If we have any kind of success outside Australia, even on a modest scale, they've got the knives out.' Derek assumed a mock Australian accent. 'Jeez, his parents have carked it, have they? Why bother to tell him? Didn't the bugger piss off to his fancy friends in Europe and ditch his old Aussie mates? Serve him right, *expatriate bastard!*'

'Derek's on his soap box again,' laughed Denise. 'Better get used to this, Pam.' Derek rubbed his cheek with the back of a wrist and was surprised to find tears.

'Shut up all of you,' said Ross. 'It's been a busy day already and we've got to get Dekka across to Heathrow in one piece by tonight. How's about a game of I Spy?'

Soon they were turning into the imposing driveway of Denross. Gibbo said: 'Welcome to Denross. Available for twenty-first birthdays, weddings and bar mitzvahs. I reckon you two should have a fancy wedding when Dek gets back from Oz. Mrs Petty could use the publicity for the next series, don't you reckon, Dekka? And a nice media wedding would be one in the eye for a few ratbags out there who still reckon you're a poofter.'

'Marriage doesn't prove anything,' said the young bride, to which no one felt constrained to reply.

There was a Range Rover in the drive which Derek recognised. Denise's 'help' – they abjured the word maid – a New Zealand girl called Bronwyn, let them in.

Ross drew Derek aside. 'Look mate,' he said. 'Sorry if I seemed to have a bit of a shitty on your Pam the other day, but to be perfectly honest with you I didn't know you were in that deep.'

'Neither did I,' said Derek.

'Look, we'd really like to give you both a bit of a bash when you come back from this shithouse trip. You haven't given us time to organise a bloody thing, you bastard, and you wouldn't feel like it anyway with your mum, and that. But there's a couple of mates of yours in there now who want to drink your health.'

The wedding party moved into Ross and Denise's Best Room. Derek seemed to remember that its original mock-Tudor features had been either picked out or disguised by a young Sydney decorator and family friend. The wainscot had been painted a glossy sky blue, and along the old curio ledge, a popular feature in houses of that period, Denise had arranged her collection of thatched cottage teapots. Over the fireplace, a large and rather garish picture of Sydney Harbour by Ken Done was illuminated by a brass picture light. Elsewhere in the room hung 'Aboriginal' paintings composed entirely of dots in beige and terracotta and bearing the signature of Malcolm Bandicoot. The furniture was in the 'retro' taste: chubby forties armchairs and couches reupholstered in maroon moquette and chrome standard lamps with chenille-trimmed parchment shades and brown Bakelite attachments and smokers' receptacles. A busy, floral wall-to-wall carpet stretched underfoot towards the lozenged lead-light doors, which opened on to a garden and swimming-pool. From its gold ceiling-rose a very new chandelier depended.

'I think you two know each other,' said Denise, as Inge stepped forward and embraced the bride. They stood holding each other for a long time as Derek greeted her husband Lionel. The famous cellist was a saturnine septuagenarian in jeans, Bally loafers and a black alpaca cardigan over a cream turtleneck. On his thin wrist Derek noticed the solid gold watch he had seen Lionel wearing in an upmarket advertisement. Lionel was probably the ugliest man Derek had ever met in his life, yet his success with young women was legendary.

'You're a fast worker,' whispered Inge to Pam. 'Yesterday you were never going back to him and today you're Mrs Pettyfer! I can't keep up with you. They might have let us know, don't you think, darling?' she cried, addressing her husband. 'I would have made a stunning Matron of Honour.'

'Not a problem,' said Ross, passing round the champagne. 'We're having an action replay for the whole mob when Dekka gets back from Oz, aren't we, Den?'

'R-i-gh-t!' said Denise.

'Inge and Li was the best we could organise at short notice,' said Ross, topping up Inge's glass. 'When I gave old Li a bell at sparrow fart this morning, I reckon I got him out of the cot, eh, Li?'

The musician politely demurred. It was awe-inspiring to observe how Ross Gibb could address a man whom he had known for less than thirty minutes by the ultimate diminutive of his name. For Derek, the maestro who had just won the *Grand Prix d'Or du Disque* for his recordings of the complete Haydn cello repertoire, would be 'old Li' thereafter.

'I'm a big fan of your husband's,' Lionel Pinkhill confided to Pam. 'But we never see each other. I'm always on tour with my fiddle and he's always running around in high-heeled shoes, stopping us from taking ourselves too seriously.' They touched wine glasses. 'I hear from my wife you are a brilliant sculptor.'

Pam was on the verge of suggesting a sitting when Ross proposed a toast.

'You see, Derek,' exclaimed Inge, 'we must love you a lot to come slumming in Weybridge and drink your health.' They all laughed except Denise who failed, quite properly, to perceive risibility in Weybridge. The help entered with some large trays studded with such Australian delicacies as asparagus rolls and smoked oysters on water crackers.

'A few wee savouries,' announced Bronwyn, taking one herself and munching it audibly. 'Help yourselves, thanks.'

While Ross went to fetch orange juice for Derek

and another bottle of Dom, Denise proudly showed the Pinkhills the glass cabinet containing her snowstorm collection.

'People think I'm mad,' she told the virtuoso, 'and I guess it's pretty whacky and unusual, but I've got eighty-seven of these from all over the world.' She delved into the case and withdrew a small dome of glass containing a miniature Sydney Opera House, which she quickly inverted. Politely, the Pinkhills peered at the toy blizzard. 'Ross reckons these are going to be worth something one day.'

'You're quite a collector, Denise,' was as far as Inge was prepared to go along the path of satire.

'R-i-gh-t.'

Pam was admiring Ross's new Bang & Olufsen sound system as she felt Derek come up behind her. 'Was it good last night?'

'Incredible,' replied Derek. He remembered the white girl, lying still beneath him, her eyes hidden by the crook of her elbow.

'Did I snore again?' he asked.

'No, you cried in your sleep though.'

'That's the only time I ever do.' She took his hand.

'Haven't you got just a bit of a chip on your shoulder about Australia, darling?' Pam had never called him that. Had never used a term of endearment before.

He kissed her lightly on her cool lips, tasting the champagne. 'Have I?'

'Yes, they love you in Australia. Well, they love Mrs Petty. Those TV shows. You might get the odd snake in the grass but that's the price of fame. It's . . .' she sought the word, 'it's *provincial* behaviour. I get it, and I've only come from Birmingham to London, and I'm not even famous! There's an art critic in Birmingham who's got it in for me. He was reasonably OK until my bust of Jonathan Miller got a nice little rave in the *Telegraph*, then he let me have it with both barrels. Australia's no different, darling. They love you, and they really want you to do well, so long as it's on a small scale.'

'That's precisely what I was saying.'

'Break it up,' said Ross. 'If you two don't look out, you'll start getting to like each other, and that's a bad start to any marriage, isn't it, Den?' Affectionately, perhaps, he goosed his wife. 'I have to break up this little party because Mr Pettyfer has a plane to Adelaide to catch, and it's my job to get him on it. To be perfectly honest with you, and speaking as his manager, I'm surprised I succeeded in locking this little event away, so I'm going to ride shotgun until the blushing bridegroom has fastened his seat-belt.'

'You'd know all about seat-belts, wouldn't you, Inge?' said Denise to the emancipated stewardess with a big smile. Mrs Gibb wasn't too stupid.

An hour later, as the Pinkhills dropped Pam off at Ashley Mansions in their Range Rover, Inge said: 'My God, Pam. I'm still in shock. When I told you to try the jealousy bit, I never thought it would work so quickly.'

'Or in reverse?' smiled Pam, slamming the door.

Peggy & Jill

'WOULD YOU LIKE to see Mother?'

The undertaker, a short freckled man in a fawn suit, looked at Jill and Derek with an expression of mournful enquiry.

Whose mother is he talking about?, thought Derek, jet-lagged. Was Peggy Pettyfer *his* mother as well? It seemed, to say the least, over familiar. He supposed all these embalmers felt on intimate terms with their cadavers. Certainly, in twenty-four hours they probably penetrated more orifices than the deceased's husband had hoped to do in a lifetime.

Derek was rather shocked by the indecency of his own vagrant thoughts under the circumstances. It must be the long flight, the culture shock. But the inside of his brain felt as though it had been briskly sandpapered, and now that he was back in Adelaide, his birthplace, there was the odd sensation that he had never been away. And a recurring dream of getting married to someone.

'I said, would either of you like to see Mother?'

Jill and Derek looked at each other.

'No.'

'No thanks.'

'Not a problem,' said the undertaker, shaking their hands. Derek had been back in Australia less than four hours, and he had already lost count of the number of times he had been the recipient of this inane courtesy. 'Not a problem' was not so much a phrase as a tic, an infestation; a virus. It raged through Australian conversation like Dutch elm or myxomatosis.

Outside the funeral home it was cold; a late Adelaide winter; but the sun shone all the same. As they got into Jill's cream Gemini in Goodwood Road, Derek was still brooding about the little, wizened mortician. It was as if he had been personally responsible for the death of his mother, four days ago.

'What a creep,' he said.

'You try a job like that sometime, Derek. His people have been marvellous. It's all very well . . .'

Derek finished her sentence: '. . . me turning up out of the blue and expecting things to be done my way!'

His sister, leaning forward at the wheel and never taking her eyes off the traffic, touched his arm with a gloved hand. 'We mustn't talk like this. Think how it would hurt Mother.'

'Since when has she been Mother? We always called her Peggy – or Peg. Did that smarmy little undertaker put you on to the "Mother" bit?'

'You're not on stage now, Derek, you're in

Adelaide – amongst decent people.' Derek looked at the pedestrians through the car window. Pushing prams, waiting for buses, pottering in gardens. He wondered if they looked any more decent than the inhabitants of, say, Ravenscourt Park. Gloomily, he decided they did.

'When I rang you up just after the doctor left, and spoke to one of your . . . arrangements, I thought to myself: he'll come out here in a minute and criticise, criticise, *criticise*.' And with that the old lady of forty-two at the wheel in a raincoat, gloves and a wild-flowers of Tasmania headscarf who was his sister, burst into floods of tears. They pulled over to the side of the road while Jill recovered herself. Awkwardly, Derek put his arm around her shoulder.

'I should tell you, Jill, in case you put your foot in it again, that the "arrangement" you spoke to in London is now my wife.'

Jill brightened perceptibly. 'So that's what did it!'

'What?'

'That's what finished off our mother.'

'I thought it was heart,' said Derek.

'It was heart,' said his sister, 'but it was probably hearing your news that brought it on.'

'Jill, I only proposed to my "arrangement" *after* I heard about Peg.'

Jill let out a wail. 'So our mother dies, and you plan a happy honeymoon. Lovely, LOVELY! You haven't changed, Derek. She said you had, but you haven't.' Jill scrubbed her eyes with a handkerchief, turned on the ignition, and the Gemini shot out rather abruptly into the stream of traffic. Derek checked his seat-belt. 'However, I'm glad mother went to her reward thinking the best of you – even if that poor darling was wrong.'

They were entering an older suburb now, and Derek recognised some familiar landmarks of his youth. They seemed smaller. Of course there were the hideous supermarkets and the raw, red and cream brick boxes on stilts – the debased legacies of that criminal, Le Corbusier; but once you got off the beaten track in an Australian suburb, nothing ever changed. There was what used to be the old tram depot, there was his old school and miraculously, a few reprieved elms still ticketed with yellow leaves. They must be in Hackney; they must be nearly home. But Jill hadn't finished.

'You may not know this, Derek, but Mother always stuck up for you.'

'Is that so?'

'Yes, she never believed those stories that she read about you . . . about . . . you know . . . the drinking, the women in the background.'

'Well, Jill, she was wrong to stick up for me, wasn't she? She was practising a bit of maternal self-deception.'

Jill delivered her trump card. 'And she liked Belinda.'

'She only met Belinda once, on her trip to London in seventy-five, and it was a disaster.'

'She liked her all the same, Derek, and she always used to send Mother a Christmas card.'

Derek suppressed his nausea.

'Actually, if you really want to know, Mother

thought you might have been a bad influence on Belinda sometimes.'

'So she didn't stick up for me all the time?'

His sister swung the car into the narrow driveway of a small suburban bungalow, faced with Adelaide bluestone. The front porch was almost overshadowed by the glossy leaves of a giant camellia, its base surrounded by a mulch of pink petals. The car stopped, but Jill was still in driving mode, hands on the wheel and staring ahead through the windscreen.

'How is Belinda, by the by?'

'She's in Devon and drunk as a skunk.'

'That's a terrible thing to say, Derek. From what I gather, she had a lot more willpower than you.'

'So how come then, dear sister, she's pissed and I'm sober?'

'Please Derek, don't be uncalled-for. We don't need that London talk in Adelaide. We never did and we don't now.'

She opened the car door and jangled some keys at him. 'Are you coming in? I could organise a cup of tea for you.' Derek was relieved to discover that, in spite of the New Sophistication, his countrymen still 'organised' things like sandwiches and cups of tea for each other. It was nice to have a cup of tea made for you, but gratitude knew no bounds when the beverage was *organised*; especially if further organisation procured a biscuit. He steeled himself as they entered the old family home and he heard the rickety fly-wire door slam shut behind him.

'Of course,' his sister was saying, 'Donald and I

could move in here now if we wished, and put Frank in a nice retirement village, but I couldn't do that to an old man, I'm sorry but I couldn't.'

'Will Frank be at the funeral today?' asked Derek, his eyes darting around the room. They were in the old front lounge. There was the smell of a dead fire in the grate and also, somewhere, the faint lingering effluvium of last week's roast.

Frank Quick was Peggy's second husband; dull and devoted. He kept her company at the bowling club, and after the death of Derek's father, the bright wiry old widow had needed a fourth hand at Bridge more than anything else on earth.

'Do you know, Derek, I think Daddy would've really liked Frank,' Jill said archly, forgetting to organise the promised cup of tea after all, and collapsing instead into a threadbare Jason Recliner.

'What's this Daddy? He's dead, isn't he, so shouldn't you be calling him "Father" now?'

'As our mother used to say: "Sarcasm is the lowest form of wit." '

'Dad would've loathed Frank, and you know it, Jill. If he'd run into him on a dark night, he would've grabbed him by the throat and got him to spit out all his Masonic secrets.'

As the grey old lady, nearly nine years his junior, expressed her outraged response, Derek looked around the dim familiar room. Where was the Hans Heysen?, he wondered. The lovely and now valuable watercolour of giant eucalypts which his grandfather had bought from the artist in the twenties was missing.

Jill read his thoughts. 'Oh, you're looking for the Heysen. Donald and I have got that at home now and we cherish it. My mother said, "Well, Jill, you might as well have the pleasure of it now as wait until I'm dead." ' Peggy was *her* mother now, Derek observed. 'Donald and I came around one afternoon and took the things we liked.'

When Derek failed to make the expected remonstration, she continued more boldly. ' "You've done so much for me, Jilly", my mother used to say, "you must help yourselves".'

'What about the camphor chest?' He remembered the carved and aromatic box which always stood in his parents' bedroom; an exotic souvenir of a voyage to Colombo, long ago.

'Don adores it. He keeps his old account books and files in it. The silver fish are furious!' Jill laughed quite merrily and for the first time. Then glanced at her watch. 'I had hoped we would have time for a cup of tea, but we might be late for the service.' She looked at her brother omnisciently. 'If you want to use the bathroom you'd better go now.'

'Good idea,' said Derek, rising. 'Sorry if I've been bit snappy,' he added. 'I can't do with those long plane trips any more. I feel wrecked.'

'We all do Derek, now hurry!'

He was looking forward to this visit to the old WC on the back verandah next to the wash house, and for the first time in fifteen years, peeing on the words, Armitage Shanks. Taking his accustomed route to the lavatory, he turned into the dark passage where that picture still hung of jolly red-faced huntsmen, quaffing goblets and smoking long pipes around the Olde Inne Fire. But opening a door, he seemed to have lost his bearings. The back of the old house, where he had spent his childhood, had been sliced off. Instead, he found himself in some modern excrescence. A 'family room' with an open-plan kitchen, cane furniture and a big TV. One glass wall with sliding doors looked on to the sad, abridged garden. After the gloom of the front sitting-room, the bleak light streamed in. He realised why. The big old peppercorn had been chopped down.

'Where's the loo gone?' Derek called, his eyes suddenly filled with tears.

'It's in mother's *en suite*,' came the shrill reply from the front of the house. 'Don't you love what Frank did to that ghastly tumbled down verandah? And my Don got rid of that old fashioned pepper-corn. It used to drop its blessed stickiness everywhere.'

Derek stormed back through the house into his mother's bedroom which, much as before, was almost filled with that dais of raspberry pink candle-wick: his parents' bed. A door had been knocked through a cupboard into a small adjacent bedroom – his old room – and an *en suite* of gold taps and shower recess installed, with a Formica vanity on which sat, presumably, Frank Quick's shaving tackle.

Kicking up a featherweight toilet seat of avocado plastic, Derek relieved himself. Swaying there in that snot-green box, with a view through louvres of a grey paling fence, he realised that tears were flowing in hot streams down his cheeks. He, the Aquarian, was regressing inexorably to his watery element.

A loud rapping on the door arrested the process of deliquescence. 'Hurry, Derek, we mustn't be late for the necropolis.'

'We won't be, God forbid!' In spite of himself, Derek gave a muculent laugh and blew his nose on a corner of Frank's reasty towel.

Derek sat in the small, defiantly ecumenical 'chapel', designed, it seemed, to discourage optimistic speculations about the afterlife, or indeed, life itself. He stared at the box in which Peggy was soon to be posted to oblivion and remembered the last funeral he had been to. It was a memorial service for Paul Baker, the legendary classical actor who had, alone in his basement flat, choked to death on his own vomit. In the packed church his 'peers' had waffled on about Paul's disdain for success, his Olympian detachment and his freedom from professional jealousy. The truth was that poor old Paul had been drunk and unemployable for the last twenty years and corroded with rage and envy, only sober enough to totter majestically through the odd chat show or cameo role.

The most grisly moment of all was the final eulogy by his doctor, a sinister medico known in certain theatrical circles for his liberal hand in the dispensation of uppers and downers. It was he who had, years before, bestowed upon Paul the diagnosis beloved of all alcoholics: 'Manic depressive'. As Derek had watched Dr Prushkin's mawkish and self-serving performance in the pulpit, he had reached the melancholy conclusion that his friend might still be alive were it not for his physician.

An electric organ whinnied something soft and secular, wrenching Derek back to Adelaide.

After the service at the Centennial Park Necropolis – the talcy embraces of old aunts, the knuckle breakers from cousins and the flirtatious hugs from distant female relations who were Mrs Petty fans – Jill and Derek, armed with a map, went to inspect Peggy's niche in the columbarium.

It had started to rain.

Derek took his sister's arm as they splashed along the gravel paths and turned back from *cul-de-sacs*, until at last they came upon the Abel-Smith Rose Garden and turned left towards a low stone wall covered with uniform bronze plaques.

'It ought to be here next to Daddy's.' Jill consulted the soggy map. 'They'll put her ashes in later, I suppose.'

'There it is,' said Derek, descrying his mother's full, new name.

Alison Peggy Quick
1918–1995
Beloved wife of Francis Clyde Quick

A rose has faded, but before my eyes
A rose will bloom again in Paradise

Camellia might have been more appropriate, thought Derek, but he said, 'Dad didn't get much of a look in, did he?'

'He has his own niche, Derek, see!' She pointed, but it was impossible here in the rain, with the imperceptible odour of grilled chops wafting downwind from the Necropolis chimney, to properly mourn or even experience a sense of graveyard irony.

Planted in the grass next to them was an official notice:

DO NOT LEAVE YOUR HANDBAG UNATTENDED.

It seemed to Derek an adjuration against single-minded grief, in case skeletal hands reached up through the saturated turf and snatched the mourners' pension books, credit cards and mobile phones.

Derek thought of Earl, his father, marginalised by Peggy's epitaph. 'Always take your hat off in lifts, son,' his father had persistently exhorted him, and it was the only piece of paternal advice Derek could ever remember. Even today, he still doffed in crowded elevators, secretly pleased that the old-fashioned courtesy went entirely unnoticed by his fellow passengers. It was at such bare-headed moments, pressed amongst louts and slatterns, looking up at the ascending numbers, that his love for his father always returned to him with a sweet intensity.

As they got back into the black Mercedes and were driven to Jill and Don's for some grisly, cake-encumbered wake, Jill said, after a silence, 'I hope you were joking.'

'About what?'

'I hope you didn't get married again. Not without telling us first.'

'Why shouldn't I? Peg's not there any more to approve or disapprove.'

'But I am, and I'm your sister, and I thought that girl on the phone sounded a cold fish.'

'She is English.'

'Do you know what Peg, I mean . . . our mother used to say?'

'What?'

'Derek could do a lot worse than a nice Adelaide girl.'

It was strange, back in his own home town after so many years, to be immured in an hotel. From the window of his hexagonal suite in the Hyatt, Derek looked out at the view. The pewter glints of the Torrens, the denuded silver poplars, the green parkland, and on higher ground, the spires and gardens of North Adelaide with a few bursts of early blossom.

Few of his old friends resided there now; and those who remembered him would probably be embarrassed to find him unannounced on their doorstep. You could not just drop back into people's lives like that after so many years and expect the red carpet. It smacked of a kind of arrogance. On his last flying visit to Adelaide – for his mother's wedding, four years before – there had, to be sure, been a big lunch party at Da Clemente in honour of his return. Only he had paid for it.

Nonetheless, he made a few telephone calls. If old

acquaintances read in the gossip columns that he'd been in town for nearly five days and not telephoned, there might be hurt feelings. As it happened, only Kym and Julie were home, but hopelessly booked up.

Derek preferred to see no one, though the PR girl at the hotel had leaked his presence to the Press, and there were importunate demands for interviews to deflect and decline. 'The price of fame,' as Pam had called it.

He phoned her once a day. It was a dispiriting exercise. The strangely inexpressive voice, the long pauses; the warmth, it seemed to him, withheld. What an unsuccessful mode of communication the telephone was. It reinforced and articulated separation – not closeness. Pam always called him 'love' now, or was it 'luv'? 'Hello, love!' and 'when are you back?' but that was all she ever said from which he could remotely infer Need, or Desire. Was she angry?

'Are you angry about something, Pam?'

'No – why?' It was the same emotional evasiveness he remembered from Peggy.

'Are you OK, Mum?'

'Fine – why?'

But he had to remain in Australia for the next few days at least. There was a meeting in Sydney he had to attend on the journey back and legal things to sort out here in Adelaide. Jill had arranged a lawyers' conference, designed, he suspected, to gently inform him that his mother's modest estate was to be carved up between her and poor old Frank.

His stepfather had been a sad figure at the service,

if such an insipid ecumenical charade could be so called. An old man with a bad shaving cut, weeping in the pew in front of him.

Phyllis Munro, his mother's best friend, had been there too; greatly aged. She had once been a teacher and taught Derek at prep school. When they met at the crematorium she had embraced him, and seemed, much to his surprise, far from grief-stricken; blithe even.

'I'm quite a celebrity now, Derek, thanks to you.'

'How come, Phyl?'

'Well, teaching you English Literature when you were ten . . .'

'Forty years ago.'

'They wanted to know what you were like then, and luckily I kept your essay on "Autumn", so I sent that.'

'You what? To whom?'

'That nice man in London who's doing the book on you. Is it Mr Hitchcock?'

'I can't imagine!'

'He's written to everyone. I think he even dropped a line to your dear mother before she passed on.'

Derek had been swept away from his old teacher by a tide of handshakes and condolences, but it disturbed him to think some busybody was plaguing these old biddies, researching him!

'Fucked if I know, mate,' said Ross on the phone. 'To be perfectly honest with you I get umpteen requests a week for the low-down on you but I'm not talking. Are you with me?'

'I need money here, Ross. I'm picking up the

funeral costs. I left in such a hurry I forgot to bring any readies.'

'What's wrong with your plastic?'

'I can't very well put my late mother on Diners.'

'Don't tell me you've spotted another of those ancient fuckin' vases?'

'Nothing like that, it's just . . .'

'I'll try mate. Don't forget most of your funds are tied up on deposit in the Bahamas. There might just be a quid in the Isle of Man production account, but I can't promise. Might take a while to whistle it up.'

'Now hold on, Gibbo. Are you telling me I can't spend my own money?'

'If you spent your own money, mate, you wouldn't have any. To be perfectly honest with you, it isn't yours to spend.'

'Say that again.'

'I've explained this before mate, but it's all part of this sexy structure I've set up for you. It's saving you a squillion in tax.'

'I paid plenty last year.'

'Well you would've paid a lot more if it wasn't for Uncle Ross. Listen, I'll try and organise you an advance on expenses for your next TV special, and we can probably lose the interest somewhere between the Zurich account and Nova Scotia.'

'I'm in Adelaide, not Nova Scotia!' Derek protested. 'And I hope you never invested any of my hard-earned cash in Lloyds,' he added apprehensively.

'You've got to be joking, mate, do me a favour!'

his manager indignantly exclaimed. 'As soon as they started to advertise Lloyds I smelled a rat.'

'How so?'

'Stands to reason, pal,' explained Ross sapiently. 'If it had been any good the Brits would have kept it to themselves.'

'I still don't quite understand, Ross. I'd just like to know where it's all going . . .'

'Hold the phone, pal, trust me. If it gets you out of a hole, I'll lend you a couple of grand from my own Norfolk Island Denross Trust Fund account. In the meantime, bash the plastic.'

'Does it all really have to be so complicated, Gibbo . . .?'

But his manager had rung off.

On his last day in Adelaide, Derek strolled up North Terrace and visited the Art Gallery. He stood before his favourites: the Conder, the Tom Roberts, the Phillips Fox, and the Samuel Palmer he had once, long ago, had a chance to buy. Then he took a stroll in the Botanic Gardens, lingering in the native flora section which his mother had loved; furtively snapping off twigs and crushing leaves to inhale the nostalgic balsam. The wattles were already exploding into yellow, powdery blossom. He felt closer to Peggy, there in the deserted gardens on a damp Adelaide Tuesday, than he had in the kitsch necropolis or the embalming parlour or even in the old vandalised house in Hackney.

It started to rain again as he walked back to the Hyatt, but he glanced up Pulteny Street looking for Beck's Second-hand Bookshop. It was now a pizzeria.

The next morning he managed to preserve a civilised equanimity during the conference with Jill's lawyer, which proceeded exactly as he had anticipated. The old house, it seemed, was already on the market and Derek had politely waived an offer to revisit it and take any small items.

Suddenly, he could not wait to get on a plane. He had the meeting in Sydney and a connection to Singapore, then London, the next day. Surprisingly, however, Jill had remembered his request of the day before.

At Kingsford Smith airport she bestowed a Laodicean peck and handed him the envelope, apparently unopened. 'It wasn't hard to find,' she said, as Derek thanked her and put the letter in his pocket. 'It was in mother's writing compendium on the nest of tables.' Then, she added meaningfully, 'It's the only letter from England she's had in years.' As she said these words, Jill smiled with unexpected sweetness but Derek, the dilatory correspondent, took the rebuke.

'Such a pity you have to go so soon,' said his sister. 'Don and I wanted to organise you a nice roast, didn't we Don?' But Don was keeping an eye on the car.

'Next time,' said Derek. 'Goodbye, Jill.'

'Bye-bye Derek. Take care.'

Antoinette

Flavoured clay, shaped like food, was placed before him.

'Can I organise you a drink before take-off, Dr Bottomley?'

Derek was on the flight to Sydney and on hearing the steward's voice, he looked up from his copy of *Time* and stole a glance across the aisle. It was, without doubt, the Adam Bottomley he had known at university, now bald, bearded and transformed by age, money and several thousand free lunches. Always plump and smug, he was now glossy; a bladder of *bonhomie.* Derek hunched into his magazine, dreading recognition. Why doctor, he wondered. Probably a 'dingo' degree at the University of Wagga-Wagga: a PhD in psychology or business administration. Australian politicians were shameless in appropriating an honorific.

With a kind of satisfaction at the symmetry of things, he observed that the undergraduate he had detested had, in thirty years, ripened and fermented into detestable middle-age. He noticed also that the 'doctor' wore on his lapel the official insignia of the Australian Republican Movement: a shamrock in enamelled metal supported by a kangaroo and a koala bear. He had read somewhere that Bottomley was a passionate after-dinner bore on this topic; not from a fervent belief in constitutional reform, but quite simply because the Republican bandwagon was a convenient pseudo-patriotic vehicle to notoriety.

'Beaut to see you, mate!'

Derek had been recognised, and his fellow traveller had heaved himself unbidden into the vacant seat beside him.

'Still destroying them O.S.?'

Derek accepted the clammy handclasp, inhaling the breath like an open grave. He observed the pursed mouth embedded in the ginger divot of his beard. 'O.S.? Ah yes, overseas. Well I'm trying.'

Adam was happy to supply Derek with a spirited résumé of his postgraduate career, from advertising man to his present illustrious post as Minister for the Arts. Throughout their colloquy he kept stroking Derek's arm and patting his hand consolingly, as if Derek had long sought an opportunity like this in which to make some shameful confession of failure. He was mesmerised by the doctor's moist pink lips, surrounded by their sparse wreath of marmalade whiskers.

'By the way, I didn't see your name on the last Republican petition.'

'I'm afraid no one asked me,' Derek equivocated.

'Too bad, mate, you ought to stick with the strength, old son. We're dishing out some pretty attractive creative incentive packages to our friends right now.'

'You mean bribes?'

The doctor laughed heartily at this. He rocked in his seat. Derek got a strong whiff of BO and Eau Sauvage. 'You satirists destroy me!' He scrubbed away the tears of merriment with the back of a porky wrist.

'Look, Adam,' said Derek, 'I keep away from politics, I'm too busy anyway, and I don't really need government hand-outs.' The Arts Minister seized his arm conspiratorially.

'It's just that if you're not with us, mate . . .' Bottomley's fuchsia lips almost brushed his ear, 'you could be seen to be against us. *Get the message?*' His eyes twinkled like the eyes of Dr Goebbels in a benevolent mood. Derek got the message.

He had never been more relieved than when the plane finally landed, but as they unfastened their seat-belts, the Minister grabbed his wrist. 'Just between ourselves, mate, how did *you* think your last series went down?'

Derek was tricked by a master into making a few modest, self-deprecating noises, as Dr Bottomley moved in for the kill.

'Funnily enough, mate, I was defending you at a party only the other night!'

Derek waited until his old friend had bustled importantly out of sight to the waiting limousine, the meetings and the lunches.

Why all those 'beauts' and 'mates'?, he wondered.

The Australian Intelligentsia – if that was not an oxymoron – all talked a kind of synthetic Oz-speak these days, and on their lips the word 'mate' could become the most malevolent noun in the English language.

His encounter with the Sydney Festival girl had not been a triumph either, and hardly worth the detour. She was a tough young lady in a black tailored suit and a henna rinse called Carmen Conroy. She looked as though she needed a man like a fish needs a Ferrari. In her grand office overlooking the glittering harbour, Derek explained that he had devised a one-man show about Ambrose Bierce which he hoped to perform off-Broadway, and perhaps also, if Ms Conroy was interested, at the Sydney Festival.

There was a long and uncomfortable silence, during which Derek suddenly began to feel like a grovelling mendicant. Stupidly, he realised that the Californian misanthropist was not on this lady's reading list. But then, neither probably were Shakespeare, Goethe, Turgenev, Stendahl or, for that matter, P. G. Wodehouse. Derek felt that he should at least have dropped the names of Anaïs Nin, Betty Friedan or Kate Millett, or a few other all-time-greats. Orwell's premonition had been wrong. Big Brother would not be watching us at Century's End: it would be Big Sister.

'Frankly, Derek, Mrs Petty was relevant in the seventies, but our demographic is the under-thirties community. These days Australian audiences are into Performance Art.'

'But surely, I mean, it might not always be Art, but I am a performer!' He refrained from adding 'for Christ's sake'. 'But I'm not suggesting a Mrs Petty show, anyway,' he said.

'This Pierce . . .?'

'Bierce!'

'Does he address gender issues?'

Derek took a deep breath and prayed for strength. We've had gender, *genre* coming up in a moment, he thought despondently, those G-words always stick together . . .

'Ambrose Bierce never stopped,' he responded to his own surprise. 'He spent his life being hounded on account of his colour and sexual orientation.'

Ms Conroy began to look interested as Derek recklessly rewrote literary history.

'To escape discrimination, poor old Ambrose had to stage his own disappearance in Mexico.'

Not wholly unimpressed by these hitherto recondite biographical details, Carmen Conroy perused a dossier. 'I hope this show you're planning is different from your Patrick White effort,' she said tartly, her eyes on the page.

Did she think she was his headmistress?, Derek wondered.

'Since you've been away, the Australian audience community has been exploring more complex genres.'

There it was! Derek was awed by his own prescience as he said, 'What was wrong with my Patrick White show? It was popular, wasn't it? It made money.'

Ms Conroy crinkled her brow and gave him a pitying smile. 'Those are hardly valid criteria, Derek. Anyway, most of us in the arts administration community found it frankly homophobic.'

'But White *was* homophobic!' protested Derek, dropping his guard. 'He was homophobia on roller-skates – he wrote the book!'

The Administrator listened sorrowfully to these heresies and returned to Derek's project.

'This Pierce – was he Australian?'

He noticed Ms Conroy's lipstick was almost black.

'Well, no. I think I said . . .'

'As a rule we don't normally encourage shows depicting overseas personalities,' she pontificated. 'Couldn't you do something on a world-class *Australian* achiever?'

'Hold on,' said Derek, inspirationally. 'Bierce wrote a lot of his stuff outside Australia, but so did Christina Stead and Germaine Greer.'

'You mean . . .?'

It wasn't exactly a lie, not yet, but Derek might have to unearth a few surprising and hitherto unknown facts in the career of Ambrose Bierce if he wanted this job.

'Ambrose was an expat, I'm afraid,' he declared sheepishly, 'but he still called Australia home!'

To his amazement, the Artistic Director of the Sydney Biennale put her lips together and smiled. It was a nun's smile on learning of a soul not totally beyond redemption.

*

Next day, he was glad to be out of Sydney. With its beautiful harbour and hideous buildings, he felt it was one of the world's great missed opportunities.

As he flew towards Singapore, Derek shuddered at the recollection of Adam Bottomley. Ross Gibb was different. Gibbo's dialogue had an authentic warmth. But why hadn't the bastard sent that cash? When he got back to London he was going to have to sit down with his friend in Roger Wainwright's office and once again get them to explain his 'structure' to him. If they could.

Derek opened a copy of the *Adelaide Advertiser* which had been free on the morning plane. Already it seemed like news from another planet. On the real estate page he was surprised to see a picture of 36 Light Street, Hackney. The caption read:

> **STUNNING ART DECO VILLA**
> Dress Circle Adelaide Suburb, Magnificent Established Garden, Superb Family Room, Period Master Bed, Stunning En suite, Ample Room Jacuzzi. May need slight reno. Ideal First Home Owner or Discerning Executive.
> NOTE: Childhood home of Derek (Mrs Petty) Pettyfer.

He slapped the paper shut. It was a bit rich, dropping his name to make a sale from which he didn't stand to earn a penny. As for 'art deco', what did they mean? The old kitchen lino? A mottled bathroom tile? The trapezoids and chevrons in the leadlight of the dining-room doors?

His table had been set and as the trolley moved towards him up the Business Class aisle, he tumbled the ice-cold cutlery on to his tray from a plastic sachet.

'Would you care for a drink with your meal, sir?' He looked up and saw a pretty 'flight attendant' with a fading love-bite bending over him and proffering a champagne bottle.

'I don't drink, thank you, but if you have some Evian . . .?'

'Not a problem.' She hesitated, still smiling. He could smell the Polo mint, and beyond that, the cigarette. 'Don't you remember me? Sandy Thomas – Gibbo's friend!'

'Why, yes, nice to see you, Sandy.' Derek's mind was a total blank.

'You can't place me, can you? We met ages ago at Brian and Helen's barbecue in London.' Derek vaguely remembered a girl who came with Ross when Denise was in Bali with the kids. 'How is he?' asked the stewardess. 'I haven't seen him since last month.'

'Last month? Ross was in London last month. No, I tell a lie,' confessed Derek. 'He had to go to LA to lock away a deal for me.' He remembered the keen disappointment he'd felt when that NBC job fell through. 'He was in Sydney for a few days too, or am I telling stories out of school?'

Sandy smiled broadly, revealing deep dimples and discreet gold inlays, as she filled Derek's glass to the brim with champagne.

'What Ross does in his spare time is none of my business,' Derek said.

'Gibbo said he'd teach me to ride,' said Sandy. 'Please keep him up to it, PLEASE!'

'I didn't know Ross could ride, and by the way, I don't drink.'

Sandy Thomas was mortified. 'Oh God! Sorry about that.' She swept away the offending glass. 'He rides pretty well for a beginner. Who wouldn't, with a stud farm like that?'

'Stud farm?'

'You must have been there, outside Bowral, it's Gibbo's pride and joy.'

Derek thought he was going slightly mad, but he decided to be crafty. 'My memory is a disaster. I think Admiral Alzheimer must have fired a few shots over my bows, but remind me Sandy, how long is it since Ross acquired this property?'

'Must be a couple of years. But of course, he keeps buying those gorgeous horses, doesn't he?'

'He must miss it,' said Derek.

'Not for long, he reckons that if he can wind up his business he can get out there full-time in about six months when the house is finished.'

She filled a clean glass with Evian water. It was freezing cold in Derek's hand.

'I don't know what I'm rabbiting on about,' the stewardess said, laughing. 'You're his friend, you'd know more about all this than I would.'

'Yes,' said Derek.

'Thank you, Antoinette, I hope it wasn't too uncomfortable for you.'

In the waiting-room, Inge looked up from her *Harpers.*

'Raewyn!' said Mr Watson. 'Please block off as many appointments as you can next Monday morning.'

Raewyn Mackle looked at the book and frowned. 'There's a wee problem, Sir Andrew Lloyd . . .'

'Please call him and offer him another time, Raewyn. If I'm not mistaken . . .' the dentist put an index finger to his cheek and smiled coyly – '. . . if I'm not *very* much mistaken, Dame Antoinette must have a pretty smile by November the first.'

'November first!' The subject of all this concern had finally spoken, albeit incoherently, through a handkerchief clutched to her mouth.

'We mustn't forget the world première of your new Anthony van Laast ballet,' said Mr Watson triumphantly. '*Les Couche-Tard*!'

Another voice excitedly chimed in: '. . . music by Françaix, sets and costumes by Patrick Procktor . . .' It was Mr Bremner, beaming cherubically from around the door of his surgery, who contributed this last intelligence.

The large, heavily-mascara'd eyes above the blood-flecked handkerchief dilated, as if, perhaps, their owner had not expected the summons of Terpsichore to arrive so soon.

'I think she's nervous,' said Hugh Bremner ecstatically. 'Dame Antoinette Diggins, nervous! Love it – *love it!*' And he went into peals of incredulous laughter at this wild improbability.

'Only the greatest artistes ever get stage fright,'

declared Mr Watson. 'Does Mr Pinkhill suffer from nerves, Mrs Pinkhill?' He addressed Inge for the first time.

'Why . . . a little I believe, when I'm driving.' Inge was not really concentrating; not at all. The scene in the waiting-room was too extraordinary.

'Till Monday at nine, Antoinette,' said Mr Watson expansively.

'Your new caps will be divine!' said Mr Bremner, and to Inge's astonishment, both balletomanes attacked those portions of their patient's cheeks unobscured by her handkerchief, with reverential kisses.

Inge hid in her *Harpers*. She had been reading a mildly diverting piece about Tom Stoppard and his recently declared admiration for the American sage, Oprah Winfrey. The headline read:

THE FAN TOM OF THE OPRAH.

Inge was so inured to this mode of journalism, it never occurred to her that its author might be insane. Moreover, she could not believe the scene which she had just witnessed.

'Excuse I, Dame!' Raewyn held out a small pink book and a writing instrument to the departing ballerina.

'Yes?'

'Listen, I hope you don't mind, Dame, but I've got a New Zealand friend who would kill for your autograph thanks.'

The celebrity seemed genuinely embarrassed, even nonplussed.

'Just your wee name thanks, Dame, Melwyn will be wrapped!'

Still clutching her handkerchief to her lips, the dancer hastily inscribed the proffered page and almost ran from the waiting-room.

'Gee, thanks,' said Raewyn, the phantom strains of *Swan Lake* surging in her ears.

Inge's eyes followed the prima ballerina with more than an idle curiosity. She observed the shabby Lotus sling-backs, the bulging calves, the navy garberdine skirt. Her gaze took in the rather short navy bolero jacket with its cheap gold buttons, beneath which the woman had chosen to wear an old-fashioned peach blouse, fastened with a necktie. It was an ensemble which a famous dancer might easily have worn who cared little for worldly things, or the exigencies of fashion, but it was not what Antoinette Diggins would have been seen dead in.

The miracle, however, was her face. Inge caught a final glimpse of it as she left the room. The resemblance was certainly uncanny. The hair, for instance, of an unreal brunette, was scraped back and secured in a tight chignon. The eyes, in that pale, almond-shaped countenance, were large, brown and emphasised with an abundance of kohl; even the celebrated mole, or *grain de beauté*, to the left of her aquiline nose, and recorded by Zoë Dominic in a famous photograph, seemed to be authentically located.

But she had given herself away completely when she scribbled her autograph in Melwyn's book. For Antoinette Diggins was left-handed, and this imposter was not.

Who better than I, the wife of Lionel Pinkhill, thought Inge with a flash of remembered gall, to be so well acquainted with Ms Diggins's manual skills.

It seemed inappropriate, even cruel, Inge decided, to rob Pinky and Perky of this roseate illusion. As Trevor Watson examined her teeth that morning she could feel the elation buzzing down his probe. He was positively resonant with excitement, like a harp string plucked by an angel and left to quiver in a slow but exquisite diminuendo. Hugh Bremner looked in at one point on some prosaic pretext, and she could see the partners from the corner of her eye, beaming at each other in mutual rapture. 'Antoinette Diggins' must have been a dreamed-for catch; a triumph, beside which the plaquey playwrights, carious choreographers and gingivitic journalists were but the *corps de ballet*, mere *figurantes* and walk-ons.

Agape in the chair, she overheard poignant scraps of dialogue.

'. . . and she's so quiet and modest . . .'

'. . . so unassuming!'

'Amazing! . . . and that skin . . .'

'She looks ten years younger up close . . .'

'. . . so petite . . . yet on stage, so statuesque!'

They needed so desperately to believe that in their chair, in their surgery, with their fingers in her mouth, had been the supine star of *Giselle* and *Les Sylphides.* It was so necessary for them to remain blind to the possibility that it was not she at all!

Rinsing, spitting, opening wider, raising a finger if it hurt, Inge thought again about the real Antoinette Diggins. The memory recurred like a toothache. It had been when Joshua, her second baby, was about eighteen months old that a friend in the LSO – it is always a *friend* – thought she ought to know that Lionel had resumed a long-standing affair with the dancer. What does she do that I don't? had been Inge's immediate reaction; is the reaction of all women.

Finally, she had decided simply to overlook the liaison, to never once let on she knew; but her heart had frozen. There had been a mad interlude when she hired a private investigator to go sniffing around their squalid trysts, but self-disgust supervened. Her only public acknowledgement of the affair was to have her long hair sliced off at Toni & Guy's, and thereafter she always wore it in the same boyish, silver-ash bob. She had also caught the worst cold of her life at that time, Inge remembered, and someone told her much later that colds were 'a way of weeping'.

When she took the children on periodic visits to Sweden to see her parents in Stockholm, she knew her husband was off somewhere chafing his old parchment-coloured loins with that pert dwarf. Or, more excusably, on one of his long concert tours groping a hostess, as he had done on the day they met.

'Would you like a rinse?' Inge shook her head, swallowed, and resumed her ringent expression.

When Lionel played the Dvořák or the Delius or even the Britten, the public assumed they were in the presence of a rarefied being; the ultimate in human sensitivity. She knew differently. They were a crude, voracious, rather scatological lot, these sensitive conduits of the Masters. Klemperer the lecher, Horowitz and his enemas.

As she left after her appointment, Inge complimented Raewyn on her hairstyle. 'How exciting for me to be in the chair straight after Dame Antoinette,' she told the receptionist. 'I used to know her quite well. Does she still live in Dulwich? I'd like to get in touch.'

Raewyn performed an arpeggio on her computer. 'Doesn't look like it, Mrs Pinkhill. The stars don't like to give out their private addresses. This is just a contact for her, I think.' Raewyn scribbled an address in Islington on a card and passed it Inge. 'It's probably her wee agent.'

Inge examined the card. 'More than likely,' she said. 'Thank you, Raewyn.'

'Thinks. Not a problem.'

'Listen to this, Poll,' said Kenneth, when he heard the front door slam. 'I think I'm on the track of something really exciting.'

He stood up from the antiquated computer at which he had been hunched all morning, and stretched. In one hand fluttered the three flimsy blue pages of an air letter. But Polly Garland was not interested in the progress of her flatmate's masterpiece that morning. The xylocaine in her gums was wearing off fast, and she threw herself whimpering into his arms.

'Steady on, Poll,' he cried. 'We don't want to get

any of your juices on this epistle,' and he rustled the letter in his hand.

'Oh Kenneth, why did you drop me in all this? I even had to sign her autograph this morning – that's forgery, isn't it?'

'Just think of those wonderful pearly whites you're going to have soon Polly, and all for S.F.A. Look at mine!' Kenneth Grocock bared his teeth at her ferociously; they were the colour and texture of Mentos. 'Basically, if I got this lot done in Harley Street it would have taken six months and cost a zillion.'

Polly looked unimpressed as she began to loosen her chignon and ease her feet out of the borrowed sling-backs.

'Pinky and Perky did all this in a bit over a week,' declared Kenneth. 'They're only in with temporary cement basically, so I can get used to them, but they'll finish the job next week. They reckoned that if I'd waited any longer, I could have got blood poisoning.'

'They told me the same story this morning and I suspect they tell everyone the same thing,' said his flatmate petulantly, sitting heavily on the beanbag. 'Thank God they haven't asked me to dance for them yet. They're all rolling up to see me at Covent Garden on November the first, by the by. I only hope they don't go backstage afterwards and ask the real Dame Antoinette to sit down and open her gob.'

Kenneth, who had an unsophisticated sense of humour, found this idea enormously funny. 'Don't worry Poll,' he reassured her between guffaws, 'we'll be well out of the picture by then, with brand new smiles. If they ever cotton on and realise they've been shafted, they won't dare to come after us. Think what berks they'd look!' He laughed uproariously. Even Polly managed a small, slightly gory grin. 'But I'd like to be a fly on the wall in Dame Ant's dressing room, when those two old minnies barge in and greet her like long lost friends!'

Polly decided it was perhaps not the best time to tell Kenneth that in the panic of the moment she had put their real address on Raewyn's form. It was better, for the time being she thought – better for both of them – to feel impervious to prosecution.

'But there's no doubt about it,' said Kenneth, shaking his head. '*You could be her!* You could sleep with her husband, Poll, and he'd never know the difference!'

'She isn't married,' said Polly, 'and I've got particular tastes in men.' She was cheering up.

Kenneth sat down in his chair back-to-front, and leaning on the back of the chair, he said: 'Now listen to this. It's a breakthrough in my Pettyfer book. A letter from his mum! Written just before she croaked!' He waved the azure pages.

Polly was slowly dismantling Antoinette Diggins, and becoming herself again. As she went into the bathroom to select a homeopathic remedy for toothache, she called back to Kenneth. 'Are you sure all of this is OK? I mean prying into Pettyfer's life. Shouldn't you ask him first?'

'No way José!' Kenneth replied. 'One of his fancy

managers would only put the kibosh on the whole thing.'

'They're not so fancy, his managers,' said Polly, returning with the magic pilules in the palm of her hand. 'Pinky said so.'

'Say on,' urged Kenneth.

'Well, we somehow got on to the subject of Mrs Petty and Pinky said his Australian business manager was a very ordinary number. Wanted his wife's teeth done for nothing too, but the boys weren't having any of it. They're not fools, you know, Kenneth.'

'Basically, Pettyfer wouldn't want me doing his life. He's probably waiting for John Lahr or Sheridan Morley, or even a three-volume job by Michael Holroyd. Mine's going to be a warts 'n' all zinger.'

'Can you do that?'

'Polly, I haven't been kicking around the journalistic traps all these years without learning a thing or two.'

'I thought you'd only been in journalism for three years – well, since you left the poly.'

But Kenneth wasn't listening. 'I'll write what I like and the *Sunday Times* will lap it up. If you stick your head above the parapet, like Pettyfer, you're fair game.'

'Who said that?' hummed Polly through closed lips as she absorbed the palliative.

'If you must know, the editor of the *Daily Mail*.'

'But Kenneth, some people don't mean to stick their heads above the parapet to be fired at by journalists. It's circumstances sometimes. I mean, what about victims of tragedy, or people who are talented, for instance.'

Kenneth felt as if his valuable time was being wasted. 'If they're talented, Polly dear, then God stuck their heads above the parapet. What's the odds anyway? They are public figures and basically the reader has a right to know!' Kenneth said this as though it were positively the last word on the subject. 'Now, do you want to hear this masterpiece of epistolatory art from Mrs Petty's mother beyond the grave, or don't you?' Polly nodded.

Kenneth smoothed out the brittle blue pages, and in a bad parody of an Australian accent intoned the following:

> Dear Mr Grocock,
>
> How nice of you to want to write a book about my son. He will be very happy, I'm sure. I doubt if I can help much and please forgive this writing. I am an old woman of 77 and my arthritis isn't getting any better. I try to look after the garden and my second husband Frank Quick, Derek's stepfather.
>
> You asked if he was a performer as a child? My very word he was! Nothing made little Derek happier than delving into our old camphor chest where we kept the fancy costumes. It was a souvenir of my parents' trip to the Old Country, many moons ago. He certainly loved that old camphor chest. He liked nothing better than dressing up and entertaining us all and having us in fits. Funnily enough there were no actors in our

> family and we sometimes wondered where
> Derek came from.

Kenneth raised his eyes to the ceiling in mock horror at the late Mrs Quick's prose style and continued to read her letter in the same Antipodean whine.

> People at Bowls often ask me nicely if Derek based that Mrs Petty skit on me. It used to worry me, but with my friend Phyllis Munro's help, I've worked out what to say now. 'Heavens!' I say, 'I hope so. I wouldn't say no to some of those nice frocks!' How they all laugh at that. 'We know where he gets it from now,' they say to me, when they've stopped laughing.
>
> Derek adored his father, though Earl passed away when he was still a lad. Funnily enough, the old hall mirror came to grief here the other day. Just fell of the wall. Frank (my present husband, Derek's stepfather) said 'Peg look, there's writing on the back.' We looked, and sure enough there was, in Earl's handwriting too. It said 'I have just plugged the wall to take this mirror. Little Derek is sitting on the floor in his Hoppalong Cassidy outfit, watching me. What a lucky man I am to have a little son like that to love.
>
> September 23, 1949.'
>
> We had to use that old mirror-back for kindling, but at least the glass didn't break, so I suppose I'm in for seven years good luck!

> I must close now as I think something might be catching in the kitchen. I hope this is of use.
>
> Yours faithfully,
> Peggy Pettyfer Quick

At this point in his performance, Kenneth could barely contain his laughter which emerged in a loud snort. He only managed, with the greatest difficulty to squeak out Peggy's postscript.

> Tell Derek I miss him, and ask him if he still remembers the camphor chest?

Doris

'I'M DORIS,' SHE said, opening the front door. 'You don't know me but I've heard a lot about you, ducks!' The plump little woman in tennis shoes, jeans and a paint-splattered, yellow tank top, held out her flabby freckled arms and pulled Derek's head into abrupt collision with her right ear. With his face buried in the grey undergrowth of her fulvous perm, and the smell of Anaïs Anaïs in his nostrils, Derek realised, with a sinking heart, that he was almost certainly in the embrace of his mother-in-law. It was not the homecoming he had hoped for.

At Singapore Sandy Thomas had got off, or was laid over. Both, more than likely, thought Derek. He had been desperately tired on the last leg, but failed to sleep, even with the aid of a mild stupefacient. The movie, unfortunately, was a *Best of Mrs Petty* compilation. He had ripped off his headset and pulled down his slumber shades, but it was impossible, every so often, not to steal a glance at his fellow passengers as they sat back guffawing at his old routines. There were also the odd travellers who seemed less inclined to laughter. Swiss, assumed Derek, or the recently bereaved.

He thought of his mother, and then, *the letter!* He struggled with the contents of his briefcase, trying to find the envelope. By then he was almost ankle deep in the detritus of flight. Tattered newspapers and discarded periodicals, duty-free brochures, tangled blankets, headset wrappings, drink coasters, serviettes, sloughed sockettes and all the unidentifiable shifting, rising, heaving wrack of Business Class travel. The letter Jill had given him at the airport was nowhere to be found.

Vaulting over the legs of a Japanese Mrs Petty fan on the aisle, Derek tottered to the locker where they had stowed his jacket and there, in an inside pocket, he found it. Back in his seat in a small puddle of light, he read 'Hitchcock's' letter. It was not sealed, as he had at first supposed. His mother had slit it neatly at the fold with a kitchen knife.

> Dear Mrs Pettyfer,
>
> Let me introduce myself. I am a senior feature writer and author, well known and respected in London, and a great admirer of your son's artistic achievement. Basically, I think his work makes Steve Martin look like a light comedian, Mr Bean a conventional, if clever, mime and Dame Edna a shrill and unsubtle drag act.
>
> Because I am basically such a fan of Derek's

> work I want the tribute I am writing to be a big surprise to him when it comes out, so may I invite you to share in this exciting secret.
>
> If you have any stories about his childhood and teenage years, could you kindly write to me at the above address. Do not hesitate to pass on anecdotes which might seem a little rude perhaps, or even stories which may not show our hero in the best possible light. Basically, I will be publishing nothing which could offend his family and friends, and I would like to thank you in advance for your help. A free copy needless to say, will be yours on publication.
>
> Excuse the pun Mrs Pettyfer when I say 'Mum's the word'!
>
> Sincerely yours,
> Kenneth Grocock.

Derek had read the letter again. It was not a perusal calculated to induce slumber. He only hoped his mother had not bothered to reply. At Heathrow there had been nobody to meet him. Not altogether surprising, since he had failed to notify the Ross Gibb Organisation or his wife of his travel arrangements. No doubt they all thought he was still in Adelaide. Moreover, Derek was not altogether sure what he was going to say to Ross when he saw him. The conversation with Sandy Thomas had been unsettling; subversive.

At length, Doris Black relaxed her pungent headlock. 'I've got a bone to pick with you, young man,' she announced, pinching the quinquagenarian on the cheek. 'What do you two mean by getting married and not inviting the in-laws?'

'It was all a bit sudden, and then . . .'

'Sorry about your mum, me duck. By the way,' condoled his new relative, raising her voice, 'when I go I don't think our daughter will be shedding a tear.'

'Come off it, Mum!' cried a disembodied voice.

'Is that you, Pam?' Derek called, setting down his suitcase and crossing the hallway.

It was, at first, difficult for Derek to recognise his own drawing-room. There was a strong smell of paint in the air, and every object and piece of furniture was draped with sheets, towels and table cloths. Pictures had been removed and stacked against the wall, and his vitrine of precious glass had been mantled with a large tartan picnic rug.

'You're back soon, love!' Pam's voice issued from the ceiling, or thereabouts. He looked up. It was hard at first to tell exactly what she was doing up there in overalls on top of a ladder. With the back of her hand she brushed aside an unruly lock of black hair and looked down at him, but she did not descend. 'We thought you'd be gone for at least a fortnight, didn't we, Mum?'

'You're a spoilsport, that you are, duck!' declared Doris, wagging her finger at Derek. 'You've ruined the surprise.'

Derek hardly supposed that his premature return had robbed the event of its surprise. He was as surprised as he ever wished to be in his life.

He saw she had put a Nescafé jar and a few mugs

on his 1897 Gallé table, inlaid with rare oriental woods in the design of an Arcadian landscape. More alarmingly, on the polished marquetry surface sat an electric kettle emitting a plume of steam.

'But Pam . . .' he exclaimed, rushing to the scalding appliance and transferring it to a square of visible carpet. 'Every time I rang you from Adelaide, you seemed . . . well, anxious for me to hurry back. Actually I cut my trip short.'

'Well you were silly, weren't you, love? You've caught us red-handed now.'

'Yes, you are are a silly boy, aren't you, Derek?' echoed his mother-in-law, rubbing the ruined surface of the table with an old paint rag. Suppressing a mild apoplexy, Derek saw the large white ring which the kettle had imprinted on Monsieur Gallé's marquetry.

'I don't know what you mean by red-handed, Pam,' he said, 'it all looks rather grey from where I'm standing.' Most of the walls and ceiling had already been covered with a coat of ashen pigment which almost exactly matched the depressing hue of the London sky outside. There was a lot more sky visible too, he observed, since his long velvet curtains had been removed. 'Where are the curtains?' he exclaimed.

'You mean those horrible brown masses of moth-fodder?' said Pam from her eminence. 'They'd absolutely had it, Derek.'

'Absolutely had it,' affirmed Pam's mother.

'Besides,' added his wife, climbing down from her ladder if not from her position of rectitude, 'this place was looking like a bloody museum. It was, Derek, it was *old-fashioned!*'

'But I'm old-fashioned, Pam, and too much light, even in London, ruins "works on paper".' He hated to call his Piranesis by that silly modish phrase, but to a young artist it might make them sound more deserving of care. He could not expect her to love them.

'Don't I get a kiss, love?' Pam, holding her grey paint-roller at arms length, leaned forward with closed eyes and proffered her right cheek and then her left. 'But don't get too near, I'm covered with paint.'

'She's covered with it,' Doris confirmed, breaking into peals of laughter. Derek was astonished to behold his young wife, so down-to-earth, so much the foe of social affectation, offering him, in the second week of their marriage, such a coy little *baiser.*

'You are rather ladylike,' said Derek, as lightly as he could manage. 'Doesn't your husband deserve a nice welcome-home squash?'

'Be your age, love! I'm not going to give you a tongue sandwich in front of Mum, am I?' Derek winced at the brutality of the expression, which would surely horrify the old woman more than its silent enactment. Perhaps 'tongue sandwich' sounded worse when juxtaposed with 'love'.

But Doris Black was still in the jolliest good humour. 'Your wife is doing you a favour, duck. This place needs to be dragged kicking and screaming into the twentieth century.'

'You should have seen the dust on those old prints of yours,' said Pam.

'Talk about dust,' said her mother, clucking.

The three sat down on an enshrouded sofa and drank their Nescafés. Doris passed the biscuits. With a sinking heart, Derek gazed around the griseous chamber that had once been his refuge; his sanctuary.

Pam was silent.

Then she said, her lip trembling: 'You know, you shouldn't come home and immediately criticise, Derek. Other people have feelings, not just you.' He was relieved she had dropped the 'love'.

'What have I said?'

'It's what you don't say.'

'It is!' supplied Doris, 'It's what you don't say!'

But Pam was getting wound up. 'Since you left I haven't stopped. I've packed up my "awful little studio" as you like to call it, I've moved my sculptures here . . .' Derek looked with a new interest at the innumerable large and swaddled objects he had not been able to identify in the room '. . . and I've nearly killed myself cleaning up this old bachelor's shit-heap! Don't I get any thanks for that?'

'I didn't mean to criticise. I was joking really. I was just a bit surprised when you did "the kiss".' He mimed her ladylike little *baiser* as comically as he could, to earn her forgiveness. Surprisingly, Doris came to his support.

''E's right, Pamela. You have got very oo-la all of a sudden.'

'If you must know,' said Pam, white-faced, 'I've

seen a bit of Inge this week. I hear from her you think I might be too common for your snobbish friends.'

'I never said anything of the kind, but even so, you don't need to overreact, it's you I married.'

' "Lady Muck"!' squawked her mother. 'She's Lady Muck these days, Derek.'

'Fuck off, Mum,' said Pam, 'you've done nothing but get in the way while I've been painting. Haven't you got something better you can do in your room?'

'That's nice talk, Derek, isn't it? Very nice talk from a daughter to her mother. She hasn't changed much since she left home. "I'll horsewhip her" her father used to say, "I'll horsewhip her!" '

'Christ,' said Pam, 'he could talk! If the police knew the half of what he got up to with us in the middle of night, he'd be the one to be horsewhipped.'

'You shut up, girlie. Shut your dirty mouth! What's Derek going to think of us, hearing all these lies? I'm going to my room.'

And with that, Doris Black marched off slamming the door behind her.

If Derek had heard anything through his jet-lagged haze, or if any of the exchanges between mother and daughter had penetrated his brain, disoriented by the transformations which had been wrought in his drawing-room, he had certainly heard two words: 'my room'.

Doris, a woman he had never met, had now apparently taken up residence in his flat!

'What did she mean, *her room?*'

'Don't panic,' said Pam, ascending once more the ladder. 'She's only keeping me company for a few days, thank Christ. I put her on the divan in your study.'

'My study is her room now, is it?'

'YES!' screamed Pam, 'IT IS! You've just buried your mother – or burnt her – so show a bit of feeling for someone else's, you selfish bastard.'

Derek decided to beat a swift retreat to the bathroom where, ducking under an improvised clothes line loaded with feminine and less than feminine attire, he ran a bath into which he decanted at least half a bottle of Penhaligon's Blenheim Bouquet bath essence. Locking the door, he undressed, submerging himself as deeply as possible in the steaming beryl-coloured water.

'It's only a dream. Let it be only a dream!' he repeated to himself, as he lay there looking up at the knickers of Damocles.

At least my bedroom hasn't been renovated, thought Derek with relief as he climbed into bed. But there were ominous signs: two mildly licentious drawings by Marquet and Segonzac had been removed from their hooks and stood decorously on the floor facing the wall.

Pam was already in bed reading something by Jeanette Winterson. Out of the corner of his eye he saw the periodically licked finger and he heard the brutalised pages snap by. It would be foolhardy to reprimand that habit now, he thought, gritting his teeth. He would reform her incrementally. Pam stopped reading. 'Nice bath?'

'I needed it. It was quite a trip.'

Discarding her paperback she turned towards him, propped up on one elbow, her cheek resting on her hand. Derek saw that she was naked. 'You'll like the new colour, even if you hate it now. You'll see.' He was taken aback by her sudden tenderness on a touchy subject.

'But if you'd only waited, it was a bit of a shock.'

'You're lucky I take an interest, love. Anyone else would've let you moulder away in all that turgid green and burgundy and brown.'

'I liked those dim old colours. Grey isn't one thing or t'other: it's the colour of indecision.' Derek had worked all this out in the bath.

'Judge it when I've finished,' his wife replied with surprising amiability. 'You won't know this bedroom either, when we've done with it.'

'I was afraid of that,' said Derek, hoping he didn't sound too afraid. 'What's this "we" by the way, can Doris be trusted with a paintbrush?'

'She's good at holding ladders. Honestly Derek, you're such a chauvinist, love; an archetypal chauvinist.' Pam put a cool hand on his shoulder. 'Was the funeral awful?'

'No – well, yes, of course it was. But I'm glad I went.' Derek gave a macabre résumé of his journey to the Underworld. His jet-lag made him feel wider awake by the minute, sliding back into Adelaide time.

They made love later. Yet again he noticed her

passivity; the strange impression she emanated of sexual autism. This love-making without a sensuous prologue or an epilogue of gratitude still disturbed him. Derek had hoped marriage and security might begin to change that. But changing Pam might take a little longer than he thought. Hoping it could not possibly be construed as criticism, Derek risked an oblique reference to the subject.

'It's all right, Pam, your mother's in the study,' he said. 'She can't possibly hear us.' Pam broke away.

'What do you mean?'

'Just that my study is at the far end of the flat. If we let ourselves go a bit, she'd be none the wiser.'

Pam flared up. 'Oh, you mean let ourselves go like whoever it was in the background when I called you about your mother that afternoon!'

Derek was angry. 'That wasn't anyone – it was only a corny video.' Whatever Pam was going to say died on her lips. Derek wished a claw could have extruded from his mouth, closed around the last thing he said and hauled it back, into oblivion. His wife's eyes narrowed and she gave him a knowing smirk.

'So at four-thirty on a Wednesday afternoon you were watching a porno movie?'

'Yes.'

'Alone? No, don't tell me! I don't think I want to know about Mr Hyde. I prefer to be married to Dr Jekyll. However, love, I presume you won't mind me getting off on the odd dirty movie in that case, with a cosy friend or two!' Derek was almost certain that during this last speech his wife had spelt it 'luv'.

'Listen Pam – it was the silliest thing, *nothing happened.* I came straight home – to you.'

'And you proposed, too, didn't you? That video must have got you really hot.'

Derek tried to change the subject. 'I met a girl on the plane who knows Gibbo.'

'Did she suck you off in the toilet?'

'For heaven's sake, Pam, give me a break. I've just got home after a twenty-four hour flight.' She threw back the covers and shielded her eyes with a crook of her elbow.

'Come on!' she commanded. 'Show me how they did it. Now!'

Derek was by no means sure he could instantly oblige. She frightened him a little, to be truthful; these switches of mood. Was Pam a bit, he hesitated to even think it . . . disturbed?

'Come on, do it, do it!' she cried hoarsely, pulling him down on her.

There was a long piercing electronic scream. Derek jumped out of his skin. 'What's that?'

'The new doorbell. I had it put in three days ago. Mum and I could never hear that piddling little buzzer.' Derek was up in seconds, improvising a sarong with a large towel. It was a heaven-sent reprieve.

'G'day mate. Are we interrupting anything?' Ross Gibb winked as he shoved his way through the door, drawing Denise after him. They were all dressed up and a bit tipsy. Denise gave Derek a big kiss on the lips and he could taste the brandy. 'Shit, mate, this place is going to be crash hot when it's finished.' His manager was already prowling around the drawing-room approvingly.

'You see!' Pam had appeared in Derek's dressing-gown looking hectic, unkempt and attractive.

'Here's your wedding present, mate.' Ross withdrew from a plastic carry bag a large box covered with gold foil. Gazing at the proffered gift, Derek observed for the first time that Ross bit his nails. The angry red skin bulged around the devoured thumbnail like the palm of a boxing glove. Wrenching his attention back to the package, Derek noticed what he believed they called an 'occasional' card, in the form of a large glitter-encrusted horseshoe. Inside, he read the message in Gibbo's small, neat backhand:

To a great mate and his sheila,
Love and congratulations,
Ross and Denise

'Open it, love,' said Pam with her chin on his shoulder. 'Open it!'

After much careful removal of bubble-wrap and layered tissue, Derek disinterred his gift. Speechless, he held it to the light. It was a greenish-coloured Greek bowl from the third quarter of the first century AD, sides slightly convex and the bottom flattened. The glass had been painted with a frieze of luxuriant vegetation in which a blue and white duck with red legs looking back, perhaps towards a source of danger, moved right towards a russet net, probably a snare. There were some pieces missing from the edges, some strain cracks and a blue enamel-like film, mostly flaking off, with iridescence on both sides, some pitting on the exterior, and a few pinprick bubbles, inclusions and minor crizzling. It was the most exquisite object he had ever seen.

'It's incredible, Gibbo,' was all he could say, and when he embraced Denise he felt as if he might cry. He thought how much kindness and planning had gone into the luxurious gift; and how much money it must have set Gibbo back at *L'art Ancien.* He was ashamed that he had, even for a second, doubted his friend's integrity. Even the equine symbol on their wedding card had revived his misgivings and sent his thoughts back to Sandy Thomas's disquieting revelations on the plane.

'Just don't break it, mate, like it fuckin' broke me!' They all laughed.

As Pam led Denise off on a tour of her renovations, Derek drew his friend into the kitchen. It would be honourable for him to clear the air, though there was an aspect of the matter which Denise should not overhear.

'Saw a friend of yours on the plane – Sandy Thomas.'

Ross Gibb grinned. 'Go on? Did she tell you about her riding lessons?'

A wave of relief assailed Derek. He had not realised how much anxiety and distrust that little scrubber had inspired. 'Well, she mentioned a stud farm. She said, "when you retired . . ." '

Gibbo gave a backward glance to see they were alone and put his arm around Derek's shoulder. 'To be perfectly honest with you, I gave her one a couple of times, or I could have given her a couple once, I don't remember.'

'But the stud farm?'

'The only riding lessons she got, I gave her, and that was at the Shangri-La Hotel in Singapore. But don't come the uncooked crustacean with me, Dekka, you know about our little patch of Aussie soil, don't you?'

Derek's shame deepened. He must have known and forgotten.

'Young Denise got left a few dollars five years ago by her aunty, so we blew it on a bit of dirt on the wrong side of Bowral with a sittin' fuckin' tenant and a few nags. End of story.'

'But you retiring? What's the strength of that?'

'Listen, mate, to be perfectly honest with you, if you're chatting up a hostie and you want her to do the dirty deed at the next stop-over, pull out a picture of horses.'

'Horses?'

'Horses, mate. The most potent sex symbol known to man since Tom Jones. As soon as they think you might sweep them off to Marlboro Country on a white fuckin' stallion, they'll part the old veal curtains, no worries!'

Derek laughed; he laughed immoderately. He looked at his maligned friend with something approaching ardour. 'But didn't I meet her with you once before at Brian and Helen's barbie?'

'Come on, you two, no dirty stories in my kitchen.' It was Pam looking for wine and three glasses. Derek did not fail to notice his wife's use of the personal pronoun.

The Gibbs stayed a little longer and finished the wine. At length they rose.

'Thanks again for the glass, Gibbo. Fantastic!' said Derek. 'Thanks for everything!'

Ross and Denise were nearly at the front door when the Apparition appeared.

'Hello, Gibbo, duck. You're not leaving without giving a kiss to your girlfriend.'

It was Doris: the study was not, after all, impervious to sound. She wore one of Derek's best custom-made, white sea-island cotton, herringbone shirts which reached beyond her knees; large, if grubby mules which Derek assumed were her own; and a dark brown painted facepack encompassing forehead, cheeks and double chins. In her Turnbull and Asser smock, her grizzled auburn peruke and the startling brown disc of her mud mask, Doris resembled a personage in a Carnival scene by Longhi.

Gibbo looked thunderstruck.

'Get back to bed, Mum! Go on, hop it! *Get out of it!*' Pam's accent was suddenly pure Birmingham.

'Have you two met?' said Denise, looking from the improbable figure of Doris to her husband.

'Of course we have. Haven't we, Doris?' said Ross, regaining his composure.

'When, prithee?' inquired Denise.

'All right, all right,' said Ross, holding up his hands in mock surrender. 'I dropped in here last week while Dekka was in Oz to get a few tips on Roman glass.'

'Don't look at me,' said Pam, then rather brutally, as though giving orders to an obdurate domestic animal: 'Mum, will you go back to bed!' Doris Black was swaying rather dangerously in the doorway, though it was impossible to read her precise expression, eclipsed as it was by her cosmetic penumbra.

'All right, m'duck, back to bed for Doris. Lady Muck says so!' She leered at her daughter, winked at Ross, and wittering cheerfully to herself, wambled back in the direction of Derek's sequestrated study. It was apparent that his mother-in-law had abused substances rather freely that evening.

'You might have introduced me,' said Denise dryly.

'It's me she's creaming her jeans for, Den,' said Ross, slapping his wife's bum. 'We're keeping these people up – let's hop it.'

'R-i-gh-t!'

'I like them a lot,' said Pam when the Gibbs had finally left.

'I rather thought you couldn't stand them,' said Derek getting into bed. It was breakfast time in Adelaide.

'Well, I like them now.'

The next morning, perched in the kitchen having their breakfast, Derek broached a delicate subject. As Pam sat munching a croissant and reading the *Independent* – she had recently abjured the *Guardian*

– he decided to deliver his introductory question as casually as possible, with his back turned, making another cup of tea.

'The stuff,' he began, clearing his throat, 'the stuff from your studio in the drawing-room . . .' Derek heard her newspaper stop rustling.

'Yes, love?'

'Where do you think, that's to say, have you got any ideas about a new studio?' He was trying unsuccessfully to fish the Waitrose tea bag out of the mug of boiling water with his fingers. Pam was watching him with an expression of amusement. With all that long black hair, those wide candid eyes and what had been his magnificent scarlet Sulka bathrobe, she looked beautiful.

'The stuff,' she began slowly, 'that you refer to, is my work. 'It's *what I do.*' He mumbled total agreement. 'My work is perfectly fine where it is, but since that's your precious lounge, and you're nearly shitting yourself with anxiety about it, I've decided the dining-room can be my studio; it's the same size and it's never used.'

'Great, great; but when we give dinner parties, how . . .?'

'They can eat off their knees in the lounge or go to a restaurant.' If Derek had ever thought that he had prepared himself for the give and take of marriage, he realised now that he had not.

'Great!' he declared lamely, 'All the same, we ought to look around pretty sharpish for a serious studio nearby.'

'There's a flat right underneath here and it's on the market. MacDermott's place.'

Derek nearly dropped his tea. 'MacDermott?'

'MacDermott.'

'Oh that, I checked it out. Don't think I haven't been on the case, Pam. It's too dark, funnily enough, and he wants an arm and a leg.'

'That's a piece of luck, love,' said Pam, 'because you've *got* an arm and a leg; Gibbo said so.'

'Have you been discussing my finances with Ross?'

'Only briefly. When he came here out of the kindness of his heart to discuss what lump of mouldy old glass you might fancy. He mentioned they were paying you five hundred thousand pounds an episode.'

'The total budget could be something like that, Pam, but it's not mine, it goes . . . well, to some entity.'

'Entity?'

'Yes, you see a division of the Ross Gibb Organisation makes the programmes and leases my services through an entity. At least, I think that's what happens. The money doesn't actually go into my pocket. You'd have to ask Gibbo.'

'That sounds like a marvellous arrangement,' fleered his wife. 'Presumably, the bottom-line is you don't pay tax that way.'

'I pay a lot of tax, at least I'm sure I do. But that's Roger Wainwright's department.'

'You're lucky you can trust Gibbo, is all I can say.'

'I hope I can.' Briefly, the cold hand of doubt touched Derek's heart and then withdrew.

'Of course you can, love. I'm a pretty good judge. What you see is what you get with Gibbo, and he absolutely adores you.' Derek was ashamed of his spasm of disloyalty.

'Where's your mother?' he enquired, changing the subject.

'Doris will be out to the count until eleven – it's her beauty sleep.'

'She could never sleep long enough for that,' said Derek, mercifully to himself. 'I have to get moving now; an appointment at ten-thirty. It's a presentation for a commercial.'

'What for?'

'A jet-lag remedy, I hope.'

'I'd better fly too,' said Pam. 'I've got to collect the rest of my things from Chiswick.'

Fifteen minutes later, they were both descending in the lift. On the floor below Derek's flat it stopped, and a slight, elderly man of military bearing in a raincoat entered. He nodded politely at Derek and Pam, then he froze, uttered a sharp exclamation, and forcing the closing doors open with his hands, bolted down the corridor. As they travelled downwards alone, Pam said, 'I'm pretty sure that was Mr MacDermott, he must have forgotten something.'

'No,' said Derek grimly. 'I think that more than likely it was something he remembered.'

Camille

'IT'S CALLED "UNTITLED Installation 3".'

Kenneth Grocock looked at the enormous sheets of perspex held together with bulldog clips. Sandwiched between them, he observed the tufts and stooks of dark brown hair, arbitrarily arranged. In front of this screen, on a kind of multiple gibbet, dangled an assortment of blue and yellow plastic knives and forks.

'It's only when I activate the lasers that you can really get the full resonance of it,' declared the artist. Kenneth was pretending to take notes.

'Very interesting,' he said. 'So basically, it's unfinished?'

'Without the lasers it loses its integrity, yes.'

'So why not turn them on?'

'Do you know how much lasers cost, man?' the artist exclaimed. 'I've applied for funding to the Arts Council for this, but they'll have to convene an Extraordinary Meeting.'

'Are you optimistic basically?'

'Very much so. They supported my Performance Art in the Sewer.'

'The sewer?' Kenneth's pen was racing across the page of his notebook, or appeared to be.

'A club in Birmingham. I used to walk across the stage backwards in the nude.'

'Is that all?'

'No, I pulled a skateboard with a ghetto-blaster on it, playing one of Hitler's speeches.'

'How?'

'On a string attached to my willie.' The sculptor was warming to his audience; this could well have been his first interview. 'It was a metaphor for the Holocaust,' he subjoined.

'Tell me, Mr Dooley, did the Arts Council ever check to see where their money had gone?'

'Very much so. Lord Palumbo himself came along to see the show.'

'Did he approve?'

'Very much so!' averred the artist, smiling for the first time and revealing an eroded graveyard of gorgonzola teeth. 'If he'd gone to the Sewer on a Saturday night and complained, he probably wouldn't have lived to tell the tale.' With immoderate laughter the journalist and sculptor contemplated the conjectural lynching scene.

Kenneth put away his notebook and discreetly withdrew a small black dictaphone from his pocket. He had, he felt, sufficiently softened up Bob Dooley with flattery to draw him on the topic which was dearest to his heart. There being no chairs, they sat, or uncomfortably reclined, on the studio floor.

'This could be a painful subject, Mr Dooley . . . can I call you Bob?'

'Very much so.'

'I'm crafting a book on Derek Pettyfer.' Furtively, Kenneth snapped on the tape and waited for the name to take effect. The sculptor plucked at his beard, rubbed his brow and scratched the nape of his neck where the pinguid ponytail greyly threshed. While the conceptualist wrestled with his memory, his self-control, or his powers of vituperation – or all three – Kenneth Grocock congratulated himself on his use of the phrase 'crafting a book'. Was he not, after all, a craftsman? He was certainly no mere journalist, and this surely was the point of affinity between these two men, who now sat in earnest colloquy on the floor of a condemned warehouse in Gunnersbury Park. It was, moreover, a cold warehouse. Kenneth almost envied the artist his soiled, mustard anorak.

'What do I actually think of him, you're askin' me?'

'Yes.'

'He's a cunt.'

'Well, it's interesting you should say that, Bob, because basically I've managed to find a few people who share your opinion.'

'You have?'

'Yes, one of them even knows him.'

'He's a cunt, Kenneth.' Bob held out a chipped teacup while Kenneth filled it from a bottle of Beaujolais he had had the foresight to pick up at Oddbins an hour before. 'He's a cunt, not because of what he does, but what he is.'

'And what's that basically?'

'Well, he destroyed a seven year relationship, didn't he? He dangled his credit cards in front of our Pamela and kicked me in the teeth.' The jilted sculptor grimaced again, revealing the necrose dentition in question.

'Have you seen her or talked to her since . . .'

'Since she threw me over and pissed off?'

'Basically.'

'Oh yes, she told me she'd met this bloke in the TV industry who'd taken her to lunch.'

'What did you say?'

'I said: "How many times did you fook him?" '

'I see.' Kenneth Grocock sucked in what little there was of his lips and frowned at the ceiling. He was wondering how much of this material, earthy and heartfelt though it was, would translate to the pages of an award-winning biography. The sculptor took a noisy suck on his cup of wine.

'You know who her idol is, in art I mean?'

Kenneth shook his head.

'Camille Claudel.'

'Sorry?'

Robert Dooley prepared himself to deliver an informative lecture. 'Camille Claudel was a nice little student who had a crush on Rodin.'

'The sculptor?'

'Very much so. You've got it, man! Well, she idolised him, she copied him and then . . . guess what?

She had to be him, didn't she?' The artist leaned forward and gave Kenneth a painful jab in the chest with his gnarled index finger. 'Then she had to be better than him, right? She had to win!'

'So . . .?'

'Some critics reckon she *did* have the edge on the old man. Personally speaking, none of that *belle époque* stuff grabs me.'

'Hang on, so basically you were Rodin and she was Camille?'

'Could be. Our Pamela had one big problem though, Ken: she could never surpass me, so she pissed off instead.'

Kenneth stole a look at 'Untitled Installation 3'.

'Pam has to be the winner, me old mucker.' The jilted sculptor took another doleful swig.

'I suppose you know they're married now, basically?'

The artist once more extended his cup for replenishment. 'That tart has got what she deserves. Always did give herself airs, our Pam. All kippers and curtains she got, whenever she had them posh folks sittin' for her. She'd go on for hours after about their fine houses and their gear and their la-de-dah friends. "We'll make it rich one day lass," I kept telling her, "when the Tate starts investing in my work." You know Kenneth me old mucker,' he confided, 'Mr Serota himself sat in the same place you're sittin' now and looked at my installations, but they're too confrontational for most. He got cold feet, the bugger.'

'It is nippy in here, Bob,' said Kenneth, hoping

not to sound facetious. He wondered if the director of that famous gallery might also have had a similar problem envisaging the effect of the lasers.

'With the art market bad,' said Bob brightening, 'I'm lucky I can teach.'

'You teach?' Kenneth Grocock, who had no knowledge of art whatsoever, hoped the sharp note of incredulity in his voice had gone unnoticed by the sculptor. Looking around at this arid, witless work, bereft of skill, derivative of a derivation, Kenneth wondered what on earth Bob could possibly teach. What did he *know*, in order to impart it? Alas, even Kenneth vaguely apprehended that the fact that Dooley's work was unsold was no vindication of taste; just an accident of Public Relations.

Bob Dooley raised his cup. 'I wish her happiness, the little slag,' said the artist magnanimously. Suddenly Kenneth noticed large tears trickling from his eyes and already beginning to irrigate the boscage of his beard. 'But she'll miss the stimulation, Ken,' he added, as the journalist rose stiffly to his feet. 'This queer fella she's with won't want to talk to her till four o'clock in the morning about Duchamp or John Cage or Yves Klein, not bloody likely!'

As Kenneth made his departure the sculptor remained cross-legged on the floor of the darkening studio, the bottle and its residue in his hand.

'Goodbye and thank you,' called Kenneth. 'Looking forward to your next exhibition.'

'Terrah!'

*

Kenneth had worked up quite a sweat on his exercise bike. It occupied nearly a third of his bedroom, and like all British appliances it had had many teething troubles since its installation. But now he 'worked out' on it every evening, and he found the exercise less boring if he listened to his Walkman while peddling. So it was that Polly's repeated knocking on his door that evening proved inaudible through the cacophony of Guns'n'Roses.

Finally she entered, as her friend, crimson-cheeked and hoarse of breath, was reaching his peak metabolic rate. Moving to the front of the bike so that Kenneth could see her, she held up before his dripping nose the 'While you were out' pad, and with her other expressive, classically trained hand, she mimed a telephone call. A few minutes later, in an exiguous bathrobe stolen from the Holiday Inn, Swiss Cottage, Kenneth joined his flatmate in the kitchenette.

'When did Derek call?' he demanded, waving the phone message excitedly.

'All morning,' she said. 'Vervain or camomile?'

'I think I'll have something off my shelf tonight,' said Kenneth, reaching for the Gold Blend. 'Did he say anything?'

'He didn't sound pleased. He asked if I was Mrs Grocock.'

'What did you say?'

'I said who I was,' Polly snapped. 'I'm two people already thanks to you and I'm certainly not going to be your wife as well!'

'Take it easy, Poll. You couldn't just ring him now

and pretend to be my secretary? It would sound a bit more up-market.'

'The answer's no. He said he was sick of you snooping around interviewing people right and left and generally getting on his wick, or words to that effect.'

'Shit.'

'You better ring him, if you put it off it'll only get harder. You never know, you might sweet-talk him round like you did me. How do you like them, by the way?' Polly bared her new teeth at the Obituarist. 'Only one more long appointment on Thursday, so I can dazzle them at Covent Garden on November first.'

They sat down at either end of the couch while Kenneth told her, with comic embellishments, of his interview with Bob Dooley that afternoon. As she wiped away the tears of laughter Polly grew more serious.

'Will you promise me something, Kenneth,' she said, patting his hand.

'Anything.'

'If you ever write a book please don't weave your sculptor into it.'

'Why not? It was pretty funny stuff.'

'Simply because there isn't a satirical novel written these days that doesn't have a dig at all those zany, whacky conceptualists with their noses in the subsidy trough. It's a cliché.'

'Promise, Poll,' said Kenneth, 'but it really happened, that's the difference.' He rose, staring balefully at the telephone. 'I better ring Pettyfer and get it over with,' he said. 'I wonder if he knows I've got a letter from his mum on file, or that I've set up a meeting with the first big agent he ever had?'

'Who would that be?'

'A big shot, the tops, Woody Weinglass. He'll spill the beans. He couldn't have liked it much when Derek sacked him for that Australian guy ten years ago, and then made it big!'

'You think so?' asked Polly over her camomile.

'Weinglass had to deal with him when he was heavily on the piss and bashing his wife. That kind of info will be solid gold, Polly, solid gold!'

'There was another message.'

'Who from?'

'An American girl called Carol or Gail or something. Said she was Mr Weinglass's personal assistant. He can't see you and he won't see you. He knows Derek socially and has no wish whatever to discuss him with a "dirty little muck-raking journalist" I quote.'

The telephone began ringing but Kenneth made no attempt to challenge the transmitter. He sat down again with his chin on his fist in the attitude of Rodin's Thinker.

'He'll talk to me,' he said finally with an enigmatic smile. 'I think I know where I can buttonhole Mr Weinglass, and he won't be wearing a buttonhole.'

Derek slammed down the phone. Naturally that Grocock fellow would dodge his calls. Of course there was a possibility, not necessarily remote, that he might even turn out a half decent book, but the prose style of that letter to his late mother was not encouraging. Moreover, there was that worrying paragraph in which he solicited 'stories which may not show our hero in the best possible light.' That boded ill. Derek felt he might need to hand this one over to Ross, and a lawyer.

Meanwhile he was excited about the commercial; everybody was excited about it.

'We're very excited to have you on board,' the people at the agency had said, singly and collectively. The Client and his representatives, who seemed numerous, had also expressed their excitement. It seemed, on reflection, a bit odd, getting as excited as this about an advertisement for a vacuum cleaner on television; even a vacuum cleaner propelled by Mrs Petty. If this excited them all so much, thought Derek, what residuum of excitement remained for their wives, their mistresses, their children or Almighty God?

He had known a ravaged Disney executive, long since purged, who had spent so many years 'being excited' by scripts, projects, movie pitches and unknown actors, that his capacity for excitement in any form whatsoever had been totally vitiated. He had become a zombie.

Ross had been there at the meeting that morning, 'riding shotgun', and in spite of Derek's jet-lag, in spite of the depredations to his flat and the installation of Doris, he had been, as Woody would have said, in 'smashing form'. They had handed the commercial to him on a golden platter.

When they left the advertising agency in Soho,

Ross suggested a coffee at some new and trendy café. Derek quickly cased the place before sitting down. After all, this was Soho and Garryl Kurdish might well pause here for refreshment in the midst of a shopping spree.

'That glass last night . . .' began Derek, 'It was the best gift. You couldn't have . . .'

'Give us a break, will you, mate? To me, personally, that vase is a load of crap, but to you it's something else – fair enough? We got a kick out of giving it to you. We love you, you silly bastard!' And with that Ross reached out across the table, grabbed Derek by the nape of his neck and gave him a comradely shake.

'I suppose this commercial pays pretty well,' ventured the artiste. Ross scribbled something on a serviette and flicked it across the table.

'And that's not a telephone number,' he declared. Derek looked at the figure. It held little reality for him. To think that he had invented Mrs Petty for a one-night stand at Adelaide University and that now they were only too happy to pay her a sum like this for pushing an appliance on television for thirty seconds.

'And what's more, mate,' Ross was saying, 'we'll be tucking that moolah away somewhere that will give you a cool eighteen per cent, no problem.'

'Isn't eighteen per cent a bit, well, greedy?'

'I hope you're joking, mate, I really do,' said Gibbo. 'To be perfectly honest with you I've put a bit of my own ill-gotten gains in the same pot, and I'm laughin' – ask Rodge.' Derek realised that his staid accountant, his man in the City, Roger Wainwright FCCA, was now, inextricably, Rodge.

'On top of the moolah, mate, you get a week in Antigua to shoot the commercial.'

'When?'

'Real soon, mate. Don't ask me why they need to shoot a Hoover on a tropical beach, but perhaps Mrs Petty will be suckin' up the sand with it!'

'They all want a free holiday in the sun, more like it,' said Derek pragmatically. 'I'd take Pam along with me but she seems pretty busy right now, settling in. By the way,' he added, 'thanks for being so nice to her, I know you had your doubts.'

'I take it all back. You kicked a goal there,' affirmed his manager. 'She's a beauty. Den reckons she's too good for you!'

'Really! But what is she doing to my flat?'

'Swings and fuckin' roundabouts, Dekka. You're married now, remember? She lives with you, she hasn't just dropped in for a quickie. She needs to give that old shitheap of yours her "touch".' Ross accompanied the epithet with a pansy gesture.

'But it doesn't feel like my place any more.'

'Look, stop whinging, will you? This girl loves you, you stupid dickhead, why can't you get that inside your skull? How much do you give her by the way?'

'Give her?'

'Yeah, you fuckin' miser. *Give her!* She's probably lucky to cop her playlunch money.'

'She's got a new watch,' said Derek self-righteously, 'her keep, of course, and I gave her a couple of hundred for clothes last week. You're forgetting that Pam is fiercely independent.'

'Pig's arse she is!' bellowed his friend, capturing the attention of the entire restaurant; then he resumed more confidentially, 'Well, I've fixed her up with a decent float in the bank and a fistful of plastic, and I'm telling her it was all your idea. Pam's not the type to go mad. You'll probably have to force her to go out and spend it at fuckin' gunpoint.'

Derek finished his cappuccino. 'I hope you're right, Gibbo.'

Doris let him into the flat. If she had a hangover, she betrayed no signs of it, or of her uliginous mask of the night before. Its cosmetic virtues seemed not to have taken effect.

Even during the few hours in which he had absented himself at the advertising agency, further changes appeared to have been wrought in his apartment.

'Close the front door again, please, Doris,' he said. 'Slam it.' She did so.

'Clack!'

'What's up, duck?' enquired his mother-in-law. This morning she had exchanged Anaïs Anaïs for Poison.

'It doesn't go "thunk" any more – what's happened to the door?'

Doris could hardly speak for laughing. 'She said you'd notice and I said you wouldn't!' She was doubled-up.

'Notice what?'

'The new door, duck. Our Pam had that old mahogany thing taken away when you was in Australia. A dinosaur, she called it. Besides,' Doris added, 'she reckons it's mahogany doors like yours is wrecking the rainforests in Brazil.'

Derek was almost speechless. 'But . . . but that beautiful door was carved out of a tree at least a hundred years ago! What good is it now to the bloody Brazilian rainforests, chucked on a builder's skip?'

'Ask her, not me, love. Anyway, this one's steel.' She rapped on the painted metal. 'It's fire-proof!'

'It's hideous.' Derek grieved for his old door on its brass hinges. 'Who wants a steel door?'

'Ask Lady Muck,' replied his capricious relative. Then she added, 'Seriously, luv, there are about half a million quids' worth of sculptures in here so I suppose our Pamela feels more secure with a modern door.'

'Who paid for this?'

'Steady on, ducks, Mr Gibb approved it.'

'PAM!' Derek yelled, but Doris put a finger to her lips and pointed up the corridor.

'Hush, duckie, she's in there with a client.' Doris sounded and looked disagreeably like a madam.

Derek peered around the corner of what had once been his dining-room. The unmistakeable, even idealised visages of Melvyn Bragg, Martin Amis and, had he but know it, Bob Dooley, looked gravely down from their wooden plinths at his wife and her present subject.

Pam's back was turned; he saw only her grey smock and her long, glossy ebony hair. Before her, on a sculpture stand, a large lump of putty-coloured clay was assuming anthropomorphic form.

In a chair, once a silk upholstered Victorian carver, sat Lionel Pinkhill. His saurian eyes flickered.

'Hello Derek old boy,' he said stiffly, 'I'm not supposed to move. I have to stay in profile, don't I, Pamela?'

Pam looked round crossly. 'Damn you, Derek! I was just getting somewhere then.'

'I'd really appreciate a comfort stop anyway,' said the virtuoso. The tall thin man in the black turtleneck and the beige cords stood up and stretched.

Over his wife's shoulder, Derek regarded the proud and sinister face. He was a good subject: the high brow, the twisted nose, the full sardonic lips. Poor Inge! Life with Lionel could not be easy, and even at his age there were rumours. His ugliness was the kind which fascinated some women and the night managers of the Carlyle in New York and the Lancaster in Paris could no doubt vouch for his popularity. On tour, Lionel was reputedly a 'tongue artist'. His was certainly a face most self-respecting women would prefer out of sight.

'I'm very proud to be sitting for your wife,' he said. 'I've been drawn by Derek Hill and Bratby in the old days, but I've never been carved.'

'Modelled.'

'I stand corrected,' said the cellist. 'But it's a brave artist who can tackle a mug like mine.'

Lionel put his arm benevolently around Pam's

shoulder and excused himself. When he had gone, Derek moved up close behind his wife and breathed against her neck. She went on working, but wriggled her bottom against him. It was enough.

'How long will you be?' he whispered close to her ear.

'Ages yet,' she said, in her back-to-business voice. 'Open a decent bottle of wine for us will you, love, and *please* find yourself a nice quiet corner out of harm's way.' He thought of the piebald drawing room, half shabby brown, half battleship grey. He thought too of his annexed study where he must now knock if he needed a book. Like a reluctant Ganymede he fetched the wine and two glasses, but before retiring to the bedroom, he lifted a corner of the rug which shrouded the vitrine and looked again at his wonderful glass. The new 'duck' bowl, Gibbo's gift, radiant in pride of place.

When he reached the bedroom he saw the bed was still tousled and unmade; there were clothes and towels everywhere.

'Doris!' he called, 'Doris! The bedroom looks as though a bomb hit it. Where's Amerika?'

Doris scooted down the hall and applied a cautionary finger to her lips. 'Shhhhh!'

'I said where's Amerika?' Derek hissed.

'Oh, ducks, she's gone. They had words, her and Lady Muck – our Pamela. She's gone for good, that Amerika. We didn't like her and she didn't like us!'

This time, when Doris started to laugh, she just couldn't stop.

Estelle

WOODY WEINGLASS WAS a Collector. He liked a theme. In his early career as an agent in Manhattan with the International Talent Organisation, he had collected weapons. In a glass case on his desk in the small apartment on East 82nd Street was a ceremonial dagger that had reputedly belonged to Von Ribbentrop. It was not an association which found much favour with his friends and colleagues in the New York world of show business.

Soon he felt constrained to dispose of these objects. The disapproval of certain friends had something to do with it, but also his own lack of enthusiasm for instruments of death, however decorative or ingenious. Instead, he began to collect nineteenth-century farming implements. Quite literally, Woody turned swords into ploughshares.

There was a resourceful dealer in Los Angeles who had cornered the market in these ambiguous and unlovely contraptions of rusted iron and weathered timber. Soon Woody and, it must be said, several other agents and producers, were covering the walls of their villas in Beverly Hills and Upper East Side Manhattan with restored butter churns from Kentucky, primitive hoes from Vermont, Wyoming wheelbarrows and, in one famous house in Bel Air, between the Hockneys and the Warhols, a 1798 reaping machine from Idaho in full working order.

But Woody Weinglass was an ambitious man; and conformity was not to his taste. The reason why a group of persons in the same world – a peer group – assemble the same things, is to show off to each other. 'You've got a Schnabel, have you? Ya boo sucks, I've got *two* Jim Dines!' or, 'That's a nice Lichtenstein, you oughta come by and see Esther's and my new Motherwell sometime'. The game only succeeds because the parties who play know what everything costs; they know the market. These are not works of art on their walls – unsurprisingly they call their possessions 'pieces' – they are inflated, hand-coloured, bank statements; legible and intimidating at fifty paces.

Woody regarded this world with displeasure. He looked, instead, towards Europe; the old Europe of his parents, German Jews from Prague. And he loved England. Everything about England was 'smashing'. Besides which, an agent, even a rich one, could not collect Stellas or Twomblys or even Bruce Naumans. Even the old farming implements were going crazy. Forgeries occasionally uttered.

When he settled into his Georgian home in Trevor Square managing the London branch of ITO,

Woody started again. The house itself, that is to say the principal rooms, exhibited no sign of his most recent enthusiasm. They were furnished well, but in the English taste, and no doubt resembled, in most respects, the interiors of other houses in the square not occupied by fugitives from the Levant. Woody's collection was contained in one large chamber at the top of the house, but it was in danger of spilling down the stairs into a spare bedroom. For Woody collected Christmas.

Since 1978, indeed, since his arrival in England, he had accumulated almost all there was of real importance on the subject of this ancient festival.

He owned an example of the first commercial Christmas card, printed in 1846 by Sir Henry Cole and J. C. Horsley. He possessed a first edition of Charles Dickens's *A Christmas Carol* of 1843. He cherished the original artwork by Norman Rockwell for a 1938 *Saturday Evening Post* cover, depicting children unwrapping presents while their parents peeked ecstatically around the door. In a glass case lay the shooting script of *White Christmas*, autographed by Bing Crosby, Danny Kaye and Rosemary Clooney, whilst beside it reposed Irving Berlin's signed copy of the eponymous song. A life-sized dummy was apparelled in the tuxedo Mel Torme wore when he first sang about Chestnuts Roasting on an Open Fire, and in pride of place, in a gold frame discreetly spotlit, was a 'Dear Santa' wants list from little Ronnie Reagan, obtained from a private source in Washington D.C.

These were just, as collectors say, the 'high spots'.

There were hundreds, perhaps thousands of lesser items, indexed and catalogued. The ensemble was dazzling, festive – in fact, like Christmas itself. Woody's garret resembled Planet Hollywood at the North Pole.

Often he would retire there to read scripts or merely to meditate on Yuletide memorabilia, past, present, and yet to come. He called it: Santa's Grotto.

He was up there that afternoon when Derek Pettyfer rang his doorbell, but he bounded down the stairs with great agility for a stout man of sixty-five, and greeted his former client. Derek was nervous.

'Hi Woody! What's the scoop?' he said, in unconvincing parody of the agent's ludicrous jargon.

'You've never been here before, have you?'

'I don't believe so,' said Derek, 'not even in the bad old days,' he added sheepishly.

'I'm glad I caught you at home in the middle of the afternoon. Was that your new wife who answered the phone?'

'Yes, it was Pam, she must've sounded a bit, well tense. She's sculpting Lionel Pinkhill as we speak.'

'She sounded smashing,' said the agent, leading the way upstairs, '. . . in terrific form.'

'I'm glad you can tell so much from her voice,' said Derek, with undetected irony, wondering if it was Woody's corrupting influence which had induced him to come out with that awful locution: 'as we speak'.

'Only one more flight, and then some little stairs,' said Woody encouragingly, as he bounded upwards.

'Not many come up here. It's where I hole up when I've got a backlog of work.'

'Don't they miss you at the office?' panted Derek. He was getting some aerobic exercise. The agent stopped at the entrance to Santa's Grotto and turned to Derek.

'I've got a smashing gal holding the fort back there, Derek, but I think you know Garryl.' Derek's heart turned over. Was this why the agent had said it was urgent he come here?, he thought. What had that ratbag told Woody? What had she invented? Was she pregnant? This last scenario seemed unlikely, given her exotic preferences.

The Collector threw open the door, touched a switch, and with a low bow ushered Derek into his garret. Fairy lights winked, a concealed projector caused snowflakes to swarm across the ceiling, a life-size and rubicund effigy of Santa Claus, formerly in Macy's store, slapped his thigh, wagged his head and repeated the phrase, 'Ho Ho Ho!' while the munchkin voice of Little Penny Blue sang 'All I Want for Christmas is me Two Front Teeth', the beloved hit of 1952. Woody also possessed the Andrews Sisters and the Nat King Cole versions of this profane carol.

Derek was flabbergasted. It was a bizarre setting in which one grown man should seek to reprimand another for sexual harassment, or staff poaching. Derek kept trying to imagine what might be the charge he had been summoned to answer: *coitus interruptus*, perhaps?

In the midst of all this jingling and ho-ho-ho-ing,

Woody projected a contrasting mood of seriousness; even gravity. 'Sit down Derek,' he said, pushing Santa's sack towards him, which proved to be a bean-bag. The agent meanwhile climbed aboard a brightly decorated nineteenth-century Austrian sleigh and prodded a remote control. The sound mercifully stopped.

'I suppose you're wondering why I brought you here.' Derek confirmed the supposition. 'What I've got to say to you has to be said, if you will, in private.'

Derek remembered, with a sinking heart, that Woody was another of those 'if you will' Americans, as in 'I feel you should know that I'm having an affair, if you will, with your wife'. Its presence in a sentence often presaged an embarrassing truth, or merely apologised in advance for a long and undemocratic word in mixed company. 'I see President Clinton is soon to undergo, if you will, a proctological exploration.'

As he was busily trying to analyse this sententious usage, Derek remembered that his former agent was saying something important. Tuning back in, he caught '. . . so for all those reasons it's better I run all this by you, if you will, *in camera*.'

'I only took Garryl to lunch once, Woody!' protested Derek. 'If she got the wrong idea I can only apologise. She's a very sweet girl.' Woody pulled his red Armani frames down off his nut-brown pate and stared through them at Derek. The black antennae in his nostrils quivered; his white designer stubble rippled like the nap on the back of an albino gerbil.

'Steady on, old man! I'm not the faintest bit

interested as to whether you and Garryl Kurdish have been, if you will, humping. I want to talk to you about Ross Gibb.'

'Gibbo? Now listen, Woody...' At this point, Derek became aware of a renewed tintinnabulation, a faint clattering, which seemed to be getting louder. Was some rogue reindeer, tricked up with jingling seasonal symbols, about to gallop through the already over-stuffed attic?, he wondered. The clinking stopped and a strong smell of cigarette smoke alerted them to a third presence in the room.

'Thank you, Estelle, that's smashing, just put it down there.' Woody carefully pushed the world's finest collection of Holy Nativities in a Snowstorm to one side of Santa's desk, as Estelle, breathing heavily, deposited thereon a loaded tray of afternoon tea.

In so doing, the pendulous ash of the cigarette between her lips dropped into a teacup with a faint hiss.

'I hope you take it with cream, old boy,' said Woody, passing Derek an infusion of Earl Grey and Peter Stuyvesant. You know my wife, Estelle?'

The woman whom Derek had assumed to be a deranged servant passionately kissed the butt of her cigarette to extract the last quintessence of nicotine and ground it into a 'Christmas Island' souvenir ashtray. Extending a bony hand, she gave Derek a flirtatious smile.

'Why, I don't believe we've ever met,' she said, the ectoplasm of her last drag still hovering before her lips. Derek looked at those lips. Perhaps, long ago, they had been normal, even pretty lips. Now they had been grotesquely enlarged by some cosmetic surgeon who had done postgraduate studies with the Kichepo Tribe on the Ethiopian border. They had been implanted with a material similar, perhaps, to the shifting, squelchy substance in the beanbag beneath his bottom. She could have loudly applauded with them. To have actually smoked a cigarette with them was an admirable feat: it was akin to picking up a strand of spaghetti with a boxing glove.

'A slice of cheesecake? C'mon, Derek, you only live once.' Two wedges of cheesecake, still wrapped from the shop, lay in a shallow cardboard box beside the teacups. Estelle, in her pink quilted 'brunch-coat', scooped up a slice and put it on his lap. 'Woody shouldn't be eating this you know,' she said conspiratorially, 'but if I didn't bake it for him he'd surely make my life a misery.'

Derek ignored the harmless subterfuge of a hostess claiming authorship of a patently bought item. Moreover, he had no wish to make more miserable a life which seemed already replete with that article.

'It's funny that you and Estelle never met in the old days when we worked together,' said Woody, tucking into the cheesecake. As he wolfed it down, Derek noticed a gold ring on his crooked pinky, embellished with the eighteen carat countenance of Kriss Kringle.

'I was pretty out of it then,' said Derek. 'Not really safe to bring home.'

Woody sucked his thumb. 'You were fine Derek.

So every now and then you enjoyed a few sherbets, you partied a bit more than was good for you – so what's the big deal?'

Derek began to see why he was there. Woody Weinglass the agent was pitching. He wanted him back; even sober he wanted him back.

'Did you see my client Nigel Fitzroy walk off with that British Film Award last month?' asked Woody proudly.

'I saw it on television, Woody, but he crawled off with it, didn't he? I seem to remember he fell over on stage.'

'Nigel's a scallywag, he'd been celebrating – who wouldn't? The food at those functions is always filthy, no wonder he was sick on Princess Margaret.'

'I didn't see that.'

'They cut to a commercial and I kept it out of the papers. But Nigel's fine; in smashing form. He can take it or leave it.'

'How come only drunks say that, Woody? Have you ever heard a normal drinker say he can take it or leave it?'

'Listen to this man, Estelle. *Will you listen to him?* These reformed lushes are all the same. I think you were better when you had a few, Derek.'

'I was waiting for you to say that, Woody,' laughed Derek.

The agent shook his head and polished off the last crumbs of cheesecake. Somewhere a long way back, between the mauve muffins of her lips, Estelle clicked her tongue.

'He'll have to own up at Weight Watchers tonight.'

'Hell, Estelle, does Derek have to know everything?'

'He goes to Weight Watchers' three times a week, Mr Pettyfer, and tells them all what a bad boy he's been, and then, my Lord, if he doesn't go right out the door and eat some more of my cheesecake, now what do you think of that?'

Derek wondered if the same surgeon who had distended Estelle's lips had also butchered her nose. It was vestigial; in the midst of an area of glossy scar tissue it stood, lonely and diminutive like a tonsil with two holes in it: an external uvula. Yet there must once have been a moment when some filthy rich rhino-plastician had handed her a mirror and she had looked at her face and said: 'FABULOUS!'

It was the Emperor's new nose.

Estelle lit another cigarette and squatted beside Derek on the floor like a ravaged schoolgirl. 'Don't you just love my husband's Christmas collection, Mr Pettyfer? Isn't it just the dandiest thing?' Derek felt suddenly as if he were in an amateur production of a posthumous play by Tennessee Williams.

So this was Woody's wife. Over all these years, he had not even known that Woody was married! He kept that one under the rug. No wonder the bimbos at Film Premières and First Nights, and Garryl in the office – what a dark old horse! Derek thought guiltily of his own wife; the first one, Belinda. She wasn't too presentable these days either. With pain he recalled that she had once been beautiful. Being painted by Francis Bacon had been a bit of a self-fulfilling prophecy. She had ended up smudged. And what about Estelle Weinglass? The poor creature was a living de Kooning.

'Why Christmas, Woody?' Derek enquired.

'I can't recall,' said the agent.

'Anything in childhood? Your family came from Prague, didn't they? Perhaps Good King Wenceslas has a lot to answer for.'

'I doubt it. I was too young to dig any of that stuff, and I didn't have a normal childhood for Chrissakes. Would you believe my father was a Rabbi? I can only remember his white beard when he put me on the last train to Paris. He gave me a toy and I never saw him again.' Woody shrugged. 'How should I know why I collect this stuff? An investment, that's for sure.'

Derek looked around the grotto. There must have been hundreds of replicated images of kind old men with white beards and red yarmulkas schlepping toys. It was so obvious; but not to Woody.

When Estelle had picked up the tray and clattered off in a cloud of smoke, Woody returned to his theme.

'Listen, Derek old boy,' he said, 'your career's taking a nose dive with that Ross Gibb chum of yours. He's not orchestrating you. How much did he get you for that vacuum cleaner ad?'

'You know about that?'

'I know everything. Shooting in Antigua next week, am I right?'

'Why should I tell you, Woody?'

'I could have doubled that money. He's an amateur, an asshole. He's not good for your image. Have you checked the books lately?'

Derek rose; he was furious. 'Thanks for the tea Woody, I'm off.' He started down the stairs.

'Take it easy, take it easy, old son!' Woody was saying behind him.

'Ross Gibb is my oldest friend in this country. He's as solid as a rock.'

'Sure, sure, I'm hearing you. It's just that you need management or you'll be toast. You need to be nurtured, you need *class*, Derek . . .'

Derek had reached the last flight of stairs. Ahead was the front door, the Georgian fanlight, a still blue sky. 'Do you seriously think that it's classy of you to sit me down in that pathetic collection of sentimental junk and bad-mouth my friend to my face? Get off to your Weight Watchers' meeting, Woody, with all those other slobs, and please don't talk to me about class!'

It was perfectly timed. One second after his last word resounded up the stairs the door slammed and Derek was in Trevor Square.

It was cool and fresh. He pulled his collar up as he strode towards Brompton Road to find a cab. He was still very, very angry.

He felt the rolled magazine still projecting from his side pocket. It was some glossy he had found on the back seat of the taxi coming over. He had once met the novelist Thomas Pynchon, and he was now halfway through a long interview with the famous author and his family, by Kate Kellaway. The headline ran:

KATE AMONGST THE PYNCHONS.

Hailing a cab, Derek thought how funny it was that men like Woody – quirky compulsive collectors – often had no insight into the origin of their obsessions, when it was obvious to all others. It was like the nun who complained of her recurring dream: being chased by a pink snake.

Derek had known another Jew. A cultivated Viennese, now in his seventies, who, as a youth, had escaped across the Frontier at night, through a forest. The signal from his rescuers which saved his life, the signal to run for it, was three owl hoots. Now he was a great-grandfather in St John's Wood and he had amassed the world's largest collection of miniature owls. Ask him why? He hadn't the faintest idea.

That same evening, before he went out, Kenneth Grocock clambered into a pair of old jeans and a leather jacket and gave himself a rather craggy, Tom Cruisey look in the bathroom mirror.

It was his custom, from time to time, to visit the Hercules Fitness Club in a basement in Westbourne Park. In response to the sound of an illuminated buzzer, the door would automatically open, and at a small and rather dark reception counter, a cheerful youth called Neil with a tattoo and an earring accepted his entrance money, deposited his valuables in a safety box, and issued Kenneth with a key on an elastic band and an abrasive towel.

It was here, with his clothes, that Kenneth was

able also to shed his parents, his school, his pallid Anglicanism, his polytechnic, and Polly. There, in that subterranean world of slimy tiles and albuminoid puddles, of lubricious collisions in tenebrous labyrinths, he felt, with a quickening heartbeat, the two things which had always seemed most absent from his other life: Intensity and Freedom. He was not a participant; he saw himself more as an Outsider like Camus, or a detached observer like Isherwood, or a nice Joe Orton.

But tonight, his visit to the Hercules had more of a sense of purpose than was customary. He might even look upon it as a professional necessity. When he pushed open the glass door of the steam room, there was the usual sudden movement within, as the occupants, seated along the tiled bleaches, hastily assumed casual, sedentary postures with their hands decorously at their sides. It reminded Kenneth of musical chairs; that mad scramble and freeze when the tune stopped.

Immediately, through a rift in the steam, he saw where he should sit, and stepped up towards it with agility before the small chamber was once again engulfed in another burst of impenetrable and humid vapour.

There had just been time for Kenneth to observe that his earlier information had been spot on. What a grapevine!

A long time seemed to elapse. The hot fog intensified and all he heard were the faint tricklings and susurrations of steam, until at length the clammy, disembodied hand settled on his pale knee. As it began its tentative journey he knew that soon, in little more than an hour perhaps, and certainly by jacuzzi time, few of his questions would remain unanswered.

Remotely, the Obituarist watched the short fat fingers, and only then did he observe the gold ring with the little face of Father Christmas.

Ms Fortune

AT THE NAPE of her neck, in the folds of her elbows, behind her knees, in the navel and at the apex of her buttocks, Inge anointed herself with a little Holy Water which had been blessed by Jean-Paul Gaultier. Wearing only this, and her peignoir from La Perla, she received her friend Derek Pettyfer in her sitting-room. It was eight in the evening, the children were at *Batman Forever*, and they were alone in the house.

'Are you sure you want this number?'

'No.'

'It's not Pam already?'

'Of course not.'

A silence.

'I won't ask.'

'All right, it's Ross.'

'You've got to be joking!'

'I know I'm wasting my money, but too many bloody Iagos have been whispering in my ear.'

'Who?'

'Well, bloody Woody for one.'

'Ross adores you, Derek.'

'Just a discreet check, Inge.'

'Why don't you simply request an audit?'

'It's the structure he's set up, it's too complicated. It's based on trust.'

'I don't really know him, but if he finds out you're snooping it'll break his heart.'

'He's a tough Aussie.'

'Aren't you?'

'No – I'm a wimp. And I'm scared.'

'Can't that accountant of yours – that Henry . . .?'

'Roger.'

'. . . that Hooray Roger. Can't he do some sniffing?'

'They could both have their hands in the till.'

'Jesus!'

'What's this investigator like?'

'Brian McColl?'

'Yes.'

'Well, not seedy or furtive like you'd think.'

'What, then?'

'Dull, ordinary, invisible, like he's supposed to be.'

'Expensive?'

'Hugely.'

'Shit.'

'That a problem?'

'Don't laugh, but every bill goes to Gibbo, I never see them.'

'He'll want cash anyway.'

'Why?'

'Because a lot of what he does is illegal.'

'Sorry, no thanks, forget it.'

'It's illegal in one sense, quite usual in another. Bribe the right person and they'll happily tap a phone for you. It's done every day.'

'Oh God.'

'Don't anguish, Derek. If you've got a few gremlins getting at you, brush them off. The best antidote to anxiety is information. Brian McColl will clear the air, hopefully give Mr Gibb a clean bill of health and you can get on with your career.'

'Don't tell Pam.'

'Sorry?'

'Don't tell her. You might be tempted, Inge, but she doesn't understand business. If she thought I suspected Gibbo of anything – and I don't, not really – she'd get on the phone and ask him straight.'

'That's women for you. Aren't we infuriatingly straightforward, honourable creatures?'

'Don't be satirical Inge, *I agree with you*! By the way, I suppose you know Pam's doing a head of Lionel?'

'Quite a challenge.'

'Really, Inge, I'm glad you said that. I thought he looked, well, preoccupied.'

'He's not well, between us. Tomorrow he's playing the Boccherini in Bristol and then he's having more tests at the Cromwell.'

'What for?'

'Heart. He's booked for a bypass.'

'My God!'

'It's more serious than he thinks; but now it's my

turn to say "don't tell Pam". He doesn't want anyone to know and that includes me.'

'Why?'

'His bloody pride, Derek. And fear of death. Lionel is pathologically incapable of taking it easy.'

'I'm so sorry. Whatever you feel for him, Inge, all this makes my problem look pretty pissy.'

'Yes, let's have a bit of light relief and consider your problem. We'll ring Mr McColl, in fact we'll ring him at home now. Who knows? By lunchtime tomorrow you might be the proud possessor of a Private Eye!'

'You're all pink and rosy, Kenneth, you look like the cat that licked the cream.'

'Nine out of ten, Miss Marple,' replied Polly's flatmate, with an uncharacteristic moue. He glanced in the mirror and patted his damp hair.

'Nothing like a work-out at the gym,' he said, feeling that to describe the Hercules Fitness Club as a gym, or even as a fitness club, was perhaps stretching a point. 'You're up a bit late.'

'I got home from the Meditation Centre and started pottering. Listen to this.' Polly darted to the CD player and touched a button. Sprightly and insouciant Gallic music issued from the small speakers.

'That's Françaix,' she said, executing a few *entrechats* and *arabesques*.

'So what, Poll?' said Kenneth, rummaging through a bulging file, which was labelled in large letters:

PETTY DISTINCTIONS, An Unauthorised Life by Kenneth Grocock.

'He's a great French composer, Kenneth. Françaix wrote the music for my ballet on November the first.'

Kenneth had been rereading his notes on Derek Pettyfer's hectic career in the early eighties. Now, as from tonight, he had a lot more anecdotal material. He looked up at his friend.

'Sorry, Poll, what was that? I've got Mrs Petty on the brain tonight. Some really hot info's come my way.'

'Not Woody Weinglass?'

'Could be.'

'How Kenneth, how? Only this afternoon his secretary told me no way.'

'I haf vays off making him talk, Polly. How does this grab you?'

The ballerina sat at his feet in the lotus position, put her pointy chin in her hands, cocked her scraped-back head, and with wide mascara'd eyes, invited him to expatiate.

'Did you know, Poll, that Pettyfer once got arrested for peeing on Victoria Station in the rush hour? Did you know he lost his licence for driving up Tottenham Court Road in the wrong direction with his feet on the steering wheel?'

'You must be joking,' said Polly.

'Did you know that once, in drag as Mrs Petty, he told Barbara Cartland to go and do rude things with a daikon radish?'

'Yuck! I use those in my Asian cooking, they've got incredible properties.'

'La Cartland didn't think so. Did you know . . .?'

Polly hugged her friend and put her fingers over his mouth. 'Enough, you'll spoil the book for me.'

'He's promised me masses more. Basically this is the period of Derek's life that will pick up the big serialisation money. It is a story that has to be told because . . .'

'. . . THE PUBLIC HAS A RIGHT TO KNOW!' They said it simultaneously, laughed, and as they always did for luck, linked pinkies and declaimed the names of famous poets.

'Helen Steiner Rice.'

'James Fenton.'

'Who?'

'He's a famous poet, Poll, basically he . . .'

'Gollywogs! I could have lost you your job!'

'What's up?'

'Your obits editor phoned about forty minutes ago. A poet called Greg Bollocks or something has died, he wants you to fax him a jolly couple of thousand words by half past eleven tonight. They're holding the page.'

Kenneth was galvanised. 'Greg Bolton! Shit Polly, thanks a bunch. That gives me twenty minutes. Jesus!'

'I'll help you, do you need *Who's Who*?' But Kenneth was already on the phone to the paper, to see if the obituary could wait. What a drag, he thought, this was the downside of working from home. Emergencies.

Then he looked at the chubby Mrs Petty file. No more hack work for our Kenneth soon, he thought.

The J. R. Ackerley Prize for Biography, dinner with Rupert Murdoch . . . Easy Street.

Derek took a radio cab to Clerkenwell. He used his taxi account all the time now, since Doris had taken possession of the BMW. It had been shopping at first. Then, several dents and scratches later, the car was practically hers. The driver's seat was pretty well locked in the far forward position, just as the sleeves of his best dressing-gown seemed to be permanently rolled up to accommodate shorter and more feminine arms.

In the back of a cab, moreover, one could comfortably read, or work, or, in Derek's case, add to his oxymorons. Opening his notebook, Derek sat back and contemplated the growing list.

An honest Cockney
A truthful Irishman
An efficient Englishman
A modest Australian
A polite New Yorker
A thin Mid-Westerner
An imaginative German
A charming Swiss
A witty Canadian
A member of the French Resistance . . .

The time passed quickly and he soon found himself in a narrow street near Theobalds Road. It was one of those wonderful London streets, fewer year by year, where you could stand and look to left and right without ever seeing a modern building. It had been overlooked by Goering, spared by Attlee, ignored by Wilson and snubbed by Thatcher. It was in such a time warp, so much in its original pre-war juice, Derek conjectured, that its inhabitants might still send and receive telegrams.

At the top of a flight of wooden stairs, and along a corridor, he finally came upon a door inset with a pane of rippled glass and a sign which proclaimed these to be the modest offices of McColl Holdings PLC. Within, all was modern. A secretary asked him to be seated. To suppress his anxiety and emotions of guilt, Derek plucked up a magazine and began to read an interview with the film director Polanski, seemingly conducted in a night-club:

ROMAN IN THE GLOAMIN'.

A woman's voice disturbed his perusal. 'Come this way, Mr Quick.'

Soon Derek found himself in a small office with a view of a brick wall. Two people behind a desk rose as he entered: a man and a woman.

'I'm Brian McColl and this is my colleague, Coral Fortune. Won't you sit down?'

Derek obliged. He looked at McColl. Inge had been right; he was *terminally ordinary.* Scrutiny seemed to slide off his smooth, unmemorable features. Even the colour of his skin, his hair, his eyes and his suit, were fugitive. Derek did not know where to begin.

'Do you use a mobile?'

'Yes, sometimes.'

'Don't,' said Mr McColl. 'It's funny how few of my clients learned their lesson from Prince Charles.'

Ms Fortune and Mr McColl laughed at this. It was meant to break the ice; had broken it before.

'Also, Mr Quick, it's better to use your real name with us. I know you probably thought it was a good idea to employ a pseudonym when you made this appointment, but we watch TV like everyone else and we can hardly help you if you insist on being someone else.'

'I was going . . . I mean, naturally!'

'If we can help you . . . thanks, Deswyn.'

A freckled redhead had entered with flasks of tea and coffee. 'A wee biscuit?' she asked Derek.

'No . . . no thanks.'

When the secretary had left, Brian McColl leant forward. 'You needn't worry. What she hears here, what she sees here, stays here. Fair enough?'

'Fair enough,' whispered Derek.

'Your assignment will be handled by my colleague, Coral Fortune.'

'But, I thought . . .?'

'She's the best in this office, Mr Pettyfer. She is one of the most experienced professionals in the country, and when she's on a delicate assignment, *no one gives her a second glance.*'

Ms Fortune smiled at the compliment, though Derek thought it was not one which would have charmed any other woman of his acquaintance. He looked at the small, spinster-like figure across the desk. About forty-five, he reckoned, neatly got up in a grey suit and blouse, dull fair hair and a small, twitching face like a washed-out rabbit. Not his, or anybody's idea of a forceful, fearless private eye. Coral Fortune took over. She put on her glasses, opened a yellow foolscap notepad and said, 'Please Mr Pettyfer, can you give us some idea of the problem?'

As the interview progressed, Derek felt increasingly ashamed of himself and increasingly convinced in his own mind that Ross Gibb was not merely squeaky clean, but downright saintly.

'. . . and this alleged stud farm in Australia?'

'It's only a few acres, his mother-in-law left . . .'

'Well, of course, the agent of a man like you,' interposed Mr McColl, with a faintly indulgent smile, 'would naturally deserve to acquire *some* assets.'

'Exactly,' said Derek rising. 'Thank you. Thank you too, Mr McColl. You've put my mind at rest. I suppose I just needed to verbalise these worries to see them in their true perspective. How much do I owe you?'

The detectives regarded him with astonishment. Ms Fortune spoke. 'Please sit down again. Where there's smoke there's fire. You could have real problems in terms of Mr Gibb, or you couldn't. Give us a month's trial. I can't say we'll come up with anything in terms of hard information, but you can be sure that whatever we do, our enquiries will not be detected.'

'Will you tap his phone?' The two detectives looked at each other in polite horror.

'That is completely illegal, Mr Pettyfer,' Coral Fortune said finally. She meant, Derek quickly inferred, that it was illegal to mention it. They all rose.

'Oh,' said Derek, 'I should point out that I haven't told my wife about any of this.'

'Why is that?'

'Well, she'd think I'd gone potty and she rather likes Gibbo.' Coral Fortune's pale eyes imperceptively narrowed.

'So he could possibly let slip something to your wife that he might not to you?'

'Could be, but really, I mean let's not get too suspicious!' Derek had experienced another slight but unpleasant intimation of fraternity with Judas Iscariot.

'You've given us these phone numbers – for our reference only, of course!' McColl added hastily. 'When do you fly to Antigua?'

'I think on Sunday.'

'Lucky you,' said Ms Fortune, looking out at the brick wall. 'It's always a good time for us to ask a few discreet questions. Suspects are generally a bit more careless when the client is abroad.'

'He's not a suspect – he's a friend.'

'Of course he is; and let us hope, very soon, a trusted friend.'

Derek shook hands, first with Brian McColl and then with the pale, tremulous little lady at his side. Her grip nearly snapped off his fingers.

'Are you really interested in this stuff?' asked Jonathan.

'Certainly,' Derek replied. 'I mean, for instance, is Haägenstrøm an old Swedish company?'

Jonathan finished the last of his wine and gave a signal to the steward. He was the president and major shareholder in Jonathan Rushing & Associates, the most successful and 'bullish' of the smaller agencies, and to Derek's slight annoyance, he looked no more than twenty-three years of age. He was wearing jeans, a Gap open-necked shirt, and a caramel-coloured jacket of some expensive synthetic, cut like a forties tuxedo with a shawl lapel. Derek observed that the executive affected long sideburns. Surely they weren't coming back?

'I'll have a Cointreau with the coffee, please,' said Jonathan. 'Are you sure, Derek?'

Derek waved his hand in polite refusal. 'Absolutely.'

On the long flight to Antigua he had had trouble keeping his end up in the conversation. The man who had wanted him, fought for his money and paid for this first-class seat, was clearly so tickled pink to be getting to know him personally that Derek just had to be awake, alert, amusing and 'raring to go'. In reality, he was so tired, so anxious, so bored, that he could barely screw his features into the vaguest simulacrum of an interested listener. Thank God for that endless meal! The chewing and sipping had prevented the muscles of his face from dropping into his lap.

'It's gratifying you should want to know so much about the product, Mr Pettyfer.'

'Please, Derek, I told you . . .'

'Derek. Well, since you're interested . . .'

If Derek had possessed a cyanide capsule then he would have bitten it.

'. . . this appliance is the result of all-British technology . . .'

Mentally Derek added a new oxymoron to his list.

'. . . a man called Jenkins – fabulous chap by the way, lives near Esher and I'll fix a lunch when we're back in London – well, this is Jenkins's baby; his brainchild, but it was our organisation that developed the name Haägenstrøm; it took us about a year.'

Derek raised his eyebrows and blew a weak whistle of incredulity. Dare he say: 'only a year?'. He dare not.

'Actually it was our top creative man who finally came up with the brand name, I think you met young Miles King, he's back there in Business as we speak. Jonathan indicated with a cock of his head an area behind them, as though Derek might have supposed that the aeroplane ended at the first class partition. Beyond, his employer assured him, in the twilight zone, travelled the rest of the agency people.

At Gatwick Derek had been introduced to most of them, and they were numerous, but it was impossible to ascertain what exactly it was they all did; whether writing, directing, art directing, client liaising or just coming along for the ride. They had two distinctive characteristics in common: they appeared to be all very, very nice, that is to say they were awestruck by Derek, and they were all, with the exception of a grizzled German camera operator, under thirty.

'This commercial is pitched at the twenty-five to forty demographic. I don't want to piss in your pocket, Derek, but basically the people who watch Mrs Petty.'

'Piss in my pocket,' said Derek.

'It's the people who wear Armani, or wish they could. It's the ones who have or want a Bang & Olufsen sound system; basically the Haägen-Dazs community at the end of the day.'

Derek wanted to interpose an interesting and complimentary observation, but none occurred to him.

'That's where Miles and his team got the "Haagen" bit of Haägenstrøm,' Jonathan added proudly. 'Naturally we've market researched this pretty thoroughly and we found that at the end of the day the potential buyer of an upmarket appliance like this responds to a Scandinavian brand name.'

'I don't think,' Derek began, hoping the act of speaking might stimulate a trickle of blood to his brain, '. . . I don't think Haagen-Dazs is actually a Scandinavian name.'

'Exactly, but what a success story! We've got very positive feedback on Haägenstrøm, particularly on how we're looking at locating it in the market-place.'

'You mean, in the shops?'

'Not altogether.' For a second Jonathan Rushing almost lost his thread. He stole the briefest of quizzical glances at his neighbour. Why, he wondered, was Mr Pettyfer grimacing like a Maori warrior with his eyes nearly popping out of their sockets?

'You see,' he continued imperturbably, 'we don't

call it a vacuum cleaner. Our research – you met Piers Forrester earlier I think, and I hope you'll get to know young Danny Mottram, he's a real East End boy but as sharp as a razor . . .' Derek nodded vigorously like Harpo Marx. '. . . our research indicates that at the end of the day, people don't really want a vacuum cleaner *per se*, they want a status symbol. That's why we call it a cleaning *instrument*.'

Derek was embarrassed to discover that he had dribbled slightly; a glittering thread of saliva swung from his lower lip like a bungee rope. 'Instrument?'

'Yes! Instrument is a user-friendly word. Your credit card is a monetary instrument, and Monsieur Chirac's bomb was an "instrument of deterrence", according to yesterday's *Herald Trib*. The punters love that word.' The president of the agency continued excitedly: 'If you built an upmarket pen say ten years ago, you couldn't sell it, Derek; you couldn't give it away. Then a genius came up with "writing instrument" and POW!!'

The ejaculation jolted Derek back into temporary consciousness. His adrenal gland had turned over but then had gone back to sleep. Do it again, thought Derek, *please* say it again!

'The Haägenstrøm cleaning instrument brings the old concept vacuum cleaner out of the closet, if you'll excuse the pun, and into the . . .'

'Market-place?'

'No, well yes, I mean the point is you can leave your Haägenstrøm in the middle of the living-room; you can flaunt it, it's sculpture. Have you seen this?'

Jonathan opened a black leather Porsche briefcase

with a solar lock. There was, Derek noticed with co-mingled envy and admiration, almost nothing in it. The president of Rushing & Associates withdrew a glossy trade manual.

'This came out last week when we announced that we had captured the Haägenstrøm account.' Proudly he pointed to the lead story:

RUSHING INTO THE VACUUM.

But Derek's head had lolled. Another liana of drool crept from his slackening lips. He had blotted his copy book, let down the side, and stone cold sober, he had brought disgrace upon the over-fifties. With a rueful shrug, the president of the agency closed his briefcase as the Talent lapsed into stertorous oblivion.

16

Karina

DEREK WAS STILL tired next morning when he awoke in his luxurious Spanish-style villa on the K-Club estate, Barbuda Island. After the long flight from Gatwick to St John's the previous day, he had not been prepared for that last twenty minute hop to Antigua's sister island. But by then he was feeling no pain. Karina, the account handler from the agency, anticipated all his needs, and at some time yesterday evening he had been delivered to the resort like a parcel, fed once again, and practically tucked up in bed.

Stepping on to his patio under a sky as blue and matt as his Smythson's stationery, Derek smelt the honeysuckle and hibiscus and listened to the crepitations of the heat. Not far away on the lawn, a sprinkler slowly revolved, so that every thirty seconds or so a comet-tail of sparkling water raked the canna lillies and the nearer bushes, drubbing on the dark glossy leaves.

On a cane table in his room, next to a cornucopia of tropical fruit and beneath a rather evil Haitian Primitive, he saw the champagne bucket and the gold foil of a vintage bottleneck, 'With the Compliments of the Management'. Beside it, Karina had left his script and his call sheet.

For the past few years, ever since he had stopped drinking alcohol, people had been presenting Derek with booze. Excellent booze. Oddly, though, when he was still on the sauce, when he really needed it, he never remembered anyone giving him more than a bottle of light ale.

In a pink bathrobe, with a plate of mangos and guavas, he ambled back on to his terrace to read the exiguous script. Before him, worried by butterflies, lay the strip of clipped turf, a low vibrant ribbon of beach, and then the peacock-green parapet of the Caribbean. Against the sky, tall palms gently chafed their amazing fronds.

Sitting in his deck-chair, absorbing the benison of sunlight, he thought of Pam. He had tried ringing her last night, but the management politely advised him that telephone calls from this area were sometimes difficult.

Now, he was completely unable to work out what time it was in London. He would find out soon, and try calling again. When he had said goodbye – was it last night? the day before yesterday? – Pam had come out of her 'studio', put her arms around his neck, and given him the softest, warmest kiss he could remember. For the first time he had sensed the depth of her gratitude. As she was about to say 'take care' he had stopped the offending words with his lips. Even old Doris had been rather sweet.

'For God's sake, don't mess around with this flat any more, Doris,' he had chided.

'It's her, ducks, it's not me, it's Lady Muck,' she said, with a thumb gesture towards what had once been his dining-room and a duplicitous wink. 'I liked it as it was.'

'Whatever,' said Derek, picking up his case. 'Put the pictures back up again, keep the blinds down when it's sunny, *and please keep an eye on my glass.*' They looked towards the vitrine and its priceless contents, still invisible beneath the dust sheet.

'Your precious old bottles eh, duck?' Doris said, daintily patting the cabinet, 'Doris will look after them as though they were hers!'

Derek may have looked uncertain.

'Now don't you fret. Get along with you and remember to bring me back a sombrero and one of those bottles of vino shaped like a bull.' Did Doris think Antigua was in Spain?, Derek wondered.

He had phoned Gibbo from Gatwick.

'What's the point of me coming and kissing you goodbye, Dekka? There'd have to be a bloody army of agency free fuckin' loaders holding your hand. By the way, mate, that lezzo in Sydney wants you to do your one-man-show at the Festival. Big bickies, and they're hot to trot.'

Derek, until then, had thought a lump in the throat was a mythological disorder, a literary affectation having no parallel in human experience.

'Are you still there, Dekka?'

'Yes.'

'Don't do anyone I wouldn't do!'

As Derek listened to his friend's voice, he had felt a wave of self-disgust. Here was a person who really cared about him. It was not money, it was a fraternal bond. He thought of the improvised drinks on his wedding day; the exquisite Roman bowl.

Before his last call to board the aircraft, Derek just had time to telephone McColl Holdings and leave a message with – was it Deswyn? – that the 'arrangements' he had made with Ms Fortune were to be cancelled.

'She'll be back in a wee while,' said Deswyn.

'Just give her that message,' said Derek, cleansed.

'Disgusting morning?' Derek squinted into the light and saw a tall youth in white Bermuda shorts and a white sweatshirt crossing the grass towards him. He carried a tennis racquet.

'Is that you, Jonathan?' he said, 'You're an early bird.'

'It's ten o'clock,' said the president from the middle of the lawn, sprinting suddenly to outstrip the next affusion of the rotating sprinkler. 'Karina, Danny, Piers and I have played a couple of sets already. Feel like a swim?'

'Perhaps later,' replied the Talent, waving his script conscientiously. 'I better do my homework first like a good boy.'

'Take your own time, Derek,' recommended his employer, patting his shoulder and looking at him over the top of his Calvin Klein shades. 'Don't knacker yourself.'

Derek wondered how many points he had lost by dropping off on the plane yesterday just as Rushing approached his orgasm of self-congratulation. He must not seem tired, *ever.*

'I'm full of beans, never better,' he asserted, 'In fact, why don't you join me for breakfast?' Derek indicated a comfortable patio lounge covered with a striped fabric which matched the interior of his 'cottage': pink and turquoise.

'We all hit the buffet pretty early, Derek; but I've booked a production brunch at twelve if you're up to it.'

What was all this 'up to it'? Had he given such an impression of enfeeblement on the aeroplane? Would the paramedics soon appear?

'I could demolish a horse right now, as a matter of fact,' he said heartily, and to his own horror.

The young tennis player concurred. 'Breakfast is my favourite meal at the end of the day.'

Having delivered himself of this inanity, Jonathan perched on the edge of the chair, his tennis racquet slung jauntily over his shoulder. Derek saw that his brow was still glistening from the morning's exertions and observed on the left of his shirt-front the small embroidered image of a polo player.

'We won't shoot anything until tomorrow, maybe even Wednesday,' said Jonathan. Derek looked surprised. 'This is a big set-up, and the weather conditions are meant to get even better.'

'Nothing wrong with today!' Derek hazarded a

juicy bite of mango but the nectar ran down his chin, and he felt a sticky trickle inching down his wrist as well. Mangos were strictly for eating in the bath, reflected the old sybarite, taking another voluptuous mouthful of the succulent fruit.

'We need that water to be like glass.' Jonathan pointed out towards the reef. Derek saw the huge Breitling Chronograph on his teenage wrist. 'Can you handle the speed you'll be moving at?'

Was this yet another aspersion on his powers of physical endurance? How infirm was he looking? Derek began to think he might not, after all, like this nice young man as much as he'd first thought. Didn't they know that he was famous for one of the longest and most energetic one-man shows in the history of the theatre?

'I always work fast. Why?'

'No, Derek, I mean when we really pull you through the water at about fifteen knots.' Derek remembered there was one thing he had forgotten to do: read the script.

'Not a problem,' he said emphatically, regressing to a ventriloquist's doll, with Gibbo's voice.

'Let's meet at the Lord Nelson lunch buffet at noon. It's a good chance for you to eyeball the team again, and tonight I've organised a barbecue on the beach. Can you live with that?'

'Not a problem,' repeated Derek, shamelessly.

Jonathan, either from an excess of physical energy or because he had seen athletes do it on television, began briskly jogging on the spot. If there had been a bottle of water to hand he might have swigged it, rinsed, and squirted it professionally over his shoulder. He then fitted the ear pieces of the canary-yellow Walkman which Derek had just glimpsed, clipped to the belt of his white kid bum-bag. They shook hands.

'Great having you aboard!' And the young tycoon jogged off across the grass as Derek subsided into his *chaise-longue.* At the far edge of the lawn, just before a break in a luxuriant hedge of cerise bougainvillaea, he saw the white figure stop and examine its right hand, rub it energetically on the wet grass, and disappear. Derek looked ruefully down at his own palm, still glutinous with mango pulp, and turned with a newly kindled curiosity to the script.

The lunch was delicious: wonderful lobster, prawns and tropical seafood. The salads were superb, the desserts, as Estelle Weinglass would have said, to die for. And the wines – excellent and expensive too, no doubt – flowed freely in celebration of the world's finest Cleaning Instrument.

'The team' was all there, their English pallor more poignant now that their recently purchased Leisure-wear exposed so much of it. There were such a lot of them. The Client had turned up as well, although the Client was plural; a small committee of polite and deferential youths and one woman. Derek was certain he could identify a familiar bulge in the men's pockets: a wife or girlfriend's autograph book waiting to be produced when they knew him better. There was some excited discussion about the small, high speed submarine, borrowed at great expense from an eccentric millionaire in Florida, upon which the script required Derek to ride.

'Rather you than me, Derek old son,' Danny Mottram had said. Derek made light of it, and gave them his all-in-a-day's-work shrug, but he was, to use a Gibboism, 'shit-scared'!

On the patio of his 'cottage' he had had to read the script several times to grasp the fact that he was being paid as a stunt man. The script called for no dialogue. Mrs Petty rarely spoke anyway, which was why she was so popular in Europe and Asia. All Derek had to do was to attire himself as the famous frumpish housewife, step into special footwear affixed to the roof of the miniature submarine inches below water level, and cling on like buggery to the handle of a Haägenstrøm Cleaning Instrument. He would then be taken on a hair-raising dodgem ride across the lagoon.

On the finished commercial, a rich, reassuring voice – at lunch everyone from Donald Sinden to Miriam Margolyes impersonating Orson Welles was canvassed – would speak over the action: 'The trouble with people who choose a Haägenstrøm Cleaning Instrument . . . is that they think they can walk on water.'

The commercial would end with Mrs Petty, seemingly propelled by her vacuum cleaner, rocketing out to sea and into the sunset. The rich voice would then intone: 'Haägenstrøm – the cleanest thing since water!'

Over the coffee, and in many cases, abundant liqueurs, Derek committed a solecism.

'I don't want to talk myself out of a job, but couldn't a stunt man do all this? I mean who'd know it wasn't *really* Mrs Petty out there?'

'I'm not with you?' said Jonathan sharply, rolling his eyes in the Client's direction and back, meaningfully.

'Well,' continued Derek, oblivious to all cautionary signals, 'you could easily shoot Mrs Petty's close-ups in a studio in London: you know, horror, joy, exhilaration, even seasickness. Then all you'd have to do is get Stanley, my stunt man in drag out here and save yourself . . .' Miles King coughed loudly and stood up, as did his colleagues, with much loud scraping of chairs.

'I'd like you all to drink to Derek Pettyfer, a great comedian and a great sport,' he bellowed. 'Derek, we're proud to be working with you.' There was a noisy and touching response from all present. Thanks to this well-timed interruption, Derek's helpful and cost-efficient suggestions had failed to reach the Client's ears, and Miles King was almost certainly in line for promotion.

In the pink and blue bedroom with its wicker and rattan appointments, Derek collapsed into a delicious siesta. The ceiling fan brushed his cheek with cool air and the brilliant afternoon outside was only visible where it leaked greenly through the jalousies. Again, before sleeping, he had tried Pam, and at length, but had only got the answering machine. He left a long, halting, and affectionate message.

Karina woke him.

'Mr Pettyfer!' She had refused his invitation to call him Derek; another 'ageist' slur. 'Wake up, Mr Pettyfer! They're all waiting for you down at the Beach Club.'

Derek, still groggy from lunch, got quickly under the shower while Karina loitered on his patio, smoking a cigarette. She was a pretty girl, he thought, tall, dark and olive skinned, with the ghost of a moustache pricked out with perspiration. She wore a purple sarong and a halter top, her spatulate toes divided by the raffia twine of her sandals. She smelled of Tuberose by Mary Chess.

'I'm so sorry . . . I slept like the dead . . . that lunch!'

'So did I,' she laughed. 'I hated waking you, Mr Pettyfer, but the chief is a bit of a stickler for meal hours and we've got a special part of the beach cordoned off for our group.'

Darkness had fallen, and as they set off across the strip of lawn Derek glanced upwards at the heavens. They looked mouldy: great stains and patches of whiteness spreading as far as the eye could see. The sky was mildewed with stars. There were too many. Not the odd glittering pinpricks one saw on a rare unpolluted night in Europe, but stars as he remembered them from his Australian childhood, swarming and pullulating.

'What a lovely night!'

'We hope you like it.'

As they passed under the low arch in the hedge and he held back the bracts of bougainvillaea for Karina to pass, they came at last within earshot of the band. He could smell honeysuckle as the back of his hand brushed her cool, inoculated arm.

Lovely Barbuda
Our island in the sun
Come to Barbuda
There's fun for everyone . . .

It was like a party, when they at last came upon it. A place of honour had been set for Derek at the head of a long table under lanterns and fairy lights. The Caribbean band was in full swing.

Lovely Barbuda
We hope you will enjoy
Our island of romance
For every girl and boy . . .

When they arrived, dodging under the lanterns, there were cheers and a couple of good-natured whistles.

'Hope we're not keeping you two up,' said Danny Mottram, and there was loud laughter as Karina made claws of her fingers and gave the ribald lads a hell-cat snarl of mock reprimand. Was she blushing?, Derek wondered.

Under a canopy and from behind a striped canvas screen, the aroma of exotic island cuisine fragrantly percolated.

'We've got a couple of little surprises for our star tonight,' announced Jonathan Rushing, after much banging on a wineglass. A well-lubricated cheer ascended through the canopy of dark stirring palm fronds to the astral penicillin above.

A pretty woman, a youthful fifty, and crowned with a chaplet of bougainvillaea, emerged from behind the screen. When Derek saw her they both laughed. It was Vanessa – his faithful make-up lady for as long as he could remember. Derek had been told she was unavailable for the shoot.

'We knew you two liked working together, so Haäg-enstrøm flew her in as a surprise!' Cheers ensued. but Vanessa looked, well, low-keyed.

'I'm not the only surprise,' she whispered as he gave her a hug. 'I nearly died when I found out, but I didn't get a chance to warn you.' A young man who could easily have played the Anthony Perkins role in *Psycho IV* and whom he vaguely recognised, placed before Derek a curious salad of radiccio, calamari and pineapple chunks with a yellow curry sauce. Karina Digby, Jock Blair, Miles King, Tom Goldwasser. Bill Wiley, Danny Mottram, Rob Maclellan, Jonathan Rushing, Anne Forbes, Peter Young, Neil Munro, Phillip Sergeant, Piers Forrester, Wolf Uecker and John Perry all looked on with big smiles. The thought that they had all put into this big surprise; the secrecy, the planning, and the Client's money!

'DINNER IS SERVED!'

There, on the beach, in an apron which would

have done an axe murderer proud and with a plate in her hand, beamed Emma: Caterer to the Stars!

'Fricassee of Hare coming up, and purée of Swede.' With her carrot-coloured hair, her leporine teeth, her dimples, she was so thrilled, so grateful, so hopelessly maladroit, that the gravy from her *chef d'oeuvre*, no doubt intended for the guest of honour, dripped copiously on to the Caribbean sand.

'Sorry about that,' she said.

It was three days before a camera turned. Derek swam and played tennis with Vanessa and Karina; mostly for the pleasure of watching Karina stoop to pick up a ball which unintentionally, but not seldom, he lobbed against the far fence.

The location was on the far side of the island; an unfrequented beach called Two Hand Bay with caves and a seventeenth-century ruin. It was rather inaccessible to tourists, which was why, Derek surmised, the company had seen fit to import a caterer, rather than convey excellent food and refreshments from the resort.

Of course, Derek's chief embarrassment was that Emma and her Myrmidon were a gift to him, the famous gourmand, so he had to regularly choke down her unpalatable concoctions and, moreover, vociferously praise them. The crew, less enjoined to *politesse* than their Star, gazed warily, and sometimes with open revulsion at skate in a parsnip batter served with a camembert and cashew nut sauce, or mushrooms stuffed with strawberry cream cheese, deep fried and served with a kiwi fruit *coulis.* Most of them, including Derek, buried their lunches in the sand and pigged out later on room service.

When they did start rehearsing, Derek began to realise that his fee was well earned. He tried the 'stunt' in his swimming costume first of all. Two cameras had been set up on the beach at a low angle and Derek was taken out to the souped-up submarine in a Boston whaler. The water was exquisite. They got Derek into his harness – it would be invisible under Mrs Petty's costume – and did a few trial runs for the cameras so that Derek could learn to feel secure.

Ankle-deep in water, the strange little craft vibrating beneath his feet, and the sleek, unsubstantial handle of the Haägenstrøm his only purchase, Derek wondered how Mrs Petty was going to fare tomorrow when they tried a 'take'. Probably much better, he decided. Mrs Petty was fearless; she could take a hazardous enterprise like this in her stride. If she fell, or flew off it would be funny; there would be cries of 'fantastic, keep that in!' from a loud hailer on the beach, whereas if Derek muffed it he would probably be beheaded by a propeller. Peter Young, the First Assistant standing in the Boston whaler, handed Derek a Walkman and helped him fit the earphones.

'They want you to try it on for this run, Derek,' he shouted.

'Why?'

'We've got a tie-in with Sony. Doesn't Mrs Petty always listen to her Walkman when she's doing the housework?' Derek grinned and gave Jonathan a thumbs-up sign like a Spitfire pilot in an old movie. The craft wobbled and his hand flew back to the security of the Haägenstrøm handle. The earphones would help muffle the din of the motor which throbbed beneath his feet.

So they had a tie-in with Sony, did they? That explained why most of the executives and hangers-on were sporting brand new Walkmans. They were getting two commercials for the price of one. So what else was new?

Derek entertained these and other cynical reflections as Peter's boat sped back to the shore. He thought, too, of the frustrations of telephoning London. When he did get through it was always the answering machine. Pam, or more likely Doris, must have forgotten to turn it off. In spite of himself, Derek was slightly relieved. His wife and the telephone were not the best of friends and he always replaced the receiver with a feeling of frustration. Down the estranging wire she transmitted a curious sense of disapproval. If he had not known Pam better, he might even have supposed it to be envy. Gibbo was no easier to locate; either busy or out.

It was lonely out there on the lagoon. The figures on the beach looked so small under the palms, with the ruined watchtower in the background; the clusters around the cameras at the water's edge seemed so tiny across the polished aquamarine. Standing to one side on the sand, her hand shielding her eyes, he could only identify Karina.

The director's voice rang out across the water with

incredible clarity. 'Stand by, Derek,' he called through the hailer. 'We seem a long way off but we're very tight on your face. Tomorrow Mrs Petty is going to have to look as though all her Christmasses have come at once, even if she feels like wetting herself. The close-ups will be critical. Now stand by and for starters, we'll try it nice and easy.'

For the rest of the day, Derek learned to get the hang of it. It was actually quite fun. Only when they tried hairpin bends at fairly high speed did he nearly come to grief, but he was surprised how quickly he retrieved his balance. He even managed a few Mrs Petty grins for the distant cameras. The Walkman proved to be an unexpected consolation. He touched a button and The Best of the Beach Boys came ringing through his earphones with astonishing clarity. There he was, Derek Pettyfer, a fifty-year-old Adelaide University drop-out, hurtling across a Caribbean lagoon on a vacuum cleaner listening to 'good, good, good, good vibrations . . .' Life was rather marvellous and tomorrow, Mrs Petty would *love* it!

The crew all applauded him when he got back to the beach a couple of hours later. Jonathan and Karina came over and congratulated him.

'You're gamer than I am,' said Jonathan.

'Did you wear any protection out there?' asked Karina. 'You would have caught a lot of sun.' Derek confessed that he smeared something on earlier, but not much.

'Try this,' she said, kneeling in the sand and producing a bottle of Aloe Vera from the Body Shop.

She patted it on his nose, cheeks, brow and shoulders. He made no protest.

'We should be getting some very nice stuff tomorrow,' said Jonathan, 'and the Client is already over the moon.' He grew confidential.

'Look Derek, I know you're a big fan of Emma's grub but the Client has chartered a chopper and invited a few of us for dinner over on Antigua at the Curtain Pluss Resort tonight. They'd be very chuffed indeed if you'd join us.'

So people did, after all, still say 'chuffed', Derek observed. He also noticed that Karina was looking at him very – how could he describe it – directly. They wanted him to say yes.

'The Curtain Pluss Restaurant has probably got the best wine cellar in the Caribbean,' added Jonathan, as a final inducement to the teetotaller.

'Sure, sounds very nice, I'd love to. I hope Emma hasn't done anything too special tonight.'

Next morning Derek woke early and had a long swim. The excursion to Curtain Pluss had been delightful from the point of view of the food, and rather hard-going in respect of the company. However, he had sat next to Karina, who had amused him, *sotto voce*, with the low-down on Rushing & Associates. She had had a few Pina Coladas, but the others had lapsed into English rowdiness and were not listening.

It seemed that most of the finished commercial would be made in London by computer; even the image of Mrs Petty Hoovering the Caribbean would be electronically faked. This whole costly excursion was just a junket for the boys; the Client was either none the wiser or couldn't care less, and the only footage they would end up using would be a few Mrs Petty close-ups and one establishing shot. Derek was not surprised, but he was beginning to enjoy this junket as well, and Karina's lips, as they breathed this intelligence close to his ear, were not its least pleasurable aspect.

'This is going to be so funny, Derek,' said Vanessa, as she worked on Mrs Petty in the make-up tent. 'We'd better pin the wig on really hard. It wouldn't be a good look if she lost her hair out there.'

'Have we got a few spares?'

'Only one, God help me, so stay erect.'

'As the actress said to the Bishop.' They said this simultaneously, laughed, linked pinkies and declaimed the names of famous poets.

'Umm . . . er . . . Christina Rossetti.'

'Dorothy Nimmo.'

'Who, Derek?'

'How long, do you think?' It was Rob, the Second Assistant.

'She should be with you in about fifteen minutes,' said Vanessa.

'Fantastic,' said Rob. 'Here's the Walkman. They want it fairly obvious on the front of the frock.' Derek and Vanessa rolled eyes at each other. Suddenly however, she stopped in her tracks.

'God, I nearly forgot. This came for you this morning. They paged you, and in the end I signed for it.' She handed Derek a small courier bag.

'I must have been swimming. Be a dear and open it.' He looked in the mirror and applied some more rouge. Mrs Petty was nearly there.

'Looks like a cassette,' said Vanessa, passing him a small plastic box.

There was no note, just a compliments slip. He read the printed name: McColl Holdings. Beneath it someone had written in ink, 'Hope you're getting lots of lovely sunshine. This came into our hands and we think it might interest you. Coral.'

'Do I know a Coral, Vanessa?' he asked, suddenly remembering with a chill that he did.

'You look gorgeous this morning, Mrs Petty, we'd like you on set immediately if you'd be so kind.' It was the director this time, beaming at the sight of his Star in all her finery.

Vanessa made a few adjustments to the dress. 'Now take care,' she said. 'We've only got two more of these frocks. Are you all right?'

'Perfectly fine,' replied Derek, feeling apprehensive nonetheless. He opened the small plastic box and slipped the cassette into his Walkman.

Out there on the glassy water, a perfect sky above, Mrs Petty steeled herself for that single word: 'Action'. The engine snarled beneath her. A man leaning across from the Boston whaler had given the Haägenstrøm cleaning instrument a last minute polish with a spray can of Windolene and a soft cloth.

'Don't forget,' said Rob, pointing towards the

shore, 'one of those cameras is going to be really tight on you.' And with stiffened palms he mimed a box around his face.

Derek took a deep breath as the countdown began, borne to him crisply over the lagoon. He remembered the cassette. This might be a good moment to find out if it was as interesting as Coral seemed to think. It would make a change from the Beach Boys, anyway. He touched the play button.

'ACTION!!'

They were off, Mrs Petty on her broomstick carving a great viridian scroll on the milky blue surface of the water. Back on the beach they crowded round a monitor. Wolf had managed to hold that big close-up of Mrs Petty's ecstatic face, despite the speed and the capricious turns made by the submarine. Why shouldn't he? Wolf was the best action camera operator in the business.

Derek heard a phone ringing and then a woman's voice.

'Hello.'

'How you doin', kiddo?'

'Not bad.'

'Any complaints about last night?'

'Why should there be?'

'You were pretty horny, the old fella's begging for mercy this morning.'

'Where are you?'

'Don't worry, Denise is having her aroma fuckin' therapy. Do you want to talk through a few things?'

'Not now, Ross, Mum's hanging around somewhere.'

'Might make it nicer. Naughtier? What are you doin' now? Where's your fingers?'

'What are you doing?'

'Well, I'm flat out master-minding. Your husband's career, that is. You thought I was going to say master something else didn't you, you filthy-minded little hornbag?'

'Mum's going to see her sister in Birmingham tonight.'

'Looks like I better start tucking into the ginseng and the royal jelly then, doesn't it?'

Derek could stand no more. He took one hand off the vacuum cleaner and fumbled with the Walkman to silence it, but the machine beneath him took a sudden, sickening turn to the left. After teetering violently for what seemed like a minute, Mrs Petty, with flailing arms and flapping red skirts, left her moorings, became airborne for a moment, then landed with a terrible smack and a spectacular splash in the middle of Two Foot Bay.

'Great!' came the director's voice on his loud hailer. 'We've got it in one take, Derek! Those close-ups were fantastic. We're coming out to pick you up.' But Mrs Petty, threshing about in the sea with her mouth full of salt, her dress billowing in the water like a crimson jellyfish, could not hear the laughter and rejoicing on the beach.

Derek had got through the rest of the morning, or been propelled through it, by handshakes, slaps on the back, and innumerable 'fantastic's and 'amazing's. The fuel of flattery. But he felt cold inside, and there was no one he could tell.

Vanessa suspected something. 'Sure you're all right, sweetie?'

'Perfectly.' She had looked slightly hurt to be excluded from his confidence. Actually, Derek had twisted something on his ejection from the Haägenstrøm, but that day he remained silent on the subject of his pain.

They had hauled him on to the Boston whaler like a slapstick Icarus, or a bedraggled red kite, irreparably foundered. Karina had been there on the shore to help him out of the waterlogged drag and he let himself, with a few jocular protests, be wrapped in towels and bundled off to his Spanish cottage for a well-earned rest. On a table in his pink and blue room reposed a gaudy and inedible collation bearing Emma's unmistakable signature.

Derek showered numbly. At first he tried to work out a plan, but he soon gave up. Should he call a lawyer? Should he fly back and confront Ross? Confront both of them? If he had not blundered into McColl's office that morning last week, he would still be none the wiser. Gibbo and Pam would have carried on their affair behind his back. What had he done to deserve any of this? Instinctively he knew that the best way to handle it was to say nothing; let them get on with it, thinking he suspected nothing. That way, with the further assistance of Coral Fortune, he could lead them into some trap and ultimately to their punishment.

Derek was not certain what the trap or the punishment would be – there would be time to work that out – but he knew that if he acted impulsively, out of affronted pride or jealousy or rage or malice, all would be lost. He would forfeit his power, and lose control of the situation for ever. Regaining control was the important thing. He had, in a short time, put Pam where she was – 'all kippers and curtains' in Doris's phrase – and as for Ross Gibb: Derek had made his fortune. They were both his creations, in a way, so whatever happened, he must restore his dominion over them. He would wait his turn.

It seemed all right in theory, of course – righteous and melodramatic – but in practice, was he vindictive enough? Or sufficiently circumspect? Derek thumped the bed and howled with rage and desolation.

He must have slept . . . an hour? Two? He had not even heard one of the louvred doors to the garden open and close, or the scratch of the rattan blind, or a rustle of silk.

'Mr Pettyfer?' It was Karina. He turned over and looked up, unclenching his fists and adjusting the towel around his waist. She stood above him in a purple silk kimono. 'I thought you might like a massage. I studied it at Holborn Aromatherapy Centre. I'm meant to be quite good.'

'How marvellous,' Derek said, suddenly feeling tears in his eyes. 'I hurt myself a bit this morning.' She looked genuinely anxious. 'Something really hurt me.'

'Turn over,' she said, 'I bought out most of the Body Shop before I left London.'

Derek obeyed. He lay there heavily with his head

turned to one side on the pillow, looking across at the rather striking Haitian primitive above the mini bar. He tried to remember what that huge villainous-looking figure in the black horn-rimmed glasses, black suit and narrow black tie was meant to represent: was it Duvalier? Marmaduke, the equally black, or as Hampstead would say, 'rather splendid' house-boy, had explained it all in superstitious whispers, but Derek had not taken much in. His head hurt. Could it be he had sunstroke as well?

He felt the cold dollops of emulsion splash beneath his shoulders and Karina's long caressing hands. He parted his legs a little and she knelt over him, one knee between his thighs. The hands fanned across his back and swept down his spine to his coccyx. He felt her fingers pull the towel down a little over his buttocks.

'Too soft, too hard? Say!'

'Marvellous.' He might have dropped off a few times but when he woke again with a start, her hands were still moving down his body.

'Sorry, did I snore?'

'A little, why not?'

'Sorry.'

'Turn over now.' There was a reason why Derek thought this should be postponed. 'Come on, Mr Pettyfer,' she whispered. As he did, the towel unravelled itself.

'Sorry!' She knelt right over him now, and Derek closed his eyes.

When she drew her fingers down from his shoulders, across his breast, she gently scratched his nipples. He felt her long hair whispering across his face. He could smell Tuberose by Mary Chess and the faint and not disagreeable odour of tobacco on her breath. She was really taking her time.

'Mr Pettyfer?'

'Please, Karina, please it's, it's . . .'

'Stand up,' she commanded. 'I need it hard now!' Almost violently she scrambled on to her knees across the bed and thrusting one hand between her legs, roughly guided him in.

Standing on tiptoe beside the bed in the dim room, his fingers resting lightly on her hips, Derek desperately sought some distracting and subduing image. He dared not look down at the girl who knelt before him like a cleft and sallow fruit; instead he fixed his eyes on that sinister image on the wall. He remembered who it was in the painting now: Baron Samedi, Ruler of Graveyards.

Outside, through the slats of sunlight, he could hear the rhythmic sparging of the sprinkler and the chittering of insects. Overhead, in the bedroom, the fan palpitated its cool zephyrs, but there was that other, more urgent rhythm of his skin slapping hers, as Karina, her head kneading a pillow, murmured a brutal litany of encouragement.

'I'd like to see you again,' he said afterwards.

'Would you?' she said, with what seemed like genuine disbelief. 'It would be nice, but your life is complicated enough.'

'Oh?' he said, remembering.

'I'm leaving with most of the others tonight.'

'Goodbye, Karina,' said Derek, holding out his

arms; he realised that they had never kissed. But she did not come to him. Slipping back into her kimono, she picked up her bottle of jojoba oil scented with apricots, and was already at the door.

'Why did you really come here this afternoon?'

She smiled. 'To give you this, Mr Pettyfer. You left it on the beach with a tape in it. Anyone could have picked it up.' She put the Walkman on his bedside table, blew a chaste kiss and went out into the warm afternoon.

17

Coral

ESTELLE WEINGLASS LIT another St Moritz and settled back into the pillows. It was five to seven in the evening and she was still wearing her quilted brunch coat from Bergdorf Goodman with its little floral sprigs. She turned down the corner of *Esquire*, for she was rather enjoying an article by a former client of her husband's, Joan Rivers, on the pleasures of spending money. It was the headline that had first caught her attention:

A RIVERS RUNS THROUGH IT.

In that overheated bedroom, with its permanently closed curtains, Estelle was never precisely conscious of the time, but as seven o'clock approached, some inner chronometer unfailingly reminded her to search amongst the ashtrays, periodicals and tousled bed-linen for her remote control. For on Sky 1 every night, William Shatner introduced *Rescue*, the Real Life Emergency Drama, and she was once more transported to a world of red and blue flashing lights, grainy streetscapes, wobbly hand-held excursions up tacky motel corridors, corpses and crying children. She had met William Shatner once, somewhere, when she used to go to parties with Woody.

On her dressing-table, amongst all the scent bottles and powder puffs, there were framed photographs commemorating her vanished social life. There they were with Frank Sinatra; the agent and his wife pressed a little too closely, too affectionately to the crooner's tuxedo'd bosom to give a convincing impression of old buddies. Another showed her twenty years before at a table with Richard Burton; she beaming, he glassy-eyed. A third photograph pictured the Weinglasses being presented to Princess Alexandra in a line-up at some Leicester Square Charity Night. The picture revealed Estelle's old Jewish profile and her previous, rather attractive smile, before she had visited the clinic in Los Angeles in search of youth, and had expensively acquired her new lips *comme negresse à plateau*, and her clitoral nose.

There was a great deal of shouting on the screen and banging of police car doors. A drug addict, pinned to the ground by two policewomen, was screaming obscenities. Nonetheless, through all this mayhem, Estelle could discern the sound of the front doorbell. It rang several times before she heard her husband's feet thumping down the four flights to open the door. Estelle dipped two raptorial fingers with their sculptured, acrylic extensions into a box of Leonidas chocolates on her bedside table, and hauled her skinny legs over the side of the bed.

She always liked to know who called. Munching the candy, she looked through a crack in the bedroom door and just caught a glimpse of Woody lumbering back upstairs, followed by a short young man in jeans and a leather jacket.

'Only one more flight and then some little stairs . . .' her husband was saying.

When her programme had finished, Estelle Weinglass lay there for a moment amongst her pillows, worrying a little about what it was she had forgotten, or meant to do. Suddenly she remembered and a vestigial sense of responsibility stirred: she was neglecting her duties as a hostess. Estelle ground half a St Moritz into a partially devoured walnut creme and tottered downstairs to the kitchen. Fifteen minutes later she emerged with the thermos, the two teacups and the cheesecake from Richoux, and with her jingling tray and a fortifying cigarette, commenced the long ascent to Santa's Grotto.

By the time she had reached the final flight of wooden steps to the garret, she could hear Shirley Bassey's version of 'Jingle Bells Rock' resounding beneath the Georgian roof. Normally, particularly if Woody was reading through one of his client's scripts, she would knock. But tonight, the door to the Grotto had sprung ajar, and all she could see with her good eye – the other being permanently shuttered against smoke – was her husband standing there, his hands on his hips, wearing the scarlet and white ermine-trimmed coat of Santa Claus and a matching stocking hat. His young visitor seemed to be kneeling on the floor doing something unusual, but whatever it was, they were both too preoccupied, it seemed, to welcome the arrival of refreshments.

Quietly, Estelle descended to the kitchen, emptied the thermos, put the cups back in the cupboard and restored the cheesecake to its box in the refrigerator. Then she returned to her bed, lit another cigarette and watched *The Return to the Valley of the Dolls* on Channel Four.

Flying home, after spending another twenty-four hours marooned on Barbuda, Derek slept like a convalescent. With Karina gone, and Vanessa also, he had been left on the island with the Inner Circle, which was dominated by Jonathan Rushing. Fortunately, Emma too had departed to cater for some Anglican bar mitzvah in Hampshire; so Derek, with a jest ever on his lips, but with a heavy heart, was forced to sit through three more costly meals, which were no more than elaborate wine tastings interspersed with food. It was at one of these Lucullan feasts that Danny Mottram confessed to Derek how dangerous the stunt had been.

'You never met that submarine pilot, did you, Derek old son?'

'We kept him well under wraps,' laughed Jonathan.

'What a nutter!' added Miles. 'I think he must have been on something. Did you see those propeller blades? My Gawd!'

They all drank to Derek's bravery, or was it his folly?, the actor wondered. Fortunately, they stopped just short of divulging the enormous insurance premium that had been taken out on his life.

After this, he had avoided the hearty and jocose tennis parties and had tried swimming and long walks, but he was now overwhelmed with a sense of flatness and accidie.

At last at Gatwick Airport, waiting for his ice-cold luggage to slither and slam on to the carousel, Derek, with fingers also like ice, found a fifty pence coin and once more tried his flat. He should give them due warning of his arrival, he felt; it would be a tactical error to barge in on anything. But this time, the line was busy.

Until the last, not only the Chief – the president and major shareholder of Rushing & Associates – but all his Associates as well, remained indefatigably excited by their enterprise. As they finally dispersed at Gatwick and put Derek into the limousine which would take about four times longer to get him home than the train to Victoria, they reaffirmed their undying excitement.

Jonathan had leaned into the car and grasped his hand. 'Derek, keep in touch, I've just had the Client on the mobile and they are still *incredibly excited.*'

Now that the bloody commercial was as good as made, thought Derek, couldn't they let their excitement simmer down a bit, to something more like quiet esteem – or even gratitude? He experienced the mixed emotions of a highly-paid whore who, having employed all her skills during the night, is informed in the morning by her proud client that he still has an unflagging erection.

Jonathan Rushing went on to mention competitive brands of household appliances, '. . . at the end of the day Derek, when this commercial airs, they'll all be *dead in the water!*' Derek felt that this was an insensitive metaphor, considering that they and their insurers fully expected him to meet an identical fate.

Before the car sped off, Jonathan added: 'The Walkman's yours by the way Derek, have fun with it!'

Creeping back to London through the traffic, in the excessive comfort of the ridiculous car, Derek, after some hesitation, once more put the miniature headphones in his ears and listened to Coral Fortune's tape. The conversation he had overheard on the Haägenstrøm – which had nearly induced a fatal accident – went on slightly longer, but contained no new information. Glumly he auditioned the unedifying dialogue, then played the whole thing through again. His brave vows of vengeance, his intricate plots, all seemed vain and pointless today. They were, perhaps, only the reactions of someone in a movie or in a work of fiction.

His car stopped at some traffic lights and he looked out at the gloom; the unbelievable shabbiness of south London in October. The desolate shops, the mean garbage-strewn streets. The city was a huge, expensive slum. The driver had taken an ill-advised short cut and Derek found himself stalled in traffic in Tooting Broadway, outside a forlorn Italian restaurant, the 'Del Capri'. Within, he glimpsed a deracinated dago skulking amongst the red-check tabletops, making passes over congealed canneloni with what resembled the leg of a billiard table. The absurd vehicle rolled on for half a block and stopped once more outside a kebab house. Across the road and ankle-deep in rubbish, a Rastafarian traffic warden loitered with ticket book poised, waiting for a housewife's meter to expire.

Slumped in his upholstered cocoon, Derek's thoughts returned pessimistically to his marriage. He realised that he was totally powerless: in spite of his arrogant schemes, his struggle for a dominant role in this impossible situation was futile. He was as autonomous as that old crumpled copy of the *Daily Mirror* blowing fitfully along the kerb and twitching beneath the traffic.

Home at Ashley Mansions at last, ascending in his own lift, to his own apartment, to see his own wife, Derek felt inexplicably guilty. If only he had got through on the telephone at Gatwick, the ice, so to speak, would have been broken – and he less apprehensive when the physical encounter took place. There was also a possibility, unconsidered by Derek until now, that Pam might immediately intend to make a clean breast of things: she might either have packed her bags, or confess tearfully to an insane fling with his manager, and beg forgiveness. There was even a third, though remote probability, that the tape had been a hoax: a cruel joke perpetrated by some nameless adversary.

Now that he stood before what had been his own mahogany front door, feeling the bevel of his own key between his fingers, Derek began to dread what he might stumble upon. He hesitated. What would be the worst scenario? To enter the flat and find Gibbo sodomising Pam on the rug? To catch them *in flagrante?* To be greeted by his wife wearing a fresh magenta love-bite? Or to discover damp and mucilaginous patches on his bed linen?

Reluctantly Derek brought himself to acknowledge the most painful bereavement of all. Alas, the above horrors would appal him far less than were he to discover that Pam had installed strip lighting in his house, or resurfaced the floor with black Pirelli rubber. It was not his wife or his friend he would mourn the most: it was his flat and its contents; the Beautiful Apartment.

Perhaps he was going mad; perhaps he had picked up something in Antigua that atrophied human feelings and enhanced his sensitivity to things. Or it could be some secretion of the soul, a kind of heroin, numbing and protecting him from intolerable pain.

It was, of course, very possible that he was about to step into a high-tech nightmare; a vision of his demonic mother-in-law sprang to mind, attired at his expense in a silver lurex jumpsuit, and on a skateboard, like garlic bread on wheels.

Derek gave the new doorbell a monitory blast, turned the key and entered. At least they hadn't changed the lock. But to his surprise, apart from the hideous steel door and *grisaille* walls, all was the same; nothing had changed. Even some of the Piranesis had been restored to their hooks. Music drifted from the drawing-room; something rather beautiful, but not Piazzolla. He had tried calling for Pam, but when he opened his mouth, no sound came.

'Is that you, love?' Her voice rang down the passage.

'Yes,' he cried. 'Surprise visit.'

'Not really,' she called. 'I rang the agency and they said to expect you about now.' His wife appeared, smiling and wiping clay-caked fingers on her improvised smock. Derek noticed the monogrammed pocket: it was one of his best silk shirts. He moved awkwardly towards her.

'Don't get too near love. I'm covered with clay.'

'Didn't you get all my messages?' asked Derek.

'I can't work the bloody machine, love, you know that.'

'You mean *nobody* can get through?'

'Gibbo always seems to.'

That was bold, Derek thought, she must feel very safe. 'How is he?'

'He's fine, well I think he is. I haven't heard from him for about three days or so.'

'Nice of him to keep in touch,' said Derek, trying to make this sound genuine.

'I like Denise, I suppose,' confessed Pam.

'You do, do you?'

'Poor love, couldn't be much fun married to that randy sod!'

'Well,' said Derek, disarmed by her bravado. 'If you ever get the answering machine working, you'll find about ten loving messages from me.'

'Sw-e-e-t!' Still keeping her distance, she put her arms around his neck.

Derek stiffened. Where did she get 'sweet' from? It was Sloane hyperbole.

'I blame that woman,' said Pam crossly.

'It's not Denise's fault, for Christ's sake!' cried Derek.

'What are you on about, love? I mean that mousey little woman who came to check the phone just after you went to Antigua.'

'Who?'

'Well it was perfectly OK before she tinkered with it.'

Derek's penny dropped. He pictured Coral Fortune with a tool bag and an overall. 'Oh, her?'

'Yes.'

'I'd been having a lot of hiccups with it,' improvised Derek, 'so I got Telecom's VIP services to come and check it out. I'm glad she showed up.'

'Fat lot of good she did, but wouldn't you know with British fuckin' Telecom!'

Derek pricked up his ears; had he just heard a hint of Gibbo? 'That's a rather crude expression coming from you, Pam.'

'I'm a working-class girl, remember? You're such a prig, and a snob and a hypocrite, love. If you don't like the way your manager talks, you know what to do, don't you?'

I wish I did, thought Derek.

She took his hand. 'Before we go to bed, I want you to see Lionel.' She led him into the dining-room. There, on his beautiful early Victorian rosewood table, mercifully shrouded with a sheet, leered the saturnine features of Inge's husband, twice life-sized. The bust was rather stylised, but unmistakable. He felt, briefly, a healing resurgence of admiration for her talent.

'It's very good, very good. But haven't you made him about twenty years too young?'

Pam bridled. 'Have I? I modelled what I saw, love, he's only seventy-two anyway; that's not so old these days. I mean, listen to him now!' Derek missed the point.

'I'm sorry?'

'*Listen* to him, love.' She ran to the gramophone and turned up the volume. He saw the control panel on his new Bang & Olufsen was heavily stuccoed with clay-coloured fingerprints. Pam stood in the middle of the room and swayed to the music, her eyes cast upwards like a rapturous Murillo Madonna. The adagio from the Beethoven Cello Sonata Opus 69 in A major, played by Lionel Pinkhill, filled the room with its epiphanous beauty.

'How about that then, love,' she said, 'isn't it fan-fuckin'-tastic!'

Ms Coral Fortune ascended to the fourth floor of Harrods on the escalator. She rarely visited the store so today was something of a treat. Later, she might find something nice for her mother, always a hard person to buy for. She looked at her watch; dead on time, she thought.

Passing through the Georgian Restaurant, she went out to the Terrace Bar, and there, seated alone at the far end pretending to read a newspaper, she saw him.

Derek glanced up from the *Telegraph* and observed the small, bird-like woman in the Aquascutum raincoat, the green umbrella and the plastic over-shoes moving towards him. He stood up.

'Thank you for coming, Ms Fortune . . .'

'Coral please, I prefer it.'

'Thank you for coming, Coral. I have to say this is all getting very unpleasant.'

'The truth sometimes is,' she replied with a dry little smile, half compassionate, half I-told-you-so. He stood and helped her remove her coat. Underneath she wore the same grey suit, the same blouse, the same cameo. Immediately she picked up the menu and brought her spectacles, secured with a gold chain, up to her eyes.

'I don't have long in terms of time, I'm afraid. At least, not for the first part of our meeting . . .' A waiter appeared as she looked up at him. 'I think I'll just have a snack, may I? Perhaps the avocado and prawn open sandwich and a nice cappuccino, if I may.'

'Just a cappuccino for me, please,' said Derek.

When the waiter had gone she delved into a rather large handbag, and produced a manilla envelope, which she passed across to Derek. 'When I said our little meeting should be in two parts, I was being rather selfish. You see, you'll need time to listen to the cassette in that envelope. It's something that recently found its way into our hands.' Again, the small desiccated smile. A cold hand entered Derek's breast and closed around his heart. 'After that, I'll meet you again, if I may, later this afternoon and discuss what next, in terms of our involvement.'

'Will, er, will it take that long, I mean, listening?'

'Oh no, not long, but I have a confession to make. I'm a bit of a collector.'

'A collector?' he said.

'Yes. Georgian Silver. There's a sale in half an hour across the road at Bonhams and I have my eye on a salt cellar. When you talked in terms of Harrods, and then the Georgian Restaurant, I regarded it as a happy omen.'

'I suppose happy omens would be a novelty in your job,' said Derek, but she ignored his sarcasm and began nibbling, rabbit-like, at the excellent sandwich.

'You did bring your Walkman as you said you would?' Derek patted his briefcase. 'A few other quite important bits and pieces in terms of information have dropped into our lap, but I'd rather talk about those anon, if I may?'

She's a bit of a 'May I' in her own way, Derek thought, without the talents or inclinations of the obliging girl in his past.

When she had hurried off to her Sale, agreeing to meet at four o'clock in the same place, Derek sat for a while staring at the trembling *Telegraph*. They were promoting a special feature in next weekend's magazine about sex and overeating. The headline, a tribute to Marquez, read:

LOVE IN A TIME OF CALORIES.

Pippa Billinghurst was slipping, he reflected.

At length he paid the bill, and taking his time, but with a feeling of dread, went downstairs through menswear to the Green Man Pub on the lower ground floor. Passing through the bar, he descended to the Gents, which was still, miraculously, as it had been in his drinking days. Solid mahogany stalls, and wooden seats like the Garrick Club before they updated it. In the bad old days he would sometimes make himself comfortable in one of these finely appointed cubicles with a half bottle of Teachers discreetly concealed in a green and gold Harrods bag.

This time he sat on the lowered lid, fitted the new cassette and adjusted the earphones. Coral Fortune had been a bit like a matter-of-fact doctor, asking him to go away and come back with a specimen. He was in the right place to produce that, but all he was likely to return with would be a specimen of his own augmented misery.

First, as before, he heard the ringing sound, then a click.

'Hello, Pam Black.'

'Pamela?'

'Yes, is that you Bob?'

'Pamela, I just thought I'd say thanks for doin' what y'did last night.'

'That's all right then.'

'No, I mean you're married to this queer fella now so I didn't expect it.'

'Let's say I gave it to you for old times' sake, Bob.'

'We 'ad a few good times then, didn't we, love?'

'Bob, have you been on the drink by any chance?'

'God, you know when I saw you in that new place of yours I thought "our Pamela's come up in the world, God love her!".'

'Thanks, Bob, is that all then?'

'No, I mean you're great, Pam. You're really great. All that kinky new underwear, and all that glam gear. I never thought you was a lady!'

'Bob, last night was great, love, but I'm working right now, OK then?'

'OK too. But Pamela, if some time . . . you know, I mean . . . like I feel I need another . . . you know!'

'I'm here, love. I'll do what I can, but only if he's away. If I answer the phone, we can arrange something, all right then, love?'

'Thanks me babs, I love you.'

'Get on with you!'

As the line went dead, Derek was stunned. Who was this Bob? A plumber or a min-cab driver, or something? He had been absent for just over a week. Was there any other recent bride in London, or in the world for that matter, who could amuse herself so energetically in the interval as his wife had clearly done? And she had even managed to knock off a piece of sculpture in her spare time.

A second ring sounded on the edited tape.

'Hello, Pamela Black.'

'Pam, it's me. What are you wearing?'

'Not much as a matter of fact.'

'I like the sound of that.'

'Wait a minute . . .'

There was a clatter as of a telephone receiver,

carelessly set down on a hard surface. Then loud classical music. It sounded like Beethoven.

'Can you hear that?'

'Of course I can. Don't you think I don't know it backwards.'

'I was just lying here listening to it when you called, you must be psychic.'

'Lying there alone and naked, listening to me? I hope you weren't being a good girl.'

'I'm not telling.'

'I can hear it in your voice; I'd like to . . .'

'Now Lionel, *you* have to be a good boy until I see you for your next sitting.'

'Sitting isn't quite the right word in our case, is it Pam?'

Laughter.

'I have a proposal.'

'I'm already married, kind sir.'

'No, a proposal for next Saturday.'

'No way, he'll be back.'

'I'll be in Birmingham playing a marvellous cello concerto by a woman who's just being rediscovered. I'll stay overnight at the Meteyard Hotel, in the Chamberlain Suite on the sixteenth floor.'

'I suppose . . .'

'Say yes.'

'I'm thinking aloud. I suppose I could easily borrow my mother's car and drive to Birmingham on Saturday morning: tell him I'm going to see my mother. She's been up there for a few days already. But she chickened out and took the train this time.'

'Would he buy that?'

'He'd rather I went up to see Mum than she came down to see me. He can't stand her.'

'Poor Pam.'

'I'll be there, Lionel, what do I do?'

'There'll be a ticket for the concert in your name at the box office at the Symphony Hall. It would be indiscreet to meet backstage. Come to the Chamberlain Suite at the hotel at exactly eleven thirty and knock three times on the door. I'll be there waiting.'

'How exciting. I love a little intrigue . . .'

Derek stopped the tape in disgust. She liked a little intrigue, did she? That was the understatement of the century! It was incredible how the bitch managed to keep these liaisons going, independent of each other. Under different circumstances, it might be a cause for admiration, even awe, but when Derek thought about how much contempt she must feel for him – what coldness, in a word, what hatred – he froze inside. A detail, trivial by comparison to all the rest, remained in his mind.

'I could easily borrow my mother's car'. That was *his* car, his BMW requisitioned by Doris. Was this the sexually reticent, women's lib, going dutch, somewhat ascetic waif he had taken under his wing, and whose teeth he had fixed? Within a few months she was screwing his manager, parading in kinky underwear for plumbers and masturbating on the telephone for the delectation of geriatric cellists. They all seemed to be interested in items of her underwear too. When he purchased them, he had never dreamed how much pleasure he would be providing, or for how many.

Derek ripped out the headphones and stuffed the Walkman in the pocket of his overcoat. He noticed a small, green Harrods bag on the floor beside the pedestal, picked it up and looked inside. It was an empty Teachers bottle. So, this was still an upmarket refuge for solitary drinkers! To think that all those years ago he had believed he was the only one: uniquely sensitive and misunderstood.

Looking at the ineffably sad and empty bottle in its olive plastic sac, he imagined that his own *doppelgänger* had left it there; this cryptic sign from the past. Or perhaps, Derek Pettyfer had just gone on drinking, and he was someone else! It felt that way sometimes.

As Derek left the cubicle, and as an instinctive ritual, washed his hands, he thought about those incredible dialogues on the tape. How would another man react under the circumstances? Well, at least today I didn't need a drink, he thought with some satisfaction, as he ascended the escalator.

Derek waited at a table in the Terrace Bar for about forty-five minutes before Coral returned. She was all smiles.

'It's your fault, Derek,' she said, rather too chattily, sitting down and immediately picking up a menu. 'If I hadn't come to Knightsbridge to see you, I could have saved myself nearly two thousand pounds, in terms of expenditure.'

'Oh?' said Derek. Did she really expect him to share in her jolly little shopping jaunts after an earful of those tapes?

'Yes,' she continued excitedly, 'I was only going to

bid for a rather modest Bateman piece, but in the end I went mad and bought a lovely pair of Paul Storr salt cellars of about 1818 – it's his best period you know.'

The waiter appeared and she looked up at him over her glasses.

'I'd really like a large scotch, may I?'

'May I too?' said Derek, reaching for the two silver objects she had placed proudly on the table between them. 'May I' was infectious. If you can't beat them, Derek thought, join them. 'Oh, of course you may, Coral. Sorry,' he said, and then to the waiter: 'A large scotch, and a cup of English Breakfast tea for me, and some cake.'

He looked at the fine silver objects.

'You've really lashed out!' To his amazement she blushed as she put them carefully back in a carry bag.

'It's an illness, I'm afraid. I can't help myself.'

'Perhaps my wife can't help it either.'

'What's that?'

'All this sex. It's like an illness. She may be a nymphomaniac. She may need help.'

Coral shook her head. 'Not from you. I think you have to protect yourself, and think in terms of your own interests now.'

'What about Ross – my manager?'

'We haven't had much luck there. He seems to be away for a few days and there have been difficulties in terms of intercepting his telephone. At least . . .' she hastily corrected herself, 'some people we know, who sometimes help us, say we won't get a report until next week. In the meantime we managed to get those recordings from your own line.'

Derek grimaced at the first sip of tea: it was Earl Grey, of course; bath salts. He spent the rest of the interview with Coral Fortune waving vainly in the direction of oblivious waiters.

'I didn't tell you to tap my phone.'

'You said, he might let something slip to your wife that he mightn't let slip to you.'

'Well, he did, didn't he?' exclaimed Derek irritably. 'He slipped her *himself*, as you have no doubt heard!'

'I can understand your anger; we began in terms of a business investigation and we stumbled on another sort of intrigue.'

'I suppose that costs extra.'

Coral delved into her bag. 'Oh, here's our charges up-to-date. They are on the high side, I'm afraid, but the people who help us take expensive risks.'

Derek opened the envelope and considered the bill. It was an impressive number. 'Cash, I presume.'

'That would be helpful.'

Glancing around the restaurant, Derek furtively counted out the money in fifty-pound notes. Prudently, he had been to the bank that morning.

'I suppose I must do my bit to help in the conservation of Georgian silver.' His sarcasm seemed to go over her little mousey head. She took the money absent-mindedly.

'Those salts are lovely, aren't they? I'm thrilled I bought them.'

He paid the infinitely smaller restaurant bill.

'We'll need to know when Mr Gibb is back in residence. He may need surveillance.'

'How should I know? They sometimes go to Paris for a few days, I'm rarely informed. I only got back yesterday afternoon and I haven't telephoned him yet – frankly, I don't know what to say; I'm still stunned, I can't trust myself.'

'Quite. Well let us know.'

Derek looked around. 'Is this really a good place to meet? I mean, people seeing us together.'

Coral actually laughed as he eased the raincoat back over her bird-like shoulders. 'Not to worry. They'll think we're a couple of scheming silver collectors, hatching something.' She peered at her unhappy client. '*You look just like an antique dealer!*'

Derek felt, on reflection, that Coral's observation was the single most insulting thing that anyone had ever said to him in his entire life.

Polly Again

IT SOUNDED LIKE the *Valses Romantiques* of Chabrier. It was.

Derek was pleased to find he recognised the music that drifted down from Inge's house into Akenside Road, Hampstead. She always had good taste. Her father had been a music critic in Stockholm. How strange that Lionel, unaware of this affinity, had latched on to her on that transatlantic flight nine years before.

Junewyn opened the door. She was taking Miranda and Joshua to a party.

'It's just around the corner,' she said. 'I'll be back in a wee while thanks.'

Inge kissed the children. 'Not too much cake, promise.'

'You summoned me,' said Derek.

'Come in.'

Over real tea and crumpets beside the Aga in Inge's kitchen, he let her speak first.

'You know Junewyn?'

'Just met her, it's only my long-term memory that's shot.'

'What is the one thing that Junewyn, Raewyn, Deswyn and Bronwyn have in common?'

'Pass.'

'They are all New Zealanders, and every Saturday they meet at Sheila's Brasserie at Covent Garden for lunch and a gossip.'

'Is that why you said this meeting was urgent?'

'Last Saturday Bronwyn, Gibbo's nanny, arrived at lunch in floods of tears.'

'Who told you this?'

'My Junewyn.'

'So?' Derek was having difficulty containing his impatience.

'Well,' began Inge. 'First you ought to know that there was a robbery at Denross two weeks ago.'

'Two weeks ago? But Gibbo would have told me!'

'Exactly. Anyway, nothing much was stolen but the office was a hell of a mess. Gibbo didn't seem too fazed, but Bronwyn felt he was very put out. Next morning he gave her a cheque for a month's pay and insisted she take a couple of days off. On the Thursday night, she went to *Miss Saigon* with Raewyn and stayed over.'

'Fascinated as I am by the social life of expatriate Kiwis, Inge, I fail to see where this saga is taking us.'

'Bronwyn got back to Weybridge on the Friday night, three days after you'd gone to Antigua, incidentally, and . . . nothing!'

'Nothing?'

'*Marie Celeste.* The house was empty because, take a deep breath, Derek, your manager Ross Gibb and his wife and children have done a runner.'

'What?'

'They've left this country – gone – vanished.'

Derek tried to seize upon the single most serious consequence of an absconded manager; was unable to do so, so merely allowed his brain to become an emotional maelstrom. Finally he exclaimed: 'McColls should have known that!'

'They certainly should have,' said Inge. 'What the hell were they doing?'

'Tapping my wife's phone,' said Derek. 'According to these tapes,' and he flung two cassettes on to Inge's kitchen table, 'Gibbo gave Pam a farewell fuck before he pissed off.'

'You really amaze me. Oh Derek!' Inge got up and put her arms around her friend. 'My God, how awful!'

'I might as well tell you, it gets worse,' he said. 'Pam is planning to spend Saturday night in Lionel's bed at the Meteyard Hotel, Birmingham – it's on the tape.'

Inge seized a cassette and looked at it wild-eyed, as though it might impart its inauspicious message through the sense of sight or touch. She had gone very white.

'I'll make a cup of tea, and you give these a quick listen.' He put the Walkman on the kitchen table.

When the tea was made, he put a cup before her. Slowly she removed the earphones. 'He'd better watch it,' she said in a strange voice. 'I've seen the test results from the cardiologist, and he hasn't yet.'

'We'll stop it,' said Derek.

'Why?' said Inge. She looked suddenly quite ugly, Derek thought. 'Would you want Pam back, would I want Lionel? Christ, I nearly threw him out over Antoinette Diggins.'

'I heard something about that,' said Derek.

'Who didn't!' fleered Inge. 'He's still besotted, even though they haven't seen each other for years, I know that. He gets all twitchy when he sees her picture in the paper.'

'But the children?'

'They cry when they see him. He's never there for them. It was the same with his first wife, poor Joan, apparently.'

'Don't you feel something for him?'

Inge, to Derek's surprise, rummaged in a drawer and produced a packet of Camel's. She lit one, inhaled, and blew a long cloud of camphor-coloured smoke.

She considered how she would phrase her next disclosure. 'He's very odd in bed, Derek, and especially *out of bed.* Let's say he's a bit of a chandelier artist.'

Derek raised his eyebrows and looked into his cup.

Inge elaborated. 'If it was only the occasional swing from a chandelier, I might have just closed my eyes and thought of Sweden.' She grimaced.

'I've met one,' said Derek, remembering the Kemble Hotel, 'only a woman.'

Inge, at the kitchen table, plucked a fragment of tobacco off the tip of her tongue.

'I didn't know you smoked,' said Derek.

'Only in times of crisis, so that's three a day.'

Inge was very upset. Derek let her ramble.

After a few minutes she brightened up. 'I had a very good idea at Pinky and Perky's last month,' she said. 'I didn't quite realise what a good idea it was, at the time.'

'Pray tell.'

'No – not yet – perhaps never. But promise me something, Derek.'

'Anything, you dear thing.' They held hands over the table.

'Today is Thursday; on Saturday, Pam drives to Birmingham, only she'll tell you she's visiting her mother. Let her go.'

'Let her go?'

'Yes, be nice to her, be vague, be unsuspecting and let her go.'

'Are you sure, Inge?'

'Just lend me those tapes. I want to check Lionel's room number.'

'You're not planning something silly?'

'Not silly Derek,' she said, dancing around the kitchen and kissing him hard on the lips. 'Not a bit silly!'

'You're a cool customer, Inge,' he said.

'I'm Swedish.'

'Is there anything in life you really dread?'

'What every woman dreads,' she replied thoughtfully.

'You mean the menopause, cervical cancer?'

'Heavens no,' she said laughing, 'going to a dinner party and being seated next to a banker.'

'Can you turn that down, Poll? You've played the same thing basically for the last hour and a half, I'm going doolally!'

His flatmate, in tights, leotard and pointe shoes was doing strenuous *pliés* against the straight back of their Conran couch, as the stereo played the rather too sprightly scherzo from the *Divertissement* by Jean Françaix.

'I'm rehearsing, Kenneth, or are you blind as well as deaf? I've got a new ballet opening at Covent Garden one week from now.'

'Oh, Poll!' He turned away from his word processor. 'Give me a break. You've flogged that joke to death. You've got your new dinner-manglers now, so you don't have to keep up the Antoinette Diggins bullshit any longer. C'mon, wakey wakey! You're Polly Garland again now.' He walked over to where she was stretching at her improvised bar and snapped his fingers in front of her eyes as he had seen hypnotists do, but she still went on mechanically executing her *pliés* like Olympia in *Hoffmann*.

'OK, OK, you win, Antoinette; flog the joke to death why don't you? Turn up at Covent Garden next week and show them how it's really done!' He returned to his computer, but Polly's obsession had unnerved him. He hoped she wasn't going to keep this up much longer. It was a bit spooky actually.

Kenneth decided he might try to divert her attention to something more important: himself.

'Listen to this.' He put his palms together, clamped them between his thighs, and rocking slightly back and forth, read his own words on the computer screen.

'Stop, Derek, you're frightening me, and you're frightening my little boy.

Give us another whisky Belinda or fair dinkum, I'll knock your teeth so far down your throat you'll have to put your toothbrush up your freckle to clean them.'

As Kenneth hoped, Polly had snapped out of her terpsichorean reverie.

'What's that?' She turned off the music.

'That's dialogue, Poll, authentic Australian dialogue. It's Derek Pettyfer drunk in 1982 talking to his first wife, in the words he would have used at the time.

'You're a flaming galah Belinda, give me that old frock of yours, I'm going to put it on and go to that audition in London under an assumed flaming name.

What's that may I ask?

Stone the crows, I've got it. My name's Pettyfer isn't it? How about Mrs Petty!?

You're brilliant Derek!

Then how about another few tubes of ice-cold Fosters, you old wowser. The last time I saw a face like yours Belinda, it had a hook in it!'

'Kenneth?'

The biographer, irritated by this interruption to his flow, turned to Polly with a sibilant sigh.

'Yes?'

'Is that how it really happened? Is that what they actually said?'

'It would be close, very close,' Kenneth declared solemnly. 'The art of biography has hit an all time low, Poll. Basically, biographers have got so bogged down in facts, in what happened to whom and why, that the life has gone out of it all. The subject has ceased to live, basically.'

Polly had now assumed her squatting-on-the-floor-head-on-one-side-looking-up proselyte's position.

'I'm making Derek Pettyfer – his family and friends – *and his enemies*, talk,' Kenneth dilated. 'I'm making them jump off the page. Basically I want the reader to think he's there, in the middle of it, sharing Pettyfer's hopes, his fears, his . . .'

'Drinks?' As the author lunged at his critic the doorbell rang.

When Polly opened the door in the small hallway, Inge Pinkhill was astonished to behold Antoinette Diggins. The likeness was so precise, she had almost to restrain herself from slapping the dancer's smug, pointy-chinned face.

'I'm afraid you don't know me but I'm Inge Pinkhill, Lionel Pinkhill's wife.'

'Oh?' said Polly, blushing.

'May I come in? There's something I have to explain, something rather private. Please?' Polly hesitated, more from surprise than discourtesy.

'I'm off now, Poll,' called Kenneth from the other room. 'See you a bit later.' He was slipping into his leather jacket as he passed them in the narrow hallway.

'Where are you off to?' She didn't introduce him to Inge – he was in such a rush to leave he did not even glance at Polly's visitor, but his voice came back to them from the landing.

'Going to get a bit more raw material – off to Knightsbridge to see Deep Throat!' And his footsteps faded down the stairs.

As he left the house in Islington and headed for a cab rank, Kenneth thought that for the sake of delicacy 'Deep Throat' was a permissible reversal of roles.

'Would you like a herbal tea?'

'No thank you.' Inge stared at Polly; then she spoke. 'I'm a patient of Mr Watson and Mr Bremner.'

'Oh are you, they're marvellous aren't they?'

'They are marvellous, and trusting.'

'They helped me recently,' Polly bared her teeth.

'They're horribly expensive, haven't you found?'

'Well yes, yes, they are.'

'But if you're famous, say a famous ballet star, I believe they can arrange things. Can't they?'

'I don't know what you mean?'

Inge pounced. 'Oh yes you do, Polly Garland, you little cheat! I know Antoinette Diggins personally! I was at school with her. She . . .'

Polly burst into tears and ran to Inge, actually falling on her knees. 'I know, I know, I shouldn't have. It was wicked, crazy, he made me do it – he got me into this!' She pointed to the door through which Kenneth Grocock had only just made his festinant egress. 'What am I going to do?'

Inge was astonished it had been this easy. She had expected resistance; grotesque alibis.

'It's a nightmare,' continued the impostor. 'I'm a very honest person, I've never even shoplifted.' In Kenneth's absence she pointed an accusing finger at the word processor. 'He's so heartless, all he cares about is his book. I'm just a doormat, a stepping-stone, a puppet, a fall girl, a patsy . . .' Polly vainly sought further epithets of abasement.

'What about those poor dentists?' persisted Inge, standing over Polly who cowered on the sofa. 'All those years of training, all that skill and caring, only to be tricked and robbed by a malicious little fraud.'

Polly howled. Inge thought she might just have pressed home her point a little too forcefully, so she changed her tack, and sat down beside the sobbing ballerina, taking her red, tear-drenched hand.

'Now I have a suggestion that might help you get out of this mess.' Polly turned towards her a face which looked as if it had been boiled for several hours on a low flame. 'When I saw you for the first time at Mr Bremner's and I realised at once that you were not Antoinette Diggins, I knew it was my duty to report you, perhaps even to the police.' Polly assumed a foetal posture.

'Then I thought, no! This is just an impressionable, over-sensitive young woman who wishes she *was* Antoinette Diggins. Is that possible?' Polly nodded. Several tears and other muculent droplets moistened the back of Inge's hand. 'If I reported you, I could never live with my conscience.'

'Why?' croaked the counterfeit.

'Because you would probably be put in jail for a long time with lesbians, and be made to pay for all that dental work as well.' Polly had become catatonic. 'So instead, I'm offering you a chance to help me.'

'I'll do anything,' the girl said. 'I couldn't dance at Covent Garden next week anyway, I haven't got enough elevation to *jeter*.'

Inge considered this statement, and the troubling possibility that this young woman really did identify, perhaps to a schizophrenic degree, with the pert dwarf of Covent Garden. 'What I would like you to play is a dramatic role. A bit like ballet, except you'll have lines to say. Not many, but important ones. And,' she added encouragingly, 'you can wear your tutu, Polly, just like Antoinette!'

'Can I? Oh thank you. I'll do anything – anything!' repeated the reprieved mimic.

'And when you've done me this silly little favour, we can all forgive and forget.'

'Really?' said Polly with an alarming sniff.

'Really!'

'What words? What will I say, wherever?'

Inge smiled, and as she spoke, she traced the words on Polly's dewy palm.

'It's me, Antoinette, here at last, Lionel. Can you get it up?'

'Is that all?'

'That's all, Polly.'

'Is that dramatic?'

'It will be, dear,' said Inge, 'it will be.'

Kenneth was running late for his appointment with Woody. It was marvellous how helpful the agent was proving to be, though the Grotto was, to use one of Kenneth's favourite words, 'Bizarre'. Woody had promised to tell him about a time in 1980 when Derek had been put in a nursing home at Potters Bar, and had exposed himself to the matron. It would be interesting to track her down, if she had survived the experience.

Kenneth was enjoying himself writing authentic dialogue for this episode; it could be a key point in the book, and the *Sun* newspaper would almost certainly snap up serialisation rights. He was entertaining agreeable conjectures of this kind as his taxi approached its destination, but a large crowd at the entrance to Trevor Square barred the way. Paying off the cab, he alighted, only to become aware of an intense and acrid smell.

His extreme shortness proved a disadvantage in this situation.

'What's up?' he besought a bystander, 'what's going on'

'A fire! One of them old houses has gone up. The brigade's trying to stop it spreading.'

Kenneth battled through somehow, until he got a better view of the square. There were two enormous fire engines, water surging down the gutters and the flashing lights of ambulances and police cars. It was rather like that rescue programme on Sky 1. Great white jets of water were playing on one of the houses. It was a house he knew.

Kenneth fought to get nearer the blaze. There was a crash, like a log in a grate, only bigger and very terrible. An immense column of sparks shot up into the London sky, which tonight looked almost maroon.

Kenneth grabbed the sleeve of an exhausted fireman. 'I'm Press,' he cried, flashing his ID. 'Basically, what happened? I know the people.'

The fireman saw that he was crying. 'I'm sorry,' he said, 'they didn't stand a chance. It was the usual thing; we reckon a cigarette done it.'

Kenneth stared at the inferno.

'It's these old narrow houses. The fire shoots up them like flames up a bloody chimney.'

Kenneth turned away, pushing back slowly through the crowds and stepping over hoses. That was it, he thought, like a chimney. It was awful, but it seemed an appropriate way for Santa Claus to take his leave.

When he got home the phone was ringing.

'Why the fuck don't you answer it, Poll?' he screamed. She was just sitting cross-legged on the floor, looking stunned. 'Hello. Grocock here!'

'Christ, Ken, where the hell have you been?' It was Dennis, his editor on the *London Evening News*.

'Sorry, Dennis,' he replied flatly.

'Listen, you heard of someone called Myron

Woodrow Weinglass, Agent to the Stars? He torched himself tonight in Knightsbridge. I'm faxing a pretty recent bio. We need about a thousand jolly words soonest, can do?'

'Can do,' said the Obituarist.

Whitney

DEREK SAT AT a corner table in the Ivy. It was a table at which he had often observed Harold Pinter and Lady Antonia Fraser holding court.

He was waiting for the arrival of his accountant and taxation adviser, Roger Wainwright. Derek consumed another bread roll. It had been deftly placed on his plate by a waiter manipulating a spoon and fork. Derek wondered if they were as fastidious behind the scenes filling those bread baskets; or did they sometimes resort to fingers?

That morning had been one of the most desolate of his life. Pam, by contrast, had been as bright as a button. They had made love the night before, against his will. The thought of what she had been up to gave his efforts a certain savagery which almost roused her from her habitual lassitude. He attempted the fantasy that he was sleeping with a famous courtesan, or Catherine the Great. Derek was determined to maintain this conjugal pretence until legal advice had been secured.

At breakfast, much to his astonishment, Pam announced that she was off to keep an appointment with the hairdresser. He had never known her to patronise such establishments; rather had he been under the impression that she despised them as 'élitist'. She had also proclaimed, in passing, and over the muesli, that it was her intention to have her legs waxed.

On the previous evening, Derek had observed that his wife's armpits, formerly rather titillatingly fronded, were now depilated to resemble the texture of chicken skin. He supposed this volte-face in her attitude towards such harmless feminine vanities was in response to the demands of one of her three current lovers; or perhaps of another, as yet unexposed.

Pam had certainly changed her ways dramatically since they had been together. Although she still diffused the same *froideur* in company, he noticed to his surprise that when introduced, she had now taken to presenting both cheeks to be kissed, at the same time making little 'muh! muh!' noises. Would that be what her mother meant by 'kippers and curtains'? Derek thought that now it was rather more like caviar and Colefax.

There remained the problem of his manager. In spite of the evidence, Derek persisted in denying to himself that Ross could be guilty of any serious misdemeanour. If he had slept with Pam, as the taped conversation implied, it was outrageous but not untypical conduct. It could even, perhaps, be ultimately forgiven. It was the story of Ross Gibb's disappearance that troubled Derek most. Surely he had just gone 'bush', as they said in Australia. He was probably holed up with Denise and the kids somewhere warm, and would surface at any moment with a grin and a handshake.

'To be perfectly honest, Dekka, I didn't think you'd miss me, you bastard.'

'R-i-gh-t,' Denise would aver.

That was what they would say, more than likely. After all, those McColl sleuths hadn't come up with much on him, had they? In his heart too, Derek knew that Gibbo would not leave him in the lurch. There were all those companies, and the Structure! No one knew how all that worked except Gibbo, and presumably Roger Wainwright.

He had to see for himself. At ten in the morning, Derek had taken a black cab all the way to Weybridge. When at last they turned a leafy corner and stopped outside the gates of Denross, Derek looked for the familiar signs of habitation. His heart had leapt at the sight of a light, visible through the venetian blinds of what Ross and Denise called the 'loungeroom'. A wisp of smoke ascended from a tapestry brick Tudor chimney. The gate was slightly ajar so, instructing the taxi to wait, he approached the front door and rang the bell.

Derek had rehearsed several short speeches and facial expressions, before he realised that when Ross opened the door, he was bound to shake him by the hand; perhaps even with a kind of gratitude.

The door opened and three people stood before him in striped Marks & Spencer's pyjamas. A father, a mother and a baby. From within wafted a strong aroma of fried onions and garlic. Derek had tried to explain, haltingly and in several languages, including loud English, that he was looking for Mr and Mrs Gibb, but the Three Bears only smiled and shrugged their shoulders. It was enough to observe that they lived there, and that in the space of a week, all evidence of the former occupants had been erased, save the mysterious name, Denross, on the gate.

Travelling back to the Ivy for his lunch appointment, it took a long time for the bitter truth to sink in: the speciosity of Ross and Denise Gibb. They had been like honorary parents. What was that story Denise had told of her friend who had gone back to the family house and found his parents dead, or gone, and the house sold and reoccupied by strangers? What were those words of reassurance?

We would have told you, but we didn't want to worry you.

But now he was at the Ivy and his accountant was approaching him through the tables. Dark suit, waistcoat, gold watch-chain, regimental tie. Roger Wainwright FCCA was a good-looking chap, Derek thought, with a florid complexion and a military moustache. He had thick, black, wavy hair, but a scalp sequinned with dandruff. When he sat down, he disconcerted Derek by removing his gold Rolex and placing it before him on the table. Was he timing the lunch? Derek wondered. Probably, he decided. He had never before seen it done so blatantly, except once by a psychiatrist who had seemed more interested in the time than the patient.

'Is that Michael Palin over yonder?'

'I beg your pardon?'

'Is that Michael Palin – chap eating the spinach?'

Derek looked across at a nearby table, a little less obviously than his guest. Palin caught his eye and smiled.

'*You know him!* God, I'm a major fan. You must introduce us later. I'd like to tell him a pretty larky thing that happened to me and Jenny down at Henley a couple of years ago, which would make an absolutely brilliant Python skit.'

Derek experienced, in advance, fraternal anguish. 'Yes, of course, Roger, please remind me to do that. It's just that I'm worried . . .'

'Do you know Cleese – John Cleese?'

'Yes, er, I do as a matter of fact. Haven't seen him lately, mind.'

'Would he be here today?'

'I doubt it, Roger. Look, I'm extremely worried . . .'

'John Cleese is my absolute idol. That man can do no wrong as far as my family is concerned. I think my favourite sketch of the lot is that parrot thing, you know, Derek, when they've got this stuffed parrot . . .' Derek's guest became so convulsed with laughter he was unable to continue. He was still mopping his eyes as he studied the wine list, which appeared to be of greater interest to him than the menu, from which Derek had selected a grilled chop.

Their orders placed, and an expensive Gruaud

Larose '75 chosen and elaborately tasted by Roger, the accountant leant forward and asked: 'As a special favour to one deeply boring accountant, would you remind me just what happens in that parrot sketch? I mean it's killingly funny and I've seen it umpteen times – we've got all the tapes down at our place in the Dordogne – but I just want to check up on a few details. Incidently, larking aside, Jenny asked me to ask you if you know Hugh Grant, she's a major fan, and I mean, a *major* fan.'

Derek saw the accountant's eyes flick towards the Rolex. Was this appraisal of Monty Python to be subtracted from the bill, he wondered, or charged at a special rate? He decided it was time to express his concerns more aggressively.

'Roger,' he began.

'Call me Rodge,' said Roger, swallowing soup. 'Gibbo always calls me that and I love it.'

'It's Gibbo I'm worried about. He's disappeared, he's not at home and I'm worried sick.'

Roger beckoned the wine waiter ostentatiously. 'I'm sorry but I'm afraid this claret might be a touch oxidised, just the teeniest bit. Mind you, it's drinkable. How is it for you, Derek?'

'I'm not drinking, Roger. I thought you might have noticed.'

'I don't mind it as a matter of fact,' continued Derek's financial adviser, 'but I'm wondering if it mightn't be fun to compare it with a Mouton of the same year. Would that be wickedly extravagant?' The *sommelier* looked at Derek. It was an eloquent look.

'Why not?' said Derek. 'Do you have a half bottle of '75 Lorenzo?'

'I'm afraid not, sir,' replied the wine waiter with a nervous laugh.

'Let's be devils,' insisted the accountant. 'If we can't drink two bottles of an excellent wine between us over lunch, there's something wrong somewhere. Eh, Derek?'

'I don't drink, Roger.'

'Not at all?'

'No.'

'Not even wine?'

'No.'

'Just spirits?'

'Nothing.'

Roger Wainwright regarded his client with a curious expression in which pity and contempt jostled for supremacy. 'You'll be getting me tiddly then, won't you?' he said mirthlessly.

'You're certainly missing something though, old boy,' he said, taking another swig and rolling it around under his moustache. 'Spike Milligan's quite a wine buff, isn't he? Know him at all?'

'Have your heard from Ross Gibb lately, Roger?'

Wainwright sat back in his chair and scrubbed his moustache with a napkin. 'Ah, dear old Gibbo. Have I heard from him? The answer, in a nutshell – no. And . . .' the accountant leaned forward, raising his eyebrows as high as he could: '. . . between you and me I don't think we will. Old Gibbo has scarpered!'

'You know for sure?' exclaimed Derek.

Roger wagged a finger. 'Finger on the pulse, old

boy, finger on the pulse. Your financial adviser is not quite the fool he looks.'

Derek was unconvinced. 'But why would he do it, why? We were friends.'

'No friends in love and war,' said his luncheon guest, as though he had just minted the aphorism. 'Now this is when you need your sense of humour, Derek.'

Oxtails and mashed potatoes arrived, but Derek gazed down at his chops with a diminished appetite.

'I'm very lucky I've got my sense of humour, I can tell you,' declared Roger, tucking in. 'Jenny says I should be in your business, she says I'm wasting my time as an accountant.'

Not just your time either, Derek was inclined to add.

'Heard of the Sunningdale Mummers?'

'No.'

'Quite a larky little outfit near us. I'm a member actually. We put on a couple of shows a year – you know, things like *Equus, Royal Hunt of the Sun, Steaming* – good family stuff!'

'Did he give you any warning? Did he ever tell you why he was leaving the country?'

'What's that, old son?'

'Ross!' said Derek, observing the rapid ingestion of gravy and mashed potatoes.

'Oh, that?' replied the ruminating number-cruncher. 'Bit of strife with the VAT people. Gibbo must have got up their nose over something. I think they raided his office, poor sod. He mightn't have dotted the odd T or crossed the odd I.'

Derek tried to take in the implications of this information.

'Do you know Whitney Houston?'

'No, I know Angelica Huston.'

'You've lost me, Derek, you bugger.' He reached out and poured himself an enormous glass of wine. 'This isn't at all bad, don't you think?'

'I don't drink.'

'Would you like a beer then, or a glass of champagne?' Roger tried to attract the wine waiter's attention.

'Nothing for the moment,' replied his host, through clenched teeth.

'Well, as I was saying, last Christmas the Sunningdale Mummers put on a kind of revue and I – wait for this – I was Whitney Houston!'

'You?'

'That's right Derek, and I killed them! She who must be obeyed, my Jenny and some of her girlfriends ran up the dress – a really glamorous number – I blacked-up of course, and we got one of those fright wigs from a shop in Covent Garden, and bingo!'

'Bingo?'

'Whitney to the life. I mimed that song of hers, you know the one, "Saving All My Love For You"? I can't say I got it perfectly, I mean, anyone knowing Whitney would probably not be fooled for very long, but I had them in the aisles *my dear!*' The accountant made a camp gesture with his wrist.

'We've got a terrific photo of me as Whitney at home – colour, of course – and you've got to see it,

Derek. Matter of fact, I've just taken it to a reliable picture framer.'

Derek, feeling disembodied, withdrew a small notebook from his pocket and wrote three words therein: 'reliable picture framer'.

'Are you quoting me?' asked Roger.

'No, just a hobby, go on.'

'Do you know Frankie Hill?'

'Who?'

'That chap in the fez who does the tricks.' Roger did a lot of loud memory-jogging finger-snapping which attracted some attention from adjacent lunchers.

'You mean Tommy Cooper? I'm afraid he's dead.'

'Ah, no he's not!' asserted the authority. 'That's Eric, you mean Eric Dawson.'

'Were his books in a bit of a mess then?'

'Frankly, I don't like what they call "drag" acts – nothing personal, Derek – but Jenny and I find them a bit sickening. And yet they all said my Whitney was tasteful; how about that for a compliment? They want me to do it again this year.'

The accountant then had an idea which inspired him to half rise from the table.

'Do you think if I asked him now, Michael Palin could come down to old Sunningdale this year for a laugh? It's right up his street.'

'I don't think so. Please Roger, let the poor devil have his lunch.'

Derek's adviser petulantly reseated himself.

'I'll ask him myself later,' lied Derek. 'But if you tell me what kind of state Ross Gibb left the books in, I'll come down to Sunningdale at Christmas and do Mrs Petty for you, on the house.'

Wainwright looked embarrassed. 'That is noble of you Derek, but . . .'

'*Free* is what I said. Just give it to me straight, Roger, how do I stand now Gibb has done a runner?'

The accountant was thinking how he could best express a matter of extreme delicacy. 'You see, Derek, you are a lucky man. You have a vast following. There are people I've met, or to be precise, Jenny has met, who think you're the bee's pyjamas. You have a large public and a heap of fans.'

'Well?'

'But not in Sunningdale.'

'Say that again.'

'You pay me to tell the truth, Derek, you pay me well, so I am bound to tell you that in the Sunningdales of this world, you are not . . .' the *sommelier* reappeared and with a cogitative expression, Roger watched the last of the wine cascade into his glass – '. . . top favourite.'

'I'm not what?'

'You're not top favourite in Sunningdale, Derek. So what! It's not the end of the world and you're laughing all the way to the bank!'

'But am I?' said Derek with feeling. 'So where do I stand? What about my Structure?'

'Offshore!' said his adviser triumphantly. 'Gibbo's department – "Offshore".' He was studying anew the wine list.

'But Gibbo's gone offshore himself. WHERE THE FUCK DOES THAT LEAVE ME?'

Roger looked disapproving. 'Don't get your knickers in a knot, Derek, people heard that. Michael over there, in all probability, so steady on!' Derek was beside himself. 'You must get a grip on yourself, old son.'

The waiter stood beside them.

'Ah yes, *sommelier*, with my bread and butter pudding I'd like to have a shot at your Bonny Doon Liqueur Muscat. Not often you see these top-of-the-range Californian dessert wines on a London restaurant wine list, is it, Derek? Met the chap who makes this once, too; name of Randall Graham, I think. Very senior wine-maker. You'll like this stuff, Derek, it'll cheer you up a bit. Where was I . . .?'

'You were telling me to keep calm; why?'

'Because you're lucky to have me to blow your nose and wipe your bum, that's why. I can be objective and detached. If I was a fan – if I liked your work – it would complicate our business relationship; it would muddy the waters.'

'Am I hearing what I think I'm hearing?' said Derek, on the brink of an apoplexy, but a tall figure was standing at their table.

It was Jeremy, the proprietor.

'Excuse me, Derek,' he said. 'We've had a little accident over there.' Derek looked across at the indicated table. A small woman of about fifty in a turban, seated with an anxious young man, was holding a napkin to her lips. She had a strained, almost mummified face and pencilled eyebrows.

'One of our best customers has accidentally broken her tooth on a lamb chop.' Derek looked down at his own uneaten lunch with a certain gratitude. 'You know a good dentist, don't you? Could you please give them a call and see if they can help her urgently?' Jeremy handed Derek a mobile.

'I'd be glad to. Bremner and Watson are the best, I'll ring them now. Who's the lady?'

Jeremy leaned closer and whispered.

'Don't worry, Jeremy,' said Derek, grateful to be back in the real world of pain and charity and fellowship and simple everyday philanthropy. 'When Pinky and Perky hear that Dame Antoinette Diggins has got an emergency, they'll clear the decks for sure!'

As Derek waited for Pinky and Perky's nurse to answer the phone, his accountant leaned eagerly across the table. 'Completely forgot to ask you, old son, but do you know those *AbFab* girls at all?'

When Derek got home, Pam was still at the hairdresser, or wherever it is that women go after the hairdresser. Waiting in the hall was a pyramid of deliveries brought up by Tommy. There were large boxes of clothes from a shop in South Molton Street, a Harrods delivery which looked like shoes and a dress in a suitbag from Vivienne Westwood.

Derek was recovering from lunch. He had managed to pin Wainwright down to a mid-morning meeting at the offices of Nimmo, Nimmo, Blackburn & Tricker on the following Monday, to review the situation. At least then there would not be the distraction of a wine list or propinquity of lunching celebrities.

He went into the shambles that had once been his drawing-room, untouched by Amerika or anyone for nearly two months. There, still smothered beneath an old picnic rug, was his display cabinet, and its treasures. Gently he unveiled it, retrieved his key and unlocked the vitrine.

For the next hour, Derek tenderly examined his collection. One by one he touched their cool and ancient patinas; enjoyed their subtle refractions and iridescences in the soft afternoon light. They were his friends, constant and changeless, and he was their protector.

The phone rang.

'Derek Pettyfer?' A girl's voice – was she crying?

'Yes.'

'Dentist will be with you in a wee minute, thinks.'

'Derek, Hugh Bremner.'

'*And me!*' Another voice came on the line. '*I'm here too!*'

'Hello Hugh, hello Trevor.'

'We've just had a nasty scene here. That woman you sent round . . .'

'You mean Dame Antoinette?'

'Dame Antoinette my foot,' said the dentists in unison.

'We cancelled Harold Pinter . . .'

'. . . and Bea Arthur!'

'To fit that cow in!'

'So?'

'So she was a phoney, trying it on!'

'What?'

'Some silly bitch breaks her upper anterior incisor,

so she reckons she can get an emergency job by trying to con us!'

'No way, José!' chimed in Trevor Watson.

'Hold the phone, fellas, she looked like the real McCoy to me. How do you know?'

'Because,' Pinky and Perky said in chorus, 'Antoinette is our patient. She's a friend, we've done her entire mouth.'

'So what did you say to this . . . this other woman?'

'We didn't say anything, did we, Trev?'

'No we didn't say anything, we just took one look at her, didn't we, Hugh? And we said "if you're Antoinette Diggins, we're the Andrews Sisters" and we chucked her out into the fuckin' mews on her big fat arse.'

Derek tried to picture the scene. 'I'm sorry,' he said. 'It's a strange con trick though, isn't it?'

'Don't worry, we're not blaming you, Derek dear, but she won't try this again in a hurry. We're getting on the blower to Covent Garden right now. Wait till the ballet world hears about this!'

The fine mist of their sibilant outrage seemed to reach Derek through the telephone.

Fanny

IT WAS A bright grey Saturday afternoon as Inge and Polly drove to Birmingham. Inge for the hell of it, wore her full length mink and Polly was apparelled in one of Inge's Burberry raincoats. It looked rather bulky over the other things she had been instructed to wear. She was muttering to herself.

'You know it by now, dear,' said Inge. 'You don't need to keep saying it over and over again any more.'

Polly closed her lips and nodded. 'I suppose I do,' she said. 'But I wish you'd tell me what it all means.'

Inge kindled a cigarette with the dashboard lighter. 'It's just a nice little surprise for a man called Lionel who is the world's biggest Antoinette Diggins fan.' Inge took her left hand off the wheel and pinched a fragment of tobacco off her tongue. 'All you have to do is go upstairs when I give you a little push . . .'

Polly took over: '. . . turn right to the Chamberlain Suite, check my watch and dead on eleven thirty, knock on the door three times. Then take off the coat . . .' Inge nodded as Polly continued, '. . . Lionel will open it. *Will* he?'

'Lionel will open it,' affirmed Inge coldly.

'I'll then walk straight towards him and say the words.' Polly put her hand over her mouth and gasped. 'Inge, you haven't told me what I do then!'

Inge thought for a moment. The Birmingham turn-off signs were starting to come up on the motorway. 'You wait a second then quietly pick up your coat, close the door and come downstairs. I'll be in the lounge. We'll have a drink and we'll go home.'

'Will I be all right?' said Polly, touching her scraped-back hair and checking her mascara in the mirror like an actress with first night nerves.

'You'll be brilliant, Polly dear,' said Inge. 'You'll kill them.'

Pamela Pettyfer took her seat in the Birmingham Symphony Hall at twenty minutes past eight. She looked gorgeous. Several men, and women too, observed the green-eyed brunette in the black, Donna Karan backless dress and smiled appreciatively.

As the lights dimmed and the conductor acknowledged the applause, Pam felt her heart beating faster; her palms moist. She had never done anything like this before. It was romantic, even a little frightening, but she deserved it. She deserved nice things and nice times and the attention of famous people. To be back in Birmingham, too, made it exciting.

With people looking at her, wondering who she was. They didn't realise it was just snotty-nosed little Pam Black from Longbridge, and if by any chance they did, they would only say, 'our Pamela's certainly done well for herself!'

Stoically, she sat through the first half of the programme; a rather long and rambling work by a contemporary Norwegian composer. It was to be an evening of musical curiosities, and as the *pièce de résistance* Lionel was to perform, probably for the first time in a hundred and fifty years, a cello concerto by Fanny Mendelssohn – the sister of Felix. It was meant to be a great musical rediscovery.

At the interval Pam had two glasses of champagne and a smoked salmon sandwich.

There was a tremendous ovation when at last Lionel stepped on to the stage. He must have known exactly where she was seated, five rows from the front, for, as he bowed, he seemed to look straight into her eyes. She bathed in the romantic music, and as he played, Lionel's gaze seemed always to stray in her direction. At the end, when the entire audience rose and cheered, he bowed, so it seemed, to her. Pam Black, the waif; the Nobody.

Lionel had promised to use his influence to get her an exhibition in New York and he knew someone who knew someone close to Harvey Keitel. There could be a commission in the offing; even a *Time* magazine cover not too far down the track.

Pam was learning to walk and wear good clothes in public. As she sipped another champagne in the Symphony Hall bar she could sense the curiosity;

feel the glances. It felt very sexy having this secret known only to her and the star of the night.

It was just after eleven. She would walk to the Meteyard; it was marvellously close. At eleven fifteen she collected her new Chanel coat and her overnight bag from the theatre cloakroom. She had left her mother's BMW in the hotel car-park.

As she entered the hotel and crossed to the lift, it was eleven twenty-five. Pam depressed the Up button.

'Pam?' She turned.

'Inge!'

'Darling!' Inge's arms were around her. 'You're looking absolutely stunning, where's Derek?' she asked disingenuously.

Pam groped for words. 'He, he's in London, I think. He's not musical.'

'Musical? What music?' asked Inge. 'Wait a minute,' she drew her friend across the foyer to a dimly lit cocktail lounge, 'We've both been to the same concert tonight. My God, what a coincidence!'

Pam was speechless.

'The Fanny Mendelssohn concerto, Lionel's concert!'

'Why yes, yes it was marvellous, but I'm really here to see my mother.' Pam, belatedly, had seized on her alibi.

'That's incredible, your mother's here in this hotel? Let's ask her down for a drink.'

Pam was trapped. 'No, mum's at home, so I came here for a nightcap, that's all.'

'Well let's have one then,' said Inge, selecting a dark corner. 'But not upstairs in the Crest Bar. Down here, where it's quiet. The upstairs bar is full of classical music rowdies from Lionel's audience; we call them "Largo-Louts".'

Pam spoke her thoughts. 'Why are you here?'

Inge shot a glance over her shoulder. 'A nice present for my husband. It's his birthday today, did you know?'

'No.'

'It's in *The Times.* However, I want to surprise him. I've been hiding out down here until he settles in upstairs.' She put a finger to her lips. 'Mum's the word, but I've got something quite special for him.'

The small side lounge was deserted except for a barman and a couple in a far corner. Pam felt deeply miserable.

'Would you like to see Lionel's birthday present, Pam?'

'Why yes,' she said, trying to conceal her wretchedness, 'and then I'll have to go, really. Mother will . . .'

Inge walked a few steps away from their table in the direction of the bar, then looking quickly to either side she turned towards Pam and opened her fur coat. Except for her faintly lewd Ferragamo shoes and another mink-like shadow, she was completely nude. Pam observed the barman obliviously polishing glasses. Then, without fastening her coat, Inge stepped towards her friend and lightly kissed her on the lips. The girl smelt the musky fur, and another fragrance.

'Now off you go,' said Inge brightly, 'and I'll tell Lionel you said Happy Birthday!'

Pam grabbed her valise and fled into the night.

*

It was less than five minutes before the lift doors opened and Polly emerged, looking rather frightened. The older woman took her arm firmly and steered her out into the fresh air.

'I hope he's all right,' said Polly. 'But I don't think he is.'

In the car back to London, Inge tuned the radio to a replay of the night's concert. Fanny Mendelssohn's music was delicious, well worth the excavation, and Inge reflected that her husband had rarely played better.

As she sat silently in the passenger seat listening to the romantic music, Polly kept remembering that strange moment when the door of the Chamberlain Suite had opened in response to her knock, and the old man had just stood staring at her. She must have looked beautiful standing there in her pink satin pointe shoes and that lovely tutu, but he was only half dressed, she recalled, suppressing a smile of embarrassment. Then she'd said the words: 'It's me, Antoinette, here at last, Lionel. Can you get it up?'

First, rather absent-mindedly, he seemed to give himself a funny little hug. Then, still looking at her oddly, he had just toppled forward on to his knees and rolled very, very slowly backwards. She had closed the door then, as Inge had told her to.

Inge reached for the Camel cigarettes. 'Would you like one after such a great performance?'

'I don't smoke. I'd hate to get hooked like Karina.'

'Who's Karina?'

'My flatmate Kenneth's sister,' said Polly. 'She

never used to smoke before she got that job at Rushing & Associates.'

Polly thought how nice it would be to get back to her barre work. There was still so much practice to do with that world première of her new ballet coming up. She must be wonderful when the big night came.

Earlier that same Saturday, Hugh Bremner and Trevor Watson had planned, as usual, to be 'At Home'. The pretty interior of their house in Glebe Place with its Colefax & Fowler curtains, its obelisks, its Lalique and its gold-framed portraits of stretched heifers, was regularly thronged with interesting people from the world of art and entertainment; guests whose even smiles of gratitude, whose dazzling teeth, masticating the delicious canapés, had been enhanced, reinforced, and not seldom fabricated by their attentive hosts. But today a funereal gloom hung in the air. The Partners had cancelled their expected luncheon guests, for the word had gone around London with astonishing speed that Dame Antoinette Diggins, in the midst of a distressing dental crisis, had been insulted and practically defenestrated at the Cadogan Mews surgery.

Within twenty-four hours the celebrated team had lost their 'credibility'. No rumour of their shame had yet appeared in any newspaper, or been bruited on radio or TV, but they were reliably informed that the *Evening Standard* and the *Daily Mail* would be running facetious stories of the affair in their

Monday editions, with photographs of its chief protagonists. Would they ever be able to hold up their heads at Covent Garden again, let alone stand boldly in the stalls in their perfect black tie, with their souvenir programmes and their nameless female appurtenances, and survey the stalls with the same *hauteur*, the same aura of distinction? The answer was never. There would be titters; raised programmes would mask salacious whisperings; and, worst of all, celebrities would take their mouths elsewhere.

The disgrace was such that the dentists had even begun enquiries, with a view to closing their Knightsbridge practice and relocating to modest premises in their native Auckland, where news of the scandal would be slow to percolate.

On a Biedermeier escritoire, a reproduction Edwardian telephone pealed. Neither dentist was inclined to answer it.

'It'll be the *News of the World*,' said Pinky.

'More like the *People*,' said Perky.

'Dempster,' groaned Pinky.

'Compton Miller,' shuddered Perky.

'Linda Lee Potter!' they squealed simultaneously.

After an interval of several minutes, during which time it was evident that the caller meant business, Trevor Watson, having taken a deep breath, lifted the receiver.

'Thank God!' came a voice down the line.

'Who is it?' enquired the dentist's companion. Mr Watson enjoined him to silence as he listened with ever increasing interest. Finally, placing his hand over the mouthpiece, and visibly moved, he said:

'Hugh, I know it's Saturday but would we be able to handle a rather painful emergency this afternoon?'

Hugh Bremner's pink jowls quivered indignantly. He was about to say 'you've got to be joking' when his partner elaborated.

'The patient is in great pain, Hugh, and it would be a sad state of affairs if we couldn't open up the surgery and do a favour for such a good client as *Mr Kenneth Grocock!*'

As he enunciated the journalist's name, the dentist gave his popular impersonation of Laurence Olivier in *Marathon Man.* At the mention of Grocock, Hugh's eyes dilated, as his belief in a Presbyterian Providence was restored to him with an epiphanous surge.

When the appointment was made and the phone replaced, the dentists looked at each other. *It was too good to be true.* The author of their predicament was voluntarily stepping back into the chair! Hugh Bremner and Trevor Watson executed a rather idiomatic and abridged version of the Maori Haka and fell into an emotional embrace which, within fifteen minutes and to their mutual surprise, reached its *dénouement* on the white shagpile of Mr Bremner's bedroom – witnessed by a bewildered shih-tzu and a King Charles spaniel called Clarice and Cliff.

It seemed to be dark outside. At first, Kenneth had no idea where he was. Bits, but only bits, came back. It was that excruciating toothache that had struck him out of the blue.

Polly had been rehearsing for her ballet all morning. She didn't seem to be aware of his suffering. Didn't care. Why should she? She was off to Bristol or Birmingham, selfish bitch. The jaunty, witty, incessant music had nearly driven him crazy; its optimism intensified the pain which seemed to run backwards and forwards down the left side of his face in an agonising circuit.

He tasted blood and he couldn't breathe. All that smoke. Kenneth kept relapsing into unconsciousness, and whenever he did he dreamed of fire: smoke and fire and Jingle Bells Rock and the sound of the sirens and the hoses. Then a tremendous crash and a column of sparks.

He burst out of his nightmare and sat bolt upright, sweating, only to discover that he was not in bed. He was in a dentist's chair in a dark room. Weakly, he began calling.

'Poll! Poll-y!'

His mouth felt numb, without feeling, and yet it seemed to throb like a huge red pulse in his face. He called again, but his throat was full of thick fluid with a taste like . . . bouillon?

'I have to go home now, you've slept long enough.'

Suddenly the room flickered and sprang to life. The light was white. The room white and brilliant. He knew it then: it was his dentists' surgery. Kenneth sank back into the chair. Thank God! He remembered it all now, the terrible pain. He had telephoned and they had come especially, just for him. They hadn't seemed to mind either, they had even been excited. What nice guys! A bit queenie, a couple of stereotypes really, but decent guys all the same.

'You've got a wee moment to put your coat on, Mr Grocock and then I have to lock up.' A young woman – he barely recognised Raewyn in her street clothes – stood beside the chair. 'The dentists went home an hour ago. They're very pleased with the work and said to let you sleep a wee while because of the drugs, but I've got a train to catch and I don't work on Saturdays as a rule.'

She wasn't being very nice, thought Kenneth struggling out of the chair. Why did he feel so weak? Raewyn definitely wasn't the nice person she used to be.

'Don't try smiling at anyone on the way home,' she said. 'They'll think they're having an interview with a vampire, you look like Dracula.' She had put her freckled ginger head on one side and looked at him before she made this appraisal.

Kenneth ran to the loo and coughed a quantity of crimson syrup into the basin. He peered at the mirror. His face was white; ashen. His mouth . . . his mouth was just a black hole – *and where were his teeth?* He darted back into the waiting-room, as though he might have left them there by mistake, but Raewyn was standing rather impatiently holding the door.

'I have to lock up now,' she said tartly. 'I won't be doing this for much longer, thanks to you. They're going back to New Zealand and I'm going to have to find another wee job.'

Kenneth made feral noises of incomprehension and distress with the wound he once used to talk with. Raewyn switched on the security system, double locked the door, and they were in Cadogan Mews. She produced an envelope.

'They said to give you this,' she said tersely. 'It's probably the bill and I hope they've charged you an arm and a wee leg.'

And with that, Raewyn turned on her heels and clicked off into the distance. Kenneth decided he hated New Zealanders, yet he supposed that such a view, expressed publicly, would be condemned as 'Kiwist'.

Although he felt like fainting, he ripped open the dentists' missive and read the following:

> Mr Trevor Watson and Mr Hugh Bremner respectfully present their compliments, and beg to inform Mr Kenneth Grocock that their professional charges are:

(Here the typewritten contents of the letter ceased. The remaining words had been scribbled in red ink.)

> *No charge as usual, the pleasure was ours. Kindly note that we have taken back the teeth we lent you – with interest.*

It was after one o'clock in the morning when Polly came home. Kenneth, still rather high on novocaine and coffee, seemed to be working at his word processor; embowered in screwed-up, crimson Kleenex tissues, like roses.

Before Polly returned, an excess of coffee and the narcotic residue in his blood had stimulated Kenneth to identify with the world's great Toothless; the edentate heroes of history. There was Churchill, for instance, whose teeth had never been seen. In spite of being frequently likened to a bulldog, he had never revealed to the camera so much as a glint of porcelain. How superior Churchill was, thought Kenneth. How much more appropriate a role model than the Kennedys! Their enormous, gleaming fangs floated grinning through American history like the 'white and ghastly *spectrum*' of the teeth of Berenice in Poe's finest tale.

The teeth! the teeth! – they were here, and there, and everywhere, visibly and palpably . . . long, narrow, and excessively white.

Smiling lips, worn over *clenched* teeth, were a wholly American invention, Kenneth decided.

But when Polly entered the room, she barely noticed him slumped there at his deliberations. She went straight to the kitchen, brewed herself a camomile, and switching on her Françaix, resumed work on her *pliés*.

After twenty minutes, her flatmate, abandoning his Amstrad, turned a woeful countenance towards the tireless ballerina.

'For Christ's sake, Poll,' he said, in a voice which Helen Keller would have been ashamed to employ. 'Couldn't you see I was trying to work? Luckily I had most of it written already.'

He went over to her and thrust his editor's latest fax in front of Polly's nose.

Kenneth,

Where the hell are you tonight? Lionel Pinkhill, the cellist, was found dead from a heart attack by the manager of a Birmingham hotel, after a big concert.

We need two thousand jolly words for the early edition. So get cracking.

Dennis

See what a pro I am,' said Kenneth, almost coherently. 'With no teeth – not that you'd notice – severe loss of blood and you going quietly bananas in your ballet frock, I can still deliver!' He waved the finished obituary in front of her nose. 'The editor needed a job done on Pinkhill, *and I did it.*'

Polly stopped stretching for a moment and turned her little pointy, perspiring face towards him.

'No, Kenneth,' she said coquettishly. 'I did it!'

Sudesh

DEREK WOKE WITH a sense of elation, attributable to no cause he could discern. When he was a boy he had never set off for school without hitching on to his back the brown leather satchel of lunch and books, ink, pens and an apple. Later, and for many years after, Derek would wake each morning, often with a hangover, shower, dress and, almost as an afterthought, hoist upon his shoulders his haversack of guilt and fear.

But this morning, at least, he felt he had a choice: today, misery was optional.

Derek rose and showered, and as he shaved he regarded himself in the bathroom mirror with more than usual interest. He was just the wrong side of fifty, but he did not look it. So many of his friends, even younger men, were grizzled, bald or tonsured. But he had only one grey hair, and that, a silver filament amongst the sparse brown copse encircling his left nipple. Was he, he wondered flippantly, going to have 'distinguished' breasts?

Naked, he mooched around his despoiled flat. His good mood did not disperse. Derek suddenly identified its cause: he was alone, and he liked it. Once more he was the sole commander of his Things.

Pamela had left a strange message on the machine to say that she was staying with her mother for several days. Hadn't he known that? Why had she found it necessary to reiterate the lie? He knew she had gone to elaborate lengths to sleep with an old man; the husband, moreover, of a friend. If his wife had left a message that she was never coming back, he would have been relieved, even overjoyed. But there, in the studio – once his dining-room – were her hostages: Martin Amis, Melvyn Bragg, Simon Rattle, and the old lizard himself, the famous cellist and chandelier man, Lionel Pinkhill.

Nevertheless, Derek still felt a curious serenity; a belief that all would ultimately be well. He lifted a corner of the rug which still draped his cabinet of glass and said 'good morning' to his collection. In the early light his favourite unguent flask refracted a glaucous sheen.

Derek thought of poor old Woody and his tragic Christmas bonfire. It was a terrible death; he wished that his last interview with the agent and his sadly reconstructed wife had been less acrimonious. Derek wondered if Woody might perhaps have died trying to protect his attic museum from the blaze, and had finally been engulfed by the black lava of melted

Mel Torme and Bing Crosby seventy-eights. Perhaps the poor man had collapsed from the fumes of a combusting acrylic Christmas tree, and perished like a chestnut roasting on an open fire.

Sometimes, Derek knew, collections could entrap their collectors. He had heard of a rich banker who, in the early forties, had created deep below his London house a bomb-proof museum to protect his collection of eighteenth-century drawings. He had not foreseen the possibility that a large conduit, which passed directly beside his shelter, would, at the height of the blitz, rupture and flood his subterranean gallery with gallons of raw sewage.

Perhaps art, even the kitsch that poor Woody accumulated, needed to be periodically culled to preserve its rarity; even its desirability. When Florence, a city glutted with art, had been flooded in the sixties, Derek pictured, almost with relief, all those sombre altar pieces, those Bassanos, Renis, Sodomas and Andrea Del Sartos, flushed out into the Gulf of Tuscany.

The telephone rang and it was Inge.

'Before you hear it from anywhere else, or read it, Lionel died last night.'

'What?'

'Pam wasn't there,' said Inge. 'She didn't even see him, though I think she went to the concert. There was no one there, he collapsed in his room.'

'I'm terribly sorry.'

'I wish I felt something,' Inge said. 'The funeral will probably be on Friday and then I'm taking the children away.'

'I see.'

'I just thought you should know they never kept their appointment.'

'Can I do anything?' asked Derek.

'Probably, darling,' she replied. 'But not at the moment. It's been a week of deaths: Woody, Pippa and now Lionel.'

'Pippa?'

'My brilliant friend, Pippa Billinghurst the journalist. She killed herself last Thursday, did I forget to tell you?'

When he had replaced the receiver, Derek wondered what headline commemorating her death might appear in the *Times Literary Supplement.*

PIPPA PASSES?

When Derek arrived at the office of Nimmo, Nimmo, Blackburn & Tricker the following morning, the accountant, paler and less ebullient than usual, greeted him in reception.

'I say, thanks for a really senior lunch the other day, Derek. I think I might have put away a little more wine than was good for me.' Derek was not going to say 'you were perfectly fine' or 'think nothing of it'; instead he said, as they ascended in the lift to Roger's office: 'You are a wine collector, after all, Roger, so lunch must always be a bit of a recce.'

'Well said, well said.' The accountant patted Derek's shoulder. Then he added, almost in a murmur, as they proceeded into a corridor flanked with calf-bound law books, 'There's been a slight glitch.'

'A slight what?'

'Just a slight glitch,' said his adviser, halting for a moment and thoughtfully stroking his moustache. 'We *were* going to have a bit of a one-to-one, you and me, about Gibbo and this and that, in one of our little conference rooms here.' Roger was doing things to his collar and smoothing his hair.

'Well aren't we now, what's up?' said Derek. 'Is there something wrong?'

'Not wrong exactly. Well, not out of the ordinary . . .' Roger stopped speaking entirely as two partners of the firm passed by them and exchanged pleasantries. 'Not abnormal,' he continued, still in a conspiratorial tone, 'but the fact is, old boy, we've got a visitor from the Revenue.'

'What kind of visitor?' said Derek.

'Well, two actually,' explained the accountant, looking almost shamefaced, 'they're a couple of bods from the Enquiry Branch who think you might have been a bit naughty.'

'Well, can't you talk to them, Roger?' said Derek. 'You know more about my affairs than I do. You and Gibbo,' he added.

'Well, it's a curly one Derek, you see, we're just your advisers but it's you they want to talk to – at the end of the day.'

As they walked past a Gents, Derek grabbed Roger by the arm and dragged him through the door. 'Now listen, Roger, do you mean to say I'm in some kind of trouble and you didn't tip me off? Is something going on I should know about? You keep the books, don't you?'

'Steady on, steady on!'

Wainwright was anxious to check there were no ankles projecting beneath the screened cubicles. Derek was almost certain that his financial consultant smelled quite strongly of alcohol.

'I, naturally, look at any documents the Ross Gibb Organisation sends me, but you have never instructed me to go through them with a fine toothed comb. I mean – what do you Aussie's say – Gibbo's a "mate", isn't he?'

'If he is, he's a conspicuously absent one. Do I really have to see these Revenue people?'

'It's not going to hurt, old boy, they won't bite. After all, you haven't done anything wrong, and fronting up makes you look good. They probably just want to look you over.' The accountant attempted a hollow laugh. 'They might even be Mrs Petty fans!'

'Unlike my own accountant, eh Roger?' said Derek. 'Well, I could do with some fans in this office. Lead me to them then!'

The conference room was small and furnished rather like a dentist's waiting-room. On the wall were prints of Leamington Spa, like framed dinner mats. Most of the space in the room was occupied by a conference table at which two people were seated: a man of about forty-five in a brown suit who introduced himself as Abbott, and a delicate looking Indian lady in an apricot-coloured sari. Derek thought she was called Sudesh Robinson. They were both very polite, even friendly. Before them on the table were rather ominously plump manilla folders.

Almost as soon as introductions were over, Roger, the collar of his Simpson blazer frosted with dandruff, and with considerable plucking at his tie, begged to be excused. 'Just for a sec.' Derek looked across the table at the inspectors with less apprehensiveness than curiosity. Mr Abbott opened the interview whilst Ms Robinson merely regarded him with a slight and not unpleasant smile. Derek gazed with his usual wonderment at the red spot between her eyes.

'As Mr Wainwright would have explained to you, we are obliged to read you an extract from Hansard dated the fifth of October, 1944.' A leaflet bearing a copy of this extract was placed before Derek as Mr Abbott's voice recited it, and another text called Section 105. Derek registered occasional phrases like 'criminal proceedings', 'full confession', 'fraudulent conduct' and 'penalty'.

'I hope all this is quite clear to you, Mr Pettyfer,' said Mr Abbott pleasantly. Derek pretended it was. In reality he was more concerned about Roger's whereabouts.

'Excuse me,' he said, 'but are you telling me this is serious?' The Inspectors looked at each other.

Mr Abbott adopted a fractionally graver tone of voice. 'We must ask you Mr Pettyfer, if you are satisfied, *totally satisfied*, that all your income tax returns and business accounts are correct and complete?'

'I think so,' began Derek, 'I mean . . . yes.'

Ms Robinson spoke for the first time. 'I presume

then you are prepared to give us full access to all your business and private records, so that the Revenue may be satisfied that all your answers to our other questions are correct.'

'What other questions? said Derek. He noticed that when Ms Robinson was speaking, there was a hint of something northern in her voice – Manchester?

The door opened and Roger entered, rubbing his hands together in a businesslike fashion.

'Hope I'm not interrupting anything,' he said heartily. 'Hands up for tea and who's for coffee.' As he stood at the end of the table grinning, Derek could not help but admire the couple from the Revenue who managed to express profound distaste for his accountant without the flicker of a change in their demeanour.

'Ah, you're back Mr Wainwright,' said Mr Abbott. 'We've just read the Hansard extract to your client and Section 105 TMA1970.'

'Jolly good!' interjected Wainwright.

'Mr Pettyfer, as I'm sure you've advised him,' continued Mr Abbott, 'would now find it in his best interest to make a full and frank disclosure to the Revenue. The alternative could be very unpleasant and drag on for many years.'

Derek looked at Roger, seriously alarmed for the first time.

'We are inclined to be more lenient with taxpayers who co-operate fully, at an early stage of the investigation. Aren't we, Ms Robinson?' Derek felt that 'Ms' did not come naturally to Mr Abbott; it was a kind of in-house anti-discriminatory form of address which he had forced himself to adopt. Derek rather liked him.

Ms Robinson opened her file and ran a pencil down a column of figures. 'Just at random, Mr Pettyfer, looking at some recent purchases, may I ask you to explain a matter of thirty-five thousand pounds paid out last month for laser equipment for Mr Robert Dooley.'

'It's a mistake,' said Derek, triumphantly.

'It seems to have been authorised by your partner, Mr Ross Gibb and paid out of your household account.'

'What household account?' said Derek.

'The account operated by your wife,' suggested Mr Abbott. 'I hope you're not going to pretend you don't know about it?'

'I don't. Really I don't,' said Derek. 'Do you, Roger?'

Roger scratched his chin and did a few side-to-side jaw exercises. 'I think we did open a credit line for Mrs Pettyfer fairly recently, but I'm very surprised you didn't know about it, Derek old top. It's pretty normal for a chap to chuck his wife a few shillings for the housekeeping, eh?' He guffawed, though the inspectors, who probably earned between twenty-five and thirty thousand pounds a year, and worked hard for it, were less amused.

Ms Robinson continued. 'And the mortgage on a large detached house in Morris Grove, Solihull, Birmingham of three hundred and seventeen thousand pounds, again from one of your production accounts and authorised by Mr Gibb. What can you tell us about that?'

'You got me mixed up with someone else,' said Derek, feeling a blessed sense of relief. 'I don't know anyone who lives in Birmingham, so there has to be another Mr Gibb.'

'But doesn't your mother-in-law live in Birmingham, Mr Pettyfer?' said Mr Abbott. 'The mortgage, it seems, has been made over into the name of Doris Black.'

Derek felt as though he was sinking into some kind of quicksand.

'Could we put this on hold for just a jiffy?' said Roger brightly, though his brow glistened and there were two bright red spots on his cheeks. 'Just a quick word with my secretary and I'll be back before you know it.'

With his protector gone, Derek blurted out: 'Look Mr Abbott . . . Mrs Robinson, this is all news to me. It looks as though you should be talking to Mr Ross Gibb, not me.'

'But Mr Pettyfer,' interrupted the lady, 'you and Mr Gibb are partners in all these companies!' And she passed him a list of exotically named 'entities', with even more exotic addresses.

'There is a recent purchase of yours that puzzles us,' she said. 'A cash payment of eighty-five thousand pounds to *L'art Ancien* of Museum Street for an antique vase of some kind.' Derek was beginning to feel very cold, despite the central heating.

'This ornament,' Mr Abbott took up the story, 'was paid for in cash to avoid VAT, yet there was a withdrawal for the same amount on the previous day from your number two trust account, on the Isle of Man, and the only two signatories on that are your wife and Mr Gibb.'

'But I haven't got a trust account,' said Derek. 'And that vase was a gift.'

'A gift to yourself from yourself, apparently,' said Ms Robinson, and for a fraction of a second it looked as though the inspectors were going to laugh.

'All present and correct!' Wainwright had re-entered the conference room looking slightly dishevelled and – could it be possible – slightly drunk. His cheeks were positively rosy; they were the colour of Shame, if shame ever visited the shameless.

'You mustn't be too hard on our Artiste. The collecting bug affects us all across the board, at the end of the day.' He beamed rosily at all three of them with his thumbs in his waistcoat pockets. 'Case in point: no prizes for guessing who went berserk at Christie's last wine auction when a couple of dozen Chateau Lynch Bages '61 came up. I paid a silly price, but at the end of the day, who cares?'

There was a silence in the room. Derek wondered how that full and frank disclosure by a card-carrying oenologist grabbed Mr Abbott and Ms Robinson, or, for that matter, assisted his case. Was he imagining it, Derek thought, or did they seem to like him a little? He decided that if they did, it was for one thing only: he represented Promotion; his ruin would be a feather in their caps.

A youthful tea lady interrupted with refreshments.

'That's the ticket, Roswyn, put them all down at the end of the table and we can help ourselves.'

'A wee sandwich for anyone?' enquired Roswyn. Heads were shaken.

'Now listen here, gentlemen,' Roger exhorted the inspectors. 'Mr Gibb, my client's partner and adviser, is temporarily on holiday at the moment . . .'

'We're aware of that, Mr Wainwright. They sold the house in Weybridge a few weeks ago to a Russian family who paid a large cash sum. That house was originally purchased by you, Mr Pettyfer, you'll be interested to learn.'

Derek was.

'Then, soon after the VAT raid, your manager felt it advisable to retire to Majorca with his family,' said Mr Abbott quietly, 'to a large villa purchased five years ago in Mr Pettyfer's name, through one of Mr Pettyfer's illegal offshore entities.'

'We think it is unlikely,' said Ms Robinson, 'that he will feel inclined to come back here and help us with our enquiries.'

'Luckily,' concluded Mr Abbott, 'we have his partner here to help us in an investigation which looks as though it may go on into the foreseeable future.'

Derek became aware of a strong and feculent smell. At first it seemed to come and go, but slowly it increased in density and rankness; it was unbearable. Roger Wainwright was drumming his fingers together and frowning intently at the ceiling. It was then that Derek realised, nor was he alone in doing so, that his accountant had farted.

'Excuse me a minute,' said Derek, gagging slightly.

'Could I have a word with Mr Wainwright in private?' The inspectors seemed only too glad of an olfactory respite.

Once they were outside the conference room, Roger said, 'God, Derek, you're going great guns in there. You're a real old trouper.'

'Bullshit,' exclaimed Derek, 'bullshit, Roger! It's a can of worms they've opened and you couldn't care less. You must have known I was in deep shit years ago. You must have known Gibbo had his hand in the till up to his *fucking armpit!* And if you didn't, then you're more of a fool than I am.'

'Steady on, Derek, they'll hear us.'

But Derek had not finished. 'I hope they do. Think of all the shits and slimy tax dodgers they spend years trying to nail. I want to come out of this clean. I need some advice and I need it fast. Who's the hot shot, who is absolutely – without a shadow of doubt – the best man to help a person like me out of a nightmare like this?'

'There's only one chap I know,' said Roger. 'He's retired but he still does a bit of consultancy work and he might be the only man on the planet who can save your bacon.'

'What's his name? What's his name?' growled Derek, grasping his accountant roughly by his Harvie & Hudson shirt.

'MacDermott, Alan MacDermott, he's a genius. Want me to give him a bell?'

Two hours later, Derek found himself descending in

the lift of Nimmo, Nimmo, Blackburn & Tricker. Mr Abbott and Ms Robinson were the only other passengers. They were still impeccably courteous, as people sometimes are at the commencement of a relationship which they expect to last for a very long time.

Fumbling with some documents he had been asked to verify, Derek dropped a copy of the *Antique Review* on the floor of the elevator, which Mr Abbott quickly picked up and returned to him.

'You *are* quite a collector, aren't you, Mr Pettyfer?' he said.

'Everyone is, aren't they?' replied Derek. 'Chippendale furniture, Beatles memorabilia, stamps, bottle-tops, spoons. Do you collect anything, Mrs Robinson?' The inspector gave him a very sweet off-duty smile, revealing one gold tooth.

'Taxes, Mr Pettyfer. Only taxes.'

As he stepped out of the lift at Ashley Mansions, Derek could smell onions cooking. His front door was open and heavy metal blared from the beautiful apartment. Inside, all the lights were blazing.

Derek was surprised to be greeted by his mother-in-law in a canary yellow Escada suit with black braid, and a large hat. She looked as though she were off to the races.

'Oh, Derek love, come in,' she said. 'Can we get you a drink?' He saw that Doris was not alone. A tall, bearded man in filthy jeans and an anorak, who looked as if he was unqualified in some branch of the building trade, sat on Derek's sofa with his boots on a chair. The Gallé table was a clutter of Guinness cans. Tea chests and swathes of bubble-wrap were everywhere and he noticed a trail of clay footprints, to and from the front door.

Doris regarded her son-in-law critically. 'Now don't give me that look, duck,' she said, giving him an unwished-for hug – she seemed to smell of Paloma Picasso. 'Our Pamela hasn't made up her mind one way or the other, but she is staying up in Birmingham for a few days with her old mum and then she's going to see some friends of hers in Majorca. She's promised me one of them wine bottles, shaped like a cow. Hasn't she, Bob?'

The man with the grey ponytail was rolling a cigarette. He merely looked up by way of reply, then returned to his fidgeting.

'Pam is a good girl, Derek, she's been very nice to her old mother lately. Hasn't she, Bob?'

The mute, cigarette ablaze, laboriously returned to his task, which appeared to be the packing and crating of Pam's busts, and lugging them out of the flat and down in the lift.

'He's been marvellous too,' said Doris in a stage whisper. 'She sent me down to clear out her stuff, but I couldn't lift none of this on my own and well she knows it.'

Derek's heart, which had atrophied during the afternoon, resumed an encouraging beat. 'She's leaving?'

'I know, love,' said Doris, shaking her head and

resuming the role of comforter. 'It wasn't a long marriage – but it's quality not quantity, as they say.'

Derek nodded.

'Don't judge her too harshly. That friend of hers dying the other night, that musical fella, what a terrible thing. Alone, too, in a cold hotel. Mind you, it's an ill wind, and as I told Pamela, I said: "That head of him you done – it's going to fetch a good deal more, now he's dead!" '

With satisfaction, Derek watched the Rasputin-like removal man heave the last box out the door.

'Well, when I said this to our Pam, you know, about Lionel's bust going up in value, she dried her eyes and had a bit of a giggle. And then she told me not to be so awful!' And Doris had another of her laughing attacks.

'It's all done,' said the Ponytail. It was the first time Derek had heard him speak.

'Terrah!' he said in a fit of garrulity, and pointed to a pile of lavish brochures on the sofa.

THE LASER OF TWO EVILS

RECENT INSTALLATIONS BY ROBERT DOOLEY

With a note on the Artist

by Pippa Billinghurst

'Give them to your posh mates.'

And he was gone.

Derek glanced at the contents, on art paper and in full colour. They must have cost someone a packet, he thought.

'Well, I'll be off too, Derek,' said Doris, patting

the back of her hat. 'You mustn't be too harsh on us now. I've done something special for you this evening that's been screaming to be done for years.'

Derek pretended to look touched.

She wagged her finger. 'I'm not telling you either, me duck, but it's the least thing a mother-in-law can do!' Another hug, and the door slammed.

Derek observed that he had not taken a breath for some time. Inhaling deeply, he sought again his mood of the morning. Surprisingly, a little serenity returned. The first thing he would do in the morning, he decided, was to make it up to Amerika and try to coax her back.

It was then that he saw the red rug on the floor, and the open vitrine. A terrible horror seized him as he stared at the empty shelves. There, propped up against a Guinness tin, was a note in a childish hand.

Don't panic, Duck. Check the Siemens!

Derek looked at the note for a long time and then walked slowly to the kitchen. He did not bother to switch on the light; there was already a small green light winking on the new appliance. A discreet threshing sound seemed to fill the kitchen and the beautiful apartment. The dishwasher was programmed at number four – heavy duty, he noticed.

Derek was disinclined to turn it off, let alone open it. With a water pressure at ten bars, a temperature of seventy degrees celsius and a big scoop of Finish, it would have been a miracle if fifteen irreplaceable pieces of two-thousand-year old, unannealed glass had survived Doris Black's thoughtful farewell gesture.

In a long coat and a muffler, Derek laboured along the boat deck against the wind, trying to find a sheltered deckchair. They were only two days out of Sydney, and the weather was surprisingly overcast and blustery.

Finally he found an isolated and protected corner, temporarily out of the breeze, and settled down with his books, both of which bore an image of himself on their dust-jackets. The first was called *Feeding the Famous* by Emma Wimbeldon, and its cover exhibited a montage of celebrities who had presumably survived the author's *fricassee* of hare. It had been sent to him by the publishers in the hope of eliciting a favourable quote. Unable to invoke any interest in this culinary chronicle, Derek permitted the book to slip from his relaxed fingertips to the deck.

He tucked the old red tartan rug that had once shielded his treasures around his legs, adjusted his glasses and pulled down his hat. He felt elderly and fragmented, like Aschenbach dissolving on the Lido. It was Derek's first time on deck since he had picked up the QE2 in Sydney.

His new one-man-show, depicting the American cynic Ambrose Bierce as a gay Aborigine, had been quite a hit at the Sydney Festival, marred only by one incident, when a female demonstrator against 'chauvinism' had leapt on the stage during a performance. It may have been a 'copy-cat' gesture, since two months before, much world-wide publicity had been accorded a mad girl, dressed identically to the star, who had run on to the stage at Covent Garden during the première of a ballet, and had to be dragged off by psychiatric warders.

Derek had got to like Carmen Conroy too, the brusque Festival Director, and Fran, her friend. He had misjudged Carmen rather badly at their first meeting after Peggy's funeral, all those months before. Of course, none of his troubles in England had gone away – if anything they had worsened – but in Sydney, beside the sparkling Harbour, care only throbbed dimly in the distance like peritonitis masked with pethidine.

The job on the QE2 was a godsend. Derek took anything he could get these days. A friend, Charles Osborne, who was to give a lecture on opera on the Sydney–Rabaul–Nagasaki–Hong Kong run, had had to cancel, and proposed Derek as a replacement. Of course the Cunard people had been pleased at the prospect of a cheap talk by Mrs Petty, illustrated with video clips from her series on high finance, *Petty Cash*; and of course Derek got the cruise for nothing.

For several days out of Sydney, he had remained in his cabin, which was large and comfortable, working up his talk. No announcements of his forthcoming show had been posted, and 'Osborne on Verdi' was still advertised in the ship's newsletter.

Derek rather enjoyed his invisibility. Invisible, that is, to all except the omniscient Mr Abbott and Mrs Sudesh Robinson. He had received a confidential communication from his accountant and decided either to destroy it or take it up on deck that evening to read in a quiet deckchair in the hope that it might be seized by a gust of wind.

Now, steeling himself, he decided to read the latest fax from Whitney Wainwright. It was short and jaunty.

> Dear Derek,
> Things here are not much different regarding you know what. I'm kicking arse, never fear. Good news and bad news. Bad news first, the Enemy wants the first instalment as soon as Ashley Mansions etc sold. Good news: we can probably crunch Pamela's lawyers to accept a five figure settlement, less costs and extras. Not promising anything.
>
> Sotheby's new catalogue with pic of you on cover 'The Pettyfer Piranesis' looks seriously larky. Big sale coming up next week, and I reckon that if your whole collection sells at the high estimate, the proceeds less Sotheby's commission will just cover the interest you owe the Enemy in arrears, and my outstanding fees. Have fun. Over and out.
>
> Roger
>
> P.S. Guess who was absolutely fabulous at the Sunningdale Mummers annual bash, dressed as Joanna Lumley?

Derek remembered that when the first tax interview had ended, with much shuffling of papers and old pal's jocularity, he had excused himself and rushed out to the Partners' loo to be sick. Then, following an ancient hunch learnt long ago, he had carefully lifted the white porcelain lid of the cistern and looked in. There, in the cool dark water beside the ball-cock, bobbed the wine-connoisseur's secret: a perfectly chilled half bottle of Smirnoff vodka.

It was getting rather cold and blowy. Derek folded the fax and placed it in an outside pocket. It was then he decided – vowed – that whenever, if ever, his troubles came to an end and he had respite from these financial cares, he would give thanks by calling on Stan the Stuntman who owed him a few favours. This old colleague who lived not a mile to the east of Lincoln's Inn would gladly arrange to have his accountant professionally 'sorted'. A little job in Sunningdale would appeal to the lads.

Derek turned to the new book he had picked up in Sydney.

PETTY-COATS
by
Kenneth J. Grocock
An unauthorised life
with a reassessment
by Doctor Adam Bottomley

The dust-jacket bore a photograph of Mrs Petty looking crestfallen, and beneath, in lurid letters, the words:

THE BITCHING, THE BOOZING,
AND THE BONKING!

On the back of the dust-jacket there was a photograph of the author smoking a large cigar and giving the victory sign, and a complementary résumé of his career: from copyboy to his present post as Arts Editor in Chief of the *Independent on Sunday*.

Derek flicked through the pages impatiently, deciding, as he had with Emma's cookbook, finally to abandon the disagreeable task of continued perusal. Soon, when he had the energy, he would discreetly deject both volumes into the illiterate Pacific.

He closed his eyes, and dozed.

When he opened them again, it was almost dark. Nearly time to return to his cabin and order an excellent supper. Two passengers now stood a few feet away, leaning on the rail, their backs towards him. A young and an elder woman, as far as he could discern. The wind snatched at their voices and flung some of their words back to the muffled figure in the deckchair.

'. . . can you remember what you once said, when I asked you if you wanted another child?'

'No, what?' said the older woman, sparks flying from her cigarette.

'You said: "I'd love a nice quiet little girl who likes having her hair brushed".'

The older, taller woman, the one with the short grey dove-tail crop, put out her hand and touched the other's dark cataract of hair, and together, with their fingers joined, they walked off down the boat deck. But Derek had already recognised the voices of Inge Pinkhill and Pamela Black.

Epilogue

I WILL TAKE up the story now in my own voice, for it is my story and there is still a little more to tell.

Till now, I have written it fancifully, rather like a novel, because the novel is a convenient form: it enables the author to reduce his own faults and follies and exaggerate the shortcomings of others.

I am, of course, strictly an Amateur, whose first profession is not authorship; and since I am also what used to be called a 'colonial' I have indulged a lifelong taste for the sesquipedalian; that unerring giveaway of the Provincial. To me, the meaning of fancy words does not matter: I merely throw them in for colour and flavour, as if I were cooking with them.

But I have to tell you that a man came to see me this morning, a man I had never met before, though once, a long time ago in another life, I knew a child who bore the same name.

'My mother died last month,' he said. 'She had been ill for a long time, as you know, and I found this amongst her things.' He withdrew a battered mushroom-coloured book from a carry bag. 'Rather the worst for wear too, I'm afraid. But it is yours, I think.'

Timothy – that was his name – handed me the volume, its cover soiled and marked where wet glasses had stood upon it. I remembered it immediately, of course. It was Piranesi's *Prisons* with the Huxley essay.

First, I looked at the end of the book, and sure enough, there was the Notice of Limitation and Aldous Huxley's autograph in ink. Then I examined the flyleaf; the blank page that had so wounded my adolescent heart over thirty years ago. I looked at my visitor.

'It's very like something I owned a long time ago,' I said. 'But how do you know it's mine?'

'There's a card somewhere,' said the bank manager. 'It's inside, perhaps stuck to one of the plates.'

We looked, and only on that second shuffle through the loose, stained pages did a card drop out. It was a Lautrec reproduction on a postcard, the one of Aristide Brouant, and there was a rectangular 'ghost' off-set on the page where it had lain all those years.

'That's it, isn't it?' he said. But I had never seen the card before. I turned it over and read the brief inscription.

To Derek,
With all my love
Yvette

'I never found it at the time,' was all I could say.

'No,' he laughed, 'it is tucked away. You could easily miss it if you didn't expect to find it.'

I stood there for a while, searching for the right words; the right way of thanking him; and he put his hand on my shoulder, that kind young man who must have reached out many times to comfort his mother.

Politely then, he left.

But I remained there still, for a long time in the empty flat, soon to be sold, reading that message of love, borne back to me out of the past.

Chalet Claire-fontaine
Gstaad
February–March 1995